Frank Edward Smedley

The Fortunes of the Colville Family

Frank Edward Smedley

The Fortunes of the Colville Family

ISBN/EAN: 9783337341558

Printed in Europe, USA, Canada, Australia, Japan

Cover: Foto ©Andreas Hilbeck / pixelio.de

More available books at **www.hansebooks.com**

THE FORTUNES

OF

THE COLVILLE FAMILY

OR

A Cloud with its Silver Lining

BY

FRANK E. SMEDLEY

AUTHOR OF " FRANK FAIRLEGH," "LEWIS ARUNDEL," "HARRY COVERDALE'S COURTSHIP," ETC.

AND SEVEN TALES

EDITED BY FRANK E. SMEDLEY

————— —

LONDON

GEORGE ROUTLEDGE AND SONS, LIMITED

BROADWAY, LUDGATE HILL

GLASGOW, MANCHESTER, AND NEW YORK

THE FORTUNES

OF

THE COLVILLE FAMILY.

CHAPTER I.

THE TWO PICTURES.

"A Merry Christmas, and a Happy New Year!"

Words, of course, in themselves good and well-chosen, and embodying a wish which all who love their neighbour should feel and communicate;—God in his mercy grant there may be very many who can respond to such a salutation hopefully; for in this Valley of the Shadow of Death there must be some who shrink from it as from a bitter mockery. Of such are those who, loving deeply, have lost, or fear to lose, the object of their fond idolatry; of such are those to whom, gifted, perhaps, with an even wider capacity of affection, such a fear would seem a blessing, for then they would not have toiled through a lifetime lonely-hearted. "A Merry Christmas, and a Happy New Year!" God comfort those who shudder at such kindly greeting!

One short month since, a little space of time, but more than long enough for the performance of many a deeper tragedy than that to which we are about to refer, an artist, glancing into the sunny breakfast-parlour of Ashburn Rectory, might have made a pretty picture of the group on which his eye would have fallen.

That *gentleman* (in rags he would equally have looked such' with the calm, high forehead, mild eye, and earnest, thoughtful mouth, must be the father of the family; for his dark hair shows many a silver thread, and the lines that appear upon his still smooth brow can scarcely be the result of mental occupation only; but, if we are right in our conjecture, whence did that curly-pated nine-year-old urchin, seated upon his knee, contrive to get his arch, merry face? for he can scarcely have "come alive" out of one of Murillo's paintings, to give light and life to our family sketch. Oh! we see, it is his mother's countenance the rogue has appropriated, only the mischief in it is all his own; for the expression of her still-beautiful features is chastened and pensive, as of one who has lived and loved, and done angels' work on earth, until the pure soul within has stamped its impress on the outward form.

But if you want something pretty—nay, we may as well tell the whole truth, and say at once bewitching—to look at, cast your eyes (you won't be in a hurry to remove them again) upon the figure seated at mamma's right hand, and recognising her facsimile (with twenty summers taken off her age, and barely eighteen left), declare whether that is not "nice," rather. The expression is not the same, we confess: more of the woman and less of the angel, you will say. We admit it; but then, how could that little rosebud of a mouth look anything but petulant? those violet eyes express—well, it's difficult to tell what they don't express that is good, and fresh, and piquant, and gay, and—must we add? a little bit coquettish also;—why, the very dimple on her chin — such a well-modelled chin—has something pert and saucy about it. There! you've seen enough of the little beauty: you'll be falling in love with her directly!

No one could mistake the relationship existing between the gentleman we have already described, and that tall, graceful boy, with his pale, finely-chiselled features, and clasically-shaped head. Even the earnest, thoughtful expression is common to both father and son, save that the curl of the short upper lip, which tells of pride in the boy, has, in the man, acquired a character of chastened dignity.

Reader, do you like our picture? Let us turn to another, less pleasing, but alas! equally true.

The waves of time roll on, and, like a dream, another month has lapsed into the sea of ages.

The sun is shining still; but it shines upon an open grave, with aching hearts around it. A good man has died, and his brave, loving spirit has gone whither his faith has preceded him, and his good works alone can follow him. "Blessed are the dead that die in the Lord."

Let us reserve our sympathy for those who live to mourn them.

When the curate of Ashburn preached a funeral sermon, recalling to the minds of those who had practically benefited by them the virtues of their late rector, holly garlands hung in the fine old church, to commemorate the birth-time of One who came to bring "peace on earth, and good-will towards men ;" but none dared to wish the widow and orphans "A Merry Christmas, and a Happy New Year," lest the wish might seem an insult to their sorrow.

CHAPTER II.

THE BROTHERS

"Percy, I *have* been quiet *so* long, and you say I must not stand upon my head, because it disturbs mamma; do come out and let us ride the pony by turns," implored little Hugh Colville in a strenuous whisper; which was, however, clearly audible throughout the small breakfast-parlour, which was the scene of our family picture.

Percy Colville, the shy, handsome boy of our sketch, looked up with a pensive smile from the writing on which he was engaged, and shook his head negatively, in token that he felt obliged to refuse the request of his younger brother, in whom the reader will recognise, with little difficulty, a certain Murillo-like urchin to whom he has been already introduced. But the petition of her youngest born had reached the ears of the widow, who (if she had a virtue which had outgrown its due proportions till cavillers might deem it a fault), was, perhaps, a little over indulgent to Master Hugh.

"My dear Percy, you have been writing for me long enough," she said, "you will be ill if you shut yourself up too much ; besides, Hugh has been so good that he deserves his ride, and you know I don't like to trust him by himself."

Percy hesitated : the writing on which he was engaged was the copy of a surveyor's report concerning that *vexata quæstio* dilapidations. Some difference of opinion had arisen on the subject between the agent of the patron of the living and Mrs. Colville's solicitor, and a copy of the report was to be forwarded by the next post to Mr. Wakefield, Mrs. Colville's legal adviser. The matter was of importance, involving a considerable sum of money. Percy was aware of these facts : he knew, also, that he could only just finish his task by the time the village post went out; and he was about to declare that Hugh must give up his ride for that day, when his mother, reading his thoughts, stooped over him, and, kissing his pale brow, whispered—

"Do not refuse him, dear Percy: remember, he will not have many more rides——"

She paused, for her composure was failing, then finished in a trembling voice—

"You know the pony must be sold when we go away."

As she spoke, an expedient suggested itself to Percy's mind, and pressing his mother's hand affectionately, he closed his writing-desk, and, carrying it off under his arm, exclaimed—

"Come along, Hugh ! we'll take old Lion (he wants a run, poor dog) as well as the pony, and have a glorious scamper."

And a glorious scamper they had, only Hugh rode the whole way, and Percy ran by his side, declaring that he greatly preferred it, which was decidedly a pious fiction, if a fiction can ever be pious.

"Oh! mamma, mamma! do make breakfast—come, quick! there's a good mamma! for I'm as hungry as—as—several sharks," exclaimed Hugh, rushing like a small express train into the breakfast-parlour, on the following morning.

"Oh, you naughty mad-cap, you've shaken the table, and made me blot ' That Smile ' all over!" cried his sister Emily, in vain endeavouring to repair the misfortune which had accrued to the " popular melody" she was copying.

We suppose it is scarcely necessary to reintroduce you to Emily, dear reader. You have not so soon forgotten the rosebud of a mouth, or the dangerous dimple—trust you for that.

"Well, I declare, so I have," rejoined the culprit, a little shocked and a good deal amused at the mischief he had occasioned; then striking into the tune of the outraged ditty, he sang in an impish soprano, and with grimaces wonderful to behold—-

"'That smile—when once—de-par-ar-ar-arted,
Must leave—me bro—ken har-ar-ar-arted.'

Oh! Emily, what a mess we have made of ' broken-hearted,' to be sure! I'm so sorry, but what fun!"

And then came a burst of ringing, happy, childish laughter, which, of course, sealed his forgiveness: no one could think him to blame after *that*.

"I wonder where Percy is; I scarcely ever knew him late before," observed Mrs. Colville, when quiet had been restored.

"Sarah tells me he is out riding," returned Emily, applying herself with very unnecessary energy to cut bread and butter.

As she spoke, the clatter of horses' feet became audible, and, in another moment, Percy cantered past the window.

"Where can the boy have been?" ejaculated Emily, holding the loaf lovingly, as though she was afraid of hurting the poor thing.

"*I* know, *I* do!" observed Hugh, from under the table, whence, having in his mind's eye metamorphosed himself into a wolf, he was preparing to spring out and devour Emily.

"*You* know, Hugh!" repeated Mrs. Colville in surprise; "come from under the table, then, and tell me."

"But, mamma, I'm a wolf, and just going to eat up Emily."

"Not now, dear," was the calm reply, as if a daughter more or less devoured by wild beasts was of little moment to that un-anxious mother; "come here, and tell me about Percy."

"Well, you know, mamma," began Hugh, emerging from his hiding-place, and assuming the grave air of a *raconteur*, "when Percy came to bed last night, he did not go to bed at all—that is, not for a very, very, very long time. Do you know, I think" —and here he put on a solemn face, and spoke with an air of mystery—"I think he was not in bed at twelve o'clock, perhaps not till almost one!" Having disclosed this frightful fact, he paused and nodded like a bird, for the greater effect, ere he continued: "I went to sleep long before, but, whenever I opened my eyes, there he sat, still write, write, writing on, as if he was writing his life, like Robinson Crusoe—only," he added, parenthetically—"only he's got no man Friday."

"But what could he be writing?" exclaimed Emily, coquetting with the large bread-knife.

"I know," resumed Hugh; then, having paused to balance himself on one leg, and spin round like a teetotum, he continued very fast, and without any stops, for Percy's footsteps sounded in the hall: "he was writing the paper he had not time to finish yesterday, because I wanted him to go out with me and the pony; and this morning he got up at six o'clock to ride over to Staplehurst, seven miles there, and I don't know how many back again, to catch the post, and make it all the same as if it had been put in yesterday; I know he did, because Sarah says so." And, having delivered himself with the greatest vehemence of this somewhat incoherent account, he rushed up to his brother, then entering the room, and, throwing his arms round his waist, exclaimed, "Oh, Percy! I've gone and told them all about your great letter, and sitting up late, and everything, and never remembered till now that you said I wasn't to mention it to anybody. Oh, I am so sorry, but what fun!" and, assured by the expression of Percy's face that his crime was not quite unpardonable, Hugh's merry, childish laugh again rang through the apartment.

The mother's heart was full: tears stood in her eyes as, pressing her elder son to her bosom, she murmured,—

"Dear, dear Percy, you must not overtask your strength thus."

The post that morning brought the following letter directed to Mrs. Colville :—

"My dear Sister,—That I have the will to aid you in your distress you cannot doubt; that the power to do so effectually is denied me, adds one more to the troubles of life. My imprudent marriage (he had run away with a pretty governess at eighteen), and its subsequent consequences (he had nine healthy children), force me to work like a horse in a mill, in order to make both ends meet. Of this I am not complaining. I did an unwise thing, and must pay the necessary penalty. But I mention these facts to prove to you the truth of my assertion, that my power is not coequal with my will. The little I can do is this: I am shareholder in an excellent proprietary school, where boys are taught everything necessary to fit them for a commercial life; Wilfred Jacob has been there two years, and is already conversant with, or, as he familiarly terms it, 'well up in' tare and tret. I trust Adolphus Samuel, Albert John, Thomas Gabriel, and even the little Augustus Timothy, will soon follow, and profit equally. I therefore propose to send your two boys to this school at my own cost; and, if the eldest distinguishes himself, as I am proud to believe Wilfred Jacob will do, a desk in my counting-house (No. 8, Grubbinger Street, City) shall reward his diligence. Clementina Jane desires her kindest regards, and begs me to say that should you finally determine upon settling in London, she shall have much pleasure in looking out a cheap lodging for you in some of the least expensive streets in the vicinity of Smithfield. I am, dear Margaret, ever your affectionate brother,

"GOLDSMITH AND THRYFT.

"P.S.—So much for habit: I have become so accustomed to sign for the firm, that I actually forget that my name is Tobiah."

Mrs. Colville closed the letter, with a sigh, and placing it in her pocket, waited till the boys had breakfasted. As soon as they had quitted the room she handed it to her daughter, saying, "Read that, dear Emily: it is very kind of your uncle, but——"

"Percy at a desk in Grubbinger Street! Oh, my dearest mamma, what a dreadful idea!" exclaimed the Rosebud, arching her brows, and pursing up her pretty little mouth with an expression of the most intense disapproval: "Uncle Tobiah means to be very kind, but he forgets what Percy is."

Mrs. Colville shook her head mournfully. "I am afraid it is we who forget, love," she said: "Percy can no longer hope to pursue the career marked out for him—with the very limited means at my disposal, college is quite out of the question; nay, if Sir Thomas Crawley persists in his demand for the incoming tenant's claim to these dilapidations, and should prove his right to it, I shall be unable to send the boys to school at all; indeed, I must not reject your uncle's offer rashly. I shall consult Mr. Slowkopf on the subject; he is a very prudent adviser."

"Oh! if you mean to ask *him*, the matter is as good as settled, and poor Percy chained to a desk for life," cried Emily. "Ah!" she continued, as a tall, thin, gaunt figure, clothed in rusty black, passed the window, "here he comes—the creature always puts me in mind of that naughty proverb about a certain person: one no sooner mentions him than there he is at one's elbow;—but, if you really want to talk sense to him, mamma dear, I'd better go, for I shall only say pert things and disturb you: he is so delightfully slow and matter-of-fact, that I never can resist the temptation of plaguing him;" and as she spoke, the Rosebud laughed a little silvery laugh at her own wickedness, and tripped, fairy-like, out of the apartment.

The worthy Mr. Slowkopf, who had held the office of curate of Ashburn for about two years, was a very good young man, and nothing else; all his other qualities were negative. He wasn't even positively a fool, though he looked and acted the part admirably. He was essentially, and in every sense of the word, a slow man: in manners, ideas, and appearance, he was behind the age in which he lived; in conversation he was behind the subject discussed; if he laughed at a joke, which, solemnly and heavily, he sometimes condescended to do, it was invariably ten minutes after it had been made. He never heard of Puseyism till Tract Ninety had been suppressed, or knew of the persecutions and imprisonments of Dr. Achilli till that amateur martyr was crying aloud for sympathy in Exeter Hall; he usually finished his fish when the cheese was being put on table; and went to bed as other people were getting up. Still, he had his good points. Unlike King Charles, of naughty memory,

> "Who never said a foolish thing,
> And never did a wise one,"

however dull and trite might be Mr. Slowkopf's remarks, his actions were invariably good and kind. The village gossips, when they were very hard-up for scandal, declared that, insensible as he appeared to all such frivolities as the fascinations of the softer sex, he was gradually taking a "slow turn" towards the Rosebud of Ashburn. Nay, the rumour was reported to have reached the delicate ears of the "emphatic she" herself; who was said to have replied, that as she was quite certain he would never dream of telling his love till he heard she was engaged to be married to some one else—in which case she should have a legitimate reason for refusing him—the information did not occasion her the slightest uneasiness.

However this might be, certain it is, that on the morning in question, Mr. Slowkopf, gaunt, ugly, and awkward, solemnly stalked into the breakfast-parlour, and that the widow, perplexed between her good sense and her loving tenderness for her children, laid before him her difficulties and her brother's letter.

The curate paused about three times as long as was necessary, and then, in a deep, sepulchral voice, observed—

"In order to attain to a sound and logical conclusion in regard to this weighty matter, it behoves me first to assure myself that I rightly comprehend the question propounded.

and if, as I conceive, it prove to be one which will not admit of demonstration with a mathematical certainty; then, secondly, to to compare the different hypotheses which m ay present themselves, that, sufficient weight being allotted to each, a just and philosophical decision may be finally arrived at."

Having, after this preamble, stated the case in language as precise and carefully selected as though he were framing a bill to lay before Parliament, and were resolved to guard against the possibility of the most astute legal Jehu driving a coach and four through it, he argued the matter learnedly and steadily for a good half-hour, ere he dug out the ore of common sense from the mass of logical rubbish beneath which he had buried it, and decided in favour of Mr. Goldsmith's proposal. Pleased at his own cleverness in having solved this difficult problem, and possessing unlimited confidence in his oratorical powers, he volunteered to communicate the decision thus formed to the person most nearly concerned therein, an offer to which Mrs. Colville, feeling her strength unequal to the task, reluctantly consented.

Percy listened in silence till Mr. Slowkopf had talked himself out of breath, which it took him some time to accomplish, for, in every sense of the term, he was awfully long-winded; when at length he was silent, the boy fixed his large eyes earnestly upon his face as he replied, " I understand, sir, we are so poor that it is not possible to send me to a public school, or to college as—as—my dear father wished; but I do not see why I am necessarily obliged to become a merchant's clerk, a position which I shall never be fit for, and which I hate the idea of; the Colvilles have always been gentlemen."

" A man may work for his living in some honest occupation without forfeiting that title," returned Mr. Slowkopf, sententiously.

" Not as a merchant's clerk," was the haughty reply: " No; let me be an artist, if I cannot receive a gentleman's education in England. I know I have some talent for drawing, let me study that, and then go to Italy, beautiful Italy, for a few years; people can live very cheaply abroad, and I will be very careful. When I become famous I shall grow rich, and be able to support mamma, and send Hugh to college, and then I shall care less for not having been there myself."

" Without attempting to regard your scheme in its many complicated bearings, or to argue the matter in its entire completeness, for which time, unfortunately, is wanting," remarked Mr. Slowkopf, deliberately ; " I will place before you, *in limine*, certain objections to it which render the commercial career proposed by your excellent uncle, if not in every point a more advantageous arrangement, at all events one more suited to the present position of affairs. Your uncle proposes to take upon himself all immediate expense connected with your education ; while, as a clerk in his counting-house, you will be in the receipt of a gradually increasing salary. Your scheme would demand a constant outlay of capital, for certainly the next five years ; nay, it would be no matter of surprise to me if ten years should elapse, ere, by the precarious earnings of an artist's career, you were enabled to render yourself independent. In one case you will be an assistance to your excellent mother, in the other a burden upon her."

Percy walked to the window ; the burning tears of disappointed ambition and mortified pride rushed to his eyes, but he brushed them hurriedly away, as he said in a firm, steady voice, " Thank you for telling me the truth, Mr. Slowkopf ; we will accept my uncle's offer."

Thus it came about that Percy and Hugh Colville were entered, as boarders, at Doctor Donkiestir's excellent proprietary establishment.

CHAPTER III.

A ROMANTIC ADVENTURE.

The Rosebud of Ashburn possessed a female friend. Caroline Selby was the daughter of Sir Thomas Crawley's agent. Sir Thomas Crawley was the rich man of the neighbourhood, lord of the manor, patron of the living, and owner of a splendid place about a mile from the village ; but although Ashburn Priory was an old family seat, the present owner of the property had by no means always been the great man he was at present ; indeed, it may be doubted whether, in justice, he had any right to be so at all ; though, unfortunately, in law he possessed a very sufficient one. The former possessor of Ashburn Priory, an irritable, perverse old man, had, in a moment of passion, disinherited an only son (who had committed the unpardonable crime of consulting his heart, rather than his pocket, in the choice of a wife), making a will in favour of a relative whom he had never seen, and of whom the little he had heard was unfavourable. It is true, he never intended this will to take effect; meaning, when he had sufficiently consulted his dignity, and marked his disapproval of the sin against Mammon which his son had committed, graciously to receive him into favour again; but Death, who has no more respect for ill-temper than for many more amiable qualities, did not allow him time to repair the injustice he had committed, cutting him off with an attack of bronchitis, and his son with a shilling, at one fell stroke. The son, an amiable man, with a large family (a conjunction so often to be observed, that, to a speculative mind, it almost assumes the relation of cause and effect), soon spent his shilling, and, overtasking his strength to replace it, ere long followed his unjust father, though we can scarcely imagine that he travelled by the same road. Before this latter event took place, however, Mr. Thomas Crawley made his first appearance as lord of the manor of Ashburn, and master of the Priory; and everybody was so well aware what he was, that they carefully abstained from inquiring what he had been. To those capable of judging, however, one thing was unmistakably apparent; namely, that neither in the past nor in the present could his manners and appearance entitle him to the designation of a gentleman. That he himself entertained an uncomfortable suspicion of this fact, might be gathered from the indefatigable perseverance with which he pursued the object of attaining to the rank of knighthood. Up the rounds of a ladder of gold he climbed into Parliament; once there, if he voted according to his conscience, that inward monitor must have been of a decidedly versatile temperament; for the way in which he wheeled about, and turned about, on every occasion, conceivable and inconceivable, was without precedent, save in the cases of Jim Crow, of giddy memory, and of Weathercock *versus* Boreas and Co. At last a crisis arrived; votes were worth more than the men who gave them: a minister stayed in who should have gone out; and Mr. Crawley became Sir Thomas. And this was the man who, with a rent-roll of £15,000 a-year, was about to avail himself of a legal quibble, in order to extort from a widow and orphans a share of the little pittance that remained to them. His agent Mr. Selby, was a better man than his master; and might have been better still, if "his poverty, and not his will," had not led him to consent to be the instrument wherewith **Sir Thomas Crawley**, M.P., transacted much dirty work in **Ashburn** and its vicinity. At the time we treat of, the will had so often yielded that it had quite lost the habit of asserting itself; and the poverty, profiting by this inertness, had gradually disappeared, till **Mr. Selby** was generally looked upon as a man well to do in the world, and respected accordingly.

And this brings us back to the point from whence we originally started; namely, that the Rosebud of Ashburn possessed a female friend. Now, the office of female friend to a Rosebud, romantic and poetical as it sounds, was by no means a sinecure; indeed, from the confidant of Tilburnia downwards, these sympathisers of all work have hard places of it. Still, there appears to be no lack of amiable creatures ready to devote themselves to the cause of friendship; the supply seems always to equal the demand. Possibly occasional perquisites, in the shape of a heart caught in the rebound, as in the case of a discarded lover, or the reversion of some *bon parti*, rejected for a more eligible offer, may have something to do with it—of this we cannot pretend to judge.

That any such sordid notions influenced Caroline Selby in her devotion to Emily Colville, we do not believe: on the contrary, the friendship arose from, and was cemented by, the Jack-Sprat-and-his-wife-like suitableness of their respective natures; Caroline having a decided call to look up to and worship somebody, while Emily experienced an equally strenuous necessity for being worshipped and looked up to. But the Rosebud was subject also to other necessities, which effectually preserved her friend from falling into the snares of idleness. First, she had a chronic necessity for "talking confidence,"—though how, in the quiet village of Ashburn, she contrived to obtain a supply of mysteries to furnish forth subjects for these strictly private colloquies, was the greatest mystery of all. Then privy councils were held upon dress, in all its branches, from staylaces up to *blonde Berthes;* and committees of ways and means had to combat and arrange financial difficulties. Again, the affairs of their poorer neighbours required much talking about, and speculating upon; and their little charities (for, despite sundry small weaknesses and frivolities natural to their age, or rather youth, and sex, the friends were thoroughly kind-hearted, amiable girls) could not be planned, or executed, without a *necessary* amount of conversation. Then there was a town, three miles off by the road, and two and a half by the fields, where everything came from; for, though Ashburn boasted a "general" shop, yet those who were rash enough to particularise any article they might require, beyond the inevitable bacon, cheese, soap, bad tea, worse sugar, starch, and hobnailed shoes, upon which agricultural life is supported, only prepared for themselves a disappointment.

This obliging town the Rosebud had a call to visit, on an average, three times a week at the very least; and of course, when the pony-chaise could not be had, which—as Hugh, by the agency of that much-enduring pony, existed rather as a centaur than a biped—was almost always the case, Caroline Selby was required as a walking companion.

Having thus enlightened the reader as to the nature of the friendship existing between these young ladies, together with other particulars, which, at the risk of being considered prosy, we felt bound to communicate to him, we resume the thread of our narrative.

Three weeks had elapsed since Mrs. Colville had accepted her brother's offer, and the day approached when Percy and Hugh were to quit the home of their happy childhood, never again to return to it. Mrs. Colville seldom alluded to the subject; busying herself in preparing their clothes, and in other necessary duties appertaining to the mistress of a family.

Now it happened that Master Hugh wore turn-over collars, famous for two peculiarities, viz., the moment they were put on, clean and smooth, they became rumpled and dirty—and the strings by which they were fastened, were the victims to a suicidal propensity for tearing themselves violently off, so that the amount of starch, labour, and tape, required to preserve these collars in an efficient condition, formed a serious item in the household expenditure.

Although the excellent factotum, Sarah, declared upon oath (not a *very* naughty one) that she had reviewed the delinquents cautiously that day fortnight, and been able to report them fitted for service, yet, at the eleventh hour, when she was actually packing Hugh's box, there were only three strings and a quarter remaining among the twelve collars, and there was no reliance to be placed even upon them. Moreover, on examination, there was discovered to have been such a run upon tape, of late, that not an inch of that useful article was forthcoming throughout the entire establishment. Under these appalling circumstances, Emily nobly volunteered to go to Flatville, and invest capital in the purchase of a "whole piece of tape." But the boys were absent on a skating expedition: and the roads were slippery, and the pony had not been roughed, and Emily, not liking to walk by herself, set off, no way loth, to enlist Caroline Selby as her companion.

Here, however, a difficulty arose. Mr. Selby was just starting in his phaeton, to drive over to the railroad station, two miles beyond Flatville, and his daughter was going with him, for the sake of a drive.

Caroline was perplexed: had it been only to give up her own plans, she would gladly have done so; but between her father and her friend, a double sacrifice was required of her, and being only a single woman, she was unable to meet the demand. Mr. Selby, happily, hit upon an expedient. He proposed a compromise: Miss Colville should do him the honour to take a seat in his phaeton (he called it phee-aton), *he* would drive her as far as Flatville; his *daughter* should alight with her: they should make their *little* purchases (the words in italics he uttered in a tone of the tenderest affection); and the phee-aton, in returning from the station, should call and pick them up.

Mr. Selby was a very polite man; and perpetually rubbed his hands together, as though he were playing at washing them, a habit possibly induced by a consciousness of all the dirty work he had performed. Emily patronised him, steadily disbelieving everything that was hinted against him, because he was Caroline's father,—a piece of scepticism, amiable, illogical, and womanly, which we rather admire in the young lady than otherwise.

Accordingly, favouring him with a bewitching smile, that a better man than he might have been proud to win, she scarcely touched the hand he held out to assist her (which he carefully dry-washed afterwards, as though the contact even of her fairy fingers had dissolved the spell of its prudish purity), and sprang lightly into the " phee-aton."

Half an hour's drive brought them to Flatville, where Mr. Selby, so to speak, washed his hands of them, and went on to the railroad station. Then began the shopping, that most mysterious and deeply-seated passion of the female heart—the one master vice which serves the ladies of England, instead of the turf, the wine-cup, and the gaming table, which mislead their lords. There can be little doubt who first invented shopping! The same hand which launched that arrow into the bosom of private life, gave to the child-woman, Eve, the apple that betrayed her—an apple which contained the seeds of shopping. It is such a seductive, hypocritical sin, too, this same shopping—one which is so easily dressed up to resemble a virtue—that it is almost impossible to distinguish its true character *till the bill comes in* : that, like the touch of Ithuriel's spear, reveals the fiend in all its deformity. Every woman (that we have known) is more or less addicted to this ruinous practice, but some appear especially gifted with the fatal talent, and, if the truth must be told, our little heroine was one of these unfortunates. The amount of shopping she would contrive to get, even out of a piece of tape, was fearful to reflect upon. In the first place, it was to be of a particular (*very* particular) texture, neither too coarse nor too fine ; then society would probably be uprooted, and the Thames be set on fire, if it were a shade too wide, or, worse still, too narrow. Again, tape was useless without needles and thread, wherewith to operate upon it; and for some time—indeed, till the obsequious parrot of a shopman had gone through his whole vocabulary of persuasion, and become cynical and monosyllabic—*all* the needles were too large ; and, that difficulty being overcome, the thread (sewing cotton Emily called it) took a perverse turn, and would by no means sympathise with the eyes of the selected needles, till the harassed shopman muttered a private aspiration in regard to those useful orifices, which would have cost him five shillings in any court of justice. But he took his revenge, did that cunning shopman, for, no sooner had Emily bought all that she required, than he suddenly recovered his good humour and loquacity, and placed before her exactly the very articles she most desired, and had not funds to purchase withal, till Tantalus himself might have appeared a gentleman who lived at home at ease, in comparison with that sorely-tempted "Rosebud." Still, what woman could do, she did, for she firmly resisted everything, till an unlucky remnant of magpie-coloured ribbon, the "very thing she should want when she changed her mourning, and which she *knew* she could never meet with again," a ribbon so cheap that the shopman declared he was "giving it away," at the very moment when he was adding two shillings to the bill on the strength of it ; though this seductive ribbon beguiled her, the little concession only proved that she was not above humanity. With which fact we are well contented, because, enjoying but a very distant and limited acquaintance with such higher circles as she would otherwise have mixed in, we might never have heard of her existence. That she possessed some power of self-denial she proved, by paying her bill and quitting the shop the moment that ribbon had conquered her; the next best thing to resisting temptation being to fly from it.

"Why, Caroline dear, we must have been an age in that shop, it is nearly five o'clock! What can have become of your father's carriage?" exclaimed Emily, glancing in dismay at the hands of the old church clock, which pointed to a quarter to five.

"Really I can't conceive," was the reply: "something must have occurred to delay it, I suppose; it will be growing dusk before we can get home if we have to walk by the road, and we can scarcely attempt the fields so late by ourselves."

"Mamma will be so frightened," suggested Emily, "if it gets at all dark before we return—had we not better start at once, and walk on till the carriage overtakes us?"

Caroline agreed to this plan, merely proposing the emendation that they should leave word they had done so, and that the groom, if he ever appeared, was to follow and endeavour to overtake them. For this purpose they re-entered the linen-draper's shop, where, while they paused for a moment to deliver the message, that vindictive shopman actually was scoundrel enough to display at arm's length a flimsy black scarf (*barège* we believe the villain called it), which, down to the very pattern itself (opaque spots of the same material, representing apparently a turnip with a cocked hat on, though we can scarcely bring ourselves to believe the draughtsman could seriously have thus planned the design), Emily had dreamed of only the night before: such is the heartlessness of men—at least of shopmen.

The two girls, having nobly withstood the scarf, started energetically on their homeward walk, nor were their tongues less active than their feet, but then they had so much to talk about. The linen-draper's stock was first done ample justice to; that "dear" silver grey *mousseline de soie*, which wasn't dear at all, but as cheap as—(the ribbon, perhaps, on which the shop-keeper only realised some fifty per cent., but then it was a remnant, and given away)—and then those gloves, French kid, oh! they must have been smuggled; how wrong it was to smuggle, at least papa (Selby) always said so, but really the price was quite ridiculous; didn't Emily think so?

Emily did not know about its being ridiculous, but it was dreadfully tempting; and if she had not made up her mind irrevocably against changing any one of the three sovereigns she had in her purse, and which must last her for pocket-money for the next two months, she should decidedly have bought a pair, really, for the sake of economy.

This fruitful and edifying topic lasted them a good mile and a half, and was not yet exhausted, when Emily interrupted herself by exclaiming—" Upon my word it's growing quite dusk; I wonder whether that carriage is ever coming?"

" I'm sure I hope so, for I'm getting dreadfully frightened; ah! what's that?" replied her companion with a sudden start; " Oh! it's only a post, how silly I am! I declare I thought it was a man with a pistol hooked—no—what is it they call it when they're dangerous and mean to go off, dear?"

" Cocked," returned Emily; " but surely that is a man, and a very uncomfortable looking one too; walk on quickly, and seem as if you did not perceive him; perhaps he may not take any notice of us."

The advice was sound, but, unfortunately, the plan did not prove as successful as it deserved to be; the individual in question, who, when they first came in sight, was lying apparently asleep upon some fallen timber by the road-side, rose as they came near, and approaching them, began in a tone half-impertinent, half-imploring, to beg of them. He was a stout, ruffianly-looking fellow, dressed in a style which accorded with his profession. The poor girls were considerably frightened: they were quite a mile from Ashburn, in a lonely part of the road; the evening was closing in rapidly, and there was no human being in sight, except their persecutor, who, walking beside them, grew every minute more pertinacious and imperative. With a most transparent attempt at dignified composure, Emily drew out her purse, and, taking a shilling from it, handed it to him, saying—

" There, that is as much as we shall give you, so you need not follow us any further—good evening."

Taking the shilling, with a look of sulky dissatisfaction, the fellow paused for a moment in irresolution; but, unfortunately, when Emily produced her purse, his eye had caught the sparkle of gold, and his cupidity was too deeply excited to be so easily satisfied: looking up and down the road, to assure himself that no one was at hand to interfere with his designs, he again followed the trembling girls; and, coming up with them, exclaimed—

"What! will you only give a poor fellow that's starving, a shilling? and you with a purse full of money in your pocket— and you calls yourselves ladies too? It would only serve you right to show you that ladies was no better than other people."

As he spoke, he pressed rudely against Caroline Selby, who, shrinking from him, whispered in an agony of terror—

"Emily, what *will* become of us? Pray give him some more money, and entreat him to go away."

Thus urged, Emily again drew forth her purse, and, trembling at her own temerity, said in an authoritative tone of voice—

"There's half-a-crown for you, and now go away, and don't annoy us any more."

"Not without something better worth taking with me," was the insolent reply, as, catching her wrist, he attempted to force the purse from her grasp; but Emily, although greatly alarmed, had a brave little heart of her own, and held on stoutly, till the unmanly ruffian, provoked at her pertinacity, used so much force that she relinquished the purse; while at the same moment, partly through pain, partly through fright, she uttered a piercing scream.

Now, albeit insolent lords of the creation exulting in strong nerves, and not possessing soprano voices, are accustomed to regard screaming as a feeble-minded practice, equally useless and ridiculous, yet in the instance before us it proved of the highest benefit, and by far the best thing, which, under the circumstances, Emily could have done; for, as if he were some good genius evoked by the Rosebud's appeal, suddenly and unexpectedly a tall, agile figure sprang through a gap in the hedge, cleared the intervening space at a bound, and, almost before the footpad was aware of his approach, struck the scoundrel, with a stick which he carried, so severe a blow over the knuckles, that he dropped the purse; while, at the same moment, seizing him by the throat, he forced him backwards, and, putting out his leg, tripped him up, and flung him heavily to the ground. Placing his foot upon the breast of his fallen foe, to prevent his rising, he turned towards the frightened girls, and, lifting his hat courteously, thereby revealing his dark chestnut curls, he said—

" Do not be alarmed, ladies, I am quite able to protect you."

Then, pointing to the fallen man with his stick, which he slightly shook at him with a menacing gesture, he continued—

" Has the scoundrel robbed you of anything but the purse ?"

As she turned to answer, Emily raised her eyes to the speaker's face. He was young, apparently not more than five or six and twenty; the exertion he had undergone had caused a bright flush to overspread his usually pale features ; even at that moment his look was calm and spiritual ; the prevailing expression of his face was power, which revealed itself in his flashing eyes and stern, compressed mouth ; his voice, when he spoke. sounded peculiarly rich and sweet. When Emily had informed him that, with the exception of the purse, they had sustained no loss, he continued—

" But he was struggling with you when I came up; he must, surely, have hurt you ; are you quite uninjured ?"

Both the girls having assured him that they were merely frightened, and that until the moment before he appeared, the man had simply been begging of them, the stranger turned to his prostrate foe, saying—

" It would only serve you right for your unmanly attack on two defenceless women, if I were to avail myself of the advantage I have gained over you to take you into custody and have you punished for the offence you have committed ; but as I wish to spare these ladies the alarm of witnessing any further struggle between us, I shall, with their permission, let you go ; but mind this, I shall give a description of your appearance at the nearest police-station ; and if you do not immediately quit this part of the country, you will have rather more attention paid you than you will find by any means agreeable. So now take yourself off while you may."

As he spoke, he removed his foot from the scoundrel's breast, and with difficulty restraining an impulse to bestow upon him a parting kick, allowed him to rise and slink doggedly away. And now the Rosebud, who, between alarm, and gratitude, and shyness, and an embarrassing consciousness that their champion was young and handsome, was altogether in a great state of agitation and excitement, felt it incumbent upon her, as spokeswoman, to express her sentiments as best she might. Accordingly, with some hesitation and many blushes, which unfortunately the increasing darkness rendered invisible, she informed **the stranger** how very much obliged to him they were: and impressed upon his mind the state of abject terror from which he had relieved them, glancing slightly at the anxiety they felt for the favourable termination of the combat, and their admiration of, and gratitude for, his heroic conduct.

The stranger received her acknowledgments with a quiet smile, partly pleased, partly amused by the young girl's eagerness; then, in a few simple, courteous, well-chosen words, he expressed the pleasure he had felt in having been able to render them such a slight service; adding, he should always consider it a most fortunate occurrence that, owing to a fancy which had seized him, to find his way from the railroad-station across the fields, he had been enabled to arrive just at the most critical moment.

The Rosebud listened to him attentively. One thing was quite evident, be he whom he might, both his language and manner proved him a gentleman. Mysterious and deeply interesting! Could it be Prince Albert, wandering about the country in disguise, for some inexplicable purpose connected with political economy, or the Admirable Crichton, suddenly "come alive," to seek for a wife in the nineteenth century?

The arrival of the "Ph*ee-a*ton," which had been taken poorly, and obliged to have its wheel oiled,—a process which, owing to the inefficiency of the blacksmith who (*faute de mieux*) had been called in to attend the patient, had occupied a longer portion of time than was by any means necessary,—interrupted Emily's conjectures.

The mysterious stranger, as soon as he understood the connection between the vehicle and the damsels he had rescued, politely handed them in; and, refusing Caroline's timid offer of a seat, again raised his hat, and the carriage driving on, was soon lost to sight.

" Oh, Emily, what a brave, handsome, courteous, interesting creature!" exclaimed Caroline, enthusiastically; "who can he be ?"

" I can't conceive; but we shall be sure to find out, for he is walking in the direction of Ashburn," was the reply. "He certainly knocked that dreadful man down very cleverly, and was extremely kind and good-natured to us; but do you think him so very handsome ?"

" Oh, there can't be a doubt about it ! Those pale, interesting features—that lofty brow—those splendid flashing eyes—the dark clusters of his waving hair !"

"Carry, you've fallen in love with the man at first sight, and are a susceptible little goose; he is by no means the Adonis you make out; and, remember, we know nothing about him; he may be a bagman for anything we can tell to the contrary," rejoined Emily.

"No, I'm quite certain he is a gentleman, and most likely something better still. He spoke just like Lord Adolphus Fitz-toplofty, when I danced with him at the race-ball, and he asked me whether I'd seen the 'Prophète,' and if I didn't doat upon that dear Mario (so lucky that he should fix upon the only opera I'd ever heard, wasn't it?), and yet you pretend to believe he's a bagman; but I know you only say so to plague me, you naughty thing;" and thus speaking, Caroline relieved her over-wrought feelings by giving her friend a playful blow, which the most fragile fly might have endured unshrinkingly.

"My dear child, I never hinted anything of the kind," returned Emily; "*au contraire*, I believe Lord Adolphus to be a thoroughly well-authenticated young nobleman, and consider him the most gentlemanly puppy I have ever met."

"Tiresome girl; you know I don't mean Lord Fitz. But I'll stake my penetration on the stranger's gentility; you only abuse him because you admire him so much that you are ashamed to own it, you mean, deceitful girl!"

"Silly child, how can you be so absurd!" said the Rosebud; but although it was so dark that, if she *had* blushed, her friend could never have discovered it, she turned away her head as she spoke.

———

CHAPTER IV

SHUFFLING, DEALING, AND TURNING UP A KNAVE AND A
TRUMP.

"TAKE this to Sir Thomas Crawley, and tell him I am waiting."

The servant to whom the above direction was given, carried the card to which it referred to his master, who, lifting it from the silver waiter on which it was presented, read the following name—"The Rev. Ernest Carrington."

"Show the gentleman into the library, and bring candles there directly," said Sir Thomas; then, thrusting his fingers through the short, stiff, grey bristles, suggestive of a venerable and well-worn scrubbing-brush, which constituted his head of hair—an action which, to any one acquainted with his habits, would have proved that he was anxious and excited—he turned, and left the apartment.

When he entered the library, his excitement seemed to have increased and taken a crabbed turn, for it was in no very cordial tone of voice that he addressed his visitor

"If, as I presume, you have come here in consequence of my letter, I must say you have chosen a somewhat late hour for a business visit, young gentleman."

"I lost no time, sir, in making the necessary inquiries," was the reply. "Immediately on receiving your letter I hastened to London, saw your solicitor, perused my grandfather's will, obtained the information I required, and came down by the first train that stopped at the Flatville station; and, as your man of business informed me time was of importance, I would not wait till to-morrow, lest the delay might cause you inconvenience. If that is not sufficient apology for my untimely visit, I have none other to offer."

The calm, respectful, but at the same time perfectly self-possessed manner of the speaker, appeared to have the same kind of effect upon his auditor that the keeper's eye has upon some savage animal, for he replied, in a more civil tone than he had yet used,—

"Yes, well—I see—yes. I am obliged to you for the prompt attention you have paid to my letter." He paused, then added, with affected indifference,—"About the entail; you find, of course, that the point raised was a wholly unnecessary one, and that your signature is a mere matter of form, to satisfy the absurd scruples of the party negociating for the purchase; some people are so ridiculously cautious, ha! ha!" and here he laughed a forced, uneasy laugh.

"Such was by no means the view the solicitor whom I consulted in town appeared to take of the matter," was Ernest's quiet reply. "So far from it, that he declared, without my signature, the title was worthless; and that, if I were inclined to litigate the question, he had not a doubt that I should gain my cause. The estates, he said, were clearly entailed; and, therefore, my grandfather could not alienate them without my father's consent, which, I need scarcely tell you, he never attempted to obtain."

Sir Thomas Crawley's brow grew black as midnight. " Preposterous," he said, " quite childish and preposterous. I have taken counsel's opinion on the point, and they say you haven't a leg to stand on. You must have consulted some very ignorant person."

" On the contrary, it is Mr. S., of —— street," replied Ernest, naming a gentleman whose reputation for legal knowledge and acumen was undeniable; " but," he continued, " it matters little, for I have no intention of raising the question. The *animus* of my grandfather's will is unmistakable; he meant to leave every acre away from my father; and I should scorn to hold the estate on no better tenure than the juggling of a legal quibble."

" Then you are prepared to sign the paper resigning all claim upon the entailed estates, are you ?" inquired Sir Thomas, eagerly.

" Yes, this very moment, if you choose," was the ready answer.

Sir Thomas paused an instant in thought ere he replied.

" There is no such extreme hurry : Mr. Selby, my country agent, will be here to-morrow morning, and can witness your signature. I am glad to find that you take such a sensible view of the matter. I feared you might have formed some rash hopes on the strength of my application ; in fact, I was most unwilling to apply to you ; but—but—"

" You found it impossible to make out a title which could sell the estate without so doing," interposed Ernest in a tone of quiet politeness, in which it would have required perceptions quicker and more delicate than those of Sir Thomas Crawley to have distinguished the covert satire that lurked beneath it.

" Exactly: one of those contemptible legal quibbles which you so justly reprobate," returned Sir Thomas ; " however, I am glad to perceive you feel with me so completely. You will dine with me ? and I have a bed very much at your service."

Ernest thanked him, but civilly declined. Sir Thomas however, persisted—he would take no denial; and at length a compromise was effected, Ernest consenting to dine with his rich relative, on condition that he might return to the inn where he had left his valise, in time to write one or two letters of importance to go by the early post the next morning.

The dinner passed off agreeably enough ; Ernest being one

of those happily endowed individuals who, without falsifying
their own opinions, or seeming the thing they are not, yet
possess the talent of adapting their conversation to those with
whom they are thrown in company, in such a manner as to set
them at ease, and draw out the best points of their characters.

Sir Thomas experienced the full influence of this fascination,
and talked largely of his schemes for the amelioration of his
tenantry; of plans for the revision and modification of the poor-
laws; of the advisability of erecting model lodging-houses for
the industrial classes, &c., &c., until he had deceived his companion, and almost persuaded himself into the belief that he was
an enlightened philanthropist, overflowing with the milk of
human kindness.

On his return to the inn at Ashburn, Ernest wrote the following letter to an old college friend, who was junior partner in
the office of the legal luminary to whom he had alluded in his
interview with Sir Thomas Crawley.

" MY DEAR MILFORD,—Since I saw you two days ago, I
have got through a considerable amount of business, met with
an adventure, and, in short, condensed more active existence
into the last eight-and-forty hours than one often accomplishes
in as many days. One thing I am delighted to tell you,—I
have succeeded in procuring employment, which will more
than provide for the few requirements without which one must
degrade from the rank of a gentleman. You can now, therefore, carry out the arrangement I explained to you, and settle
the small residue of my poor father's property upon my sisters;
—my mother, as you are aware, having (I own, against my
wishes) married again. Thanks to those unnaturally amiable
railroad shares which my father bought just before his decease,
and which have turned out a really good investment (I look
upon any one who, having gambled in railroads, leaves off a
winner, as I should at a rat, who, nibbling at a baited trap,
carried off the cheese scatheless), they will thus be able to live
in comparative comfort, especially on the Continent, which
their tastes lead them to prefer. The employment I have
obtained is not exactly to my liking, but I shall look out for a
curacy if I find the duties of my position unbearably irksome.
Owing to my wrangler's degree I distanced some half-dozen
competitors, and obtained the post of classical and mathematical
master at Doctor Donkiestir's well-known school, almost as soon

as I had entered my name as candidate. I begin my new
duties the day after to-morrow, at which time the school meets.

"Having been thus enabled to place my sisters beyond the
reach of poverty, my last scruple, in regard to that which you
are pleased to call my absurd Quixotism, about the entailed
estates, has vanished; and I, this evening, signified *in propriâ
personâ* to Sir Thomas, my willingness to 'do a little bit of
Esau,' as you irreverently term signing away my birthright—
and here, *par parenthèse*, let me observe that you are too much
addicted to this style of scriptural jesting—a fault the more to
be reprehended because (as I find to my cost) it is decidedly
infectious: *verbum sat!* The aforesaid ' Sir Thomas ' seems,.
as far as one can judge on so short an acquaintance, by no
means so black as he is painted ; indeed, upon many of the great
social questions of the day, his ideas coincide wonderfully with
my own : he was polite in the extreme, though I must confess his amiability *followed* my declaration that I was willing to
meet his wishes in regard to the entail.

"This epistle has run to such an unexpected length, that I
have no room to detail my adventure, and will merely stimulate
your curiosity by adding that it was intensely romantic, and
that it contained the elements of the two things which, in the
old Trinity days, we esteemed the greatest pleasures in life—
viz., a fight and a flirtation.

"In consideration of my cloth, I indulged in the first spar-
ingly, and abstained from the last entirely ; though, as far as
the twilight enabled me to judge, the provocation was a very
fair one. I know the epithet this confession will obtain for me ;
but I had rather bear the ignominy of being considered a
' muff,' than merit the designation of a ' fast parson ; ' and so
fare thee well.

" Yours ever,

" ERNEST CARRINGTON."

"P.S.—Remember, my sisters are not to know that I am
sacrificing anything to add to their income ; you are merely to
inform them that, my father's affairs being at length arranged,
they will for the future be in the receipt of six hundred and
fifty pounds per annum, instead of the four hundred which you
before paid to them ; and the delightful mist through which all
women regard business matters, will effectually prevent their
making any further discoveries."

Having sealed his letter, Ernest betook himself to bed, and fell asleep as contentedly as if he had not sacrificed an estate worth £10,000 to a chivalrous scruple, and a patrimony of £200 a-year to brotherly affection.

Sir Thomas Crawley might consider him a weak-minded, good-natured fool; Milford designate him a "muff." But if there were a few more such muffs and fools in this realm of good King Mammon, that same kingdom might be better worth living in.

By ten o'clock the next morning he was again at Ashburn Priory; signed the deed relinquishing all claim upon the entailed estates; shook hands cordially with the rich man who was thus scheming to defraud him; and started with a light heart, and still lighter purse, to carry his own carpet-bag seven miles to the railroad. About a mile from the station, a pony-chaise overtook him, driven by a stout serving-lad, and containing two gentlemanly-looking boys, dressed in mourning, and a ponderous trunk, carefully corded and directed. As this vehicle approached, Ernest, who had walked fast, paused to wipe his brow, at the same time resting his carpet-bag—which he had carried on a stick over his shoulder—upon the top of the last milestone.

The elder of the two boys regarded him attentively; then whispered something to the younger, who nodded and smiled in reply; making a sign to the driver to stop, the elder boy, addressing Ernest, began—

"I beg your pardon, sir, but you seem tired : we are going to the Flatville station, and have a vacant seat at your service, if you please to accept it."

"I will with the greatest pleasure," returned Ernest, "if you are sure we shall not overweight the pony."

"Oh, you needn't be afraid—you need not be in the least afraid of that, sir," interposed the younger boy confidently. "Samson can draw us; Samson is as strong as——"

"His Israelitish namesake, perhaps," suggested Ernest, placing his carpet-bag on the top of the trunk, and springing lightly into the pony-chaise.

"Well, *I* was going to say, as strong as the Elephant and Castle," remarked the younger boy, with a look of profound sagacity; "but, perhaps, the original Samson will do as well. What do you say, Percy ?"

"I say that you are an absurd little chatterbox, Hugh, and I have little doubt the gentleman thinks so too," returned his brother,—for the reader need scarcely read the direction on the trunk, albeit written in Percy's plainest hand, to inform him that the boys were the two young Colvilles, then leaving home for the first time in their lives.

The parting had been a trying scene for all the persons concerned; and poor Hugh had only just recovered from the hearty cry, in which even his incipient manly dignity could not preserve him from indulging, when they overtook Ernest.

" A chatterbox, perhaps, but not an absurd one," was the good-natured reply. " I feel particularly interested about the pony, I can assure you ; have you had him long ? I daresay he is a great favourite."

This speech, which was addressed to Hugh, was too much for the poor little fellow's fortitude, and, after a vain struggle to repress them, his scarcely dried tears sprang forth anew.

Percy threw his arm around him, and drew him affectionately to his side, as he said, in an explanatory whisper, " He is going to school for the first time, sir ; and before he comes back, the pony we are so fond of must be sold."

" And you?" inquired Ernest, interested by the boy's manner and appearance.

" I am older, and therefore better able to bear such little trials," was the reply. " Besides," Percy continued, in a lower tone, " my mother depends upon me to take care of him, and keep up his spirits, for he has no father now to protect him."

Ernest glanced involuntarily at their deep mourning, and there was a pause ; for the circumstance brought vividly before his recollection a similar period of sorrow, when death had been busy among his own loved ones, and his father and a younger brother, of whom Percy strongly reminded him, had been called from this world of care, and sin, and sorrow, to that better land, " where the wicked cease from troubling, and the weary are at rest." The silence was at length broken by Hugh, whose grief was a very April kind of affair, even at the worst of times.

" I suppose you are not going to school, sir, too ?" he said, addressing Ernest, while a merry sparkle in his eye belied the simplicity the question indicated.

" Perhaps I may be," returned Ernest, smiling at the applicability of the question to his own situation. " If I should tell you that I were going to do so, would you believe me ?"

" I don't think I should," replied Hugh, regarding him attentively. "People don't usually go to school when they've these things on their faces;" and, as he spoke, he, with a gesture half coaxing, half arch, gave a gentle twitch to Ernest's curling whiskers.

Percy, afraid Hugh's sudden rush into intimacy might annoy the stranger, attempted to restrain him, but Ernest, with a good-natured smile, prevented him.

"Do not check him," he said; "our friendship will not end any sooner because it has begun rather rapidly." He then entered into conversation with the boys, choosing subjects in which he imagined they would feel interest, and enlarging upon them so cleverly and amusingly, that ere they reached the station, he had completely captivated the fresh, warm hearts of his young companions.

"What will you say if I guess where you are going to?" he inquired of Hugh, as they drove up to the station.

"Why, if you guess right, I shall say you must be a conjuror," was the reply.

"I think you are going to Doctor Donkiestir's school, at Tickletown. Am I right?"

"Quite, quite right," exclaimed Hugh, clapping his hands in delighted surprise; "but you *must* be a conjuror; how did you contrive to find it out?"

Ernest enjoyed the mystification for a minute or so; then, casting his eyes on the box, observed quietly, "I was taught to read when I was a good little boy; and your brother has written that direction so plainly, that I must have been blind if I had not been able to decipher it."

"Oh, you cheat! anybody could have done that," returned Hugh, contemptuously; "and I to think you a conjuror! Why, I expected to see you take twenty eggs out of an empty bag, and make a boiled plum-pudding in your hat, like the man we saw perform last year. I say, Percy, it strikes me I've been making a goose of myself."

"Very decidedly," was Percy's quiet reply.

CHAPTER V.

A FAST SPECIMEN OF " YOUNG ENGLAND.

THE railroad station at Flatville was a large and central one, two or three branches converging at that point and joining the main line. A train from London was due before that by which the Colvilles were to proceed would start. Almost at the moment our little party arrived it made its appearance, the engine snorting and puffing, as though it were about to burst with spite at having been forced to draw so heavy a train at the rate of fifty miles an hour.

" This is the train by which our cousin, Wilfred Goldsmith, was to arrive; but it is so long since I last saw him, that I scarcely expect to recognise him," observed Percy.

" Oh! I hope we shall not miss him, for he will take care that they don't put us into a wrong carriage, and carry us off to some desolate island, where we shall never be heard of any more till we have been eaten by the savages like Captain Cook; and then you know it will be too late," suggested Hugh.

" I will ensure you against that catastrophe," observed Ernest, " even if your cousin should not make his appearance; for I am going as far as Tickletown, and we will travel in the same carriage; see, they are bringing them up now—follow me."

So saying, and having committed the important trunk to the care of an amiable and intelligent porter, Ernest selected a carriage, and the trio took their seats. Just before the train was about to start, an individual bustled up, followed by a porter carrying a writing-desk and a railway-rug glowing with all the colours of the rainbow. The moment the door was opened, he sprang in with such energy as nearly to overturn poor Hugh.

" Beg your pardon, little boy, but 'pon my word I didn't see you—you ought to grow a couple of sizes larger to travel safe by rail; it was nearly a case of infanticide—a *spoilt* child, as somebody calls it. That'll do, Velveteens" (this was addressed to the porter); " gently with that writing-desk, if *you* please; there's all my personal jewellery, and several £500 notes in it. That's the time of day! Sorry the directors set their faces against tipping; but the first occasion on which we meet in private life, half-a-crown awaits you; till then, Velveteens, as the Archbishop says in the play, ' Accept my blessing.' "

The speaker was either a very small man, or a large boy dressed in adult clothing—at first sight it was not easy to determine which—till closer observation detected, in the breaking voice, now hoarse, now shrill, the youthful complexion, and straggling, unformed figure, sufficient evidence that the latter hypothesis was the correct one. His outer boy was encased in a rough, very loose pea-jacket, with preternatural buttons, a pair of the very "loudest" checked trousers, *real* Wellington boots, with heels not above three inches high, a shawl round his neck, in regard to which Emily's perfidious shopman might have been believed, had he declared the colours to be indisputably *fast;* while a velvet travelling-cap, with a bullion tassel, completed his costume. Having wrapped his rug round his lower limbs, and gone through a most elaborate pantomime of making himself comfortable, he condescended to favour his companions with a glance of patronising scrutiny; apparently satisfying himself, by this means, that they were sufficiently respectable to be honoured by his conversation, he turned to Ernest, saying,—

" Fine open weather this, sir—jolly for the hunting—none of your confounded frosts to-day—regular break up yesterday evening, and been thawing like bricks ever since—fond of hunting, sir ? "

" I consider it a fine, manly sport, but too dangerous for little boys to be allowed to indulge in," returned Ernest, drily.

Either not detecting, or more probably purposely ignoring, the covert satire of his speech, the fast young gentleman appeared to agree in the sentiment.

" Yes, that's true enough," he said; " for instance, I wouldn't advise this small shaver " (indicating with a motion of the eyelid Hugh, who sat watching him with breathless astonishment) " to trust himself across country outside a horse; but when one has come to—ahem! years of discretion, and learned how to take care of oneself,—the purpose for which divines tell us we are sent into the world,—why the more hunting one gets the jollier, I say."

" Have you ever been out hunting yourself, may I ask ? " inquired Ernest, fixing his penetrating glance full on the boy's countenance; who, despite his fastness, was not, when asked a straightforward question, prepared to tell an actual lie, though to adhere to the exact truth would have made his previous remarks appear singularly inconsistent and uncalled for; accordingly he answered—

"Ar—well—yes—oh! of course I've been out hunting—ar —not exactly on horseback, perhaps, but it's just the same thing, you know;—what a shocking slow train this is, to be sure!— —they hardly do their five-and-thirty miles an hour; I shall certainly write to the *Times* about it, if they don't mind what they're at."

During this speech Hugh's sharp eyes had deciphered the direction on the important writing-desk, containing the jewellery and the incalculable number of £500 notes, and he promulgated the result of his discovery thus :—

"'Wilfred J. Goldsmith, Esquire :' what! are *you* our cousin Wilfred? why I took you for a gentleman !"

"Oh, Hugh !" exclaimed Percy, scandalised at his brother's rudeness.

"No, I don't mean that," continued Hugh quickly, while Ernest turned away his head to hide an irrepressible smile ; " I mean, I took you for a grown up gentleman, and not a boy like Percy, you know."

This involuntary tribute to the man-about-town-like adultness of his manners and appearance delighted Wilfred Jacob more than the most elaborate compliment courtier could have devised ;. at length he had found some one to believe in him, and to take him at his own valuation, and he adopted and steadily patronised Hugh from that time forth. He was much too wide awake, however, to allow this to appear; replying in the off-hand manner which he affected—

"Rather an equivocal compliment that, young 'un; but I expect it was better meant than expressed ; so I'll take the will for the deed, as the lawyer's clerk did after he'd mixed the 'dog's-nose' rather too stiff at his early dinner. 'Always give credit for good intentions,' is a copy old Splitnib (so called from an analogy between his professional avocations, and the fact of his having, in by-gone hours, fallen over a form, and divided the bridge of his own proboscis) will set you writing before you are many days older; and in me you behold a living embodiment of the precept."

"How was it we did not see you at the station, Cousin Wilfred ?" inquired Percy; "we waited as long as we dared, till we thought we should lose the train looking for you."

" Why, you see, my dear boy," began Wilfred, stretching
out a boot beyond the rainbow-coloured wrapper, for the purpose
of tapping it admiringly with a dandyfied little cane, "leaving
the modern Babylon by the seven o'clock A.M., I necessarily
breakfasted early; and as, according to Cocker, the interval
between six A.M. and one P.M. embraces seven hours, I experienced, on my arrival at the Flatville station, the very uncomfortable sensation of nature abhorring a vacuum in my
breadbasket; and, as even Curtius himself could scarcely have
contrived to fill up a similar gulf by jumping down his own
throat, I walked first into the refreshment-room, and then into
a basin of mock-turtle soup. A deucedly pretty gal it was
who handed it to me, too; uncommon attentive she was, to be
sure : in fact, *en're nous*," he continued, leaning confidently
towards Ernest, "it strikes me she wasn't altogether insensible
to the personal attractions of 'yours truly'—do you twig?"

Ernest smiled as he replied, " Of course she charged for the
admiration as well as for your luncheon."

" Real turtle as well as mock, eh? I hope you don't mean
any insinuation about a calf's head too ! But, now you mention
it, I *do* think seven-and-sixpence was rather high for a basin of
soup. Ah ! the women, they make sad fools of us youth; but
as the old lady piously remarked, when her pet dog died of
repletion, 'Such is life, which is the end of all things:'—
heigh-ho !"

Having relieved his feelings by venting a deep sigh, Master
(he would have annihilated us for so calling him) Wilfred Jacob,
who appeared gifted with an interminable flow of conversation,
and an insatiable delight in listening to his own voice, again
addressed his companions, exclaiming—

" I tell you what it is, gentlemen : the cares of existence, and
the heartlessness of that deluding mock-turtle soup gal, are
weighing upon my spirits to such a degree, that nothing short
of a mild cigar can bring me round again: that is, always
supposing you, none of you, entertain a *rooted* aversion (you
perceive the pun?) to the leaves of the Indian herb."

" I presume you are aware that smoking in a first-class
carriage is against the rules of the railway company," suggested
Ernest.

" I know that some such prejudice exists in their feeble
minds," was the rejoinder; "but they are not obliged to learn anything about it, are they? 'Where ignorance is bliss,' you know."

" The first porter who opens the door is certain to perceive the smell; and of course, if he inquires whence it proceeds, I shall not attempt to disguise the truth," returned Ernest.

" Never fear," was the reply; " even if such an alarming contingency were to accrue, I know a safe dodge to throw him off the scent."

" If I possessed any authority over you, I should strongly remonstrate against your violating such a wise and useful regulation," observed Ernest, gravely.

" That fearful moral responsibility not resting upon your conscience—for which, as a philanthropist, I feel humbly thankful—I shall, with your leave, waste no more precious time, but go ahead at once." So saying the young pickle drew from his pocket a small neatly finished leather case, well filled with cigars; having politely offered it in turn to each of his companions, who were unanimous in their refusal, he selected a cigar, lighted it by means of a piece of German tinder, and, placing it in his mouth, began puffing away with equal zest and science.

Having set it going to his satisfaction, he removed it for a moment, and, emitting a graceful wreath of smoke, resumed— " Capital good cigars these—came from Fribourg and Pontet's —I never smoke any others—better change your mind and take one, Mr. ——, 'pon my word your name has escaped me."

" Are you quite certain you ever knew it ? " inquired Ernest, whilst a smile of quiet intelligence curled his handsome mouth.

In no degree disconcerted, Master Wilfred took another long pull at his cigar ere he replied, " Not to be done, eh, sir ? Well, I respect a man all the more for being unpumpable ; dodginess, in all its branches, is the virtue I most venerate."

" And what *is* dodginess, please, Cousin Wilfred ? " inquired Hugh, upon whose youthful intelligence slang was, for the first time, dawning with all its fascinating eloquence.

" Dodginess, my verdant young relative, is a psychological attribute compounded of equal portions of presence of mind and fertility of resource, which enables every ' cove ' (cove is a generic appellation for indiscriminate male humanity) thus happily endowed, to rise superior to all the minor obstacles of existence ; as, for example, when I, trying to pump the gentleman opposite in regard to his patronymic, was by him foiled in my attempt, and convicted of the logical absurdity of having declared myself to have forgotten that which I had never known; or, again,—when, this morning, my governor, your venerable uncle, who, benighted innocent that he is, hopes to coerce me into giving up smoking, took from me my cigar-case, but allowed me to regain it by picking his pocket thereof, while squabbling with the cabman for an extr sixpence;—mind you recollect all this; for, in these days slang is completely the language of fashionable life. Were I that epitome of slowness, 'the father of a family,' I should have the young idea taught to clothe itself in slang from the cradle upwards. And now, as I've a notion the train is approaching a station, and my cigar has arrived at its terminus, you shall witness a specimen of dodginess with your own eyes;—be silent, and observe me attentively—ahem!"

He then flung the end of his cigar out of window, and, assuming an air of great consequence, waited till the train stopped; the moment he did so, he summoned a porter.

"Porter, open the door!" The man obeyed. "Put your head in and tell me what this carriage smells of."

The porter, looking surprised at the request, complied—"It smells tobaccer-efied like to me," he observed, after a minute's investigation.

"Tobaccer-efied, indeed!" repeated Wilfred Jacob, in a tone of the deepest indignation; "some brute has been smoking in this carriage, I'm certain of it! a first-class carriage, too. I tell you what, porter, when gentlemen pay for the comfort and convenience of a first-class carriage, they expect to enjoy what they pay for, and not to be poisoned alive with the odour of tobacco."

"Smoking ain't never allowed in the fust class, sir," pleaded the embarrassed porter.

"It may not be allowed, but *it has been done*," was the captious reply: "I'll take my oath some one has been smoking in this carriage; I'm as certain of it as if I'd seen them myself; my nose never deceives me;—what's your name?"

"My name be Johnson; but I'll call the station-master to speak to you, sir."

"By no means; it's no fault of his," replied Wilfred, hastily, feeling anything but desirous that a more enlightened intellect should be brought to bear upon the question: "no, I shall write to the directors, to complain, and call you to witness that I mentioned the fact at the first station we stopped at. It's absurd to pretend to make rules, and then suffer them to be broken in this way. Shut the door. I shall remember your name—Johnson!" and as he uttered the last word, the train started.

His companions exchanged glances: Percy's expressed disapproval; Hugh's, mingled surprise and delight; while Ernest was so much amused at the boy's ready wit and cool impudence, that, for the life of him, he could not reprove him for the deception.

When the recollection of this little incident had, in some degree, worn off, Percy asked his cousin how he liked Doctor Donkiestir's school; and begged him to tell them a little about the manners and customs of the place to which they were going.

"Put you up to a thing or two, eh? Give you some small insight into the time of day? Well, I suppose, as it's all in the family, and you're Tickletonians yourselves, or about to become so, it's no breach of confidence. *You* won't split, sir?" he continued, appealingly, to Ernest. "Honour amongst thieves, eh?"

"You may trust me," was the concise reply.

"First promise me, upon your honour, that you will not tell any of the masters, then," stipulated Wilfred.

"Upon my honour I will not tell any of them," was the slightly Jesuitical reply; "nor will I make an unfair use of any information you may please to communicate to my young friend."

"That's all right, then. You look like a brick (I'm a bit of a physiognomist, you see), so I'll trust you. In the first place, masters: there's the Doctor, *alias* old Donkey, *alias* (his name is John) Jackass, with sundry other derivatives, more caustic than complimentary. Well, he's not altogether a bad sort of fellow, only he makes a fuss about trifles, and is especially jealous if he fancies that any one appears likely to interfere with what he calls his prerogative; in fact, he would be a stunner if his temper did not stand in his way: but, on the whole the boys like him, and so look over his little failings. Then, there's a sort of second master, 'Mat. and Clat.' we call him, which is short for mathematical and classical; but we are changing horses in that quarter, so, till we have tried the new animal (pretty well tried he will be, too, before we've done with him, I expect), it's impossible to say how he may suit us; only, if he ain't a tolerably wide-awake cove, I pity him; for, between master and boys, he'll have a sweet time of it, poor devil! Then there are two ushers—Hexameter and Pentameter (familiarly Hex. and Pen.) so termed because one is six feet high and the other scarcely above five : they are not gentlemen, therefore they don't act as *sich*, so of course we 'chouse' and bully them as much as we dare. Then there's old Splitnib, a coach of the most unmitigated slowness, but who writes a wonderful hand; and, finally and lastly, Monsieur Beaugentil, the French master, who is more involuntarily comic than all the rest of his frog-devouring nation put together. These worthies rule, and are ruled by, a floating capital of some two hundred boys, more or less, of whom the eldest may be about seventeen or eighteen, and the youngest on a par with this juvenile shaver here."

" And do you work very hard ?" inquired Percy.

" Not we," was the reply. " Of course, for decency's sake, we do something. It don't pay for a fellow to be quite an ignoramus in these days, unless he happens to have been born a lord, or experienced some such jolly dispensation at starting ; but as for hard work,—no, thank ye. What's the use of having a fag, if you can't get your exercises done for you, I should like to know ?"

" What's a fag ?" inquired Hugh.

The first effect of this apparently simple question was to throw the person to whom it was addressed into a state of the most violent laughter. As soon as he could recover breath, he gasped out, " Oh, lor ! it's very fatiguing ; you'll be the death of me with your blessed innocence, that you will."

After a less severe relapse, he continued, " *You*'ll soon know what fagging means, you poor, unfortunate, green little warmint ; though I think I shall honour you by taking you myself. I've a right to a fag now I'm in the fifth form ; and the chap I had last half has left. You seem a jolly, good-tempered little beggar, and I shouldn't like to see you made miserable."

" He shall never be ill-used while I am alive," exclaimed Percy, with flashing eyes.

" That's a very proper and plucky sentiment on your part, my dear boy," returned Wilfred ; " but it's a precious deal easier to talk about than to act upon. You can't thrash a whole school, especially when some of them are almost men grown. Such chaps as Biggington or Thwackings, who can polish off a coalheaver in sporting style, for instance ; your namesake Hotspur himself would have found such fellows as them tough customers. All you can do with **them is** to keep 'em in good humour while you can, and get out of their way when you can't."

"But all this time you have not told me what a fag is," interrupted Hugh.

"Well, a fag is a small boy, taken possession of by a larger boy, according to an old established precedent, against which the masters set their faces in vain. The small boy thus enslaved is termed a fag, and his duties are to do everything the larger boy finds it impossible or disagreeable to do himself. If the small boy performs these duties zealously and good-humouredly, he is only kicked and driven about like a dog, and survives to become a fifth, and ewentually a sixth form boy, and takes his change out of fags of his own. If he sulks, or neglects orders, he is either half or three-quarters murdered, according to the hands he falls into, and is usually taken away from the school, or otherwise expended, before he reaches hobble-de-hoy's estate. And now, have I made that clear to your juvenile capacity ?— Yes ?—Then mind you profit by it, or I shall have to show you practically how Tickletonians tickle," and as he spoke, he pointed suggestively to his cane, though a good-natured twinkle in his eye contradicted the threat.

Having thus broken ground, he favoured the company with a series of dissolving views, illustrating various episodes of Tickletonian life, wherein were vividly portrayed scrapes got into and out of with much ability, and more impudence, by certain scholastic heroes, past and present ; but the gist of each anecdote lying in the discomfiture or mystification of one or more of the masters, it is scarcely to be supposed, giving Wilfred Jacob credit for the most open disposition imaginable, that he would have been quite so communicative, had he divined the capacity in which Ernest Carrington was then journeying to Tickletown.

When they reached the station at which they were to alight, an omnibus, provided by Doctor Donkiestir, was in waiting to convey any of his scholars who might arrive by that train. Ernest, who was not to present himself till the following morning, and had availed himself of the opportunity to accept the invitation of an old college friend, from whom he had originally heard of the vacancy, here took leave of his young companions, saying, as he did so—

"Good-bye. As I should not much wonder if we were to

meet again sooner than you at all expect, I wish you to remember, that if at any time you require advice or assistance, you will find a friend in Ernest Carrington."

He then touched Wilfred's arm, and drawing him aside, observed,—"I have allowed you to run on in a way which I am sure you would have endeavoured to avoid had you known who I was. I did so, not from any mean wish to entrap you into confessions of which I might afterwards make use to your disadvantage, but simply in order to gain some insight into your true character; and now I will make a compact with you : as long as you behave kindly towards your two cousins, who interest me exceedingly, and befriend them as your superior knowledge of the world" (the slightly ironical emphasis with which he pronounced the last few words was not lost upon his auditor, who, for once in his life, felt conscious that he had made himself ridiculous), "and especially of the little world comprised in a boys' school, will enable you to do, I shall forget anything peculiar I may have heard this morning. I will only add, that I have misjudged your character if you consider the condition I have proposed a hard one."

"Before I attempt to make a suitable reply to your mysterious and startling communication, allow me, sir, to inquire, in the most respectful manner possible, first, *who* you are? secondly, *what* you are?" returned Wilfred Jacob, in a quieter tone than he had yet made use of.

"The Rev. Ernest Carrington, classical and mathematical master (or, familiarly, Clat. and Mat.) in Dr. Donkiestir's school at Tickletown, at your service," was the reply.

The first effect of this announcement was to elicit from the "fast young gentleman" a prolonged and expressive whistle; next came an aside, "Well, if I haven't gone and put my foot into it deepish *rather*, it's a pity." Then, turning to Ernest, he asked, abruptly,—

"'Pon your honour as a gentleman, Mr. Carrington, if I stick to the young Colvilles like a trump, you won't peach?"

"Upon my honour," was the frank reply.

"It's a bargain, then," rejoined Wilfred. "And now, sir, before we sink the amenities of social life in the less jovial relationship of master and pupil, allow me the honour of shaking hands with you, while at the same time you must permit me to express my opinion, that your conduct has been brickish in the extreme."

With a smile called forth by the peculiar school-boy phraseology, and strange admixture of good feeling and never-failing impudence, of his new ally, Ernest shook hands with him good-naturedly, and turned to depart; but Wilfred Jacob detained him.

"One slight additional favour would oblige," he said. "A discreet silence in regard to the cigar episode 'would be a desirable addenda to our compaet. Our friend Donkiestir has prejudices—*verbum sat*—a nod is as good as a wink. Farewell ' we meet again at Philippi.' "

So saying, he bowed low, removing a very shining new hat, wherewith he had replaced the gorgeous travelling cap, and hurried after his cousins, who were by this time seated in, and sole tenants of, the omnibus, where they presented, so to speak, a very forlorn and cast-away appearance.

CHAPTER VI.

THE CONSPIRACY.

"Oh, Percy, have you heard the news?" inquired Hugh, eagerly, some five weeks after his arrival at Tiekletown; and as he spoke, he began dancing and clinging round his brother in a state of the greatest exeitement.

"What news, Hugh?" returned Percy, who, seated at his desk, was writing with the greatest assiduity.

"Oh, then you haven't heard," resumed Hugh. "Well, you know that a company of aetors are performing at the Tickletown Theatre, and that all the boys are mad to go and see them; and no wonder, either, for, from what Wilfred and others, who have seen one in London, say, a play must be the most wonderful, glorious, jolliest, briekish-est thing going." Hugh was making surprising advances in slang, under his cousin Wilfred's able tuition; his progress in dear Dr. Valpy's Latin Delectus was by no means equally rapid.

"I know what you have told me; but I know, also, that the Doctor has expressly forbidden any of the boys, even of the sixth form, to go to the theatre, on pain of expulsion. His reason—and it seems to me a good one—being, that he cannot exereise any surveillance (that means care, or watchfulness) over them, if they are allowed to be out late at night," returned Percy, gravely.

"Yes; but you don't know that the manager has written to the Doctor to say that he will give a morning performance, and select only pieces of which the Doctor shall approve, if he will allow the boys to go ; and the dear, good, jolly old Doctor has said 'yes,' and granted a half holiday next Thursday for the purpose ; and I'll never call him old Donkey any more, if Biggington kills me for refusing. But Percy, dear Percy, do you think there is any chance that we could go ?"

Now, although at first sight this question would appear a very simple one, it was by no means so easy to answer as might be imagined. In the first place, Percy had a vague and indistinct notion that his mother disapproved of theatrical entertainments ; certainly, as far as his own personal feelings were concerned, the recent loss he had sustained, with all its painful consequences, rendered him indisposed to enjoy any such amusements.

Then, again, on the score of expense: their pocket-money was very limited, Hugh being allowed sixpence, Percy a shilling a week,—a sum which was barely sufficient to supply slate-pencils, ink, peg-tops, clasp-knives, "toffy," and all the other innumerable and incomprehensible *sine quâ nons* of a public school-boy's existence.

Although he had suffered both obloquy and inconvenience on account of the paucity of his funds, Percy had resolved that, during their first quarter, nothing should induce him to apply to their mother for more ; and, when Percy had resolved upon a thing, because he considered it a matter of principle, Hugh was aware that Gibraltar itself was not more immovable.

It was, therefore, with rather a blank expression of countenance that he replied to his brother's inquiry of what it would cost,—

"The admission is to be half-a-crown each."

"Then we cannot go," returned Percy ; "for I have not been able to save any of my allowance, neither do I imagine have you."

One reason why Percy found a difficulty in saving was, that Hugh was for ever losing things which must be replaced, or breaking things which required mending, or earnestly desirous of something or other which Percy could not bear to see him wishing for in vain ;—for be it known, that unless some matter of deep feeling, or right principle, were concerned, his elder brother spoiled Hugh as thoroughly and unconsciously as anybody. Thus, in point of fact, Master Hugh spent, in addition to his own sixpence, some ninepence out of every shilling of Percy's.

But Hugh's selfishness was a fault of which he was himself perfectly unaware. Not being of what minor treatises on Christian ethics consider it the thing to term " an introspective habit of mind," and knowing that if Percy required such a sacrifice, he would willingly allow his right hand—the hand with which he played marbles—to be cut off in his service ; he was so accustomed to consider that, because he was the youngest, everything was to be given up to him, that he forgot the injustice of such an arrangement.

" Not a halfpenny," was Hugh's reply; "that cake woman cleaned me out yesterday! What a goose I am to be so fond of cakes! but I like to have enough to give some to the other fellows too, and all we little chaps have a weakness for cakes ;— but have *you* got no money ?"

Percy shook his head. " Breaking windows, and losing other boys' balls, are expensive amusements, Hugh," he said. " Remember, I have got you out of several scrapes of that kind since we have been here. Of course, I was glad enough to do so ; but I only mention it to account for my being nearly as poor as yourself. A shilling a week is soon exhausted."

Hugh paused in deep perplexity ; at last he said slowly, and in a hesitating voice, " Mamma would send us the money, I think, if you would not mind writing to tell her that you had no objection, and that I wish to go so very, *very* much."

" But I should mind writing for such a purpose," returned Percy; " and I will explain to you why: since dear papa's death, mamma has been very poor, and she is likely to be poorer still, I am afraid, for she writes me word that Sir Thomas Crawley still persists in his demand, and Mr. Wakefield is afraid she will have to pay it whenever a new clergyman is appointed."

" How wicked! how cruel of Sir Thomas!" interrupted Hugh, vehemently ; " and he is as rich as an old Jew, too ;—I hate him !"

" Gently, Hugh, you must not speak in that way ; every man has a right to obtain anything the law of the land will award him. But now I have told you this, I am sure you would not wish me to write and ask mamma to send us money to be spent in amusement, which she must deny herself and Emily the actual necessaries of life in order to procure." Percy waited for an answer with some anxiety, but, in a matter of feeling, Hugh would never have been likely to occasion him disappointment.

"Do not write, for the world, Percy," he said; "I would rather never see a play in my life than grieve dearest mamma. Oh, Percy! I wish I were a man, then I'd work hard, and keep her and Emily, and give them pleasures and luxuries, and make them quite happy; and as for that wicked Sir Thomas, I'd punch his head for him, as Wilfred says."

So saying, Hugh returned the caress his delighted brother bestowed on him, and walked off manfully. But his courage only lasted till he had made his way into an old hayloft over a large rambling stable, capable of holding twenty horses, but now devoted to the use of the doctor's fat pony, and a cow and a calf, also the property of that dignitary. Having reached his hiding-place, his fortitude gave way, and he bewailed his disappointment with a hearty cry; for he was but a child after all, poor little fellow! and a spoiled one as well, and to such, however differently far-advanced Christians may appreciate the quality, self-denial appears a very harsh and uncomfortable virtue.

On the morning of the important day, a fresh trial awaited him; Wilfred Jacob, who had thoroughly fulfilled his promise to Ernest Carrington, by saving Hugh from ill-usage, and Percy from many of the annoyances to which his proud, sensitive nature rendered him peculiarly susceptible, as soon as breakfast was concluded, shouted vociferously for his fag—

'Hugh, Hugh Colville! where has the young warment hidden himself? Oh, there you are; come here, you imp of darkness, I shall have to give you that thrashing I've owed you so long, I know I shall, and when it does come, old Bogie have mercy on your precious bones! for I shall have none. Now, listen to me; the moment morning school is up, cut away like a flash of greased lightning, and turn out my things to dress. Let me see—I shall wear—hold up your head, sir, and look attentive!—I shall wear—ahem!—my white d'Orsay overcoat; the light-blue coatee with fancy silk buttons; the pink satin under-waistcoat; the green embroidered vest with coral buttons; the blue necktie with crimson ends; the MacFerntosh plaid trousers, those with the green ground and broad red, and blue, and white checks over it; and the polished boots—do you twig? Now, then, repeat it all, that I may be sure you've taken it in correct."

"D'Orsay wrap; blue coatee; pink under, green and coral over-vests; blue and crimson choker; MacFerntosh sit-upons; and japanned trotter-cases," returned Hugh, gabbling over the different items with the velocity at which tradition has decreed it proper to inform society that "Peter Piper picked a peck of pepper."

"Bravo, young'un, you improve apace; but you took to slang uncommon kindly from the first, I will say that for you. Well, when you've looked out the toggery, and — ahem! brought me my shaving water;—I've felt, for some time past, a tickling sensation at the sides of my face, which, I am sure, indicates the approach of whiskers. Ar—I should be rather a good-looking fellow if I had but got whiskers, I flatter myself; wouldn't I wear 'em bushy, that's all. As soon as you've done all I've told you, jump into your own juvenile habiliments, and be ready to go with me at a moment's notice."

"But—but you know, Wilfred, I'm not to go," faltered poor Hugh.

"Not to go, why not? Who says so? What! has Percy cut up rough, with his sanctified, Puritanical, Puseyitical, Pontifical, Hieroglyphical notions; oh! leave him to me, I'll soon talk him round;—I've the highest possible veneration for morality and piety, and all that sort of thing, particularly on Sundays; but to fancy they've got anything to do with going to the play, is an association of ideas little short of downright sacrilege, to my notion."

"No, it is not that," returned Hugh; "Percy would have let let me go, only——"

"Only what?" inquired Wilfred, "come, make haste, I've got thirty lines of Terence to knock off before I go up to Carrington."

"Only we've both spent our allowance, and I've not got money to pay," replied poor Hugh, fairly driven into confessing his poverty.

"Phew!" whistled his patron, "no assets forthcoming, eh that's unfortunate, all the more so, because just at the present epoch my own financial arrangements are in a somewhat embarrassed condition—ar—banker's account over-drawn—owing to their confounded free-trade, I expect, I can't get my rents paid up,—in fact, to be frank with you, when this play business was first started, I, with incautious liberality, volunteered to make one of a jovial crew of fifth-formers, who intend to follow up the theatrical entertainments with a sort of extempore *déjeuné à la fourchette* of oysters and porter. Well, sir, when I came to examine into the state of my funds, I, after much deep and intricate calculation, arrived at the following result viz., that I had contracted liabilities to the amount of one pound five, while to meet them I possessed the exact sum of two shillings and threepence halfpenny—the halfpenny being scarcely an efficient coin of the realm, by reason of my having that morning punched a large hole in its centre, in pursuance of a mechanical experiment which failed. Under these circumstances I immediately wrote to the governor, saying that several unusually distressing cases of charity having come under my notice since I had last received his blessing and a ten-pound note, the blessing alone remained ; adding that another case more urgent than any of the former now appealing to my sympathies, I trusted he would not object to replace the money without unnecessary delay. They say it is a wise child that knows its own father ; certainly in this particular instance I seem to have formed a strangely mistaken estimate of the manners and customs of mine, for yesterday morning I received from him the following heartless reply :—

" ' DEAR WILFRED JACOB,—As I happen to know your charity is of the kind which begins and ends at home, and as two pounds a week is rather more than I wish you to spend on lollipops, I strongly recommend total abstinence from such delicacies for the next fortnight, at the expiration of which period you may look for a five-pound note (the last you will receive before the holidays), from

" ' Your affectionate father.'

" Well, my father being thus obdurate, the only alternative that remained for me was to apply to my uncle, in consequence of which application, my watch will have a little extra *ticking* to do for the next fortnight ; my relation, on the security of that valuable, favouring me with the loan of five and twenty shillings. Thus, the admission to the theatre being two and sixpence, you will perceive, by a reference to ' Bonnycastle's Arithmetic,' or ' Smith's Wealth of Nations,' I am still twopence-halfpenny behind the world, which sum I must beg, borrow, or otherwise realise before two o'clock to-day, at which time the doors open. So, you see, young 'un, I literally cannot treat you, for which, without chaffing, I'm really uncommon sorry; but never mind, put your trust in jollity, and depend upon it something to your advantage will turn up some day;" and with this well-meant, but slightly vague attempt at consolation, Wilfred Jacob passed on to have, as he termed it, a "go in" at Terence.

In the meantime, a solemn and important discussion was being held among the boys of the sixth form (some of whom were lads of seventeen and eighteen, and considered themselves young men), as to whether these morning theatricals, being got up solely with a view to the juveniles, were not *infra dig.* Biggington, who had grown up to fit his name, and stood six feet one in his stockings, and who, moreover, in virtue of the date of his entrance, as well as from his strength and prowess, was looked upon as leader of the school, decidedly set his face against it, and declared, with unnecessary vehemence of expression, that the play might be—that to which its author would have especially objected—before he would go to see it.

Stradwick quite agreed with him, which fact possessed every advantage but that of novelty; Stradwick being a mere reflection, and by ho means a brilliant one, of Biggington.

Fowler also considered the thing would be infernally slow, nothing sporting about it; besides, Jackass (alas for boy nature, that so could paraphrase the respectable name of Doctor John Donkiestir!) was going himself, and would have nothing to do but to watch them, so that if a fellow happened to sneeze, he would be safe to get an imposition for winking at an actress; for his part he'd rather be in school at once.

Norman and Piper followed on the same side; Swann, Pitt, Kitely, Martin, and Jones, agreed with the foregoing, but had an original opinion of their own, that old Donkey was growing superannuated.

On the other hand, Warmingham, Gaston, and some dozen others, although considering that an exception ought to have been made in favour of the sixth form, thought the measure a judicious one, as far as the little fellows were concerned, and were, therefore, prepared to pocket their dignity and go;—unless anybody had got anything better to propose.

" I tell you what, Gaston, that was not a bad notion of yours about an exception being made in favour of the sixth; surely, if that were properly placed before old Jack, he could never be so besotted as to refuse," observed Fowler.

"Bravo, Fowler," exclaimed several voices; "let us draw up a formal representation of the affair, and send up a deputation with it to Jack."

"What do you say, Biggington?" inquired Fowler.

"Simply that I'll have nothing to do with it; I'll neither sign the address, nor head the deputation," was the sulky reply; "I consider I have demeaned myself too much to Jack already, in submitting to his absurd prejudices."

"Biggington and I view the matter exactly in the same light," observed Stradwick: "you'd all better give up the notion directly."

"Speak for yourself, stupid!" returned Biggington: "if Fowler and the rest like to try, let them, and they'll see what will come of it; my own feelings are purely personal. Don't you see, fool," he continued, drawing his satellite aside, "by the plan I adopt, they will do the dirty work, and, if they succeed, I shall profit by it; if they fail, I avoid the slight of having my request refused."

"Then what shall I do?" inquired Stradwick, who possessed just intellect enough to perceive that the rule of blindly following his leader would, in this case, annoy rather than propitiate the autocrat.

"Why—a—you see, you are—that is, we are differently—a —in fact, in your position I should decidedly sign the address; though—stop, wait a minute—on second thoughts it strikes me it may look odd to have every name but one on the list: Jack may think I've got some dodge in my head. Well, never mind; if you like to follow my example you can," returned the slightly selfish Biggington.

Accordingly, Gaston, who was famous as a scribe, wrote the address; and Fowler, and some half-dozen others, carried it up to the Doctor.

Dr. Donkiestir, who was a tall, fine-looking man, of about fifty, with a clever, energetic countenance, marked, however, by the stern, worried expression common to schoolmasters, received the deputation courteously, read the address, and then observed—

"All the sixth appear to have signed this, except Biggington and Stradwick: why are their names absent?"

There was a moment's pause, and then Fowler, who was naturally of an open, fearless disposition, replied—

"I believe, sir, Biggington preferred giving up going to the theatre, to asking a favour which he considered it unlikely you would grant ; and Stradwick generally does whatever Bigging-ton does."

As Fowler announced this well-known fact, a general smile, which even the Doctor's presence could not entirely restrain, went the round of the deputation.

The Doctor seemed not to notice it, though a twinkle in the corner of his eye revealed to those who knew his every look, that he was not so unobservant as he appeared.

"Biggington and his friend are very prudent," he said, with a slight ironical emphasis on the last word. He then paused a moment in thought ere he continued, "I am very sorry that I consider it my duty to refuse your request, for the straight-forward, gentlemanly way in which you have preferred it has much pleased me; but I cannot believe that I should be fulfilling the trust reposed in me by your parents, if I were to allow you to be exposed to the temptations of a theatre, in a town, at night, when it would be impossible for me to exercise the slightest vigilance over you ; and this applies more strongly to the sixth form than to the younger boys, as many of you are almost young men, and peculiarly liable to the evil influences to which I allude. As some compensation I will grant a whole holiday, either for skating, if the weather permits, or boating, or cricketing, later in the season, whichever you may prefer. I hope, as a proof that you do not think I have been unneces-sarily strict, the sixth will think better of it, and that I shall see many of their faces at the theatre this morning."

The Doctor's harangue was not without its effect, for Fowler (who, though somewhat of a pickle, was of a warm-hearted, generous disposition) thanked the head master for the promised holiday, and declared his intention of going to the morning performance. Gaston, Warmingham, and the rest of that party, followed his lead, and the deputation withdrew.

"So you've eaten humble pie for nothing, been humbugged into promising to go to a childish affair you ought to be ashamed to be seen at, and been choused out of the only bit of fun and jollity that has come in our way this half. I wish you joy of your promised holiday, you good little boys," was Biggington's sarcastic speech, when he learned the result of their mission.

"Chaff away, Big-un" (a familiar abbreviation of Biggington's patronymic, of which only the *élite* of the sixth were permitted to make use), returned Fowler, good-humouredly. "Jacky's a stunning good old fellow, after all, and I, for one, shall go, to show him I don't bear malice; you'd better pocket your dignity for once, Big-un, and come too!"

"Not if I know it, to please either old fools or young ones," was the unamiable reply; and, turning on his heel, Biggington walked angrily away, followed, at no great distance, by Stradwick and two or three other recusants.

In spite, however, of their disapproval, the morning performance went off with great *éclat;* and those who attended it, amongst whom were a large proportion of the sixth form boys, raved about their delight to such a degree, that even Biggington, albeit he pretended to take the matter with a high hand, felt intensely provoked, and thrashed most unmercifully a small boy, who, in the innocence of his heart, incautiously promulgated his opinion, within the tyrant's hearing, that "any one who could have gone and did not, must be a precious slow coach, and no mistake."

As for the fictions founded on facts, upon which the prolific imagination of Wilfred Jacob delighted to expatiate, they had such an effect upon poor Hugh, that he fairly cried himself to sleep that night, from sheer vexation and disappointment.

The next morning, a flashily dressed, sharp-looking young man, who was none other than the usher introduced by Wilfred Jacob into his description of the Tickletown masters by the nickname of Pentameter, but whose proper appellation was Sprattly, and who was, as Wilfred had truly stated, anything but a gentleman, approached a group, consisting of Biggington, Stradwick, and one or two others, with whom he appeared on the most intimate and confidential terms.

"I say, old fellows," he began, "is it actually true that the Doctor won't let you go to the theatre at night?"

"Yes, worse luck," was the reply.

"And are you going to stand it quietly?" continued Sprattly.

"Eh? why what can we do to help ourselves? If the whole of the sixth had stuck together, we might have made something of it; but that ass, Fowler, was talked over. He says Jack appealed to his feelings, or sympathies, or some such disgusting rubbish. So Fowler went, and took half the form with him; and altogether, if I was to express my true opinion,

I think the whole affair is about as absurd, not to say disgraceful, to all parties as it well can be."

Norman, the speaker, was a tall, slender stripling about seventeen, with well-cut features and beautiful glossy hair of a raven blackness, which he wore long, and evidently bestowed much care upon ; but his cold, grey eyes, and the immovable expression of his mouth, gave a clue to his true character—viz., a clear, vigorous intellect, but a total deficiency of that which is commonly called heart. He was very anxious to leave the school, as a rich relation, who had taken a fancy to him, and intended to make him his heir, had purchased for him a commission in a cavalry regiment, on the strength of which he affected a *pococurante* air ; and possessing great natural powers of sarcasm, made himself feared and looked up to by the other boys. Outwardly he and Biggington were the greatest allies possible, but beneath the surface lay hidden a mine of envy, hatred, malice, and all uncharitableness, which only required the application of a match to cause an explosion, the effects of which could scarcely be foreseen.

"It's an awful bore, really," replied Sprattly, "for my cousin Courtenay Trevanion——"

"Which, being interpreted, means Jack Sprattly," interrupted Norman, sarcastically.

"No ! come, really Norman, 'pon my life you're too bad. I told you of his being my relation quite in confidence. All theatricals have a professional name, and a fellow may as well choose a spicy one as not, while he is about it," continued Sprattly ; "but I was going to tell you about to-night. They are going to do the ' Beggars' Opera,' Juliet Elphinstone——"

"*Alias* Betsey Slasher," put in the incorrigible Norman.

"Plays Polly Peachum," continued Sprattly, not heeding the interruption ; "Coralie, the French girl, does Lucy Lockit ; and Courtenay—or Jack, if you will have it so," he added quickly, perceiving that Norman was again about to speak—"Jack himself is cast for Macheath ; stunningly he'll play it too, for I heard him last winter—can't he just tip 'em, ' How happy could I be with either ' in style !—Uncommon well he looks, too, in the highwaymen's dress—red frock-coat, with gold frogs, and high shiny leather boots ; but Jack's a regular spicy-looking fellow."

"Little too much of the lamps and sawdust about him," returned Norman, superciliously

He paused a moment, then turning to Biggington, he said abruptly, fixing his piercing glance upon him as he spoke—

"Big., we must go to this affair."

Thus appealed to, the cock of the school, who at heart was more dunghill than game, like most other bullies, turned rather pale as he replied in a low voice—

"How is it to be done?"

"I have ideas on the subject," returned Norman, confidently; but we need not trouble other folks with our private affairs. I don't exactly agree with Solomon about the advisability of a multitude of counsellors."

"If you're good for a spree I'll stick to you to the backbone!" exclaimed Terry, a boy nearly sixteen, who lived only for mischief, and worshipped Norman, as Stradwick did Biggington, only with enthusiasm, instead of servility.

Stradwick, the remaining member of the party, was beginning slowly and gravely, "I shall do whatever Big——" when a shout of laughter from Norman, Sprattly, and Terry, cut him short. As soon as Sprattly had sufficiently recovered from the effects of his hilarity to be able to speak, he observed—

"Well, if you naughty boys are determined to plot mischief, of course I must not hear it: only, if we *should* meet by any accident behind the scenes of the theatre, I shall have much pleasure in introducing you to Polly Peachum and the fascinating Coralie;—by-the-bye, let me give you a hint! that stuck-up parson, young Carrington, is a precious sight more wide awake than the Don, so keep out of his way as much as you can." And having thus spoken, Pentameter Sprattly carried off his five feet four of vulgar humanity, with the most conceited air possible of underbred pretensions.

"What a thorough snob that unfortunate little Pen. has improved into!" observed Norman, as soon as the amiable usher was out of earshot.

"He never was anything else since I've known the animal," returned Biggington, surlily; "that's him all the world over: he'll give a fellow information which he knows will set him raving to do a thing, and then come out with his humbugging, 'Well, you *would* do it; I *told* you you'd get into a scrape.' I wonder what his object now is?"

"Oh! merely to help his cousin, or, more likely brother Jack," was the reply; "they're as much alike as two men can be, only ou. Spratt left off growing a couple of years too soon:

if Jack draws a good house his salary will be raised. And now I'll explain to you my plan, as far as it is at present matured;" and so saying, Norman unfolded to them a scheme—with the details whereof we need not trouble the reader—which, from his intimate acquaintance with the manners and customs of both masters and boys, he had been enabled to adapt to circum stances so cleverly, that even the cautious Biggington confessed he could only discover one flaw in it.

"And that is," he continued, "supposing everything to have gone smoothly up to the moment of our return, pray how are we to get in, when every door and window will be carefully closed and barred, and the Doctor's six-barrelled revolver, which he is so proud of, awaiting us if we make noise sufficient to rouse him ?

"I've ideas on that point, too," returned Norman, meditatively ; " I'm certain I remember a window in that old loft over the stable, by which I used, when a little shaver, to get in and out through the school-room skylight : I must contrive to make some excuse for inspecting the premises."

"I'll tell you who knows more about the loft than all the rest of us put together," exclaimed Terry; " and that is little Colville : he has a pet cat which resides in those parts, and he is constantly climbing and scrambling about up there, and has the place pretty much to himself, I suspect ; for most of the juveniles have faith in a ghost, which Hugh Colville seems too plucky to care for."

"That was exactly my case some ten years ago," returned Norman : " find little Colville and send him here to me, and let us meet again in Biggington's room after morning school, when I will report progress, and the affair shall be finally arranged. Now be off with you different ways : we must not be seen talking together too long."

And so with breasts more or less burdened by a conscious-ness of their evil secret, the conspirators parted.

CHAPTER VII.

TEMPTATION.

"COME here, Colville. How is your cat this morning?" inquired Norman, as Hugh approached, a good deal puzzled, and rather alarmed, at his summons, by reason of the fact that when a sixth-form boy sent for one of the little fellows, the interview, however it might begin, generally ended by the juvenile coming in for a thrashing.

"Thank you, sir, she is very well," replied Hugh; then, judging from Norman's face that no very adverse fate awaited him, he continued, "If you please, sir, she caught a rat to-day all her own self; such a monster, sir."

"Indeed! she must be a most meritorious and praiseworthy animal," returned Norman; then, anxious to set the little fellow at his ease before he began to pump him, he continued—"How did you like the play yesterday? were you very much charmed?"

"I did not go, if you please, sir."

"Ha! how was that? Did the Doctor keep you in for a punishment, or don't you care about such things?" inquired Norman, pretty well foreseeing the answer.

"No, it was not that, sir," returned Hugh. "I should have been delighted to go; but I had spent all my pocket money, and so could not pay for entrance."

"Unlucky for you—very," rejoined Norman; "I wish I'd known it sooner, I'd have tipped you the half-crown; more particularly as I want you to do something for me. You know the loft well?"

Hugh grinned, as he replied, "Every inch of it, sir"

"So used I when I was your age. Is not there a little square window, or trap door, by which one can get on the top of the school-room, near the part of the skylight which opens? and which can be reached by standing on the doctor's desk?" inquired Norman.

"Yes, sir," was the reply; "I often get up that way if the boys are plaguing me; and they don't dare to follow me because it is dark inside that part of the loft, and they are afraid of a ghost; but I'm sure there's no ghost, or else Puss would not leave her kittens there: if the kittens are safe, why should not I be?"

Norman smiled at this specimen of juvenile logic

"That's right," he said, stroking Hugh's curly pate, "you're plucky little fellow; and now show me this window. I want to see if I have forgotten the way."

"I'll show it to you, and willingly, sir," returned Hugh, whose affections were easily won, more especially when one of the sixth condescended to lay siege to them; "but you won't be able to get through yourself, now. You were a little fellow like me, I suppose, when you used to do so."

This information was what the immortal Dick Swiveller would have termed "a staggerer," and for a moment, Norman began to fear his scheme was knocked on the head; but possessing two main elements of greatness, namely—presence of mind and fertility of resource, an alternative occurred to him, which, although by no means so safe or easy as his original plan, might yet be practicable. Everything depended on the character of the child before him : of its strong points he had already some experience, and felt satisfied that he might rely on them. The boy possessed pluck enough for his purpose : he had now to test his weakness.

"Suppose," he begun—"mind, I only say suppose—there were yet a chance of your going to the theatre, what should you think of it ?"

"Think! why I should be ready to jump out of my skin for joy, to be sure!" returned Hugh, his eyes sparkling, and his cheeks flushing at the bare idea.

Norman had gained a step : he perceived the strength of the temptation he had to offer.

"Well," he said, after keeping Hugh in an agony of expectation for a minute or two, "there *is* a chance; but it must depend on whether you do exactly as I wish and approve. In the first place, promise me not to say a word to anybody about this conversation, or even mention that I have been talking to you ;—in the second place, come to me in Biggington's room, as soon as dinner is over."

"Please, sir, may not I tell Percy ? I always tell him every-thing," pleaded Hugh.

"Did you tell him who broke the Doctor's inkglass ?" inquired Norman, sarcastically.

Now this inquiry referred to a little affair which had occurred within a week of Hugh's first arrival at school. Indulging in that propensity common alike to boys and monkeys, viz., of examining everything with their fingers' ends, Hugh had allowed to fall, and thus broken, Dr. Donkiestir's own peculiar inkglass. Overwhelmed with the awful nature of the offence he had committed, and expecting, at the very least, to be flogged for the same, the poor child sat down by the side of the devastation he had caused, and commenced the uncomfortable operation of crying his eyes out.

In this forlorn condition he was discovered by Norman, who, without being really kind-hearted, possessed that not uncommon species of negatively selfish good-nature, which leads people to dislike to look on distress, physical or mental. Moreover, the fact of Hugh being a very pretty boy pleased his taste, and therefore interested him. Accordingly, he first inquired the cause of his grief, and then devised a remedy.

It so happened that Norman's own inkbottle and the one which Hugh had just broken, were, as nearly as possible, similar. He knew, moreover, that the Doctor was by no means observant of such minor particulars. He, accordingly, substituted his bottle for the broken one, assisted Hugh to clear away all traces of the accident, and, advising him to keep his own counsel, left him greatly consoled. But Hugh felt a consciousness that there was something in this transaction of which Percy would not approve ; and, fearful lest, in his strict sense of honour, he should pronounce it necessary to acquaint the Doctor with his delinquency, his moral courage failed him, and, up to the moment in which Norman asked him the question, he had never revealed the misdeed to his brother. It was the first time he had ever been guilty of that mildest form of lying— suppression of the truth ; but the stone of dissimulation, once set rolling, soon gathers force, which the feeble hand that sufficed to put it in motion is powerless to restrain.

Nor was Hugh's first " little sin " fated to prove an exception to the rule. Of course he was obliged to confess to Norman that he had not told his brother, and of course Norman replied that what he had done once he could do again : and that if he cared to go to the play, he must not tell Percy or any one ; and Hugh, not having a word to say in denial, the discussion ended by his promising to preserve a strict silence on the subject, and to come to Norman in Biggington's room.

In that same apartment was assembled, that afternoon, a solemn conclave. Biggington took *the* chair (there was but one); Stradwick drew a box from under the bed, and seat himself upon it, in an attitude exactly copied from that of Biggington; Norman, resting his elbow on the chimney-piece, remained standing; while Terry turned a wash-hand basin topsy-turvy, and perched himself, monkey-like, on the apex of the semi-cone thus created. After a moment's silence, Biggington exclaimed—"Well, Norman, how are we going on? have you brought your plan to perfection yet?"

"Unforeseen difficulties have sprung up," was the reply, "but none which the three Ps—patience, perseverance, and pluck—will not carry us through."

"Difficulties be hanged!" rejoined Biggington, impetuously. "I tell you one thing, go *I will*, by fair means or foul; the fact is, Trevanion" ("Jack Spratty," murmured Norman. "With a great pair of dyed moustachios on him," urged Terry) "has been here, and promised to take us behind the scenes, and to come and sup with us at the Bull afterwards, and induce Coralie and the other girl to come too."

"Ay! and Coralie's a stunner, and no mistake," observed Terry; "such a pair of black eyes, by Jove! they go through a fellow like—like——"

"Bradawls," suggested Stradwick, complacently.

"A *pointed* illustration, decidedly," resumed Terry; "but I was walking the day before yesterday with old Beaugentil, when we met this said Coralie, taking a constitutional for the benefit of her complexion; the moment Beaugentil set eyes upon her, he went off into an ecstacy, throwing up his arms and capering about like a bear on hot bricks. '*Mais, ce n'est pas possible!*' he exclaimed, 'vot shall I be'old? *Est-ce toi, Coralie?* Am it thou, Coreliar, zie daugtaire of thy mama, zie beloafed *de ma première jeunesse! et quelle ange!* vot an angle! *vrai ange du ciel*, a right angle of 'eaven! *Voyez donc, Monsieur Terrie; permettez que je vous présente mon cher éléve, Monsieur Terric, june homme charmant; mais n'est-ce pas que Mademoiselle est jolie;* ees not Mees *superbe*, beautifu', *magnifique*, pretty vell!' and so the old boy ran on till I was in fits."

"What is your confounded difficulty, Norman?" inquired Biggington, abruptly.

"Why, the window in the loft turns out to be too small for anything bigger than a boy to get through," was the reply.

Biggington muttered something unintelligible, which it would be the height of charity to consider a good word, as he continued—"What do you mean to do, then?"

"Put a small boy through it, who shall open the back door into the school-room for us, whereby we shall enter and walk up to bed," returned Norman, stroking the raven down on his upper lip, where the "cavalry moustache" was just beginning to show itself.

"And what chance is there of finding a boy whom you can trust to do such a thing?" asked Biggington, gloomily.

"He is already found, or I am much mistaken," was the answer. "Moreover, properly handled, he'll do the thing well, and *con amore;* I'd sooner work with *one* willing agent than with twenty forced ones."

"And his name?"

"The younger Colville."

Biggington mused. "He might do it; but his brother will not allow him," he said after a pause.

"His brother will have no voice in the matter, for he will know nothing about it," returned Norman; "but you shall judge for yourselves, for I have appointed the boy to come to me here. Only leave me to talk to him, and don't bully or frighten the little fellow, else you will defeat your own object. If, when you have seen him, you wish me to persevere with the plan, Biggington, stroke your chin thus."

As Norman raised his hand to indicate the appointed signal, a modest tap at the door was audible, and, on the bolt being withdrawn, Hugh made his appearance, and, at a sign from Norman, entered. The door was closed and fastened by Terry, who resumed his seat on the inverted wash-hand basin, with the air of a monarch ascending his throne. Hugh bore the scrutiny to which all the plotters, Biggington in particular, subjected him, unflinchingly; he looked rather more grave and anxious than was his wont, but did not appear intimidated or abashed, though he stood in the awful presence of the cock of the school.

"Come here, Colville," began Norman; then, as the boy approached, he continued, fixing his piercing glance upon him, "have you mentioned what we were talking about this morning to anybody?"

"No, sir," was the unhesitating reply.

"Not to your brother, even? don't attempt to deceive me!"

"No, indeed, sir, I would not tell a lie; if I had mentioned it to Percy, I'd say so at once," returned Hugh, colouring at his assertion being doubted.

"I believe you," replied Norman, glancing towards Biggington as he spoke to attract his attention. "I am sure you are a brave, honourable boy, who would neither tell a lie nor betray a secret, which is worse, if anything."

At this commendation, Hugh's eyes sparkled, and a bright, honest smile lit up his innocent, childish face, which ought to have touched the hearts and disarmed the purpose of those who, for their own selfish ends, were thus deliberately leading him into evil; it probably would have done so, were it not a well-established fact in pathology, that, during the phase of public schoolboyhood, the human heart remains in a torpid or chrysalis state; the animal, at that period, consisting of a head, a stomach, and (fortunately for those who have the control of it, as well for its future chance of developing into a reasonable mortal) a tail also. Not being actuated by any such tender feelings, or indeed by an feelings at all, except selfish ones, Biggington replied to Norman's look by stroking his chin. Stradwick stroked his at the same moment, giving involuntarily a slight shudder at the alarming future to which he was thus committing himself. Terry only grinned, which indeed was his invariable custom on all occasions, solemn or comic.

"As I am now convinced that you are trustworthy," resumed Norman, "I am going to tell you a secret; *the* secret, in fact, upon the safe keeping of which depends your going to the play."

"Or getting every bone in your skin broken," muttered Biggington in an aside, which was, however, sufficiently audible to convey to Hugh a knowledge of the alternative which awaited him.

"Mr. Biggington, these other gentlemen, and myself," continued Norman, "mean to go to the theatre this evening, and if you will do exactly as we tell you, we will take you with us."

"But the Doctor!" exclaimed Hugh, aghast.

"That is the very point I was about to touch upon," rejoined Norman, in no way discomposed: "the Doctor not approving of the younger boys being out at night, thought himself obliged to give a general order to the whole school; but at the same time he contrived to have it hinted privately to *us*, that if the elder members of the sixth form chose to go, he should not make any inquiries about it; the only point he insisted on being, that such an expedition must be managed privately, and without his being supposed to know anything about it. Now in order to contriv 'his, we had thought of making our way in at night (we can easily get out unobserved after five o'clock school), through the window in the loft ; but, as you say, and as I now remember, it is too small to render that possible,—we want you to get through the sky-light into the school-room (as we were talking about this morning), and unfasten the little door which opens into the playground ; it is only secured by one bolt, which is not above your reach, so you can easily undo it. If you will undertake this, and promise faithfully not to breathe a word about it to anybody, you shall go with us to the play."

Poor Hugh was sorely puzzled ; and his sense of right and wrong entirely confused; one idea, however, soon extricating itself from the chaos, he immediately gave it utterance. " The Doctor," he said, " will be angry with *me*, sir, though he may not be so with you, for I am only a little fellow, and a long way off the sixth form."

Norman hesitated ; he knew that if they were discovered he should be quite unable to protect the child from punishment, and a sense of self-respect made him adverse to pledge himself to anything which he could not perform.

Biggington was trammelled by no such scruples. " Never fear, young 'un," he said ; " if the Doctor should by any chance speak to you on the subject, just refer him quietly to me ; merely say,—Biggington desired me to go ; Biggington will explain everything ;—and you'll have no more trouble from the Doctor. Don't you think so, Stradwick ?"

" Oh! certainly," was the reply : " refer him to Biggington, by all means ; say—Biggington desired me to go ; Biggington will——"

" That will do," interrupted Terry, grinning. " Shut up, Slow-coach, we didn't *encore* the sentiment ; moreover, I can perceive by the expression of our young friend's optics, that he is awake to a sense of his sitiwation. The play, a jolly good supper, and immortal honour and renown on one hand ; and an awful thrashing from Biggington, with a gentle refresher from myself appended, on the other ; between such a Scylla and Charybdis he will hardly be inclined to forestall Jack Sprattly by singing, ' How happy could I be with either.' So now, young'un, favour us with your sentiments."

" If I might but tell Percy ! " pleaded Hugh, glancing appealingly towards Norman.

That individual shook his head.

"If you do," he said, "you will have broken the trust reposed in you, and proved yourself a mean-spirited, cowardly child, quite unfit for the service we require of you, or the pleasure with which we propose to reward you;—tell your brother, and you lose the play."

Poor Hugh! his better nature made one final struggle, but he had dallied with the temptation till it had obtained too firm a hold on his imagination to be shaken off; and so, like many folks older and wiser than himself, who have indulged in a reprehensible longing for some forbidden fruit till the appetite has grown too strong to be resisted, he fell.

"I *will* promise," he said. "I do so want to see the play, and you will take care of me if the Doctor is angry, Mr. Biggington?"

"Oh, decidedly; both myself and Stradwick," was the reply. "Stradwick and the Doctor are hand and glove just now, because Straddy's such a dab at Euripides."

This insinuation referred to the uncomfortable fact, that the head-master had that morning informed Stradwick, in consequence of his total inability to construe the works of the ancient Greek in question, that if after another week he did not perceive a very decided improvement, he should be under the disagreeable necessity of degrading him to the fifth form. Stradwick, therefore, hung his head sheepishly as he echoed—

"Oh yes, decidedly."

"We understand each other, then, and had better agree to meet here, prepared to start, at a quarter to six," observed Norman.

A general assent was given, and the conspirators separated. Norman glanced at his victim; there was a determined look in the boy's face, which gave assurance that he would go through with the task he had undertaken. Resolution was one of the few qualities Norman reverenced, and for the moment he repented the evil into which he was leading the child; but the two strongest passions of his nature, ambition and revenge, were linked with his scheme for that evening, and he could not relinquish it.

"Courage, little one," he said, laying his hand on Hugh's curly pate; "if you and I live, and, as something here"—and he touched his forehead as he spoke—"tells me will be the case, I achieve greatness, I will not forget this evening. Silence and courage!"

CHAPTER VIII.

NORMAN'S REVENGE.

WHEN the devil suggests some pleasant but wrong scheme to frail humanity, his dupes generally find him a most amiable and efficient patron at the beginning of the enterprise, however he may leave them in the lurch when the fatal catastrophe approaches. To give that much-abused personage his due, on the occasion to which we are about to allude, he adhered to his word like the gentleman Shakspere has declared him to be, for, as at seven o'clock the very small curtain of the very " minor " theatre at Tickletown drew up, and the limited orchestra, with a hoarse, eccentric, and *ad libitum* bass, left off playing, four distinguished-looking young gentlemen entered the stage-box, and arranged the drapery in such manner that, themselves unseen, they might alike be able to witness the performance and criticise the house, which, in virtue of its being the fascinating Courtenay Trevanion's (*alias* Jack Sprattly's) benefit, was crowded by all the rank and fashion of Tickletown.

Any person who had very closely observed this same box, might have perceived peeping from under the corner of the red curtain nearest the stage, a little, eager, restless, excited face, watching with the deepest and most engrossing interest every trifle that occurred, as though it presented some great and striking novelty. Had the looker-on been of a speculative turn of mind, he might have wondered why this little, bright face, which ought naturally to have expressed nothing but childish delight and surprise, should have had this expression marred by an anxious, scared look, which occasionally passed across the boy's intelligent features. To the reader, however, this evidence that Hugh Colville was feeling slightly ill-at-ease, even in the midst of his enjoyment, need present no mystery. But as the play proceeded, and Polly made her appearance, looking like a single angel, and singing like a whole covey of them, interest and delight overpowered conscience; and when Jack Sprattly came on in jet black boots and moustachios, and bright red coat and cheeks, and swaggering about the stage as Macheath, and looking so charmingly impudent, sang in a rich rollicking tenor, " How happy could I be with either," toll-de-rolling at the end with a devil-may-care joviality, which pro-

duced him three several encores, Hugh Colville's delight waxed
to such a pitch that he mentally decided, if the Doctor had
suddenly appeared, armed with his stoutest cane, and then and
there varied the performance by flogging him before the faces
of the assembled audience, the exquisite pleasure he enjoyed
would have been cheaply purchased at even that frightful cost.
Then followed a pantomime! Hugh's first pantomime!

Juvenile reader whose first pantomime is yet to come, mark
my words, the words of one who speaks from experience! You
look forward eagerly, no doubt, to the wonderful time when you
shall be a grown-up man, and do as you please, which you
firmly believe will involve always sitting up till three o'clock in
the morning; riding a prancing horse all day; eating unlimited
plum-pudding without uncomfortable consequences; and having
that very pretty little girl next door, with whom you danced—
and, in your small, unassuming way, flirted also—at the children's ball last Christmas, grown up into a beautiful wife for
you, who will always do exactly what you wish with her, and
never go near Howell and James's at any price. You have
heard poets and other licensed story-tellers rave about there
being

> " Nothing half so sweet in life
> As love's young dream ; "

or prate of the delights of ambition ; the charms of fame ; the
pleasures of hope and of memory ; the satisfaction of a good
conscience ; or the inestimable blessings of domestic felicity—
which, in a general way, means buying cradles, paying taxes,
and settling bills :—you may have heard all this, and believed
much or little of it, as your bump of veneration happens to be
largely -veloped or otherwise. But what I am going to tell
you is a real "great fact;" and do you remember it, and act
upon it accordingly. The happiest time of your life ought to
be, and probably therefore will be, the glorious night on which
you, a light-hearted, merry child, witness your first pantomime!
—and you may go with my compliments to Papa and inform
him that I say so.

At all events, Hugh Colville felt strongly that until he had
seen a clown he had been ignorant of the real dignity of human
nature, or the sublime heights to which, properly cultivated, it
was capable of soaring. Columbine also (as enacted by that
houri, Rosetta Matilda Slammock) impressed him with a deep
sense of the sylph-like grace and ethereal purity of woman,—

all but the very pink calves of her seraphic legs, in regard to which, beautiful and praiseworthy as they were, viewing them in the abstract as mere bounding, pirouetting, sliding, and gliding machines, he could not help indulging some scruples of conscience, mentally classing them with unpaid-for toffy, clandestine nine-pins on Sunday, and the few other examples of the "pleasant, but wrong" principle, which had come within the limits of his juvenile experience; and he was just considering that, if Heaven had vouchsafed to place him in the proud and enviable position of her elder brother, he should have mildly remonstrated against her making such a very prominent feature of her legs; when to his surprise and regret, Virtue suddenly triumphed amidst a blaze of fireworks, and Vice being punished in the person of the Lurid Wizard of the Forty-locked Murderer's Cavern, who was dragged by three supernumerary fiends to a naughty place under the stage, the curtain fell, and all was over.

The next phase of the evening was to Hugh one strange and uncomfortable scene of inexplicable confusion. Biggington, Norman, and his companions, went behind the scenes, under the auspices of Jack Sprattly, who did not look nearly so brave and glorious out of his scarlet coat; and Hugh followed them for fear of being lost, receiving at their hands much the same kind and degree of attention that a little dog would have met with.

Of all miserable, desolate, chaotic-looking places, the stage of a theatre in *dishabille* is one of the most forlorn. The incomprehensible machinery for scene-shifting, the frightful backs of all the brilliant effects, the dirt, the smell of the lamps, the ropes, the rubbish, the dangerous trap-doors, the tired, sleepy carpenters, the haggard, snobbish actors, and, worse than all, the pale, hollow-eyed actresses, with their forced, heartless laughter—a very mockery of mirth—of all places for destroying illusion, commend me to the region behind the scenes as the most dismally effectual.

Biggington, Norman, and Stradwick, having disappeared somewhere within the mysterious precincts of the green-room, where they remained long enough for Terry to jump over everything, and tumble down everywhere, and set wrong bells ringing in all kinds of unexpected places, and have a terrific combat with nobody in virtue of a "property" sword and buckler wherewith he had illegally armed himself—the party re-assembled, and without further delay proceeded to "The Bull."

This remarkable quadruped must have been, in his interesting lifetime, a most rare and wonderful creature, at least, if he at all resembled his portrait, which hung creaking on a species of jovial gibbet in front of the hostelrie bearing his name. The picture certainly *may* have been a likeness, but as it represented the bovine original got up, regardless of expense, in richly-gilt hoofs and horns, with his tail twisted over his back in the shape of a horizontal figure of eight, ending in a bright golden flame, while such a cluster of Hyperion curls waved over his massive brow, as involuntarily to suggest the idea of his wearing one of those false fronts, paraded by self-deluding old ladies in the forlorn hope of deceiving society on the score of their undesirable longevity, we can scarcely conceive the artist to have adhered to nature with a proper degree of pre-Raphaelite severity. Be this as it may, the present proprietor of the Bull had exerted all his energies to provide a supper commensurate with the dignity and gullibility of the givers of the feast; and Hugh Colville's eyes sparkled with delight, when the goodly array of nice things first met his gaze; for, though by no means greedy, he was still almost a child, and was a hungry school-boy into the bargain—need we say more?

Then arrived Courtenay Trevanion (*alias* Jack Sprattly) and the young ladies, who, from a strict sense of propriety, which was one of their marked characteristics, had refused to come unless they might be allowed to bring with them Mrs. Belvidera Fitz-Siddons as *chaperone*. This great lady, for such she was in every sense of the word, had done the heavy tragic business for many years with immense *éclat*, until latterly she had grown too heavy even for that, which fact had been painfully impressed upon her by reason of her constantly, at harrowing moments of heart-rending despair, disappearing suddenly from before the streaming eyes of the astonished audience down traps calculated to support mortals of moderate (but not immoderate) weight. Finding that these unexpected disappearances tended to impart a burlesque character to her acting, rather than to increase the pathos thereof, Mrs. B. Fitz-Siddons had wisely restricted herself to such parts as suited her advanced years; and now having, by the trifling addition of sixpence weekly to his salary, bribed the call-boy to chalk B. T. (beware traps!) upon all dangerous footing, she still shone in the elderly comic line, and played

Mrs. Malaprop and Mrs. Backbite to delighted audiences. For the rest, this illustrious woman rejoiced in a pair of large, bold, uncomfortable black eyes ; a man's voice, slightly the worse for wear, and —— and a little failing she had in regard to liquor ; stiff horse-hair-like curls, which might have been her own only that she had a harmless scruple against wasting money on paying her bills ; and a generally hooked outline, so essentially Israelitish, that her green-room cognomen of "Mother Moses" appeared by no means inappropriate. Of the young ladies we will only say that, like *all* young ladies, they were irresistible.

Just at first starting, matters appeared a little dull and unpromising ; the fact being that the two elder Tickletonians, not finding, when put to the test, that they were quite such thorough men of the world as they imagined themselves, suffered under an uncomfortable inability to make small talk ; while Jack Sprattly, possessing a most inconvenient appetite, was so engrossed with the good cheer before him, that conversation, under the circumstances, became a physical impossibility.

As the supper progressed, however, and more especially when the champagne (which really was not bad for Tickletown) had made two or three rounds, affairs began to brighten. Mrs. Fitz-Siddons, unlike the voracious Macheath (which hungry highwayman still continued to demolish a supper more fitted for forty thieves than for one), was able to eat, drink, and talk at the same moment ; and soon, by the cheerful, not to say jolly, style alike of the sentiments she expressed and of the manner in which she expressed them, succeeded in placing the "young people," as she called them, upon a more friendly footing.

"Cora-lee, my love," she began (and be it observed, parenthetically, that this noble woman spoke with a slight Irish brogue—a philological fact to be accounted for only by the hypothesis, which she herself had started on a particular occasion, when she was suffering from a temporary nervous affection which confused her speech and imparted a slight unsteadiness to her gait, viz., that her mother must have been an Irishman), "Cora-lee, my love ! don't ye see Mr. Biggington waiting to take wine with ye ; thank ye, sir, since you're so very pressing I'll not refuse ; only up to my thumb, if you please, sir " (as she spoke, she, with delightful unconsciousness, ran her thumb up the glass as the wine advanced, until her digit and the champagne reached the brim simultaneously). "Your health, Mr. Norman, sir ; O-phaliur, my darling, the same to you ;—it's the cavalry you're going into, Mr. Norman, they do tell me, and it's an ornament you'll be to the ridgimint—fine men they are, the Lancers. I'd a brother in them once ; maybe you'll have heard tell of Major Fitz-Siddons ? Six feet six did he stand in his stocking-soles, till he fell gloriously leading a forlorn hope at the siege of—of—bless the name of the p'ace ! now I can't for the life of me lay my tongue to it."

" Troy, perhaps," suggested Terry, politely.

" Belleisle, more likely," put in Jack Sprattly ; it was the first word he had uttered since they sat down, and he had a largish tartlet in his mouth as he spoke ;—swallowing the morsel, he continued in a whisper to Biggington, next to whom he was seated—

" The major was no major at all, but only a private, and was drummed out of the regiment for stealing the captain's shirts."

Having once found his tongue, which was not until he had more than satisfied even his uncompromising appetite, Jack pro- ceeded to make use (we can scarcely in conscience say, good use) of it, to relate all sorts of anecdotes, theatrical and other- wise, of which the wit was so small as scarcely to deserve the name, while what ought to have been the moral was rather the reverse.

Then, quite by accident, another gentleman connected with the theatre called to speak to Mr. Sprattly, so of course he was invited to join them, and proved a great acquisition to the party, as it was generally reported of him that there was no subject, grave or gay, human or divine, on which he could not perpetrate a bad pun ; and certainly on that evening he did his best, or more correctly, his worst, to justify popular opinion. And thus a vast amount of nonsense was talked, and many bottles of wine drunk, until Norman conceived that the time was ripe for the execution of his project.

It has before been intimated that the apparent friendship existing between Biggington and Norman was based upon a most false and hollow foundation,—the truth being that the cock of the school, who was older than Norman, had, in times past, availed himself of his superior strength to bully, and impose insults and indignities upon, his junior, under which the proud spirit of the embryo lancer had chafed, until a deep thirst for revenge was excited, which he only waited a favour- able opportunity to satisfy. During the previous year, a change had taken place in their relation to each other. Biggington

having grown up, was, by the immutable laws of nature, prevented from growing any higher, while Norman, in obedience
to the same laws, grew steadily after him until he also had
attained the full stature of man ; while, although of a slighter
build, he had so strengthened his frame by athletic exercises,
that he was now no contemptible antagonist even for the colossal
Biggington. That the bully himself was aware of this fact,
may be gathered from the extreme care with which he avoided
giving Norman an opportunity of picking a quarrel with him—
a line of policy which, until the evening in question, had proved
most successful.

Norman, although apparently enjoying himself to the utmost,
and constantly hastening the circulation of the decanters, contrived to drink very little wine ; Biggington, on the other
hand, who was essentially animal in his tastes, indulged freely,
until the effects became unmistakably apparent in his flushed
cheeks and rapid, thick utterance. During the earlier part of
the evening he had devoted his attentions to the amiable and
accomplished Juliet Elphinstone (*alias* Betsy Slasher) as he
found that young lady, who was of a singularly affable, not to
say free and easy, disposition, least trouble to get on with ; and
Biggington hated trouble. But as Coralie's diffidence vanished
before the influence of the champagne, and the polished compliments which Norman from time to time addressed to her not
unwilling ears, she laughed and displayed her white teeth and
uttered piquant nothings in the prettiest broken English
imaginable, till she appeared altogether so fascinating, that
Biggington began to perceive he had made a mistake, which
the wine he drank rendered him determined at all hazards
to remedy.

Norman, who watched him closely, remarking this, redoubled
his attentions to Coralie, and Biggington's dissatisfaction and
ill-temper became so unmistakable that they were observed
even by Mrs. Fitz-Siddons, whose troublesome nerves were
again beginning to inconvenience her, as was evinced by a
slight disposition towards the unromantic spasmodic affection
popularly termed winking, with which she punctuated (so to
speak) her sentences. Feeling desirous that so agreeable an
evening should end as harmoniously as it had begun, she tossed
off a final bumper of claret (Mrs. Fitz-S. was great at claret),
and, turning to the young ladies, began—

"Cora-lee, my love—O-phalinr, my darling, all that's bright

my dears, must (*wink*)—the fondest hearts must part; 'parting is such sweet sorrow,' you remember! Not another drop, I'm obleeged to ye, Mr. Biggington, sir—well, if you will have it so I suppose I must (*wink*); we weaker vessels you know—"

"Hold as much as the strong ones," interposed Jack, "and carry it off a precious sight better too, and no mistake," he added *sotto voce* to his punning friend, glancing towards Biggington as he spoke.

In the meantime, the young ladies having risen, were looking for their bonnets and mantles. Terry, whose strong point was activity, had discovered Miss Ophelia's shawl, and, with many grimaces as of a polite monkey, had placed it over her shoulders; and Norman was about to perform the same friendly office by Coralie, when Biggington sprang to his feet, and advancing with a slight unsteadiness in his gait, exclaimed in a hoarse, angry voice—

"Give me that shawl directly, Norman; I intend to escort Miss Coralie home."

"Excuse me," was the quiet reply; "having found the shawl, I shall not yield the privilege of placing it over the fair owner's shoulders, to you or any one."

"Won't you?" returned Biggington, with an oath; "we'll soon see that!" and as he spoke he grasped the shawl with one hand, while he attempted to push Norman aside with the other.

Drawing back to avoid his grasp, Norman whispered to Terry, "Watch and see who strikes the first blow, and then lock the door and put the key in your pocket."

Irritated at the tenacity with which Norman still retained his hold on the shawl, Biggington pressed angrily forward, when, by putting out his foot, Norman contrived to trip him up, while, by a slight push, he caused him to lose his balance, so that he reeled and would have fallen, had not Jack Sprattly caught him just at the critical moment. Rendered furious by the laugh which followed his discomfiture, and losing sight of his habitual caution from the effects of the wine he had drunk, Biggington's savage nature blazed forth in all its full ferocity, and, springing forward with a bound like that of some wild animal, he aimed a blow at Norman's head, which if it had taken effect as it was intended, would have ended the struggle at once.

But Norman was prepared for such a salute, and, dodging aside, received the blow on his shoulder, whence it glanced off innocuously; then, before his antagonist could recover his guard, he rushed in and planted a well-directed hit on his face, in a direction which was certain to render him the proprietor of a black eye for the next week to come, at the very least. Thereupon ensued a grand shindy. Terry, in obedience .o Norman's directions, having recorded in the tablet of his memory the fact that Biggington had struck the first blow, hastened to lock the door and secrete the key; having accomplished these feats, he called out, "A ring! a ring!" at the same time exhorting the combatants to take it sweetly and easily, and to fight fair, and like gentlemen of the sixth form.

The two girls, frightened out of their affectation, shrank into the farthest corner of the apartment, where they clung to each other in speechless terror. Mrs. Belvidera Fitz-Siddons, considerably flustered (no other word could express her exact state of mind so graphically), in trying to get out of the way, fell first over, and finally upon, a sofa, where, after making one or two abortive efforts to rise, she remained uttering incoherent ejaculations to which no one paid the slightest attention.

Jack Sprattly made a feeble and futile attempt to bring about a reconciliation; but his friend—who, from being invariably cast as the benevolent uncle, or philanthropic benefactor, in all the genteel comedies, had, by a not unnatural reaction, acquired a sanguinary and democratic habit of mind—drew him back, muttering in a theatrical whisper—

"Let the serpent-brood of haughty aristocrats prey upon each other, Jack; there will be more room in the world for the honest sons of labour."

In the meantime, after a short but spirited rally, the combatants came to the ground together, when Terry picked up Norman and gave him a knee, while Stradwick, frightened out of his wits (the few he possessed), did the same by Biggington. Five or six rounds ensued; but as Norman, who was, to begin with, the most scientific pugilist, appeared perfectly cool and self-possessed, while Biggington was furious with rage, and excited and bewildered by the wine he had imbibed, each round terminated in Norman's favour; he having escaped any disfiguring blow, while his antagonist's countenance already showed marks of severe punishment. When the seventh round commenced, and Norman again succeeded in planting a well-directed hit on the bridge of his adversary's nose, it became evident that the bully's temporary courage was failing him, and that one or two more rounds would completely exhaust it.

By this time the landlord of the inn and his myrmidons had been aroused by the noise, and were clamouring at the door demanding admission; but so effectually had Terry hidden the key, that Jack Sprattly, unable to find it, was reduced to shout to them to burst the door open. This, however, was more easily said than done, for the door was made of stout oak, and he fastenings were strong and in good repair.

In the eighth round Biggington, rendered furious by pain, pressed so hard upon Norman that, in avoiding his blows, he entangled his foot in the carpet, and stumbled, while at the same moment a left-handed hit from his opponent catching him on the side of his head, brought him to the ground so violently that, when raised on his second's knee, he stared wildly about him and scarcely appeared conscious where he was; but a few moments served to restore him, and when time was called, he sprang to his feet with an expression of countenance which showed he meant mischief.

Biggington, elated by his success, fought with more energy and spirit than he had shown in the last round or two; but in attempting to end the conflict by a tremendous hit, he over-reached himself, and Norman, seizing his opportunity, drew back his arm, then flinging it out from the shoulder, with the force and rapidity of a sledge-hammer, caught his antagonist a crashing blow between the eyes, before which he went down like a shot, and when time was again called, he remained stunned and insensible. At the same moment the fastenings of the door suddenly gave way, and the landlord and his wife, supported by the entire *dramatis personæ* of the establishment, appeared upon the scene of action in various attitudes of terror and amazement.

CHAPTER IX.

THE DISCOVERY.

ERNEST CARRINGTON sat in the retirement of his little study, and gave himself up to thought. His scholastic labours were over for the day, and with a head too tired for mental occupation, and a heart too full of the great problem of existence to find pleasure in frivolous amusements, he sat resting his aching brow upon his hand, pondering the mighty enigma of human life in general, and his own individual experience of it in particular. He thought of the aspirations of his boyhood, of the bright hopes of his later youth, and mentally compared them with the dark reality of his manhood; he called to mind the dreams of greatness which he had pictured to himself—not the false and hollow greatness of mere rank and riches, but the true greatness of living to become a benefactor to his species; the greatness which he sought when he took upon him the duties, and privileges, and responsibilities of his sacred calling; greatness the praise whereof is uttered by the lips of widows and orphans, and written on broken and contrite hearts, to be transferred thence, by an angel's hand, to the Book of Life. And then, for he was young and loving-hearted, he thought of softer, brighter visions; of a fair ideal being, with an angel's brow and a woman's form, who should pass by his side through life, and, loving him more than all things else save the GOD who gave them to each other, should meet him again, and be his reward in Heaven, where perfect bliss could be ensured by the certainty that they should part no more. And in what had these bright visions ended?—a life of solitary drudgery. Even independence, the one thing that sweetens labour—the power of carrying out his own ideas of right and wrong—even that, by his subordinate position, was denied to him. And why was all this? What wrong had he committed to deserve so severe a punishment? Why was he condemned to this mental prison-discipline, this alternation between psychological oakum-picking and solitary confinement? Nay, was not his present position the result of his own unselfishness and liberality? If he had not given up his patrimony for the benefit of his sisters, nor relinquished his claim upon the entailed property, he would have possessed a fair income, on which he could have lived comfortably until he should have met with some ecclesiastical preferment, the duties of which would have afforded him the opportunities he sought of devoting himself to the good of others. If not permitted to exercise the talents committed to him to the glory of God, why was he born into this world at all? Poor Ernest! he had yet to learn that hardest of all lessons, to an eager, energetic spirit: he had yet to acquire belief in the great truth, that—

> "——They also serve
> Who stand and wait."

But his trial was more nearly ended than he was aware of

even as he sat there late into the night, pondering on the evils of his position but perceiving no means of escaping from them, the very fact of his unaccustomed wakefulness constituted the first link of the chain of events which was to bring about his deliverance. Days afterwards this idea struck him, and taught him a useful lesson.

The great clock in the school-room had just proclaimed, for the benefit of the blackbeetles, crickets, and mice then tenanting the apartment, the interesting fact that it was two A.M., and Ernest, weary and dispirited, had just determined to put himself and his troubles to bed, when he recollected he had left some Greek exercises, which he had to look over before the school opened the next morning, lying on his desk in the school-room. Anxious not to disturb any one, he substituted a pair of soft slippers for his boots; and knowing exactly the spot in which he had left the papers, he determined to dispense with a candle. Feeling his way cautiously, he descended the stairs and reached the school-room without any *contretemps*—but here a difficulty arose, for some one had moved the papers. Recollecting he had some lucifers in his desk, he was preparing to light a taper which he kept there for the purpose of sealing letters, when a sound, as of footsteps in the play-ground, caught his ear :—he paused to listen ;—the steps appeared to come nearer, till at length they approached the outer door;—from the sound it was evident that there were two or three persons. When they reached the door, they paused and spoke to each other in a low whisper; then Ernest became aware, from the altered nature of the sounds, that some one was climbing into the loft over the stable ; his first idea was, that they were common pilferers, intending to steal the Doctor's oats; but it occurred to him that there might be some communication between the loft and the dwelling-house, and that they were burglars attempting to effect an entrance ; desirous of obtaining a more certain knowledge before he gave any alarm, Ernest remained motionless, listening to the sounds without. Suddenly, a noise above him caused him to look up ; as he did so, a small window in the skylight was cautiously opened, and a boy's head and shoulders were thrust in ;—seeing this, Ernest stooped down so as to become hidden by the rails of the desk. Having reconnoitred the apartment, and imagining it untenanted, the owner of the head and shoulders noiselessly drew in the rest of his small person ; then, hanging by his hands, he allowed his legs to drop, till, with his feet, he was enabled to reach the Doctor's desk, which was considerably higher than any of the others; he next closed the window, and silently gliding down the slope of the desk, by the aid of a high stool gained *terra firma*.

Ernest's first impulse was to collar him, but on second thoughts he determined to wait, and let the affair develop itself a little further. Having reached the ground, Hugh (for of course the reader has long since surmised that it was that misguided child) crept cautiously to the outer door, and withdrew the bolt; as he did so, Ernest noiselessly crossed the apartment, and, when the door opened, seized the first person who attempted to enter. A short, but severe struggle ensued, which ended in Ernest's favour: finding himself foiled in his endeavours to free himself from the young tutor's grasp, Norman (for he it was) observed quietly—

"Let me go, Mr. Carrington, you have half strangled me : I shall not attempt to escape."

"I'll take good care of that," returned Ernest drily, releasing his grasp on his antagonist's throat, though he still retained his hold on his collar. "Oblige me by walking across the room," he continued : "I must take measures for securing your companions in this nocturnal adventure, as well as yourself."

So saying, he conducted Norman to the door of the schoolroom which led to the interior of the house—this he locked—then, still retaining his hold on the prisoner's collar, he rang a bell which communicated with the Doctor's private apartments. In the meantime, perceiving farther concealment to be impossible, Biggington, leaning on Stradwick's arm and Terry's shoulder, entered considerably the worse for wear, and flung himself doggedly on a bench. The sound of approaching footsteps soon broke the uncomfortable silence which followed the capture of Norman. Ernest unfastened the door, and Dr. Donkiestir, followed by a man-servant with a lantern and a thick stick, hastily entered.

"Ha! Mr. Carrington! Norman! What is all this? What is all this?" he exclaimed, as his eye fell upon the two most prominent figures.

In a few words, Ernest explained his own share in the matter ; then setting Norman at liberty, he crossed his arms on his breast, and, leaning against a high desk, left the Doctor to finish the adventure.

"In the first place, who have we here?" inquired the

head-master, sternly. Receiving no answer, he took the lan-tern from the servant, and held it so that the light fell in turn on the faces of the different delinquents, remarking as he did so—"Norman! I believed you to have been too much of a gentleman to have been mixed up in an affair of this kind—you have disappointed me; go to your room, I shall speak to you to-morrow. Biggington! why what is the matter with him?" throwing the light of the lantern full upon his swollen and discoloured features, he continued—"Why you've been fighting, sir, and are partly intoxicated! Disgusting! you shall disgrace my school no longer. Stradwick! with Big-gington, of course. At all events, I am glad to perceive you are sober—fighting is a vice I never suspected you of. Terry! have all the pains I have taken with you led to no better result than this? but I suppose you chose to copy Norman, even in his faults! And lastly, who is this poor child you have suborned to aid you in your nefarious practices? The younger Colville! your brother should have prevented this!"

Poor Hugh, his worst fears realized, had been crouching close to Terry (the most goodnatured of the party) in an agony of apprehension; but, at this insinuation, all his love for Percy, together with the innate sense of justice which was one of his best traits, rose up within him, and, at any cost, he hastened to repel it.

"Percy knew nothing of it; knows nothing yet," he said; "I have deceived him; and it will serve me right if you flog me to death, sir, but do not be angry with dear Percy!" and here a burst of tears chocked his utterance.

The Doctor was as much affected as a school-master can be

"Poor child!" he replied; "do not be alarmed for your brother; if he is, as you state, ignorant of this business, he has nothing to fear. You may all," he added, raising his voice—"you may all depend upon my acting with the most strict and impartial justice; and now to your dormitories instantly. I shall investigate this affair most scrupulously to-morrow."

So saying, the Doctor withdrew, courteously but stiffly bow-ing to Ernest; leaving the man-servant, with the thick stick and the lantern, to see the delinquents safely to bed; where it is but charitable to desire for them a good night; a consolation we can scarcely expect them to obtain, however much we may "wish they may get it."

CHAPTER X.

THE TRIBUNAL OF JUSTICE.

IT cannot be a pleasant thing to be going to be hanged —however thoroughly you may be aware that you deserve it—however clearly you may perceive that it will be for the good of society, nay, possibly, looking beyond the present moment, for your own good also; yet the stubborn fact must ever remain the same—it cannot be a pleasant thing to be going to be hanged!

Now, although as the law at present stands they do not exactly hang refractory or disobedient schoolboys, yet there is a process analogous thereunto, though milder in degree, termed flogging, to which such juvenile offenders are occasionally subjected; and this process it was which, as Hugh Colville sobbed forth his penitence and remorse on his brother's neck, loomed large in the distance, and hung over him, and weighed upon him, and crushed him down into a very abject and desponding condition indeed. It was not simply the pain (though that constituted a large and uncomfortable item in his depression) that frightened him, but the publicity, the exposure, the disgrace, were more than he could bear to contemplate;—while Percy, cut to the heart by his brother's misconduct, yet sympathising with a bitter intensity in his dread of the probable consequences, could only comfort him with feeble hopes of commutation of punishment, which his reason belied.

Poor little Hugh! how deeply did he repent having yielded to the temptation; how bitterly did he reproach himself for having deceived Percy; what vows of amendment did he register, if only he should escape that dreaded flogging; and how pale did he turn, and how sick at heart with apprehension did he feel, when the bell rang for morning school, and he knew that, before it broke up, his fate would be decided!

As the boys assembled in the great schoolroom, it was evident by their eager, excited faces, and by a general amount of subdued whispering, that the news of the *escapade* of the previous night had transpired, and all eyes were fixed on Norman, Stradwick, and Terry (Biggington did not appear); even Hugh Colville came in for a degree of observation which served still more to embarrass and distress him.

As the clock struck eight, the Doctor, followed by the other masters, entered; and the cloud that hung upon his brow was without the smallest vestige of a silver lining, and appeared so awful and portentous as to strike terror into the stoutest hearts The moment prayers were ended, the head-master rose and said, in a clear, stern voice—

"Before school commences, I have a painful duty to perform. Regardless of my express prohibition, certain scholars of the sixth form have ventured to break through the regulations of the school—which do not permit any of the boys to be out at night—and have been to the theatre, taking with them one of the younger boys, who, on their return, was put through a window, and made to unbolt the school-room door, in order to admit them. How they employed their time after they quitted the theatre, I have yet to discover; but they did not return till two o'clock in the morning—one of them in a disgraceful state of intoxication. As the whole school is aware of my orders, and the manner in which they have been disobeyed, I consider it salutary that they should also be witnesses of my method of dealing with the culprits, so as at once to vindicate my authority, and to mark my disapprobation of their rebellious and ungentlemanly conduct."

The Doctor then resumed his seat, and continued—"Let those whose names are mentioned step forward—Biggington!"

There was a moment's breathless silence, and then, with trembling knees, downcast eyes, and guilty, sheepish manner, Stradwick replied, that "Biggington was too ill to leave his bed."

"I am not surprised," was the reply. "Let Norman, Stradwick, Terry, and the younger Colville stand forward."

With a proud, haughty bearing, Norman advanced, and placed himself immediately in front of the head-master's desk. Crestfallen and sulky, Stradwick shambled after him. A moment's delay took place ere Hugh could muster sufficient physical strength to tear himself from his brother's side: while Percy was near him, he felt some degree of security; but Terry put his arm round him, and whispering, "Cheer up, young 'un, flogging's nothing when you're used to it, and I dare say the Doctor will let you off easy—never say die!" half led, half carried him to the tribunal of justice.

"You are the eldest, Norman," observed the Doctor, fixing his stern glance upon him; "and I will therefore deal first with you. Whatever faults you may possess, I have never known you tell me an untruth, and therefore I shall, for the satisfaction of myself and of those around me, ask you one or two questions, which you are at liberty to answer or not, as you may prefer. In the first place, do you admit the truth of the accusation brought against you ?"

" Yes, sir," was the quiet self-possessed reply, in a tone neither disrespectful nor penitent.

" Have you any objection to give me an account of the expedition, especially how you passed the evening after you quitted the theatre ?" was the next inquiry.

Norman paused for a moment, in thought, ere he answered, " My only objection, Doctor Donkiestir, would be the possibility of betraying my companions; but it appears to me that as you saw and recognised us on our return, and are acquainted with the main facts of the case, the little I shall have to add will tend rather to help than to injure them. For private reasons of my own, I proposed to Biggington to go to the theatre last night, and devised a scheme by which we might accomplish our purpose; but the loft window being too small to admit the passage of a man's body, I bribed little Colville to accompany us by a promise of taking him to the play, which he had missed the other morning, forbidding him to tell his brother lest he should prevent him. We slipped out after five o'clock school, Stradwick and Terry accompanying us; went to the theatre, and supped afterwards at a tavern with some of the actors and actresses; towards the end of the evening, Biggington insulted and struck me; I returned the blow, and we fought; in the last round, a hit I made stunned him, and it was some little time before he recovered sufficiently to walk back; as soon as he was able to do so, we returned—of the rest, you are yourself aware, sir."

When Norman had left off speaking, Doctor Donkiestir paused for a moment ere he replied.

" Your account completely agrees with all the facts I have been able to acquire in regard to this disgraceful affair. You admit the truth of the accusation brought against you, and by your own statement confess that you were the originator of the scheme; you have also demeaned yourself so far as to quarrel with a youth in a state of partial intoxication, and as it appears to me, availed yourself of his incapable condition to punish him most severely. It has always been a chief object with me, and

one in which I have been in many instances most successful,
to induce the elder scholars to set a good example to the
younger ones; up to the present time, I have been well
satisfied with you upon this point; I am the more surprised and
disappointed at your late gross misconduct. My duty is clear
No kind of subordination could be kept up in the schoc , if I
were not to visit such an offence as that of which you have been
guilty, with the most severe punishment it is in my power to
inflict—I have, therefore, resolved to expel you and Biggington.
You may now resume your seat, and, when school is over, come
to my study, where I shall acquaint you with the arrangements
I propose to make for your immediate departure. Stradwick,
have you anything to say in your defence ? "

Stradwick, thus appealed to, remained uneasily shifting
from leg to leg, until at last he bleated forth, in a half-crying
tone of voice—

" If you please, sir, I went because Biggington went."

As the abject parasite uttered these words, a furtive smile
went the round of the school, but the Doctor's face relaxed not
a muscle as he said sternly—

"I have long observed with displeasure the weak and servile
manner in which you have imitated the worst points in Biggington's character; I, therefore, cannot do better than afford
you a practical lesson how, by participating in his vices, you
must also share in the punishment they entail. You I shall
also expel—sit down. Now, Terry, how came you to be of
this party ? Heedless and imprudent I have long known you
to be, but disobedient I have never before found you."

For a moment Terry hung his head, and a tear glistened in
his clear, blue eye; dashing it away, he raised his face to that
of the Doctor, as he replied earnestly—

" It was the fun and excitement of the thing tempted me,
sir ; and I never thought about how wrong it was, till it was too
late for thinking to be of any use. I am most of all sorry to have
disobeyed you and forfeited your good opinion, and, if you will
but give me a chance of regaining it, I'll cheerfully bear any
punishment you like to inflict."

The head-master paused ere he answered—

" I will take you at your word; I shall not expel you, but
degrade you to the lower school. On every holiday and half-
holiday during this half-year, you will remain in, and employ
your time in construing and learning by heart six hundred lines

of Greek tragedy; and, lastly, you are forbidden to contend
for any of the prizes before the holidays. If it were not against
my rule to administer corporal punishment to boys in the fifth
and sixth forms, you would scarcely have escaped so easily.
Resume your place, sir. Now, Hugh Colville, tell me the
truth : did the elder boys force you to accompany them, or
merely induce you to do so by promising to take you to the
play ?"

Poor Hugh ! all eyes were turned upon him as, hastily swallowing his tears, he replied—

" Biggington promised me a thrashing if I refused to go;
but it wasn't that, sir ; it was the play did it, sir : I did so want
to see a play."

For a moment a faint gleam of pity passed over the Doctor's
face, but had vanished ere he resumed—

" I am sorry that I feel it impossible to look over this, your
first offence ;—you are so young a child that I believed and
hoped you had scarcely been in a position to exercise your own
free will in this instance ; that, in fact, you had been merely a
passive instrument in the hands of your elders ; but this does
not appear to have been the case—you evidently, being aware
of my orders to the contrary, were persuaded to share in this
expedition in order to witness a play ; and you studiously concealed your intentions from your brother, because he, being
older and steadier than yourself, might have interfered to prevent you from going, which you well knew that he would
disapprove of. I consider this so reprehensible that, in justice,
I am bound to punish you for it, and the only punishment likely
to make much impression on one of your age and character,
and to inspire you with a salutary dread of, and respect for
properly constituted authority, is a flogging, which will be
administered to you in private, as soon as morning-school
breaks up."

Hugh, who had listened to the Doctor's address as if life or
death hung upon his words, clasped his hands together in an
agony of supplication as his worst fears became realised ; the
head-master, however, who had hurried over the latter part of
his speech, as though he had mistrusted in some degree his own
resolution, turned hastily away, and began arranging the papers on
his desk ; and poor Hugh, finding all hope shut out from him,
crept back to his brother's side, and burying his face on Percy's
shoulder, gave way to a burst of passionate but silent weeping.

During the Doctor's address to Hugh, Norman, wh: during the whole of his own examination and sentence had appeared perfectly cool, self-possessed, and almost indifferent, began for the first time to evince symptoms of uneasiness :—when the decree for the flogging was promulgated, he unconsciously bit his lip, and clenched and unclenched his hand convulsively ; but when Hugh burst into tears, he rose and said in an eager, excited voice—

"I beg your pardon, Doctor Donkiestir, but I believe, in fact I am certain, this poor child was assured that if the affair came to your knowledge, he should be protected from the effects of your displeasure."

"By those who, for their own selfish purposes, were leading him into evil, I presume?" inquired the Doctor. Norman making no reply, he continued :—" Did *you* tell this little fellow such an untruth—pledging yourself to that which you knew you were unable to perform ?"

"If I did not actually say so, I allowed it to be said in my presence without contradicting it, which amounts to the same thing, sir," replied Norman, colouring.

"I am glad to see that you have sufficient right feeling left to be ashamed of your heartless and unmanly conduct," resumed the head-master ; "and I can devise you no more fitting punish- ment, than to show you by practical experience, how powerless you are to counteract the evil consequences of the wrong you have committed. Your appeal only confirms my decision in regard to little Colville."

Norman had hitherto succeeded beyond his expectations in his cleverly-devised scheme. His object had been to secure two points : first, to wreak his revenge on Biggington, by forcing him into a struggle, for which he had been for some weeks past privately training himself under the auspices of a retired pugilist, who kept a public-house in the neighbourhood ; and, secondly, to be expelled for so doing, by which event he should be enabled to join the regiment to which he had been appointed, and upon which all his hopes and wishes were just now centred, four months sooner than he otherwise could have done. Accordingly, till Hugh Colville, for whom he had taken a decided liking, was sentenced to be flogged, Norman had been inwardly congratulating himself on his success ; but the fact of being unable to protect this child, to whom he had by implica- tion pledged himself, wounded his pride and self-respect to such a degree, that, as the Doctor had truly observed, no more effective punishment could have been devised for him

In the meantime Percy had been working himself up into a dreadful state of mind. The reflection that Hugh, his lost father's darling, who had scarcely had a cross word spoken to him in his lifetime, and even since he had been at school (owing to his own watchfulness, and the rough good-nature of their cousin Wilfred Goldsmith), had never received an angry blow—the reflection that Hugh, his pet, everybody's pet, was sentenced to be flogged, was more than he could bear with equanimity. What could be done to save him? He glanced inquiringly towards Wilfred, but that knowing young gentleman shook his head despondingly—the case was beyond his skill; determined to risk a last appeal, he half rose from his seat, but the Doctor's quick glance detected the movement, and he said in a decided, but not an unkind tone of voice—

" Sit down, Percy Colville; I am doing what is best for your brother's future interests, and my decision is irrevocable. I will not hear another word on this subject from anybody," he continued angrily, perceiving that Percy still seemed inclined to remonstrate.

Ernest Carrington's desk was so situated that he could not only see each movement of the two Colvilles, but could actually hear every word they spoke to each other; thus he became aware that, at the moment in which the Doctor addressed Percy, Hugh started, and made a manful effort to subdue his tears.

" Hush, Percy," he said, in a broken whisper, " hush, dear, he will be angry with *you*. I daresay I can bear it; it's only the disgrace I'm thinking of, and that somebody may tell mamma of it, and make her nnhappy, perhaps." And here, despite his efforts, a sob choked his utterance.

Ernest caught the import of the whisper, and at the same moment he became aware of a timid and appealing glance from Percy, which Hugh also observing, a new light broke in upon him; for the first time,—believing equally in Ernest's will and power to assist him,—a hope of deliverance suggested itself to him; and, with a piteous, expressive little face, in which every passing thought and emotion could be read as in an open book, he also fixed his large tearful eyes imploringly upon Ernest's countenance.

And Ernest?—in his own private mind, he had all along

considered the Doctor injudiciously severe in regard to Hugh—
he had duly estimated the strength of the temptation, and the
poor child's weakness—he had also perceived the depth and
sincerity of Hugh's repentance ; and now his promise to do his
best to befriend the orphan boys, and the recollection of the fact
that he had been the involuntary instrument of Hugh's detec-
tion, recurred to him with a force that was irresistible, and
springing from his seat, he said—

"Doctor Donkiestir, I fear the petition I am about to urge
may be opposed to the etiquette of the school, but I ask, as a
personal favour, that Hugh Colville may not be flogged."

The Doctor's brow grew dark, but self-restraint in speech
had long since become habitual to him.

"I believe," he said, "I believe I have clearly signified my
wish that no further attempt to influence me in Hugh Colville's
favour should be made."

"I am aware of your prohibition, sir," returned Ernest, completely carried away by feeling, "but I have pledged myself to
befriend these orphan boys, and I will not fly from my word ; I
therefore again ask as a personal favour that Hugh Colville shall
be let off."

The Doctor's lips worked convulsively, but by a great exertion
of self-control he a second time restrained himself from any outward expression of anger.

"I grant your request, Mr. Carrington," he said gravely,
"your position as second master in this school necessitates my
doing so. How far your having urged it proves you to be unfitted
for that position, is a question which I have yet to consider.
Hugh Colville, you may thank Mr. Carrington for your escape
from a well-deserved flogging : I hope the narrowness of this
escape may impress you for the future, and that, while under
my tuition, you may never again merit so severe and disgraceful a punishment. And now let the sixth form come up to me
in mathematics."

And so the scene ended. Ernest had redeemed his word,
and saved Hugh from a flogging, but at what amount of personal sacrifice remained yet to be proved.

CHAPTER XI.

LOSS AND GAIN.

SIR THOMAS CRAWLEY paced up and down his handsome library, a prey to anxiety!—much depended on the turn events might take over which he had no control, but which yet must exercise a great and lasting influence on his future career. A ministerial crisis was at hand, and the party to which Sir Thomas belonged would either be turned out, or would retain their position reinforced by a coalition with some of their opponents, and thus become stronger than they had ever before felt themselves. If they went out, Sir Thomas was prepared, cleverly and respectably, to " rat," and come in again with the opposition ; but if they remained in, he was equally prepared to adhere to them with the most unshakable fidelity, and to make himself as generally useful and agreeable as in him lay : either way he trusted to see his services rewarded by a baronetcy, and he was only waiting for this desirable consummation, to make an offer of his bad heart, and dirty hand, to the ugly younger daughter of a very aristocratic, disagreeable, old nobleman. If he succeeded in all this, he told himself he should have reached the height of his ambition, and mentally promised his conscience (for, reader, he had a conscience as well as you and I, though we, in our superior sanctity, regard it as a poor limp, damaged, washed-out piece of goods, and look down upon it accordingly, like two fine old English Pharisees as we are) to give up sneaking and shuffling, which he called tact and policy, and live virtuously ever after, as became a member of the aristocracy—thus fitting himself to proceed, *vid* the family vault, to take possession of some equivalent for the Ashburn estates in another world, in regard to which he was fain to own that his title at present was a little—just a very little—doubtful. What a bad man Sir Thomas was, to be sure ! How lucky, dear reader, that you and I are so much better than he !

But Sir Thomas had two friends in the ministry, Messrs. Tadpole and Taper (the Right Honourable Benjamin Disraeli knows them, and has made notable mention of them in his tale of " Coningsby "), whose views were exactly in accordance with his own, *i.e.*—to take the best possible care of their own interests, and (whenever that purpose could be best insured by their so doing) of each other's also; and Sir Thomas had that morning received the following note, marked "private and confidential," from his friend Tadpole :—

"DEAR SIR THOMAS,—I have just learned, from an *unmistakable quarter*, that it is Lord ——'s (naming the Premier for the time being) intention to apply to you for your living of Ashburn for the nephew of Mr. ——, the colonial Bishop of Boreanigger. The coalition is still quite upon the cards, so it would scarcely be advisable to say 'no;' while, if they go out, which is more than probable, to say 'yes' would be certain to give offence where you would least wish to do so. I would therefore suggest that, if you have not already filled up the vacancy, it would be *most desirable* to do so without delay, and you will thus avoid the difficulty—*verbum sat.*

"I am, dear Sir Thomas, yours very faithfully,

"A. TADPOLE."

"P.S. You will kindly bear in mind that clerkship in the Woods and Forests; young Grig, Mrs. Tadpole's nephew, is a very promising lad, and in good hands might do credit to his patron."

Sir Thomas read and re-read the letter. How fortunate that Tadpole had ferreted out this information! but for that he might have been forced to commit himself irrevocably to the wrong side—horrible idea! Yes, Tadpole was right: the living must be disposed of without an hour's delay: who should he give it to? It must be some one without political influence or connection, lest he should give offence to either party! At this moment, from one of those strange chances which occasionally appear to determine the whole destiny of a lifetime by the agency of a mere trifle, Sir Thomas knocked some papers off his desk, and as he stooped to pick them up, the card Ernest Carrington had sent in some weeks before fell from among them. He raised it, and regarding it fixedly, as though he were scrutinizing the person whose name it bore, muttered—

"Young Carrington, he is in the Church—why should not he do? He might, of course, be had at a minute's notice;— £800 a year would be a fortune to him;—besides, there's policy in the thing—I find North Park (a farm of some five hundred acres) is in the entail; if he were to get scent of it, and could obtain access to the papers, he might claim it any day; his boyish, chivalrous scruples are sure to wear out; this would bind him to me by the tie of gratitude: he is just one of those hot-headed, romantic dispositions that are always absurdly grateful. Gad! I could not have hit on a fitter person; I'll write to him at once: I've got his direction, somewhere;"—as he spoke, he began tossing over papers and letters in search of the missing direction. "A very good thought," he continued; "I could see through that young fellow in a minute; he may be managed as easy as a child, if you only take advantage of his weak points. I like 'em of what they call an open disposition; they show you their whole hand at starting; it's your close, crafty, quiet dogs that are the hardest to deal with. I shall make a point with him that he gets every farthing out of that proud, haughty Mrs. Colville, and her conceited, stuck-up minx of a daughter; they've looked down upon me, and never liked me, I know: they'll be sorry for it some day."

Ernest Carrington, when he returned to his rooms after morning school, found two letters on his table. The first he opened was from Dr. Donkiestir, and ran as follows:—

"My Dear Sir,—It is with considerable pain that I feel it my duty to urge upon you the propriety of resigning your position, as Mathematical and Classical Master, at the school of which I have the honour to be Principal. As regards talent and acquirements, I have never before had so able an assistant, but there are other qualities necessary in the onerous position of second-master of such a school as that over which I have, since its establishment, presided, which are equally important. In these qualities, the injudicious manner in which you this morning allowed, what I admit to have been an impulse of generous feeling, to hurry you into a breach of scholastic discipline, which a more hasty man than myself might have construed into a personal insult, proves you to be utterly wanting. It is to avoid the possibility of your again placing both yourself and me in such a false and difficult position, that I thus reluctantly press upon you the advisability of your immediate resignation. When a few more years shall have passed over your head, maturing your judgment, and tempering your impulsive disposition, I can conceive you will prove eminently qualified for the responsible, yet interesting office of an instructor to youth. In the meantime, I would advise your looking out for a curacy, or a situation as tutor to some young nobleman about

to travel. I shall have much pleasure in giving you unexceptionable testimonials for such a purpose, or in furthering you.
interest, to the extent of my power, in any other manner yo‘
may point out.—Awaiting your reply,

"I remain, dear Sir,

"Yours very faithfully,

"JOHN HANNIBAL DONKIESTIR, D.D."

"So that is my reward for my philanthropy, is it?" was
Ernest Carrington's mental comment as he finished perusing
the Doctor's letter. "Well, I daresay I did wrong to interfere,
but I should hate myself if I could have sat by and watched
the expression in that boy, Percy Colville's, beautiful face, or
listened to that poor little child's heart-broken sobs, and not tried
to help them—I'm glad I've saved the little fellow, at all events;
no more teaching for me; I'd sooner go out as a missionary,
and try to wash blackamore heathens into piebald Christians
than that. Well, now for a curacy, hard labour, and genteel
starvation on £80 a year; never mind, I shall be my own
master, at all events, and may do some good amongst the poor
people : no drudgery can be worse than this horse-in-a-mill life
I have been leading of late. A letter from Sir Thomas Crawley ;
What can he want of me? I've no more birthrights to sell for
a mess of pottage;" and with such hard, but not unnatural,
thoughts running in his brain, he broke the seal, and read as
follows :—

"MY DEAR YOUNG KINSMAN,—Ever since I had the pleasure
of making your acquaintance, and learning the very sensible
views you hold on all topics, political and religious—views
which agree so remarkably with my own—I have been turning in my mind how best I may assist you, and have come
to the conclusion that I cannot better discharge my duty as a
patron of ecclesiastical preferment, than by offering you my
living of Ashburn, now vacant. The parish contains from six
hundred to six hundred and fifty souls, and the living is worth
eight hundred per annum, with a parsonage-house and glebe
attached; you will thus be rendered independent of any pecuniary difficulties, and able to apply your mind entirely to that
deeply interesting subject, the religious and social improvement
of the labouring classes. I have only two provisos to make :—
one is, that if you approve of the position I offer you, you will

signify your acceptance of it by return of post (my reason for this I will explain satisfactorily when we meet); the other, that you promise to urge your claim upon the estate of the late incumbent for dilapidations in the house and glebe. I am sure you will agree with me, that the Church is bound, in this latitudinarian age, to protect her property ; and I can bestow my living upon no one who will not give me a distinct pledge upon this point.

"I remain, my dear young kinsman,

"Your affectionate friend and relative,

"Thomas Crawley, K.C.B."

Poor Ernest! The revulsion of feeling was almost too much for him, and in his contrition for the hard thoughts he had entertained of Sir Thomas Crawley, he dashed off a hasty letter, full of generous feeling and overflowing with gratitude, in which he thankfully accepted the living, and pledged himself to see full justice done to the interests of the Church as embodied in the Ashburn Rectory dilapidations : he was sorry for it afterwards, when——but we must not anticipate

* * *

CHAPTER XII.

THE ROSEBUD SKETCHES FROM MEMORY.

Reader! dear reader! nay, on the chance of your being a young lady, and, therefore, necessarily charming, we will go the whole length of the adjective, and say at once, dear*est* reader! (of course, asking your pardon for the liberty, and feeling quite sure you are only too ready to grant it, because you are such an amiable sex);—don't you think—(by the way, how very becoming that new plan of plaiting a pig-tail of your back hair, and twisting it round like a coronal over your front hair, is to you—it gives quite a Classical, Grecian, Etruscan, and all that sort of thing, style to your *contour*)—don't you think, dearest reader, that we have for much too long a time lost sight of, and practically ignored, and altogether cruelly and abominably deserted, and neglected, the Rosebud of Ashburn ? and she all the while, in the self-denial of her nature (a species of self-denial, by the way, which would be very generally practised and become exceedingly popular, if we were but sufficiently philanthropic to divulge the recipe), has only been growing prettier and more fatally fascinating every day.

Oh, that dangerous, irresistible little Rosebud! There she sat, looking as demure as if she wasn't always ready to smash any amount of hearts into the smallest possible pieces, on the shortest notice imaginable, toiling busily over an absurd little crochet purse, which she was manufacturing literally " by hook and by crook," against Mr. Selby's birthday, when she intended to present him with it "to keep all his sovereigns in ;" though if he could have kept *all* his sovereigns in that pretty little folly, the said folly would very soon have had a sinecure, and poor Mr. Selby have been a ruined snob, instead of a prosperous one.

Now, we do not object to mention in confidence, though we should not wish it repeated, that the Rosebud, albeit a most dutiful and affectionate daughter, had, since the boys went to school, found her life very dull and monotonous, and was getting decidedly "hard up" for excitement ;—pleasurable excitement would, of course, have been her choice, but even a little mild persecution would not have come amiss, in this dearth of variety: she had expected Sir Thomas Crawley would have given away the living, and some horrid interloper have arrived to turn them out of house and home long ere this, but no ; day after day passed by without producing even the ghost of an incident, and the unfortunate and victimised Rosebud was reduced to sit by herself and look pretty, without any one to reap the benefit thereof. What a cruel situation for a vivacious Rosebud !

Mrs. Colville had been absent nearly an hour, and Emily, who stayed at home to get on with her crochet (for the next day was the eventful birthday, and she was alarmed lest her offering should not be ready in time), had been all by her small and pretty self, and had croched away so hard that she had croched herself into a headache ;—perceiving this to be the case, she laid down her work and fell a thinking, and having nothing agreeable to reflect upon in the present, she began to "try back," till she had mentally jibbed as far as the day when she, and her friend Caroline, had been frightened by the footpad, and rescued by an interesting young stranger, whom you and I, dearest reader, know to have been Ernest Carrington, although the Rosebud was still in ignorance of that fact. From sheer listlessness and want of anything better to think about, Emily began speculating as to whom her deliverer could possibly have been, and whether, by any odd chance, she should ever meet him again, and if so, whether he would recollect her, or she him, when it occurred to her to try if she could remember his features well enough to sketch them. Emily had rather a talent for taking likenesses, so she provided herself with a pencil and a piece of paper, and drew away till she had produced, what an auctioneer would have termed, a "splendid portrait of a nice young man." Having accomplished this feat, she held up her performance to scrutinise it, drawing back her head and bending her slender neck from side to side, like some graceful bird, till she got the light to fall properly upon her sketch,—" Yes, I think that is very like him," she said, " only it hasn't got quite his expression—there was something so calm and—spiritual, I suppose it would be called, in his look; he was very handsome, certainly ; I wonder who he could be !" Resuming her pencil, she added two or three finishing touches, then appended to it her initials, and the date, with the intention of adding it to a select gallery of portraits of remarkable ball-partners, and other heroes of her imagination, which reposed inviolate within the sacred precincts of her writing-desk ; but, at this moment, the house-door opened and Mrs. Colville entered, so hastily that Emily had only time to thrust her portrait between the leaves of the nearest book (which happened to be a volume of Blair's Sermons), ere her mother had joined her.

" Mamma, you are tired," she said, as Mrs. Colville, hurriedly drawing off her gloves, seated herself on the sofa; observing her more attentively, she continued, " You look pale, and—— You are not ill ? Has anything happened ?"

Mrs. Colville smiled faintly. " I am not ill, darling," she said, " but—but—the new rector is appointed, and we must leave this house next week;" and overcome by the idea of quitting the home where she had passed so many happy years with him who was no more, but whom she had loved, nay, *still* loved so well (for hers was one of those rare and true affections which only *begin* on earth), the widow burst into tears. In an instant, Emily flew to her side, quietly removed her bonnet, and then, with the delicate instinct of a true woman's nature, feeling that her sympathy could best be shown by silent tenderness, she gently drew her mother's head towards her till it rested on her bosom, and suffered her to weep unrestrained. But Mrs. Colville, although on this occasion the suddenness of the

shock had overcome her habitual self-control, was by no means
a weak character, and she soon recovered herself.

"I did not mean to distress you thus, dearest," she said
"but the announcement was made to me so abruptly; Sir
Thomas—I do not wish to speak against him—but he is not a
man of any delicacy of feeling."

"He!" interrupted Emily, "he has no more feeling than the
most obdurate old paving-stone that ever refused to be mac-
adamised."

"He has certainly not shown much consideration towards us
in our sorrow," returned the widow, "but I bear him no ill-
will : he only exacts his legal rights, and I have no business to
blame because nature has not gifted him with delicate perception. But I was going to tell you : Mr. Selby received a note
from him this morning, saying—but here it is ; Mr. Selby gave
it to me to show you."

As she spoke, Mrs. Colville placed the note in her daughter's
hands. It ran thus :—

"DEAR SIR,—I have at length found a suitable person on
whom to bestow the living of Ashburn. The new incumbent
will read himself in on Sunday next. I presume, from the
length of time which has elapsed since the late rector's decease,
that his family have quitted the parsonage. Should this not be
the case, will you apprise Mrs. Colville of my desire that she
should do so with as little loss of time as possible. The gentleman to whom I have given the preferment, holds most strongly
the same views as myself, as to the necessity of guarding against
the deterioration of Church property, and has, at my suggestion, written to Mrs. Colville's solicitor, to announce his intention
of claiming, to the utmost farthing, the sum due for dilapidations ; which debt I depend upon you to see liquidated. You
will oblige me by doing everything in your power to facilitate
all arrangements the new rector may wish to make. I leave
Ashburn early to-morrow for London ; therefore shall be glad
to see you this evening, when I can explain my intentions
more fully.

"I remain, dear sir,
"Yours, &c.,
"THOMAS CRAWLEY, K.C.B."

"What a cruel, heartless letter!" exclaimed Emily; "and
this horrible new rector appears to be as unfeeling as his patron

but of course Sir Thomas has picked out some dreadful old creature like himself; he had better have given the living to dear, tiresome Mr. Slowkopf than to this unpleasant man. But mamma, dearest, what is to become of us?"

" Mr. Selby advises my taking the cottage on the common," was the reply : " it will just hold us and the boys, and I do not wish to quit this neighbourhood, at least till Percy is old enough to leave school."

" Well, the plan has its advantages; it would break my heart to leave dear Caroline, certainly," rejoined the Rosebud, musing ; " the worst feature in the case is this dreadful new rector—I've taken a thorough aversion to him already—it is so unpleasant to dislike one's clergyman ! I know he will be horrible, I've a presentiment about him, and my presentiments always come true."

And so the Rosebud chatted on, partly to make up for her long silence, and partly to divert her mother from the sad thoughts which she could see were still depressing her, till Sarah coming to lay the cloth for their frugal meal, she tripped off to get ready for dinner, quite forgetting a certain portrait she had sketched ; and Mrs. Colville, being of a neat and orderly disposition, perceiving a stray volume of Blair's Sermons lying about, put it, and all it contained, away in its proper place in the book-shelves.

Saturday came, and with it the new rector ; he was to stay at Mr. Selby's till the rectory was ready for him. Despite her prejudices and presentiments, the Rosebud was decidedly curious to see him, and actually made a pretence to gather some flowers for the drawing-room (although they were to leave on Monday), in hopes that, hidden behind the great laurel, she might catch a glimpse of him in the act of arriving, Caroline having told her by what train he was to travel. But unfortunately, after waiting a quarter of an hour, she had just gone into the house for the garden-scissors, when the railway fly drove past, and her utmost endeavours only enabled her to catch the retreating outline of—a black leather portmanteau. Before she went in, however, Mr. Slowkopf, who in his heavy way was always extremely gallant towards the Rosebud, made his appearance, clad in his best suit of black (which was inferior to any other clergyman's worst), on his way to dine *chez* Selby, and be introduced to his new rector ; and hearing from the young lady (who looked upon him in the light of a half-childish grandpapa, or thereabouts) that she wished to learn something of the appearance, manners, habits, customs, zoology, pathology, ethnology, and general statistics, of the illustrious strangei, he promised to look in for five minutes on his way home (being Saturday night, he should come away very early), and report progress.

Of course Emily told her mamma of this arrangement, and of course Mrs. Colville smiled, and called her a silly little goose for not having patience to wait till to-morrow; adding that, for her own part, she was used to Mr. Slowkopf, and should be sorry to see any one else in his place; and then with a sigh she quitted the room.

Ten o'clock came, and with it Mr. Slowkopf, who looked and felt rather peculiar, which might be accounted for by the fact that his usual beverage was spring water, but that, on the evening in question, he had been prevailed upon to drink two or three glasses of wine. Instead of creeping into the most lonely corner of the apartment, and finding something uncomfortable to sit upon, he advanced boldly into the room, and saying cheerfully, "Well, you see, ladies, here I am," he drew an arm-chair exactly between Mrs. Colville and the fire, and seated himself thereupon, chuckling with the air of a man conscious of a good joke, but completely in the dark as to what might be the nature or subject thereof.

The Rosebud was so deeply affected (in what manner we leave our readers to guess) by this unaccountable behaviour, that she dared not trust herself to speak; so Mrs. Colville, seeing that the curate appeared likely to chuckle himself to sleep without making any further attempts at conversation, began—

"Well, Mr. Slowkopf, are your never going to satisfy our curiosity?"

Thus abjured, that individual started, looked round in confusion, and then in some degree relapsing into his usual manner only smiling vacantly all the time, he said—

"Before I can comply with your request, my dear madam, I must inquire to what particular subject the curiosity to which you allude especially applies?"

"Oh! Mr. Slowkopf, you're only trying to tease," exclaimed Emily, recovering her voice and her curiosity simultaneously. "Of course about the new rector: what's he like? come tell us—quick!"

"He's like," replied the curate, pausing on each syllable, as if conversation were an electric telegraph office, and he had to pay extra for every additional word he uttered—"he's very like —most other young clergymen."

"Then he *is* young?" continued Emily interrogatively: "is he tall, gentlemanly, handsome?"

"He's not, at least as far as I observed—but such things don't make much impression on me" ("I wonder what *does!*" was Emily's *sotto voce* comment)—"but I should say, he's not what would be generally called—hard-featured. I only hope," he continued solemnly—"I only hope that he may turn out sound: there was something I didn't like about that Hock."

"Indeed!" returned Emily, looking very grave, with the exception of her eyes, which were laughing wickedly, "incipient spavin, perhaps."

For a moment Mr. Slowkopf gazed at her in sheer amazement; then a faint consciousness of her meaning gradually dawned upon him, and he replied—

"Similarity of sound has not unnaturally misled you in regard to the import of my observation, Miss Emily: the Hock to which I alluded was not, as you conceive, the elbow-joint of a horse's hind-leg, but a choice sample of Rhenish wine, hospitably produced by Mr. Selby for our gratification; in regard to which Mr. Carrington was pleased to observe that it was not the only good thing that came from Germany—a remark which I conceived might refer to the German school of theology, whence, by logical progression, I was led to doubt the soundness of the new rector's doctrinal views."

And having delivered himself of this ponderous explanation, Mr. Slowkopf rose up as suddenly as if he had been propelled by a spring, after the fashion of that much-enduring public character Jack-in-a-box, and abruptly taking leave of the two ladies, broke his shins over a chair, and was gone.

"Why, mamma dear, what has come to the creature?" exclaimed Emily: "is he going entirely to take leave of the few senses wherewith nature has so scantily endowed him?"

"You're too pert to him, my love," was the reply; "he's a very excellent young man; and always drinking water at home, is naturally more elated by a glass or two of wine, than a less abstemious person would be."

"Oh! that is the secret, is it—the wretch; I shall send him some teetotal tracts to-morrow. I've got 'A Voice from the Pump,' and 'Cold Comfort for chilly Christians,' still left: they'll suit his case charmingly."

And so saying, the incorrigible Rosebud tripped off to bed, where, straightway falling asleep, she dreamed, that being in church, and the new rector turning out to be a fine young piebald centaur, she clearly perceived, as he cantered up the pulpit stairs, whisking a most unclerical switch tail, that he was decidedly spavined in the off hind-leg.

CHAPTER XIII.

AN ' ELEGANT EXTRACT " FROM BLAIR'S SERMONS.

An unfortunate necessity existing to compress this our veracious history of "the Fortunes of the Colville Family " within the limits of one small volume, a great many incidents on which we would gladly expatiate can merely be sketched in outline, while we must leave the reader's imagination to fill in the details.

Amongst these " fancy portraits " must be included the pretty face of our little heroine, characterised by the look of astonishment with which she recognised, in her new spiritual pastor, the handsome hero of the footpad adventure, together with the becoming blush consequent upon the discovery.

Another leaf of the sketch-book must be devoted to Percy and Hugh's first return for the holidays, and their delight in renewing their acquaintance with their kind friend and protector at Tickletown, together with the consequent intimacy which ensued between the cottage and the rectory.

The new incumbent soon won " golden opinions " from rich and poor. Sir Thomas Crawley, who had wriggled himself into the new ministry, and obtained the appointment of envoy to the court of one of the German potentates—a position which he hoped would secure for him the baronetcy as a retiring pension—had taken up a superstitious notion that his success was a reward for the good action of appointing Ernest Carrington to the living of Ashburn ; and in order still to propitiate the fickle goddess, he continued to heap favours upon his *protégé*, till worthy Mr. Selby, unaccustomed to such freaks of benevolence on the part of his patron, began to fear the air of Germany had produced some strange effect upon Sir Thomas's brain.

Mr. Slowkopf, too, had gradually arrived at the conviction that Mr. Carrington was " a most praiseworthy and remarkable young man," and, once assured that he had no lingering affection for modern Teutonic heresies, he yielded himself to the fascinations of his rector's manner and address, and became one of the most devoted of his admirers.

Faithful to his pledge, Ernest exacted every farthing of the dilapidations to which he had a legal claim; but then he took at a valuation Mrs. Colville's furniture and live stock (comprising Samson the pony, an orthodox and superannuated cow, some fine old Protestant cocks and hens, the annual pig, and the perennial yard-dog, which latter individual always barked at the wrong time, *would* go to church, and howl at the singing-psalms, whenever he could get loose, and cost rather more to feed than did his new master), and, trusting to the widow's ignorance of business matters, contrived to pay a sum for these conveniences which made the dilapidations fall very lightly upon her pocket.

Whether Mrs. Colville was more clear-sighted than he expected, or whether his kind interference to protect Hugh from punishment, of which she heard an account from Percy, had won her heart, certain it is that the dislike with which the widow was prepared to view her lost husband's successor, soon changed to an almost maternal regard for the young man who so well performed the duties which Mr. Colville's death had left unfulfilled. The only person who appeared insensible to the merits of this general favourite, was the capricious little Rosebud; but she, very early in the session, seceded to the opposition benches, and constituted in her own pretty person a formidable minority of one.

Nearly two years had elapsed since our tale began, and Percy and Hugh were again at home for their Christmas holidays. The party, consisting of Mrs. Colville and Emily, the two boys, their cousin Wilfred—now promoted to tail coats and a stool in the paternal counting-house—and the rector and curate, who, having *happened* to look in, had been asked to stay to tea, were gathered round the fire in the snug little drawing-room in the cottage. There had been a pause in the conversation, of which Mr. Slowkopf availed himself to address the Rosebud.

"It is a singular and remarkable fact, Miss Emily," he began in his usual deliberate manner : "it is a most singular and remarkable fact, that, intimate as I have long had the privilege of being in this family, I never, until this morning, when Master Hugh obligingly gave me an account of the transaction, was aware of your having been alarmed by a footpad, and providentially rescued by the benevolent interference of our excellent rector here;" and as he spoke he indicated Ernest by a flap of his larboard fin, with about as much grace as a seal might have displayed under similar circumstances.

"Ay, what was that?" inquired Wilfred Goldsmith, eagerly. "Tell us about it, Shortshanks" (an elegant Tickletonian sobriquet for Hugh): "I like to hear of shindies."

Thus appealed to, Hugh, nothing loth, proceeded to give a full, true, and particular account of the adventure; which, as Ernest was aware that he must have derived his information originally from the Rosebud herself, he listened to with a quiet smile,—more particularly when he heard himself described as a tall and graceful young man, of singularly prepossessing appearance.

"Well, it was a plucky thing well done, and I give you credit for it, Mr. Carrington," was Wilfred's comment, as Hugh concluded.

"Really I'm quite overpowered," returned Ernest, with an affectation of extreme humility: "my poor exertions were a great deal too humble to deserve an eulogium from Mr. Wilfred Goldsmith." Wilfred, who since we last heard of him had altered only by becoming in every respect "rather more so," winced slightly, for he knew that Ernest was laughing at him: —lest any one else should make the same discovery, he hastened to divert attention by attacking his fair relative.

"You must have been finely astonished, Cousin Emily," he said, "when you recognised the interesting knight-errant peeping over the pulpit-cushion."

"Did you know him again directly, Emmy?" inquired Hugh.

"Of course she did," rejoined Wilfred. "Do you think she did not dream of the features of her gallant deliverer twice a week regularly for the next half year, at least?"

"Indeed, I did nothing of the kind, you absurd boy!" exclaimed the Rosebud, eagerly. "As well as I remember, I did happen to recognise Mr. Carrington, but I really wonder that I should have done so; for I was so dreadfully frightened on the first occasion, that I could think of nothing but the horrible man who had attempted to take my money;" and as the proud Puss uttered this slightly apocryphal statement, she gave her head a little pettish toss, which meant a great deal, and expressed its meaning unmistakably—at least so thought Ernest Carrington ; and the grave expression of his face became graver than ever.

"Talking of falling among thieves," began Mr. Slowkopf, addressing Ernest, " reminds me of the last time I met you."

"Complimentary, very," muttered Wilfred, *sotto voce.*

"We were then discussing the subject of white lies, as they are called," resumed Mr. Slowkopf; " now I have since recollected a passage in one of the sermons of that learned and excellent divine, Blair, which affords a curious commentary on what we are saying.　I cannot remember his words, but you'll find it in the fourth sermon in the second volume."

" We have Blair's Sermons," remarked Mrs. Colville; " they are on the book-shelves by you, Mr. Carrington, if you wish to refer to the passage."

"The second volume, I think you said, Slowkopf?" inquired Ernest, taking down the book as he spoke.　Receiving an affirmative grunt, the young clergyman turned his chair, so that the firelight fell strongly on the book, leaving his face in shadow, which circumstance prevented the fact from transpiring, that scarcely had he opened the volume when he gave a sudden start, then coloured violently, and then examined the page before him most carefully and minutely.　Having completed his investigation, he turned over two or three leaves, and, in his usual voice and manner, read aloud the paragraph to which the curate had referred.

In the meantime, Hugh, by dint of coaxing, had inveigled his mother into providing the materials for a bowl of snapdragon, wherein, to his great delight, Mr. Slowkopf was induced solemnly, heavily, and perseveringly, to burn his reverend fingers in fishing out almonds and raisins, which he invariably dropped, for Hugh to pick up and eat.　Just when the fun was at its highest, and even Mrs. Colville joining heartily in the chorus of laughter, Ernest approached the Rosebud, with the volume still in his hand, and said quietly—

" Pray, Miss Colville, do you ever study Blair's Sermons ?"

"Oh, I have read some of them," was the reply ; " but why do you ask ?—are you afraid I shall find you out if you appropriate the worthy man's ideas ?"

"On the contrary, he appears to have appropriated something of mine," was the answer.

" Indeed! and what might that be ?" returned the Rosebud, wholly unconscious of the dangerous ground upon which she was treading.

" Only, as Mr. Slowkopf judiciously observed, a very singular commentary on the subject we were discussing—white lies !" was the reply; and as he spoke, Ernest opened the volume he held in his hand and disclosed to the eyes of the horrified Rose-bud, a certain pencil-sketch, with its tell-tale date and initials, which possibly the reader may not have forgotten as entirely as the fair artist had done.

In an instant a crimson blush suffused her face and neck, and turning away her head, she struggled successfully against a strong inclination to burst into tears; recovering herself, she said hastily, and in a tone which indicated a mixture of wounded feeling and of anger—

" I consider you have insulted me, Mr. Carrington ; it is most unkind—unworthy of you !"

What Ernest might have replied to this especially unpleasant address, can never be known; for at that moment, Mr. Slow-kopf, in an agony of digital combustion, overturned the bowl of snapdragon, and, during the confusion which ensued, Emily contrived to leave the drawing-room unobserved.

For some reason or other, Ernest did not sleep very well that night; and the first thing next morning he wrote a note explanatory and apologetic, to the Rosebud, and having despatched it, sat down to finish his sermon, but got no farther than " Dearly beloved," till the messenger returned. The answer contained his epistle unopened, and the following note :—

" Miss Colville presents her compliments to Mr. Carrington, and begs to say, that as any discussion of the occurrence of yesterday evening must be equally useless and painful, she has thought it most advisable to return his note unread. Miss Colville trusts Mr. Carrington will not allow this silly affair to influence his manner towards Miss Colville or the boys, as such an interruption to an intimacy which is so agreeable and bene-ficial to them, would prove a source of deep and additional annoyance to her."

Ernest was very sorry for what he had done, but he saw this was not the fitting time to endeavour to repair the breach ; so being a sensible young man, he let the Rosebud have her own wilful way; and when the boys returned to school, informed Mrs. Colville he was about to prepare a volume of sermons for publication, which would occupy all his leisure hours; and that she must not think he meant to cut her, if his visits assumed the angelic property of being "few and far between;"—as he said this, he observed the Rosebud's eyes fixed upon him with a peculiar expression in them—could it be regret?

* * *

CHAPTER XIV

CONTAINS MUCH DOCTOR'S STUFF, AND OTHER RUBBISH.

ERNEST was true to his word—all that spring and summer he worked at his sermons and his parish, like an ecclesiastical galley-slave, till the volume was finished, and all the people had become so good, that if it had not been for christenings, weddings, and funerals, they would scarcely have required the services of a clergyman at all. Indeed, carrying out the doctrine of self-denial logically, and to its fullest extent, we doubt whether a rectory might not be regarded as a superfluous luxury, a kind of canonical pomp and vanity, and therefore a stumbling-block to be removed from the spiritual highway of that super-excellent community.

But writing sermons, and instilling pure and heavenly principles into the decidedly earthly minds of small shopkeepers and needy agricultural labourers, albeit a high and sacred calling, considered abstractedly and as a whole, is yet, taken in detail, a very trying vocation to a man possessing, in no common degree, a taste for intellectual pursuits, and a strong appreciation of refined society. Thus it came to pass that one fine morning (it was the 12th of August) Ernest, having written a report of a district meeting for the propagation of the Gospel in parts so very foreign that the propagators themselves would have been puzzled to find them on the map, leaned back in his chair and wondered how sundry college friends of his were getting on among the grouse, when a note in the Rosebud's handwriting was brought to him. With sparkling eyes and a slight accession of colour to his pale cheeks, he read as follows :—

"DEAR MR. CARRINGTON,—Mamma is very ill—how ill I do not know—and fear to learn. Mr. Pillanbill (do you consider him clever?) tells me not to be alarmed, which frightens me terribly. May I hope you will come to us—poor mamma is able and anxious to see you, and you will tell me whether anything else can or ought to be done. Yours sincerely,

"EMILY COLVILLE."

Within ten minutes after the note had reached him Ernest was at the cottage. Emily received him with a blush and a smile. "How kind and good of you to come so quickly!" she said. Tears trembled in her eyes. Ernest had never seen her look so pretty.

"How good of *you* to send for me!" he replied: "I hope," he continued—"I hope it proves that I am forgiven?"

Emily hung her head—"If you please, we will never refer to that again," she said, entreatingly; "I was very proud and foolish, and behaved very ill; but you are wise enough to forgive, and kind enough to forget: is it not so?"

Ernest took her hand and pressed it warmly, nor was it immediately withdrawn.

Mrs. Colville was seriously ill; and having sat with her for some time, the rector obtained her permission to inquire whether Mr. Pillanbill would object to meet Dr. Twiggit, and learn if they agreed in their view of the case, just to satisfy Miss Colville's natural anxiety.

Mr. Pillanbill graciously consented. Dr. Twiggit resided ten miles off, and had too good a practice near home to make it worth his while to poach upon his (P.'s) manor for the sake of a single outlying patient with a limited purse. So Dr. Twiggit was summoned, and came; he was a little man, with a large hooked nose and an ornithological cast of countenance, as of a shrewd fowl. Having strutted and clapped his wings, and, so to speak, crowed over the apothecary and the Rosebud, and looked as if he would have liked uncommonly to fight Ernest for a handful of barley, he entered the sick-room, where first, with two little bright bead-like eyes, he looked clean through poor Mrs. Colville into the mattress and feather-bed; next, he stretched out a claw to feel her pulse; then he pecked at her to make her put out her tongue; then he shook his feathers and crowed over *her;* and then he chased Pillanbill round and out of the room for the consultation, which ran thus:—

Twiggit.—"Clear case!"

Pillanbill.—"No mist

Twiggit.—" Hepatico-cerebreosistosis, first stage."

Pillanbill.—" Quite so."

Twiggit.—" What have you thrown in ? "

Pillanbill hands prescription. *Hydrarg:*—mysterious cipher, looking like a 3 with two heads—*Rhei: pulvo :*—another cipher, worse than the first, &c., &c.

Twiggit reads—" Hum ! yes, ha ! good !" (returns prescription), " can't be better—ar—I think that is all to-day, ar—needn't send for me unless any symptoms of spiflicatio appear, and then it will be too late ; keep the feet warm, head cool, nourishing slops, bland puddings—but you know—good morning."

So saying, the talented M.D., who was in himself a modern instance of the mythical relation existing between Esculapius and the cock, strutted out to his carriage a richer man by five guineas than he had been when he quitted that vehicle.

Mrs. Colville's was a very severe illness, and at one time her state was most critical ; but, thanks to a patient and resigned spirit, and an excellent constitution, after three weeks of intense anxiety to those who watched over her, she began to show symptoms of amendment. From the day on which Ernest had received the Rosebud's summons, to the happy moment when Doctors Twiggit and Pillanbill took their leave, he had shown the unceasing affection of a son towards Mrs. Colville, and of a brother towards Emily. Hour after hour had he attended the sick woman's bedside, reading to her or conversing with her on those all-important subjects that, at such seasons, become invested with a deep and solemn interest which in our happier moments they too often fail to excite in our weak and fallen natures. And as Emily sat by, and heard the words of the inspired volume, rendered yet more beautiful and impressive by the correct taste, true feeling, and rich mellow voice of the reader ; or listened, as, with a wisdom beyond his years—a wisdom not of this world—Ernest explained away difficulties, and threw the clear light of a strong and vigorous understanding on the great truths of our Holy Religion, what wonder if some of the reverence and affection, which such teaching must excite in every pure and gentle bosom, grew to cling around the teacher? Or what wonder, either, that when Ernest saw the scornful, capricious, half-childlike little coquette, whose sparkling beauty had charmed his fancy, change, the instant sorrow laid its chastening touch upon her brow, into the thoughtful, tender devoted woman,—the ministering angel beside the couch of sickness, whose gentle, never-failing tact and quiet power of steadfast, patient endurance, man's stronger, more energetic nature, may envy, but can never attain to;—what wonder if, where he had before admired, he now grew to love?

It is a good thing to love! So much mawkish sentimentality and bombastic nonsense, so many white-muslined tears and boarding-school sentimentalities, have been heaped around its counterfeit, that healthy minds not unnaturally scoff at the passion—until they feel it! and thus has one of the highest emotions of which our nature is capable, been brought into undeserved disrepute. A deep, true, earnest, unselfish affection, such as an honest man ("the NOBLEST work of God") is capable of feeling for a woman worthy to call it forth, raises, purifies, and spiritualises his whole being, enlarges his sympathies, and (by affording a new motive for exertion) stimulates his faculties, and thus causes him to do the work he may lay his hand to, better than he would have executed it without such an incentive. The Apostle tells us, "If a man say, I love God, and hateth his brother, he is a liar;" and a great truth is embodied in the text;—a nature capable of forming a deep, unselfish attachment to one of God's creatures, raises its possessor in the scale of creation, and enables him to adore his Maker and love his fellows with a zealous earnestness and reality, of which a self-engrossed character is incapable—therefore, as we began by saying—it is a good thing to love!

As Mrs. Colville's recovery progressed, it was Ernest Carrington who drew her about in her garden-chair, and as she grew yet stronger, it was on his arm she leaned when, with feeble steps, she began once again to resume her daily walks; and as, with grateful heart, Emily watched the colour slowly returning to her mother's pale cheeks, she almost felt as if it was to Ernest that she owed her beloved parent's restoration.

One morning, about a month after Mr. Pillanbill had finally taken leave, and when every vestige of his first syllable had been swallowed, and his last syllable (which was a very long one) had been paid, Ernest, whilst waiting until Mrs. Colville was ready for her accustomed walk, had a letter with a foreign postmark put into his hand. Emily, who watched him while he read it, saw him start and change colour.

"Is anything the matter?" she inquired, as he refolded the letter.

"Yes—no—that is, I think you cannot any longer be anxious about Mrs. Colville: her health, thank God, is perfectly restored.

"Oh yes, I trust so," was the reply, "but why do you ask?"

"Because I must leave you for a time; and if you felt nervous or uncomfortable about your mother, we could arrange for Percy to return a week or two before the holidays—what do you say?—he might be a comfort to you?"

As Ernest spoke, he stooped to pick up the envelope of the letter, and thus failed to observe that Emily started and turned pale when he said he must leave her. The letter was from Sir Thomas Crawley's valet; his master was very ill—dangerously ill, he was afraid; he had been unwell for some time, and had gone to Baden for change of air; but instead of recovering, he had grown worse every day, until finally, after a long interview with his medical advisers, he desired Hemmings to write to Mr. Selby and Mr. Carrington, begging them to come out to him without delay, and bring with them some clever English physician. When Mrs. Colville appeared and learned this intelligence, she fully agreed with Ernest that no time should be lost in setting off; and after a few minutes' conversation on the subject, the rector rose to take his leave, saying that he should probably start the next morning.

"Mamma has persuaded me to go for an hour or two to the Selbys this evening; Caroline would take no refusal, and Miss Plainfille is coming to sit with mamma. Shall I see you there?" asked the Rosebud, quietly.

"Well then, farewell, dear Mrs. Colville," exclaimed Ernest warmly, having answered Emily's question in the affirmative; "I leave you in very good hands, and expect to find you stronger than ever when I return."

The evening at the Selbys was a very pleasant one, both to Emily and to Ernest, only instead of two hours, it appeared to last about ten minutes.

"Mr. Carrington, I'm afraid I must be rude enough to ask you to step into my office and look at the arrangements I have made for our journey to-morrow," observed Mr. Selby, late in the evening.

"Certainly, I will follow you in one moment," was the reply.

There was a small apartment opening out of the drawing-room, fitted up as a boudoir for the benefit of Caroline Selby. In this snuggery the two young ladies had been looking over some water-colour sketches, but Caroline Selby had just been called away, and the Rosebud was left by herself. At that instant Ernest joined her.

"Emily," he said, and his voice was low and tremulous—"Emily, I have come to bid you good-bye."

"Must you go already?" was the rejoinder.

"Indeed, I fear so," returned Ernest. There was a pause, and then he resumed, in a voice which trembled with emotion, "Emily, we have been very happy of late."

"Oh, yes!" she murmured, almost unconsciously.

"And you," he continued—"you have been very kind and gentle. Emily, you will not forget me—will not grow cold towards me again?"

She made no reply, but her silence was more eloquent than words. At that moment Mr. Selby's footstep sounded on the stairs.

"I *must* go," Ernest resumed: "Emily, dear Emily! good-bye;—God bless you!" He took her soft, warm little hand in his own; she allowed him to retain it unresistingly: he pressed it, and his heart beat quickly when he felt the pressure faintly but unmistakably returned. With a sudden impulse he raised the little hand, still imprisoned in his, to his lips, kissed it, and tore himself away. As he paused to close the door, a slight sound caught his ear: could it be a sob?

How long it might have been after his departure ere the noise of approaching voices roused Emily from the mental abstraction into which she had fallen, that young lady herself never knew—it might have been one minute, it might have been ten. When she did awake to a sense of outward things, the following speech from the lips of Mrs. Selby, a good-natured, vulgar woman, arrested her attention :—

"And so, ma'am, if Sir Thomas Crawley dies, which my husband fears is only too probable, Mr. Carrington is as likely to be his heir as anybody I can think of."

"And then he'll go and marry that pert stuck-up Emily Colville, I suppose" (the speaker was Mrs. Pillanbill, who owned three awful daughters, unattached); "that girl's played her cards well, and no mistake. It was easy to see she set her cap at him from the first—probably calculated on his being Sir Thomas's heir all along. Oh, she's a deep one, trust her!"

And as the speakers passed on, their words became inaudible in the distance; but Emily had heard too much for her peace of mind. All night long she lay awake weeping—for she resolved, if Ernest should be Sir Thomas's heir, and asked her to become his wife, she must and would refuse him, if the resolution broke her heart.

Oh, Rosebud! Rosebud! beware of pride—the sin that peopled hell!

CHAPTER XV

SETTLES THREE OF THE DRAMATIS PERSONÆ.

Sir Thomas Crawley had sneaked and shuffled through life, and, by doing so with a degree of talent which if exerted in a righteous cause might have gained him the love and respect of good men, had obtained the world's prizes—rank and riches. But tact and cleverness, rank and riches, were equally useless to him now, for he had met with an opponent whom he could neither bribe, nor cheat, nor intimidate, nor cajole. Face to face with death, all his worldly wisdom failed him. Dying! he could not believe it—so much yet remained for him to do. If he could but live for two months longer he should be a baronet —for two years, and he might have married the proud peer's daughter, and transmitted the rank and honours he had won to a long line of descendants. Then, indeed, then, when he had accomplished his desire, then the idea of death might not have appeared so monstrous, so impossible. But even then he should have required a little time to prepare for death. Poor, self-deceived fool! as if every hour you have lived, every word you have spoken—ay, and every thought you have thought, were not preparing you for death and for eternity! It is not what you have achieved that will help you now; it is what you have been—what you are! The meek and lowly of heart will compose the aristocracy of Heaven; and the lame, and the halt, and the blind, who have borne their cross patiently, shall be its mighty ones: he who best has loved God and his neighbour— he whose life has been one unconscious preparation for death —he shall reap the reward;—else is Heaven but a mockery, and death, the "long dark day of nothingness," the sceptic's idea of death, extinction, annihilation, is the only reality.

Sir Thomas Crawley was dying; he knew it before Ernest Carrington brought the English physician; he knew it when the physician's eye first met his own; he knew it when Mr. Selby urged him to sign his will. But he could not, he would not believe it. He was weak, he said; Germany did not agree with him; he had worked too hard, and required rest and society: that was his reason for summoning Mr. Carrington. Had Selby brought the papers he required?—old Sir Ralph Carrington's will?—good! and his own will?—good! Let that be destroyed now, before his eyes—good!—he should make a fresh one when he reached Ashburn Priory. But he did not do so, for the very good reason that men in their coffins cannot make wills, and Sir Thomas reached Ashburn a corpse, and took up his abode in his family vault, handsomely bound in mahogany and black velvet, ornamented with a real silver plate, whereupon were engraved a goodly list of virtues, of which nobody had suspected him when living, but of which the undertaker always kept a large ready-made supply on hand, for the benefit of such of his customers as were rich enough to afford them. Nothing was said about his vices, perhaps because the silver plate was not half long enough to contain them.

Dear reader, shall you like to have a silver plate? For myself, a little one of Britannia metal, with "PECCAVI" engraved upon it, will suit me well enough; but then I am only a poor author, and if any of my works should happen to survive me in morocco covers, I shall care little what sort of boards the hand that traced them lies bound in.

During the time Ernest was in Germany, the Rosebud was decidedly out of spirits, restless, and anxious; and when the news of Sir Thomas Crawley's death arrived, she became so nervous and dejected, that Mrs. Colville grew quite uneasy about her.

One fine morning Mrs. Selby paid them a visit, evidently full of news. It soon came out,—she had heard from Mr. Selby; he and Mr. Carrington would be home the next day; and— would Mrs. Colville believe it?—poor dear Sir Thomas had died without signing his last will and testament; so all the property would go, under a former one, to his heir, Mr. Peter Crawley—a very fine young man, in a large way of business in Manchester, though of course he'd give up all that sort of thing now. She, Mrs. Selby, was only sorry on one account, she had never been able to get it out of Mr. Selby, he was so ridiculously close, but she was almost certain Sir Thomas had left £20,000 to Mr. Carrington in his last will, and he would have spent the money so well, it certainly was a thousand pities; but Mr. Peter Crawley would benefit, and he was such a very fine young man; a fortunate family the Crawleys were, certainly.

That day at dinner, Mrs. Colville remarked her daughter's appetite was returning, and that she began to look like herself again; which she attributed to a certain quinine mixture wherewith the Rosebud had been victimised, and which she canonised accordingly.

Ernest and Mr. Selby arrived when due, and the legend of Mr. Peter Crawley's heirship remained uncontradicted—nay, was confirmed, by that very fine young man's arrival, in high health and spirits, to enact the part of chief mourner. Ernest was much occupied by parish affairs, and by the arrangements for the approaching funeral (in regard to which Mr. Selby appeared resolved to consult him much more than he wished, or Mr. Peter Crawley seemed to relish); but all his leisure moments he spent at the cottage, and had no reason to complain of the reception he met with from either mother or daughter.

And so, in due course of time, the day for the funeral arrived. Now, it is an acknowledged fact that funerals and weddings are the two dullest and most sombre occasions on which human creatures assemble themselves together, and are therefore equally insipid to describe; only a funeral labours under the additional disadvantage, that it is against every rule of good taste and right feeling to poke fun at it. We feel, therefore, that we have "our public" with us, when, without entering into detail, we beg them to consider Sir Thomas Crawley handsomely and appropriately interred, with the necessary amount of black crape, crocodile tears, and funereal foppery.

After the ceremony was over, Mr. Selby ate an excellent luncheon at the expense of the estate, to provide against the possible contingency of requiring the performance repeated on his own account, after a verdict of "died of inanition," and then prepared to read the will—only, after searching high and low, and in every intermediate altitude, no will was forthcoming; so the next best thing was to inform a small and select coterie of ravening wolves, and daughters of the horse-leech, there met together in bombazine and black sheep's-clothing (*alias* broadcloth), and styling themselves relations of the dear departed (which in more senses than one, they certainly were), all that he (Selby) knew about the matter. This was—that since his accession to the Manor of Ashburn, Sir Thomas Crawley had made two wills:—the first bequeathing the bulk of the property to Mr. Peter Crawley, he had duly signed, sealed, and delivered; the second he had never completed. That, when Sir Thomas, in his last illness, summoned Mr. Selby to Baden, he had desired him to bring with him three documents, viz., old Sir Ralph Carrington's will, under which he had originally inherited the property; his own completed will; and the draught of the more recent one, then incomplete. That Sir Thomas had carefully perused every clause of Sir Ralph's will; then, begging Mr. Selby to take especial care of it, he desired him to destroy both the others in his presence; adding that they neither of them carried out his present intentions, and that, on his return to the Priory, he should give instructions for a fresh one. That he (Mr. Selby), declining to destroy the wills without witnesses of his doing so, by Sir Thomas Crawley's express desire, the valet and the English physician were summoned, and in their presence he burned the wills. The property must, therefore, be disposed of according to the will of the late Sir Ralph Carrington.

We will save the reader (and ourselves) the trouble of wading through the mire of that most senseless abuse of the Queen's English, and her subjects' common sense, yclept "legal phraseology," which ought to be rendered illegal without delay; and proceed at once to state that, in the event of plain Thomas Crawley (not then be-knighted) dying intestate and without issue, the property was to revert to the eldest son of Reginald Carrington, &c. &c., which Reginald, as the reader may probably conjecture, was the "cut off" son of Sir Hugh, and the father of the present rector of Ashburn.

Ernest Carrington, therefore, the *ci-devant* mathematical and classical master of Dr. Donkiestir's school at Tickletown, was now lord of the manor of Ashburn, patron of his own living, and owner of Ashburn Priory, besides, if he chose to revive the dormant title, a baronet also.

On hearing this announcement, that fine young man, Mr. Peter Crawley, said a naughty word, and then tried to look as if somebody else had done it, frowning portentously at the oldest ravening wolf, who, with the rest of the pack, appeared eager to turn and rend somebody, and were only restrained from an outbreak of ferocity by the tightness of their (black) keep's clothing; while the Misses Horse-leech, despite their bombazine and flounces, cast sanguinary glances on Mr. Selby, and would probably there and then have fixed upon him and exhausted his vital fluid, albeit his personal appearance was scarcely suggestive of an agreeable esculent, but for the presence of the bystanders.

The Rosebud heard the news before she slept that night—slept, did we say?—poor little self-tortured victim to a delusion of the arch-enemy—if agonised sobs, threatening to part soul and body; if pale cheeks, throbbing bosom, streaming eyes, and burning brow, be signs of sleep, then indeed was the expression rightly chosen. Ernest also, either by some strange vibration of the sympathetic chain which unites those who truly love—(my dear strong-minded old gentleman, albeit you are the "father of a family," and a fair specimen of the ancient Turk of private life into the bargain, your saying "Pish! folly! German rubbish!" does not affect me in the slightest degree—probably because the sympathetic link which so much offends you, does *not* unite our spirits, which will, I fear, always more or less effervesce rather than mingle, by being brought in contact with one another)—Ernest also, either from some sympathetic influence, or from the natural impetuosity of his disposition, was so restless and excited that night, that he determined the next day should decide whether he was to be more happy, or more miserable, than anybody had ever been before—except, perhaps, the *few* other ardent young men who have "lived and loved," and got into desperate states of mind about it, since the days when Noah went a-yachting.

Accordingly, being aware that Mrs. Colville had usually breakfasted in her own room since her illness, and seldom made her appearance in the drawing-room till about twelve o'clock, Ernest (as soon as he had finished his breakfast, and written two or three business letters, which were fertile in mistakes and erasures, seeing that his hand had written them while his mind was "far away") walked down to the cottage, let himself in, and without announcement made his way into the drawing-room, as he had often done before, where, opening the door, he found, as he had fondly hoped to do, the Rosebud "blooming alone;" only that she was not blooming at all, but looking especially pale and washed out, by reason of the tempestuous night she had passed. Not but that the storm of feeling which had swept over her maiden soul, and left its traces behind, had added a depth and (if we may use the term) pathos to her beauty, which it wanted previously. She turned, if possible, still more pale as he entered; then, by a strong exercise of self-control, she strove, with tolerable success, to receive him in her usual manner. After a few commonplace inquiries and responses had passed between them, Emily, by a great effort, felicitated him on his accession of fortune. He smiled mournfully.

"Do not congratulate me, Emily," he said : "it is a vast and fearful responsibility. My career would have been a simpler and happier one without it ; but it is God's will to call me to a more prominent position, and I must not shrink from the cares and duties it will impose upon me." He paused, then with a forced smile, which most ineffectually concealed his agitation, continued, "I should make but a poor advocate, I fear ; for here am I setting forth all the evils and difficulties of my new position, when my object in coming here—an object in the attainment of which the whole happiness of my existence is centered—is to ask you to share it." He then in a few simple, truthful, and therefore eloquent words, told her of his deep affection for her, and of his earnest desire to do what mortal might, to guard her from, or to mitigate, all the sorrows which more or less fall to the lot of each of us, confident that, in striving to provide for her happiness, he should insure his own.

Emily heard him to the end without interruption, and, save that she grew paler, and that her features assumed a more fixed and immovable expression, she evinced no sign of being in the slightest degree affected by his appeal. When he had concluded, she thanked him for the compliment he had paid her, but informed him that, although she should always regard him in the light of a dear and valued friend, and hoped he would not deprive her of a privilege she so highly appreciated, yet that she could never become anything more to him than a friend—in fact, she decidedly and unequivocally refused him.

Ernest was thunderstricken! He was no coxcomb, but neither was he devoid of penetration ; and he knew her so well —had traced, as he believed, so clearly the rise and progress of her affection for him—an affection ripened, and, as it were, sanctified, by their joint attendance beside her mother's sick bed—that, although from a slight tendency to waywardness which he was aware lurked in her disposition, he anticipated some little difficulty in obtaining her consent to their union, yet the idea that his offer should be met with a calm and deliberate refusal, had never occurred to him even as a possibility. After a minute's pause, he exclaimed—

"I am grieved,—pained beyond expression!—nay," he con-

tinued, gaining courage from the strength of his convictions,
"I will even dare to add, surprised. Emily, I cannot bring
myself to believe that my offer has come upon you unexpectedly; you *must* have been aware of my affection for you?"
Receiving no answer, he continued in a sterner tone, "I am
then to understand that, perceiving my attachment, without
returning it, you have led me on merely to gratify your heartless vanity, till, in my weak trustfulness, I have placed it in
your power to inflict this blow upon me—a blow, the effects of
which years will fail to counteract. It is not my pride that is
wounded: the little pride I ever possessed has been pretty well
taken out of me by the drudgery of life ere this; but that
such deep, unselfish love, such entire boundless trust, should
have been thus bitterly deceived, thus heartlessly rejected, and
by one who seemed all truth, innocence, and gentleness—Oh! it
is unnatural, incredible!" He sprang from his chair, and
began pacing the room with rapid strides, then continued,
"But I will overcome it; it is unworthy to be thus affected—to
feel thus for one capable of such deception. No! cost me what
it may, I will crush——!"

Gently, my dear sir, gently: you may crush exactly what
you please of your own—your outraged affections, your rejected
heart, or that very nice new hat which you purchased in
your way through London—though that would be the most
wantonly extravagant act of the three; but you mustn't crush
our Rosebud, albeit she is such a heartless little tigress. Ay!
you may well stop and look at her! You ought to be ashamed
of yourself, Mr. Carrington! so you ought! And you a clergyman, too!

Stop and look at her! Why, what was there to see in that
calm, expressionless face, that cold stoical exterior?—only that
the said stoicism had turned out a dead failure, broken down with
its would-be professor at the critical moment, and there she was
crying her woman's tender heart out, through her woman's
beautiful eyes, more like Niobe than Plato, by long odds.

When Ernest perceived this, he experienced what dear
Mrs. —— would call, in her very affecting third-volume style,
"a tremendous revulsion of feeling," under the influence of
which he seated himself beside the weeping Rosebud, and taking
her poor, cold, little hand, said—

"Emily, dearest Emily, what is the meaning of all this?
Why! you are making yourself as miserable as you have

made me! Come, treat me as a friend—a brother: confide in me. You must have some reason for what you are doing. Tell me"—-and here, despite his best efforts, his voice faltered—"tell me—your happiness is ever my first consideration, and, even though it involve the ruin of my dearest hopes, I will strive to secure it—do you love another?"

She did not speak; in fact, she could not just at that moment, by reason of the swollen state of the *globus-hystericus* interfering with the action of the *larynx*—to write technically—or because of a choking sensation in the throat, if any reader prefers the colloquial style; but she had very expressive eyes, and they said " no " just as plainly, or rather as prettily, as her lips could have done.

Ernest felt better; if she did not love anybody else, she must in time love him. Such affection as his must produce a return—he knew, he felt—but you see the line of argument, dear reader. Well, then, what was the hitch? Ernest pondered; at last, a bright idea occurred to him. The change in Emily had taken place since the previous day. Yes, *that* was it! So he half muttered aloud, half thought to himself, " Some absurd, romantic, generous scruple about this confounded" (I am afraid he said confounded) " fortune." He then continued aloud, rather in the tone in which he talked to the very little children in the Sunday-school,—

" Now listen to me, dear Emily. The happiness of my life, and, as I cannot but hope " (charitable hope!), " of yours also, is at stake. I once again tell you that I love you, as I have never loved before—as I shall never love again ; that I love you with the one, deep, enduring passion of my lifetime. And I ask you—I adjure you—for both our sakes, to tell me, as truly as the fact will appear on that solemn day when the secrets of all hearts shall be known, do you return my affection ? —Emily, dearest, do you love me?"

Well, of course she could not say " No," for that would have been false ; she must say something, for, Sunday-school manner and all, Ernest had become rather awful at last, so there was nothing left for her but to say " Yes,"—-which she did accordingly. That, in fact, settled the question ; for, naturally, Ernest decided if she loved him, she must and should marry him ; and then he elicited from her that it *was* the fortune, upon which he observed—

" Very well: that he *had* hoped and intended to send Percy

to college, and to buy Hugh a commission, and to build a
church at Satanville, and to despatch a bran-new missionary
to Sambobamboo, and to erect some very uncomfortable model
cottages for the poor people, and to double Mr. Slowkopf's
salary; but that if Emily persisted in refusing him because of
the fortune, he would that very afternoon make it over by a deed
of gift to that fine young man Mr. Peter Crawley, and marry
her on the £800 per annum which he received as Rector."

And so, as it was quite clear that he meant what he said, and
was prepared to act up to it, the poor Rosebud was obliged
to give in, and consent to accept him fortune and all.

Thus the interview ended as happily as it had begun miser-
ably; and if Ernest didn't steal a kiss ere he took leave, it must
have been because he was a clergyman, and had the fear of the
bishop before his eyes;—though if the bishop had been a good-
natured one, he would have winked at such an offence—certainly
an *arch*-bishop would have done so!

CHAPTER XVI., AND LAST.

THE MORAL—DRAWN VERY MILD!

ONCE again it was Christmas-day. At Ashburn Priory the
plum-pudding was a "great fact;" Hugh Colville said so, and
he ought to have known, for he ate enough, not to say too much,
of it to test its merits—at least, if there be any truth in the
old proverb, that "the proof of the pudding is in the eating."
But there were other good things at Ashburn Priory beside
plum-pudding. Love and Joy and Peace dwelt there, and pure
Religion shed her mild light upon that happy household. The
cloud which had hung over the fortunes of the Colville family
had passed away, and the silver lining alone remained to testify
that, although

> "In every life some rain must fall,
> Some days be dark and dreary,'

yet that rain falls only to fertilise the ground, and enable it to
bring forth fruit and flowers; and the metaphor holds good in
the case before us. The sorrow which had fallen upon the
Colville family had been a chastening sorrow, and its effects were
to be recognised in a goodly crop of virtues.

The proud and sensitive disposition of Percy had been strengthened and fitted for intercourse with the every-day world, by the rough teaching of the commercial-school, and he was about to enter on his Oxford career, a wiser and a better man than a more refined mode of education would have rendered him.

Hugh's volatile and impetuous disposition had been also favourably acted upon, by the misfortune which caused him to be placed under Doctor Donkiestir's firm and judicious rule ; and he had learned one essential requisite for a soldier's profession, on which, since he had been to spend a day with Norman (now a captain in the —th Lancers) at the Flatville Barracks, he had set his heart, viz., obedience.

Mrs. Colville was almost perfect when we were first-introduced to her ; but the loss of one she had loved so well had taught her to place her affections still more firmly on " things above."

As for the Rosebud—bless her !—all that the cloud had done for her was to make her the most charming little wife that ever has been, or ever will be ; and if Ernest Carrington had not thought so, and doated upon her accordingly, we would, even at this eleventh hour of our tale, have procured her a divorce, and married her to a duke. But if we had been compelled to take so decided a step, we should have been sorely puzzled how to dispose of an autocratic and imperative baby, with a loud soprano voice, a decidedly dangerous temper, and a general tipsiness of appearance, which had established itself at the Priory, and was said by everybody to be the image of its parents—a statement which, unlike the plum-pudding of immortal memory, was not a great fact, but to speak mildly, an enormous—'tother thing !

If any one cares to know what became of Mr. Slowkopf, we beg to state that after Emily's marriage, he grew day by day more and more heavy and dejected, till at last he—died of a broken heart?—by no means—married Caroline Selby, on the principle of the Persian saying : that if she wasn't the Rose (bud), she had dwelt near the Rose (bud). Moreover, they are very happy together, and live at the Rectory ; Ernest having, on Mr. Slowkopf's marriage, resigned the living in his favour, although he still generally preaches once every Sunday in Ashburn Church, and once at the new chapel-of-ease at Satanville ; for, in Ernest, riches had wrought no change, save, that by enabling him to extend his charities, his sphere of usefulness

was enlarged.   His darling wish is now fulfilled : he is free to
devote his whole time and talents to the welfare of others ; and
his position, as both lord of the manor and spiritual pastor,
affords him opportunities for carrying out his schemes for the
amelioration, moral and physical, of the labouring classes, with a
degree of success which few philanthropists are so fortunate as
to obtain.

Reader, our tale is told.   Should it assist you to while away
some rainy morning of life, and at the same time lead you to
remember that, above the clouds which lour so heavily, the blue
heaven lies in its deep tranquillity, and the glorious sun still
shines brightly, able, when it shall be God's good pleasure, to
dispel the darkness that oppresses you, and again shed its light
and warmth into your spirit—the end for which this sketch has
been traced will be answered.

THE

MYSTERIES OF REDGRAVE COURT;

A STRANGE EPISODE IN THE LIFE OF EDWARD CHICHESTER, GENTLEMAN.

BY FRANK E. SMEDLEY.

CHAPTER I.

I DO not by any means consider myself particularly nervous—in fact, I rather pride myself upon being the reverse; but a man must be utterly devoid of feeling, and possess a defective organisation, *not* to have jumped under the circumstances.

But I beg your pardon, dear Reader—really, I am very forgetful!—I see now, you're not in a position to form any opinion about the matter, because—I can't think how I could be so forgetful!—because I have not yet told you what the circumstances were! Well, that's soon remedied. It was exactly this day two months—that is (it's as well to be correct, you know), it was on Tuesday, the 16th of May last, that I was walking down Piccadilly, about four o'clock in the after-noon, buried in thought. I *could* tell you what I was thinking about, and I will too; for that was rather a curious coincidence, considering—Well, never mind what, you'll find out the coincidence if you will but have patience. I was thinking what a very singular thing it was that all my friends and acquaintances seemed to have taken it into their heads that some imperative necessity existed for me to be married; in consequence of which idea they were incessantly preparing matrimonial pitfalls for me, so that I absolutely led the life of a hunted animal amongst them. I could not poke my nose into a ball-room but some marriageable female was there, ready to snap it off for me. At dinner-parties I was sure to be seated next a girl who "would make *such* a wife;" while the country houses of my friends were each, in turn, converted into a monster man-trap, baited with an heiress, for the special purpose of effecting my capture.

Not that I had any insuperable objection to matrimony: 1 knew that some time or other every man had to die, and most men had to be married—nor did I expect to be exempted from the common lot; but, just as 1 should have disapproved of being called upon to die all in a hurry for the amusement of society, so did I dislike the idea of being married in haste, with the prospect of repenting at leisure, merely because my friends chose to consider that I wanted a wife. I was pondering all this in my mind, and reflecting on the advisability of making a tour in Turkey, where the women are as sedulously kept out of one's way, as in England they are thrust into it, when suddenly —without the slightest warning—somebody gave me a violent slap on the back!

And now, having afforded you all the necessary data to go upon, I ask you once again, must not a man have been utterly a hardened character, *not* to have jumped under the circumstances? At all events I know I did, for I sprang clean off the pavement into the horse road—when I say *clean*, I use a figure of speech, for the road had been watered—with blacking I should imagine, to judge from the effect produced on a pair of white duck trousers, in which my evil genius had seen fit to clothe me for the occasion.

I'm naturally one of the best tempered men in the world, but I confess it was in anything but an amiable frame of mind, that, standing on an isolated paving stone in the midst of the black sea before alluded to, I glanced from my no longer spotless trousers, to the face of my assailant, which, to the discredit of human nature, was, I am sorry to say, convulsed by a hearty laugh. It was a countenance with which I was well acquainted, being, in fact, none other than that of my old friend and schoolfellow, Harry Stapylton; accordingly, seeing that I had not been insulted, but only victimised, I executed that intricate evolution commonly termed a hop, skip, and jump, and succeeded in reaching the *trottoir* without adding to the injury already sustained by my unfortunate white trousers. As I accomplished this feat, Stapylton seized me by the hand, and shaking it heartily, exclaimed, still laughing—

"Why, Ned, old fellow! did I make you jump?"

Now, I'm aware that it's a weakness, that the thing is in itself of no consequence, and that it is extremely foolish of me to care about it, but I honestly confess I don't like to be addressed as "NED;" it was all very well when one was a boy, and wore a jacket without a tail, to be called by a name without a second syllable, but such a mere stump of an apellation (if I may be allowed the expression) seems to me derogatory to the dignity of manhood. The members of my own family were aware of this little peculiarity, and at home I was always Edward at full length; so that now there was scarcely any one who called me Ned, except Harry Stapylton. It was not then in the most cordial tone of voice that I replied—

"That's a question, Mr. Stapylton, to which the answer is so self-evident" (and I involuntarily glanced at my ducks), "that I may save myself the trouble of replying to it."

"Phew!" whistled Harry, "what's the matter now, *Mr.* Chichester? is it the damaged ducks? Never mind, man, they're warranted to wash, and laundresses are a hard-working generation and deserve patronage; so never look black about a splash or two—more particularly when I've some good news for you."

There's an indescribable something about Harry Stapylton which renders it impossible to continue angry with him for five minutes together, so linking my arm in his (for it appeared we were walking in the same direction) I replied—

"Good news, eh? let's have it by all means."

"Most excellent news," returned my companion, "and you'll say so too, Master Ned" (Ned again!), "when you hear it: I've found you a wife with a clear two thousand a year in the Three per Cents! what do you say to that, my boy?"

"Say," rejoined I testily, "that as you've found her, you had better keep her yourself."

"Unfortunately," was the reply, "a law against bigamy is in force in this feeble-minded country, or I should be delighted to comply with your suggestion; if one wife is a good thing, two must be better. But do you really mean to say you did not know I was married?"

"I should as soon have expected to hear you were hanged," returned I. "When did the catastrophe occur? and how do you feel after it?"

"The great event came off some six weeks since, and the results are most satisfactory: Mary is as good a little girl as ever wore crinoline, and I'm jollier than I ever was in my life before. I tell you what, Chichester, a fellow does not know what happiness is, till he is married—it's a fact, I can assure you."

"Now, tell me the truth, Harry," returned I ; "you've been calling at our house, seen my mother, or one of the girls, mentioned your marriage, and they've put you up to this ; confess —is not this the case ? "

"Upon my honour, no !" was the reply ; "the thing is just as I tell you : I married a girl I loved, and finding how much it has increased my happiness, wish you to follow my example."

Seeing I made a gesture of impatience, he added,—

"'Pon my word, I am quite serious ; you and I have been friends from boyhood, I always liked you, and I do so still, because, although you have a few little oddities about you, you're a right good fellow at heart, and that's the chief thing after all. And now I'll tell you how the idea occurred to me :—Mary was talking to me the other day about an old schoolfellow of hers, who she had asked to come and stay with us, telling me what a sweet girl she was, and lamenting her position. It appears that she is an heiress, without any near relations belonging to her, and is living in desolate grandeur at an old country house, with a superannuated governess and a paid companion ; so Polly expects her to bolt with the first insinuating fortune-hunter who comes in her way, out of sheer *ennui*. Well, it struck me directly, she might be just the wife for you ; so I examined Mary about her particularly, and she says she's right in every point—good principles, good temper, good looks, in fact, a regular Phœnix ; and the long and the short of it is, she's coming to stay with us next week at Redgrave, and we want you to run down and meet her. What do you say ?"

What could I say ? the thing was an awful bore ; but without appearing unfriendly and ill-natured, I could not well refuse. The heiress, I felt sure, would prove a failure ; but I liked Harry, and had a sort of curiosity to be introduced to his little wife, and to observe for myself the practical working of matrimonial felicity ; so, before we parted, I had accepted his invitation, and stood committed to meet the heiress at Redgrave Court that day week.

And now, perhaps, before I relate how I fared for my temerity, the reader will like to learn a few particulars concerning the individual, with an episode in whose life he is about to become acquainted. Like most other people, I once possessed a father and mother. My father might have been poetically described as one of the merchant princes of the great metropolis of Europe; in plain prose he was a large sugar-broker, and sat in a large chair, in a large counting-house, in a narrow street, in the heart of the City, where he made a large fortune, which he very obligingly left behind him for me to spend; and, as he died when I was about five years old, and my chief recollection of him is, that he boxed my ears soundly for tumbling over his gouty foot in my childish gambols, it would be affectation on my part to pretend to any very deep feeling, in regard to his highly respectable memory.

My mother and three sisters, older than myself, did their best to spoil me—and succeeded, as far as the inherent excellence of the material upon which they had to work would allow; fortunately, their efforts were in some measure counteracted by a judicious course of bullying which I underwent for two years at Eton, whence I migrated to the abode of a very bland private tutor in a small country village, where I vegetated upon Euclid and bread and butter for three years, returning at nineteen to the maternal apron-string, as conceited a young prig as female fondness could desire. Since that period, six years had elapsed, during which I had been master of one mother, three sisters, four horses, eight servants, £2,000 per annum, a large rambling mansion in Portland Place, and my own actions; I had made the grand tour, and several minor ones, and had done all the other necessary things of life—except marrying a wife. And now I was actually going to Redgrave Court to inspect a real live heiress! Book of Fate, with the iron clasps, is Benedict written against my name on thine inscrutable pages?

CHAPTER II.

REDGRAVE COURT belonged to Sir Geoffrey Stapylton, Harry's uncle. Sir Geoffrey was a thorough specimen of the class of old "gentlemen of England who live at home at ease,"—which aforesaid ease he appeared to appreciate so intensely, that he had never chosen to run the risk of endangering it by taking to himself a wife; consequently Harry was heir to the title and property. Being a great favourite with his uncle, and having pleased the old gentleman by marrying into a good county family, Sir Geoffrey had made it his request that the young couple should reside with him ; and Harry, who looked upon the property almost as his own, was so strongly in favour of the arrangement, that his good little wife never for a moment opposed it, although she was particularly afraid of the gruff old baronet. Nor, if report spoke truly, were her fears altogether unreasonable. Sir Geoffrey, naturally of a violent temper and eccentric disposition, had lived so much alone, and been for so many years entirely his own master, that the slightest opposition to any of his caprices was said to irritate him beyond control ; and rumours were afloat that, on such occasions, he would relieve his feelings by flinging decanters at the servants' heads, kicking them down-stairs, and otherwise forcibly demonstrating his intention of proving himself absolute " monarch of all he surveyed."

These particulars I gleaned on that hot-bed of scandal, the top of a stage-coach, which vehicle was hurrying me, at the rate of ten miles an hour, towards Redgrave Court and the desirable heiress—against whom, by-the-bye, I had conceived a greater prejudice than I was usually accustomed to indulge in on any subject. I had fully made up my mind as to the style of woman she would prove to be : she would either be tall, with light hair, grey eyes, pink and white cheeks, a deep voice and a tragedy manner, or she would be short, with black hair and eyes, plump, puddingy cheeks, and a jollity of demeanour most excruciating to one's feelings. It is a singular fact, that I had never yet met with an heiress who did not belong to one of these classes. As these reflections passed through my mind, for the five-hundredth time since I had formed the engagement, the railway omnibus pulled up at the old-fashioned gates of Redgrave Court, which, in accordance with a whim of Sir Geoffrey's were always kept locked and barred.

After a very aged woman had spent five minutes in withdrawing bolts and unlocking locks, and an unexpected boy had popped up, like a jack-in-a-box, to carry my carpet-bag, I was admitted, and a walk of nearly a mile up an avenue of magnificent elms, brought me in sight of the house. It was a glorious old edifice, built in the Elizabethan style, round three sides of a quadrangle, the fourth side being occupied by the servants' offices. As I reached the porter's lodge, Harry, who had been on the watch for me, sprang forward, and grasping my hand, exclaimed—

"Bravo, old fellow, this is famous! I never felt sure of you till I saw you coming up the avenue. I was dreadfully afraid you'd be playing me false, and bolting at the last moment. Now, come in. Will you like to dress before you're introduced to the ladies? It's just dinner-time." I signified my assent, and Harry, as soon as we had reached the room destined for my use, continued—"Well, it's all serene, the lovely Julia arrived last night—and a splendid creature she is!"

"I expected as much," said I; "if there's one thing I hate more than another, it is a splendid creature."

"Growl away, old Cynic," replied Harry, laughing, "we shall have you 'sighing like furnace' before a week is over; and at her feet in a fortnight, despite your grumbling."

It was useless to attempt to argue him out of his infatuation, so I merely shook my head in sign of dissent, and inquired of whom the other members of the party might consist.

"Oh, there is your *belle amie*, Julia Walsingham, and her companion, Alice Woodford; young Marston, an artist who is down here sketching; and Monsieur Cazotte, a French advocate, who was very civil to me last year when I was in Paris then my uncle, my little woman, yourself, and myself, make up the party."

"Ah! about your uncle, by the way; it does not do to argue with him, does it? He's a little hasty at times, isn't he? Just give me a hint, and I shall know how to get on with him."

Harry's brow contracted as he replied, "So they've been telling you that confounded nonsense, have they? Billy Haimes, the 'bus driver, lets his tongue run too fast. I shall have to speak to him rather seriously one of these days, if he does not take care. My uncle is as fine a specimen of a real old English gentleman as you would wish to set eyes on, and would never dream of treating a guest otherwise than with the utmost attention and courtesy; but the fact is, when he was a younger man, he received a very severe fall in hunting, and pitched upon his head, and since that time a very little wine affects him, and he is obliged to be extremely careful. I fancy, when I was abroad last year, he exceeded rather one night, and kicked old Wilkins the butler, down-stairs, when he wanted to persuade him to go to bed; but the whole thing has been very absurdly exaggerated. So put out of your head any nonsense you may have heard, and form your opinion of my uncle for yourself." Thus saying, he left me to complete my toilette.

On entering the drawing-room, I was introduced by Harry to the gentlemen of the party, the ladies not having yet made their appearance. Sir Geoffrey, who shook me warmly by the hand, and expressed himself delighted to make the acquaintance of any old friend of his nephew's, certainly justified, as far as appearance went, the description of a fine old English gentleman. His age might have been sixty-five or sixty-six; he was tall, and powerfully built, and, excepting his hair and whiskers, which were as white as snow, showed few signs of age. His manner was particularly urbane and courteous, and, save a strange, restless look in his prominent grey eyes, I could discover no symptoms of the irascibility which was said to have found relief in kicking the unfortunate butler down-stairs. Mr. Marston, the artist, was a quiet, gentlemanly, young man, with a clever, sensible face. M. Cazotte was rather handsome, with very black moustaches, and very white teeth, and spoke English unusually well, for a foreigner.

I had scarcely had time to make the foregoing observations, when the door opened, and Miss Julia Walsingham entered, leaning on the arm of a bright-eyed animated little brunette, in whose good-natured smile I read evidence of the "best little woman in the world," *alias* Mrs. Harry Stapylton;—a third young lady, who I rightly imagined to be the companion, followed. One glance sufficed to show me to which class of heiress the fair Julia belonged,—tall, with flaxen hair, and light blue eyes (I can't bear tall women; and light blue eyes are so very unmeaning). She was handsome,—there was no denying it—regular features, good bust, small waist, erect carriage, but there was a something—a want of breed about her: her hands, though well-shaped and white, were large, in proportion to her size; she had not an aristocratic air—in fact, though there was much to admire, and nothing decidedly to find fault with, I felt at once she was a woman I *never could* marry. It is true, this was only what I had expected; yet so inconsistent are we, that I experienced a sensation of disappointment at thus finding my expectations verified—all the more so perhaps, because Harry, in describing his own wife, had rather underdone the thing than otherwise; for she was not only the best, but one of the prettiest little women in the world. I could have married *her* on the spot, if it had been necessary.

Of course at dinner I found myself seated near Miss Walsingham, and, as a matter of course, obliged to talk to her; so, resolved to do my duty thoroughly, and not to allow Harry the chance of accusing me of mere unreasonable prejudice, I exerted myself to draw her out. 'Twas no very difficult matter—up to a certain point she was voluble enough, but beyond that all was a blank—"*ex nihilo nihil fit*"—where there was nothing in, nothing could be drawn out; her mind was as insipid as her person. The gentlemen did not sit long after dinner; and, before we joined the ladies, I proposed to Harry to stroll round the flower-garden; as soon as we were *tête-à-tête*, I plunged at once *in medias res*.

"Harry, it's no use; I would not marry her, if she were a princess."

"Nonsense! my good fellow, you've scarcely seen her yet; don't form such hasty judgments."

"I've seen enough of her; she is of the regular heiress stamp; and—in short, nothing should ever induce me to marry that woman. Don't look so aghast!" continued I, laughing at his solemn face; "I'm not going to start for town to-morrow morning, or do anything desperate; on the contrary, I shall be happy to stay with you as long as you like to keep me; but just explain to your wife, who, by the way, is charming (but you always have the luck of it), that there's no use in trying her match-making skill in this instance. I could not marry that long-legged female Crœsus, if my life depended on it!"

As I uttered these words, we reached a wider path, and came suddenly upon a lady who was walking therein, and who, unless she might turn out to be providentially afflicted with deafness, must have overheard my last words.

"Pleasant this!" whispered I to Harry, "who is she?"

"Miss Woodford, the companion," was the reply; "I don't think you have spoken to her yet. She's a very quiet, ladylike young person." Then addressing her, he added, "Mr. Chichester and I were taking a stroll, by the light of the moon; I'm afraid we have disturbed you, Miss Woodford?"

"By no means," was the rejoinder; "Miss Walsingham and Mrs. Stapylton were discussing some very confidential affair together" (talking *me* over, no doubt, thought I); "and, as they did not appear to want me, I strolled out to enjoy the beauty of the evening."

At this moment, a man's voice from the house shouted, "Harry! Harry!" in somewhat impatient tones, and my companion, exclaiming, "My uncle's calling me; will you excuse me? I shall join you again in two minutes," ran off, leaving me *tête-à-tête* with the heiress's *dame de compagnie*.

Now, I always feel the greatest compassion for the whole class of governesses and companions: nine times out of ten they possess infinitely more refinement and cultivation than their employers; and while their position renders them acutely sensitive to every slight, they are often treated with less consideration than is accorded to that most irritating blessing, a thoroughly respectable servant. These being my ideas, I immediately endeavoured to set Miss Woodward at ease in my society, by infusing into my manner what I hoped would appear a judicious mixture of respect and cordiality; nor were my efforts thrown away; her shyness, which at first was painfully apparent, soon wore off, and ere ten minutes had elapsed, we were chatting away as comfortably as if we had been old acquaintances. We strolled onward, in the soft moonlight; and still Harry did not return; and still, as I started fresh subjects, my companion proved able and willing to converse sensibly and agreeably upon them. At last the conversation turned upon painting; and Miss Woodford asked if I had not admired the face and figure of Vashti, in a painting by one of the old masters, which hung over the dining-room chimney-piece, exactly opposite to the place where I had been seated at dinner.

"There is not a doubt of its being a very fine picture," replied I; "the grouping is excellent, and the light-and shade most skilfully arranged, but I confess the particular figure to which you allude does not suit my taste; in the first place, she is so abominably tall, she quite looks down upon the unfortunate Ahasuerus."

As I spoke my companion turned away her head quickly, but not in time to prevent my discovering that it was to hide a laugh she did so. After a moment's pause she said, in a tone of voice which gave an arch meaning to her words—

" I am afraid, Mr. Chichester, you do not admire tall women?"

Now, as she herself was, although higher than Mrs. Harry Stapylton, yet, by no means a tall woman, the " afraid " having no personal application, could only refer to Miss Walsingham, it was clear my new friend had overheard my remark regarding the long-legged female Crœsus, and had me at her mercy. My resolution was instantly taken—the time (after dinner), the scene (a garden by moonlight), the situation (a *tête-à-tête* with an agreeable, sensible girl, who could understand one), were all favourable to my purpose, and I determined at once to make a confidant of her; accordingly I began :—

"Although our acquaintance has not been a very long one " (it must now have been nearly a quarter of an hour since Harry had left us), "I feel sure from the very sensible view you seem to take of—of—things in general—that in mentioning the cause, —in fact, I may say the reason—of my being at this moment so unpleasantly situated ;"—a little toss of the head, and a slight acceleration of speed, made me aware of the uncomplimentary construction the young lady might put upon my words, and I hastily continued—"No, I assure you I don't mean *that*—in fact, quite the reverse; but I was going to say that, as it is evident you must have overheard my remark about that horrible Miss Walsingham—— "

"Really, sir!" began my companion, in a tone of remonstrance.

"Yes, I quite understand," continued I, not heeding her interruption ; "but I'm certain you can't be fond of her; with your quickness you must have discovered long ago that—in fact, there is nothing to discover in her—the woman's a perfect nonentity ! It seems, however, that my friend Harry's charming little wife was at school with her, and, for the sake of old associations, and out of her natural amiability of disposition, continues to feel a great regard for this giantess; so by way of securing her future happiness, she has generously determined to make her a present of an excellent husband, paying me the compliment of selecting me as the victim. Harry put me up to the whole thing in town last week, and tried to persuade me into it, wanting to bribe me with her consols; so I agreed to come down and inspect the young lady, because I did not like to vex him ; but I knew how it would be directly I heard she was an heiress—they're all alike. Dame Nature is sufficiently a woman of the world to be aware that beyond pounds, shillings, and pence, no charms are needed to get husbands for heiresses, so she has reserved all other attractions for the unendowed portion of the sex. Well, the moment I saw your Miss Wal-

singham, I perceived she was not likely to shake my faith in
my theory. I plumbed the shallowness of her mind during
dinner, and having perfectly satisfied myself on the subject, I
walked Harry out just now, to tell him the thing was utterly
impossible, and you overheard my concluding sentence.—And
now, my dear Miss Woodford," continued I, " having explained
the affair to you, I'm sure you will stand my friend, and take
every opportunity of abusing me to your—ar—to Miss Walsingham, save me from victimisation in *téte-à-tétes* with her—
Oh, there are a hundred little things you can help me in, if you
will only be good-natured,"—and having at length exhausted
my eloquence, I paused, and looked into her bright eyes (I forgot if I mentioned before, that she had beautiful eyes) for a
reply ; it came at last.

 "Really, sir, your frankness has taken me so completely by
surprise, that I scarcely know how to answer you ; one thing,
however, I may venture to say, I will never betray your
secret to Miss Walsingham, more particularly as I have
heard that gentlemen can change their minds, as well as
ladies."

"No chance of that, in this instance, my dear Miss Woodford," returned I earnestly ; " when I marry Miss Walsingham,
I'll give you——"

"What ?" she inquired, quickly ; adding, in half a childlike
tone of voice, " I always wish to avail myself of the most remote
chance of getting a present."

"A dozen pairs of the best French gloves," was my reply.

"Mind they fit properly," returned the young lady, extricating a pretty little white hand from the recesses of her thick
shawl, and holding it up coquettishly in the moonlight.

Simplicity of character is a point on which I have always
prided myself ; the natural thing, of course, was to seize her
hand and press it to my lips, so I *did it ;*—at the same moment
that wretch Harry, who, from his knowledge of the ground,
had been able to approach us unperceived, suddenly made his
appearance, in an abominable state of laughter, and Miss Woodford, uttering a little cry, snatched away her hand, and ran off
towards the house as fast as her legs would carry her.

I leave the reader to imagine all the ironical congratulations
to which I had to submit from Harry, on my sudden conversion
from woman-hating ; suffice it to say, that I detained him in
the garden until he had exhausted his merriment, and promised

to behave properly, and we then joined the ladies. After tea,
music was proposed, and as Harry was unfortunately aware of
my vocalising propensities, I was forced to sing duets with, and
turn over leaves for, Miss Walsingham, for two wretched hours.
The creature's singing was of a piece with her other accomplishments. She had a good contralto voice, and sang in time
and in tune, but without a shadow of expression, or a spark of
feeling ; however, man is made to endure, and I bore it.

As the ladies were preparing to retire to their rooms, Miss
Woodford approached a table near which I was standing, for
the purpose of lighting her candle, an exertion which I obligingly saved her ; she thanked me for my civility, and then
added, demurely—

"Good-night, Mr. Chichester, I hope you have passed a very
pleasant evening."

As she said this, she glanced for a moment at my face, with
such an expression of mischievous glee in her dark eyes, that
I did, what I had not done about any woman during the last
five years,—I dreamed of her half the night.

<hr>

CHAPTER III.

TEN days had elapsed since my arrival at Redgrave, and still
my departure was a thing undetermined ; and sooth to say, I
was so well pleased with my present quarters, that I was perfectly willing to let events take their own course, without any
interference on my part.

Then, Mr. Ned Chichester, it appears, in spite of all the fuss
you have made about it, you were trying to fall in love with
the heiress after all ! Passing over the "Ned" question, dear
Reader (though I must observe, parenthetically, that, knowing
my feelings on the subject, it would have been better taste to
have addressed me as "Edward"), allow me most decidedly and
emphatically to inform you that I was *not*. Indeed, so far from
trying to fall in love with *any* body, I was endeavouring, and
as I then believed successfully, not to fall in love with—well, I
suppose I may as well own it at once—with Alice Woodford,
the heiress's *dame de compagnie*. But really she was so sensible, so amiable, so clever and fascinating, and right minded,

and pretty, and altogether so everything tha. a woman ought to be, and that Miss Walsingham was *not*, that it was by no means such an easy matter to keep heart-whole in her society as you may imagine ; still, of course, I was not, at my time of life, going to make a fool of myself for a pretty face, though there were such a sweet pair of eyes in it, and a mouth (you can t think what a dear little mouth she had,—I should say it was clear to the meanest capacity what purpose nature had in view when she made such a mouth as that)—no, the idea was too preposterous. I, the *bon parti* for whose benefit half the mothers of England were parading their daughters at "opera, party, and ball," to marry a penniless damsel, who probably never had a grandfather of any kind ! Bah ! And yet when I came to think of it, what did I want with money ? I was well off, and was neither extravagant nor avaricious—I would not marry a woman I did not like for the sake of money; why, then, sacrifice one I did like, for the want of it ? No, it was the force of habit, and a deficiency of moral courage, which led me to dread the sneers of worldly men whose opinion I all the time despised. I knew this, and felt rather ashamed of myself, and yet I could not make up my mind one way or the other ; so, as thought was disagreeable to me, I strove by every means in my power to banish it, and gave myself up to the fascination of the hour. I am aware this was neither right, wise, nor heroic, but I'm afraid it was intensely natural.

I had been in great measure relieved from the *onus* of doing the polite to Miss Walsingham by M. Cazotte, who was evidently smitten by the Juno-like exterior of the heiress, or the "*beaux yeux de sa cassette*," and I had availed myself of his attentions to secure many a delightful half-hour's conversation with Alice Woodford, who, although she never in any way directly encouraged me, at all events appeared to have no distaste to my society. Things were still in this state, when, about a fortnight after my departure from London, an expedition was proposed to visit the country town, about ten miles distant, where a flower-show was to be held. The proposition was agreed to, *nem. con.*, and soon after one o'clock the vehicles which were to convey the party made their appearance. Both Harry and his uncle were famous whips, and one of their chief amusements was coaching in all its varieties. The conveyance department consisted, on the present occasion, of a drag with a handsome team of bays ; a tandem with a splendid roan in the shafts, and a spicy-looking chestnut as leader; and a low phaeton, drawn by two saucy little grey ponies.

In and about these vehicles did the party, reinforced by the wife and daughter of an adjacent clergyman, dispose themselves according to their several inclinations. Harry drove the four-in-hand, Sir Geoffrey chose the tandem, and persuaded Miss Walsingham to accompany him, a step of which it was evident she repented when M. Cazotte, going into ecstacies about the "gra-ponies," as he was pleased to call them, volunteered "*conduire ces braves petits chevaux.*" As it was, the clergy-*woman* was allotted to him as a companion, and the rest of the company took possession of the drag. The drive, save for the beauty of the scenery, was dull enough, the sun being so power-ful that the ladies all preferred inside places; for the same reason Harry, who was very careful of his horses, drove so slowly that we were above an hour and a quarter doing the ten miles. The flower-show was much like other flower-shows—rather a bore than otherwise: there was plenty of heat and dust, and gay parasols and muslin-dresses, and variegated bonnets, and many people, great and small, from my Lord A. and his right honourable daughters, to Farmer Z. and his right vulgar ones; and sesquipedal *Græco-Latin* compound names of bran-new annuals, were "shockingly mangled" by would-be botanical old ladies; and horticultural hearts beat high with gratitude to Heaven for the blessings of colossal strawberries, and gooseberries, suited to mouths as capacious at that of "The Monster Polypheme." In a word, it was a very legitimate and orthodox flower-show. But in this sublunary world all shows come to an end, sooner or later, and the time for returning drew near. I was walking with Miss Wilson, the rectory young lady, on my arm, Harry and his wife being just before us, when Sir Geoffrey came up hastily, and tapping Harry on the shoulder inquired—

"Would you mind going round by Cuffley, on your way home? Old Wotton's taken seriously ill, and wants to see one of us, I suppose in regard to his son keeping on the farm. I've no objection to the young man having it, I hear very good accounts of him."

"Then I may promise him the farm, if that is what he wishes?" asked Harry.

"Certainly. You'd better take the tandem, and one of the grooms, and I'll drive the ladies home," returned his uncle.

"Very well. You must keep a tight hand on Zantippe, for she's rather fresh, and pulls hardish. You might drive her in the lower bar, if you want to put 'em along at any pace. I'll try and get back by dinner-time;" so saying, Harry bespoke my vacant arm for his wife, and left us.

This change of arrangement produced sundry alterations in the order of our going. Cazotte secured Miss Walsingham for a companion, and drove off whisking his whip about the ears of " *les braves petits chevaux;*" and squaring his elbows as a Frenchman alone could do. Mrs. Wilson and her daughter were " timid," and preferred the inside of the drag to the outside. Mary was obliged to accompany her friends. Miss Woodford, looking bored, was about to follow them. I approached her, and urged a change of plan.

" You'd much better come outside, it is such a lovely evening, and the country is looking so pretty."

" Mr. Chichester is advising me to go outside," said she, appealing to Mary.

" Yes, certainly, pray do, if you prefer it. You will find it much cooler," was the reply. She still hesitated; but the horses were fidgety. Sir Geoffrey uttered an exclamation of impatience, and Marston and I, without waiting for her decision, handed her up as a matter of course. The seat at the back of the drag was the most comfortable for a lady, and this we had, therefore, selected. As soon as she was seated, I sprang up also. Marston was about to follow, when Sir Geoffrey shouted—

" Marston, here is the box for you."

" Thank you, sir," was the reply, " I shall do very well where I am."

" Nonsense, man ! come along, there are three or four views I particularly want to point out to you, that will make your fortune on canvas in next year's Exhibition."

Thus appealed to, there was nothing for him but to obey, which, after indulging us with a short pantomimic insight into his feelings, he accordingly did. The groom jumped up also in front, and Alice (by the way, it is a very dangerous symptom when one begins *to think* of a woman by her Christian name) and I were left virtually *téte-à-téte.*

It was very interesting and delightful that conversation, as we rolled easily along the smooth road, the cool breeze playing around us refreshingly after the heat of the day, and an ever-changing panorama of wood and hill, field and river, chequered by the soft lights and shades of evening, seeming to glide by us as we still passed onward. A very charming conversation it was. I've not the most remote conception what it was about. I don't think I ever knew very clearly; but I recollect we went *deeper* than we had done before, and at last talked ourselves into an eloquent silence; and then she sat, with her soft eyes fixed upon the blue sky above us, thinking no doubt of heaven, like an angel as she was; while I remained gazing on *her*, and thought of nothing higher, or brighter, or purer, than the fair girl beside me. And yet the time and scene were not quite without their hallowing influence on me also, for I fought an inward battle with my worldliness—and conquered; and owning to myself, that the love of such a pure-minded, warm-hearted woman as Alice, was worth more than any pleasures gold could purchase, I resolved no effort on my part should be wanting to secure the only thing which I now felt was essential to my happiness.

As these thoughts flitted through my brain, I was aroused from my day-dream by the clatter of a horse's feet, and immediately afterwards perceived a kind of two-wheeled chaise, drawn by a horse, which was evidently a famous trotter, rapidly approaching; the driver, a fellow in a rough great-coat, who looked like a bailiff or cattle-dealer, leered impudently at my companion as he passed, and then, touching his horse with the whip, rattled by us, startling the bays, and enveloping us in a cloud of dust. "That fellow would be the better for a sound caning, whoever he is," observed I.

"He has been a bailiff of Sir Geoffrey's, and was discharged for dishonest practices the very day you arrived," returned Alice; "but look! what is he going to do now?" As she spoke the man, holding in his horse so as scarcely to let it proceed beyond a walk, forced us to pass him; but no sooner had he done so, than, slackening his rein, he again dashed by, causing our team to start and plunge in a manner which banished the warm blood from the fair cheek of my companion.

"Don't be frightened," observed I, "Sir Geoffrey is an excellent whip, and I do not apprehend the slightest danger." I was, however, far from feeling as confident of our safety as I would fain have had Alice believe; for our tormentor was again holding in his horse with an intention of repeating his offensive manœuvre, when Sir Geoffrey exclaimed, in a voice that quivered with suppressed anger—

"Either go on with that chaise at once, or keep behind ; I won't be passed and re-passed in this way."

"I suppose I may drive at what pace I like ; the road's as free for one gentleman as another," was the reply, accompanied by an insolent laugh.

To this impertinence Sir Geoffrey made no answer, but waiting until the fellow had allowed us to pass him, threw out his whip-hand, and drawing the lash lightly across the leaders' backs, allowed the spirited horses to increase their pace, with the view of leaving the chaise-cart behind ; but our persecutor was not so easily to be got rid of. As I have before observed, his horse was a remarkably fast trotter, and the chaise was lightly built, with very large wheels ; still, for some little time, Sir Geoffrey was able to prevent him from passing us, by keeping in the centre of the road, which at that point was not very wide ; this plan, however, was rendered abortive by the intervention of a strip of smooth green sward, running parallel with the road, on to which Roberts (for such I afterwards found to be his name) immediately turned, and giving his horse the rein, endeavoured once more to dash by us. For some few yards Sir Geoffrey attempted to race with him, but the risk was too great ; excited by the rattling of the chaise, Zantippe, the near leader, began to plunge violently, her companion broke into a canter, and the wheel horses, snorting and setting up their heads and tails, pulled so strongly that it was evident their driver could scarcely hold them. Indeed, for a minute, it was very doubtful whether or not they could be restrained from running away ; but, fortunately, Sir Geoffrey was an unusually powerful man, and by a strong and continuous effort, he once more got his team under command.

Apparently satisfied with the annoyance he had caused, or, possibly, afraid of proceeding to extremities, Mr. Roberts contented himself by keeping a short distance ahead, and favouring us with his rejected dust. In this order we proceeded until we arrived at a turnpike, which event afforded our tormentor a fresh opportunity for the display of his powers of aggravation. Stopping in the middle of the gateway, so as to preclude the possibility of anything passing him, he began, in the coolest way imaginable, a conversation with the turnpike man, as to the state of the crops, the market-price of live stock, and the

like, while he searched, or pretended to search, in his pockets
for the toll Sir Geoffrey, after waiting for a few seconds with
exemplary patience, gave some orders to his groom, who
jumped down, and going round in turn to all the horses,
tightened their curb chains (that of Madame Zantippe in particular), and buckled each rein in the lowest bar. Having
resumed his seat, his master, addressing the turnpike-keeper,
said—-

"Why don't you make that man go on ? it's your duty to
see that no one obstructs the public road."

On hearing these words, Roberts turned his head, and pretending to recognise, for the first time, his late employer,
slightly raised his head, saying, " Ah, Sir Geoffrey ! sorry to
keep you waiting ; but the sixpences always get out of the way
just when one wants 'em. Here, Pikey, here's your money.
The bays seem fidgety to-day, Sir Geoffrey ; you give 'em too
much corn, I expect."

The impudent leer with which these words were accompanied
overcame the small remnant of Sir Geoffrey's patience ; and,
thundering out an oath, he vociferated—

" If you stop there another moment, you thieving rascal !
I'll get down and horsewhip you with my own hands."

" Will you like to do it now, or wait till you can catch me ?"
was the impertinent reply ; and whipping his horse, the fellow
drove off.

There was a look of furious resolve in Sir Geoffrey's face, as
settling himself firmly in his seat, he gathered up the reins, and
started his team, which I did not half like ; fortunately, Miss
Woodford did not appear to notice it. As the horses steadied
down to their trot, their driver gradually increased their speed,
till at last we were bowling along at between ten and eleven
miles an hour. This pace soon brought us up with Mr. Roberts,
who seemed determined not to yield the mastery of the road
without a struggle, and urged his horse to display its fullest
powers. Still the distance between us continued to decrease ;
the bays were splendid steppers, and had now got into a long,
slashing trot, which few horses could have equalled. Roberts,
however, knew the ground well, and determined to avail himself of it.

After proceeding about a mile at this pace, the chaise keeping ahead, we came to a very long and tolerably steep hill ; as
we began to descend this, the ex-bailiff, calculating that with a

heavy carriage it would be most dangerous to preserve the present rate of speed, far more to increase it, and trusting to his own skill to drive his light chaise safely down, whipped his horse into a furious gallop; but he had not calculated upon the daring courage, or rather, I should say, the insane recklessness of Sir Geoffrey Stapylton: to my horror, I again saw the snake-like lash of the four-in-hand whip playing round the leaders' ears— Zantippe broke into a gallop, her yoke-fellow followed her example, the wheel-horses could not hold back the carriage, and in another moment we were flying down the slope with the speed of lightning. Instinctively I turned to my companion, who up to this moment had behaved admirably; even now, although her face was pale with terror, she preserved her presence of mind so far as to be aware that the wisest thing was to endeavour to keep her seat, which, from the frightful rocking of the coach, was no easy matter, and she accordingly leaned back, grasping the iron rail with convulsive energy. It was no time for ceremony; placing my arm round her waist, I drew her to my side, saying—

"Trust yourself entirely to me; and if it is in the power of man to save you, I will do so; at present there is nothing for it but to sit still, and hold on."

My intention was, in the event of an overturn, to take her in my arms, and, leaping clear of the carriage, endeavour, as far as possible, to break her fall, at whatever risk to myself. She did not attempt to repulse me; but, on the contrary, clung to my arm, as if even its insufficient protection served to reassure her. The rate at which we were proceeding once more brought us up with the chaise; and all the efforts of its driver, stimulated by the knowledge that the race had now become one for life and death, scarcely sufficed to enable him to keep ahead of us. I was, however, glad to observe that Sir Geoffrey, although, of course, he could not have stopped his horses, yet kept them well together, and evidently had them, in some measure, under control. As we approached the bottom of the hill, I perceived that a stream crossed the road at right angles, over which was thrown a bridge with a low, stone parapet, the ground, of course, rising up to the centre of the arch; to cross the bridge before us, Roberts was now straining every sinew; and he punished his horse, which was rapidly becoming exhausted, most cruelly, to attain his object; but in vain. At the foot of the hill, the taper lash of Sir Geoffrey's whip again played round the now reeking sides of the horses; as we neared the bridge, the leaders were neck-and-neck with the gig-horse. Now they have passed it; at the centre of the arch, the hind-wheel of the drag strikes the nave of the chaise-wheel with the force of a battering-ram; the shafts snap like touch-wood, the horse falls, and the driver is shot over the parapet into the stream below.

With such rapidity did all this take place, that I had scarcely time to turn my head and ascertain that our late tormentor had sustained no bodily injury beyond a good ducking, which he thoroughly deserved, ere our speed began sensibly to diminish, and it was evident (thanks to an opportune rise in the ground) that Sir Geoffrey had recovered complete control over his horses. On turning to inform my companion (from whose slender waist I had as yet only partially withdrawn my arm) of Roberts's safety, I perceived the tears were coursing each other down her pale cheeks. Now, if there is one thing more than another that I cannot stand, it is to see any woman, for whom I have the slightest regard, cry—it's all over with me then, and I must do the best in my power to comfort her, at all hazards. Accordingly, I took her little, trembling hand in mine, and exclaimed—

"Miss Woodford!—Alice, *dearest* Alice!—you're not ill?"

She suffered me to retain her hand for a minute, then, disengaging herself from my supporting arm, she replied—

"No, no; it is only the revulsion of feeling. A moment ago on the brink of eternity, now comparatively safe! Oh, it was very terrible!" She paused, then, smiling through her tears, she added,—"You were very kind; I believe I should have fallen, if you had not supported me. I was fast losing my presence of mind. I really do not know how to thank you properly."

"I will tell you," replied I; "give me a right to protect you always, as I have done to-day. Alice," continued I, "this is no sudden resolve, no mere ebullition of feeling, called forth by the excitement of the moment; but the expression of a far deeper sentiment, the declaration of a passionate attachment, which must constitute the joy or sorrow of my future life. Alice, as you sat gazing on yon pure blue vault above us, I looked into my own heart, and read there that I loved you better than any created thing on the face of this fair earth; and when, during the peril from which God in his mercy preserved us, I believed that another moment might plunge us into eternity,

my only care was for you, for I loved you better than myself."
Seeing she appeared much affected by my words, I added, " I
would not distress you for the world : if what I have said is
displeasing to you, if you feel unable to return my affection, I
will leave this place to-morrow—I will "——I paused abruptly,
for I saw that my companion, who had been struggling against
her emotion, had so far succeeded as to be able to speak, and I
waited, with trembling eagerness, the words which were to
decide my fate.

" You know not to what you are pledging yourself," she
began : " you speak from an impulse of pity, called forth by
my desolate position. I should be most ungenerous to take
advantage of your disinterested kindness of heart."

" Alice, on my word, it is not so," interrupted I ; " dearest,
—I have thought,—I have reflected "——

" Have you reflected what would be the opinion of your
mother and sisters, when, instead of the well-born, richly-
endowed bride they wish you to possess, you tell them you
have engaged yourself to a poor, friendless girl, with nothing
to recommend her—— "

" But the fact that she has every perfection a man could
dream of in a wife—that she is the only woman I have
really loved, the only woman I ever shall love. Alice," I
continued, " I am happily my own master. My mother and
sisters are well provided for. I myself possess what you, dear
one, with your simple tastes and habits, will deem an ample
fortune ; if, therefore, I may hope for the deep joy of believing
that you are not altogether indifferent to me—"

Well, reader, unless you are particularly addicted to love-
scenes, I should think you have had about enough of this sort
of thing by this time.   Love, like a pair of shoes made to order,
is (if it fits nicely) very agreeable to the happy couple for whom
it is intended (who, to carry on the metaphor, usually find
they've put their foot in it, and learn, from the sad realities of
smoky chimneys and crying children, where the shoe pinches),
but it is an awful bore to every one else. In the present instance, the damsel brought forward more scruples, which I
combatted successfully, and before we arrived at Redgrave
Court, the affair was satisfactorily arranged, and I found myself
in the enviable position of accepted lover to Alice Woodford.

Up to the present point the reader of this "o'er true tale "
may, with some justice, have complained of a want of incident

therein. Should this have been the case, he may console himself, as from the moment of my offer to Alice Woodford, events followed each other in rapid succession.

When we reached Redgrave, Miss Walsingham, M. Cazotte, and "*les braves petits chevaux*," were reported missing. Harry returned about seven o'clock; still no tidings of the lost sheep. At eight we went to dinner in despair, having despatched mounted grooms in search; at a quarter to nine one of the messengers returned with a letter for Miss Woodford, on perusing it that young lady beckoned Mary Stapylton out of the room; next, Harry was sprighted away; and lastly, to my intense mystification, I was summoned to Mrs. Stapylton's boudoir. Then the murder came out—Miss Walsingham had eloped with Monsieur Cazotte! "Good-luck and joy go with her!" was my mental comment; but I only said, I was afraid Mrs. Stapylton must be distressed at the young lady's conduct, as they had been such particular friends; whereupon that animal, Harry, burst into what seemed to me a very uncalled-for fit of laughter; and Alice hid her blushing face on Mary's shoulder, and that best little woman in the world, *but one*, told me, with an April face of smiles and tears—well, reader, have you guessed what? if so, you are quicker than I was, for, like an oaf, even up to the last moment I had never dreamed of such a thing—told how, when Harry spoke of the model husband he had found for her old schoolfellow, the two naughty girls laid their pretty heads together, and devised a plot against the "coming man," which, had he been as much bent on marrying an heiress, as he was prejudiced against it, would have ended in his complete discomfiture. The scheme, then, so cunningly devised was, that Alice Walsingham, heiress of Walsingham Manor, should, for the time being, change name and station with her *dame de compagnie*, Julia Woodford, by which metamorphoses both ladies had, as has been related, obtained for themselves that desirable thing—a husband; the real Miss Woodford having availed herself of her temporary elevation to secure the venal affection of M. Cazotte, though the character of her "little deception" was, it must be confessed, in more senses than one, the exact opposite to that of her charming patroness. And thus, you see, Alice bid fair to *win* her French gloves, and Fate seemed to have decreed that I am to marry an heiress after all.

CHAPTER IV.

A WEEK had elapsed since the occurrence of the events related
in the last chapter, and I no longer remained an inmate of Redgrave Court, having run up to town for the purpose of communicating my matrimonial intentions to my mother and sisters,
as well as to make certain necessary arrangements preparatory
to Alice's introduction to my family. Harry had accompanied
me, having business of his uncle's to execute, which obliged
him to visit the metropolis.

There had been a grand *embrouillement* between the Cazottes,
the lady having kept her own counsel till the fickle imp, Cupid,
had been bound in the iron fetters of Hymen, was obliged to
confess that her landed estates lay chiefly in the immediate
vicinity of certain castles in the air (a vague species of property
it would clearly have been unwise to build upon), while her
expectations were only that this information would put "Adolphe"
into a thundering passion, and in these, we grieve to say, she
was not mistaken. But "Adolphe" was a practical man, and
did not confine his indignation to mere words; having escorted
the lady on her homeward journey as far as Derby, he availed
himself of the fact of her being a very sound sleeper, and bidding her farewell after the fashion of his country (*i.e.* taking
French leave), he purchased a first-class ticket, and ere the fair
Julia awoke to the painful consciousness that she was rather a
widow bewitched than otherwise, was far upon his road to London. The deserted Julia, however (being blessed by nature
with very little delicacy of feeling, in compensation for which
deficiency she was gifted with a double portion of impudence),
immediately started for Redgrave Court; went down upon her
knees to Alice, shed a very heavy shower of tears, and appealed
to her compassion; which manœuvre answered perfectly : the
fact being, that Alice felt herself somewhat guilty in the matter,
as it had been in compliance with her wishes that Miss Woodford had originally assumed the character of heiress. Accordingly, wise heads were laid together, and their cogitations
resulted in Harry undertaking to discover, and negotiate with,
M. Cazotte. On reaching town he had succeeded in tracing
the fugitive, and having proposed to him financial arrangements,
which brought back all his affection for his " *chere et belle Julie,*"

had sent him down to Redgrave to make his peace with Madame, and await the drawing up of a certain deed of settlement.

This matter being happily disposed of, Harry and I had agreed, after dining together on Sunday, to return to Redgrave on the following Tuesday. Whether the said dinner was unusually indigestible I know not, but for that or some other reason, I dreamed, when I went to bed that night a most vivid and horrible dream.—Methought that I was at Redgrave, and the party were assembled in the drawing-room before dinner, when, suddenly, a fearful monster, something like an exaggerated edition of a hyena, with glaring, fiendish eyes, rushed into the room, and seizing one of the party (Marston, I think it was), carried him off bodily. Having, as I imagined, devoured his first victim, the creature returned for another, and no one appearing ambitious of the unenviable distinction, a hurried flight and pursuit took place, which continued through the suite of rooms, and the innumerable passages of the old house. Amongst the rest, Alice and I ran for our lives, and, after witnessing the capture and destruction of two or three of our companions — all the details presented themselves with horrible distinctness to my sleeping fancy—we finally took refuge in the housekeeper's room, a small apartment into which I had once been introduced, to be shown a portrait of Harry, as he appeared in a hat and feathers, at the tender age of four years. Our hiding-place, however, proved no defence against the savage cunning of the monster, for scarcely had we congratulated ourselves on our escape, when the window was dashed in, and in another moment Alice was struggling in the creature's reeking jaws; while, on attempting to advance to her rescue, I found my limbs were paralysed, and that I was immovably fixed to the spot. The scene that ensued I will not attempt to describe; suffice it to say, it was so intensely horrible, that, with a cry of agony, I awoke, to find the perspiration pouring down my face like rain, and my whole frame trembling with agitation.

So vivid had been the dream, that at first I could scarcely persuade myself it had not been real, and even on the following morning it haunted me to a degree which was perfectly ridiculous. I tried to forget it—that was impossible; I endeavoured to reason myself out of it, but the attempt proved a failure; and, as a last resource, I set off to find Harry, and persuade him to start a day sooner than we had intended: of course, he

thought me a fool for my pains, and laughed at me accordingly; in fact, I could not but laugh at myself. He was
however, unable to agree to my plan, as he had fixed an important appointment for the following morning.

" Well, I daresay you will think me a complete idiot, Harry,
was my reply to this announcement, " but I've worked myself
up into such a fidget about this confounded dream, that if you
won't consider me very shabby, I shall run down by the last
train to-night, and surprise them to-morrow morning by appearing at breakfast."

" I see how it is," returned Harry, laughing, " the poor
youth is love-sick, and has hit upon this particularly unreasonable reason as an excuse for returning to his *inamorata* twelve
hours sooner than he otherwise would do. Go your ways,
Master Ned (*Ned*, of course), and warm yourself in the sunshine
of the fair Alice's smiles. Tell Mary I shall be down to-
morrow night;"—and so we parted.

I can generally sleep as soundly in a carriage as in a bed,
but during my journey that night, I never closed my eyes; a
weight hung upon my spirits—a vague presentiment of coming
evil which I could neither banish nor account for, rendered me
anxious and uneasy, and I chid the lagging hours, which seemed
as if they would never come to an end, and deemed, in my impatience, that the train which conveyed me was the slowest
coach it had ever been my evil hap to travel by. Although
the sun had scarcely appeared above the horizon, it was quite
daylight, when at about a quarter before 5 A.M., I was set down
at the iron gates of Redgrave Court.

" Vell!" exclaimed the driver as I handed him his fare, " I've
drove by these here blessed gates here fifteen year next mid-
summer, but this is the first time I've ever seed 'em open at
this time in the morning."

Attracted by his words, I turned to look—'twas true; the
gates were wide open, and stranger still, the key was remaining
in the lock! " What an extraordinary circumstance!" thought
I, as I tried in vain to account for it in any satisfactory manner; it was, however, useless to puzzle my brain about it, no
one being at hand to afford a clue to the mystery, as the old
woman who usually acted as gate-keeper was accustomed to
sleep at the village, a quarter of a mile distant.

This little incident, unimportant as it may appear, did not
tend to allay my anxiety, and I ran, rather than walked, up the

avenue, so great was my impatience to prove my fears groundless. As I approached the house, the whining of a dog became audible, and in another moment a favourite spaniel of Harry's came bounding towards me, and fawned upon me; as I stooped to caress the animal, my hand encountered something damp and sticky, and, on examining the creature more closely I perceived, to my horror, that his coat was in places stained, and his paws stained, with blood. Pushing the dog from me, I ran hastily on, and in another minute had reached the porter's lodge, the door of which was usually most carefully barred. To my surprise and alarm, this was also standing wide open. Fearing I knew not what, I entered, but had scarcely done so when I started back aghast, for I perceived traces which evinced clearly whence the animal had contracted its ensanguined stains. This confirmation of my worst fears coming upon me so unexpectedly, made me feel very faint, and I was forced to return into the open air, for a minute, to recover myself. As I threw my eye along the range of buildings, not a living creature was visible, nor was there the slightest indication of the mansion being inhabited. The fresh air having in some degree restored me, I again entered the porter's lodge, determined to prosecute my search, though I dreaded each moment to encounter the ghastly evidences of some hideous tragedy.

On examining the lodge more closely, I perceived the footprints of several people, mixed with crimson drops and stains, while ensanguined marks upon the handles and panels of the doors seemed to indicate their having been dashed open by murderous hands. From the larger spots, tracks of the same nature were discernible in a passage leading towards the servants' offices. Following this horrible guide, I reached the kitchen. Here, although the marks never entirely ceased, they became less frequent; the room appeared untenanted, either by the living or the dead; there was no fire burning in the grate, but on the table stood what, to my astonishment, I soon made out to be the second course of the yesterday's dinner, untouched, and arranged in the exact order in which it should have been put upon the dining-room table. This struck me as a most inexplicable circumstance, as it indicated that the mysterious fate which seemed to have annihilated the family, must have overtaken them suddenly, and that, moreover, the catastrophe had not occurred during the hours of darkness, but early in the preceding evening. It was clear, however, that the clue to the mystery could not be ascertained without farther investigation; and though I am free to confess that the situation was one which inspired me with the most vivid sensation of fear, I determined, come what would, to go through with it, if but for the sake of avoiding self-reproach afterwards. Accordingly, feeling by no means certain that I might not at any moment be attacked by some of the unknown agents in the tragedy which I could scarcely doubt had been enacted, I armed myself with the heavy kitchen poker, and proceeded in my search. The ensanguined traces now became more distinct, and led towards the dining-room. As I approached the door of this apartment, the marks of a man's hands, with the fingers spread out, were distinctly traced in crimson stains on the walls of the passage, as if some one had pressed against the wall to save himself from falling.

The dining-room door stood ajar; I pushed it open, and entered. The table was laid for dinner, the chairs for the guests stood round it, and the first course had been served; but the covers were still on the dishes, and the whole was in the most exact order, but untouched. While making these observations, my back had been towards the sideboard; but on turning to leave the room, such a scene of destruction met my sight, that I instinctively rubbed my eyes to convince myself I was not dreaming once more. The sideboard, and the oil-cloth for some feet round it, were covered by fragments of broken glass and china, with knives, forks, articles of plate, large and small, lying huddled together in the wildest disorder; whilst among, and about, and upon everything, were spots, and stains of gore, which appeared to have fallen from the victims in some desperate and mysterious conflict. Still, strange to say, there appeared no signs, either living or dead, of the actors in the hideous drama. Everything was alike silent and terrible. Having overcome a shuddering sickness which the sight had produced, I hastily left the dining-parlour, and hurried through the suite of sitting-rooms. In each and all the same phenomena presented themselves; silence, unbroken but by the sound of my own footsteps, solitude, and traces of violence.

Having gone through most of the rooms down-stairs, I determined to examine the sleeping apartments. The first room was the one commonly occupied by Harry and his wife. The door stood open; but I could observe nothing unusual in the apartment, except that the bed had not been slept in. The next room, which had been Alice's, presented much the same appearance, the bed also being undisturbed. The door of Marston's sleeping apartment had, however, evidently been exposed to some most violent assault; the lower hinge was broken, the upper one bent and strained, and the lock was literally *dashed to pieces*, the floor being strewed with fragments of iron and splintered wood. On entering, there were ensanguined stains upon the carpet, the bed was undisturbed, but the window, which might be eight or nine feet from the ground, stood wide open, and on the sill was the red print of a hand, as if some person had leaned on it in order to jump out, while on the soft border beneath, the traces of footsteps were distinctly visible. The adjoining room was that of M. Cazotte. The door was fastened on the inside; but the lock had been partially destroyed, and the two lower panels were dashed in, so that, by stooping down, I could look into the room. Nothing, however, was visible which could throw light on the affair, though I could perceive the bed had not been slept in; while, from the current of air, I imagined the window to be standing open.

There now only remained one more chamber to examine, viz., that of Sir Geoffrey Stapylton himself. The door of this apartment remained firmly closed, and the fastenings on the inside resisted any efforts of mine to open them. On applying my ear to the key-hole, however, the heavy, but regular breathing of some person in a deep sleep became distinctly audible. Under these circumstances, I paused for a moment to decide on my next step. The sleeper I had little doubt was Sir Geoffrey. The question then was, should I endeavour to arouse him at once, and demand from him an explanation of these ghastly evidences; or should I leave him undisturbed, while I made the best of my way down to the village, to obtain assistance, and ascertain if anything could there be learned of the fate of the other inmates of Redgrave Court? Many reasons induced me to adopt the latter alternative, amongst which, by no means the least influential, was a terrible doubt which, despite Harry's assurances to the contrary, had more than once occurred to my mind, in regard to the baronet's sanity. The fearful expression of his face before the finale of the drag adventure, had impressed itself indelibly on my memory, and there was a half cunning, half ferocious look in his cold, grey eyes, which seemed to strengthen the supposition. Nay, was it not even possible that he might be in some way connected with the frightful traces around me?—Might not some fit of anger have induced a sudden outbreak of insane fury, in which, perchance——The idea was too vaguely horrible to realise, but it settled the question; and merely delaying to glance through the servants' sleeping rooms, all of which were empty, and the beds unslept in, I hastily retraced my steps. The course which I pursued in order to effect my exit, happened to lead me past the housekeeper's room, and an irresistible impulse led me to investigate it.

Accordingly, I pushed opened the door and entered. Scarcely had I done so, when I started back terror-stricken and aghast, for, accustomed as my eyes had now become to objects of dismay, the appearance of the room corresponded so exactly (as far as things inanimate were concerned) with my dream of the preceding night, that I could scarcely believe the evidence of my senses. The reader may remember that in my dream, the creature with the fiendish eyes dashed in through the closed window, and seizing Alice, devoured her in the centre of the apartment. Imagine, then, my dread and amazement, to perceive that the *window-frame, glass, and everything were literally smashed to pieces*, while on the floor were again traces of—— But the description is too horrible! There were further marks of violence about the apartment, yet, shocked and sick at heart, I could not stay to examine them. My pulses throbbed, my brain reeled, and had I remained a minute longer I must have fainted. The cool air served once more to restore me, and turning my back upon the scene of horrors, I fled as from a charnel-house. How I contrived to reach the village I know not; it must have been solely a matter of instinct, mind had nothing to do with it; for at that moment I was utterly incapable of thought. The first thing that recalled me in any measure to myself, was the sight of Marston, who, with his forehead bandaged, and his arm in a sling, was standing at the door of the little inn watching the sunrise. My appearance, I imagined, afforded some clue to my state of mind, for, starting as he saw me, he exclaimed—

"Good heavens, Chichester, you here! you have not been up to the house, surely?"

I managed to gasp out an affirmative, adding, "Tell me— what of Alice?"

" She is here, safe and well," was the reply.

I uttered an exclamation of thankfulness, and sinking on a bench covered my face with my hands, and—I am not ashamed to own it, for since I left off pinafores, it is the only time I have so misconducted myself—cried like a child. The relief was instantaneous, and ere five minutes were over, I was walking up and down with Marston, listening to his explanation of the horrors which had so affected me. It appeared that on the previous day, just before the usual dinner hour, Marston had accidentally entered the parlour in search of a book, when he perceived Sir Geoffrey (who had complained in the earlier part of the morning of feeling ill, and out of spirits), in the act of filling for himself a glass of brandy at the sideboard. Marston, being aware of the necessity which existed for his host to abstain from all exciting liquors, had ventured to remonstrate with him, but to no purpose ; he was obstinately bent upon having his own way, and as a last resource, Marston, pretending to do so by accident, knocked the glass out of his hand.

It was a dangerous experiment, and, as the event proved, a most unwise one ; for the baronet, irritated beyond control, seized a decanter, and flung it with tremendous force at Marston's head, who only avoided the blow by the greatest quickness. Thus foiled in his attempt, Sir Geoffrey struck Marston a violent blow on the face, which set his nose bleeding, and appeared inclined to follow up the attack so vigorously, that, in self-defence, Marston was obliged to use his fists also. M. Cazotte and the servants, attracted by the noise of the scuffle, hastened to the scene of action, and the combined forces threw themselves upon, and endeavoured to overpower, the baronet. This, however, was no such easy matter. Sir Geoffrey, at all times an unusually powerful man, was now animated by the strength of frenzy, and being, moreover, by no means scrupulous in his choice of weapons,—flinging a knife at one, a plate or decanter at another, as opportunity offered,—it could be little matter of surprise, that the battle ended by his fairly beating them all out of the room, and elate with victory, pursuing them up and down the passages, and through the suite of apartments.

In such a conflict as I have described, with fragments of broken china and glass flying in all directions, it may be easily imagined that hands and faces would be cut, and the effusion of blood considerable : and such in fact was the case. At the first onset, the ladies of the family, and the female domestics, with one exception, had sought safety in flight; the men-servants soon followed their example; and Marston and Cazotte, having by that time had quite enough of it, rushed up to their respective bed-rooms, Sir Geoffrey following hard upon their traces. This, however, proved of little avail; the infuriated madman—for such, at all events at the time, he was—kicked in the lower panels of one door, and smashed the lock and hinges of the other—hostile demonstrations which determined the tenants to escape by their windows, and make the best of their way to effect a junction with the main body of fugitives.

The only person now remaining in the house, besides the victorious baronet, was the old house-keeper, a faithful servant of the family, who had known Sir Geoffrey from his youth up, and having ere now witnessed somewhat similar explosions, entertained no personal fear of her master, and had therefore ensconced herself in her own room, to wait till he should "come round again," as she termed it. Her anticipations were soon verified. Sir Geoffrey, having satisfied himself that he had made a clear house of it, and that no more enemies remained to contend with, became in a degree tranquillised, and at last entered the housekeeper's room, and asked her to bind up one of his hands, which had been severely cut with the broken glass. In complying with his wishes, she accidentally pressed against the wounded part, and hurt him. The pain brought back all his scarcely-extinguished anger, and striking her violently across the face with the back of his hand, he set her nose bleeding violently, then seizing the poker, he commenced breaking the furniture, and, by way of an appropriate finale, smashed the window to shivers. Upon seeing this, even the old housekeeper became alarmed for her life, and while his attention was engrossed by the demolition of the window, made her escape, trotting off as fast as her legs could carry her, having paused, however, in the porter's lodge for a minute or two, to stanch her injured nose. By her advice, it was decided to leave Sir Geoffrey alone in his glory until the morning. She was well acquainted with his habits, and declared that if he were allowed to remain undisturbed, he would most probably betake himself quietly to bed. Accordingly, an express was despatched to inform Harry of all that had occurred, Marston had his wounds bound up, and the whole party took possession of the little village inn for the night. And in this manner was the fearful and horrible scene, which had shocked my eyes and filled me with the most dire forebodings, accounted for more satisfactorily than I could have deemed possible.

Little else remains to be told. Harry, who had started for Redgrave the moment he became aware of what had taken place, arrived in time to give directions as to the most advisable course to pursue with regard to his uncle. This was, to set the servants and workmen to clear away all signs of the late *fracas,* 'and restore the house to its former state of order. Sir Geoffrey's valet was then desired to call his master, having been previously cautioned to avoid all reference to the occurrences of the preceding evening. The plan answered perfectly. The baronet appeared either entirely to have forgotten his late exploit, or else, aware that it did not exactly redound to his credit, he chose to appear oblivious of it, and for the time the thing passed over. Harry, however, in accordance with his wife's wishes, made my approaching wedding a pretext for removing the family to London, and I believe it is not his intention to allow Mary again to reside at Redgrave during his uncle's life. He has also, under pretence of hiring a new butler, contrived to introduce into the establishment a man accustomed to the care of persons whose eccentricities occasionally assume a dangerous character.

And now, shortly to return to my more immediate concerns : most of my readers have doubtless partaken of the good cheer provided by that " mighty master " of the art of gastronomy " Gunter," on the occasion of a wedding breakfast. Let each, then, recall his or her brightest recollections of orange flowers, white satin, and Honiton lace, *ad libitum*, no end of kid gloves, inexhaustible ices, and unlimited champagne ;—let him add to the catalogue half-a-dozen pretty bridesmaids, in a very dangerous state of pink bonnets and fascination, and twice the number of young gentlemen (mild, nineteenth-century Cæsars), got up for the occasion regardless of expense,—prepared to come, see, and conquer, but who are each safe to play Antony to some bridesmaid's Cleopatra, ere the sitting is concluded ;— batteries of smiles, most ably served, that set hearts on fire, which bucketsful of tears, shed because every one is so *very* happy, are unable to extinguish ;—long *impromptu* speeches, carefully studied beforehand, and dead failures after all ;—tipsy waiters, white-favoured post-boys, eager horses, one bridegroom in the seventh heaven of confused ecstasy, and the most lovely, and lovable bride that ever existed:—let the reader remember, or imagine, all this, and he will, even then, have arrived at a very insufficient and tame conception of the sayings and doings of that most glorious morning, which beheld me the proud and delighted husband of the once-dreaded heiress, Alice Walgham.

"And that is all about it, eh, MASTER NED ? "

"It is so, dear Reader ; except that, perhaps, as a concluding remark, you will allow me to state my very decided opinion, that—*under the circumstances*—it would have been better taste in you to have called me a married man, EDWARD !"

Note by the Author.—The strange incident related in the last chapter of this tale is founded on fact, and occurred almost exactly as the author has described it. If this is not deemed sufficient reason for introducing the unpleasing details without which the facts of the story could not have been related, the author can only apologise for his choice of a subject. The principal actor in the affair was an eccentric Baronet, well remembered by many of the inhabitants of B——shire, while the gentleman from whom the account is derived, and who performed the part assigned to Edward Chichester in the matter, is still living, to vouch for its truth.

NORFOLK AND HEREFORD.

BY G. P. R. JAMES, ESQ.

PART I.

THE woods were echoing with the music of hounds,—for many
a deep throat was pouring forth the fierce but melodious cry of
eager pursuit, as the deer started away from the thicket and
bounded over the brushwood of the more open part of the
forest. Waving up and down was a sea of gentle hills and
dales, with streams flowing through the valleys, and castles
perched upon the summits. On the one side, where the country sloped away towards the banks of the Wye, a wide extent
of wavy lines of every hue, of purple and of yellow, might be
seen stretching afar till they were lost in misty nothing; whilst,
on the other hand, over the tall tree-tops rose up the blue heads
of some distant mountains. On a spot where this scene, so fair
in itself, was rendered doubly beautiful by the effect of the
sky, which, though it was full summer, was now partly over-
shadowed for a few instants by a broad heavy cloud, stood a
young lad of some fourteen or fifteen years of age. He was
dressed in a light tunic of green, bordered with a gold lace,
with breeches, stockings, and boots of untanned leather. No
cloak was upon his shoulders, but under his left arm hung a
quiver full of arrows. In his right hand was a bow, taller than
himself: and with his foot he kept down the leash which confined two tall speed hounds, which stood with arched backs and
raised ears gazing along a broad road running through the
midst of the forest. In the same direction the boy's eyes were
also turned, and the same eager and impetuous look might be
seen in the human face and in the faces of the dogs.

A moment after a large fine deer bounded across the space

where the wood was low, and was crossing the road into the thicker part of the forest on the other side, when, in an instant, an arrow was laid upon the string, the bow raised, the shaft shot, and the noble beast fell over and over, with the missile piercing his side, through and through, just behind the shoulder Close upon his track came the hounds and a large body o huntsmen; and the youth ran eagerly forward, exclaiming, with a sort of deprecatory look, "You gave me leave to shoot!"

"Yes, I did, Walter," replied one of the new comers, turning towards him; "but you should be careful: you might have shot man or dog."

"Oh, no fear of that, noble lord," replied the boy; "I never miss my mark;" and gazing upon the prostrate carcass of the stag, still quivering with animal life, while the huntsmen flogged the dogs back from it, he said, in a musing tone, to himself, "The old man told me, I should some day shoot the highest beast in all the forests of England; and I think I have done it, and the fattest too."

"This is the fourth brought down this morning," said the gentleman who had just spoken, turning to another who accompanied him. "You see, Ralph, that we have venison in Herefordshire as well as in Norfolk."

"Ay, truly," replied the other; "and this is the tallest buck of all. 'Tis a shame to have it slain by a page's hand."

"Nay, nay," replied the first; "Walter Tyrrel is the best marksman amongst us; and the Norman bow was never better than in his hand. Some day he will do good service therewith. Envy him not his stroke, but let the foresters break the deer, for I have had enough of such work, and come along with me. I will show thee a hind which is better worth thine aim than all the harts of the forest."

"Have with you, my good lord," replied the other. And turning their horses' heads, they rode away, followed by a part of their attendants, but not all.

It had not been difficult to see that the two gentlemen who had spoken, while the rest maintained silence, were Norman nobles of a very high rank. They had all the distinctive marks of their class and their nature: the long dark hair, hanging in ringlets over their shoulders,—the close shaven face, leaving not the slightest particle of beard that could be removed,—the long tunics, apparently more fitted for a court than a hunting-field, and not only embroidered with gold round the edges, but ornamented n various parts with precious stones,—and, above all, the furred rheno, or gorget, as I believe it may be called, which, rising partly round the neck, descended thence over the chest and shoulders. Both were young men in the early pride of life; and both were peculiarly handsome, especially the one who had spoken last. He was tall, graceful, powerfully made; and the features, slightly aquiline, displayed all that peculiar delicacy of outline which marked the Norman race, and often deluded the enemies opposed to it into the dangerous fancy that the spirit would be found as soft and delicate as the countenance.

As they rode along, at a slow pace, the one called the other Ralph, and the other addressed him again by the name of Roger; but when any of the attendants spoke to either, it was with lowly reverence, and with the addition of, my Lord the Earl. Sometimes, indeed, though but rarely, the first of the noblemen I have mentioned would call the other " Norfolk; " and the other would in turn address his companion as " Hereford; " but they seemed upon those intimate and brotherly terms which frequently existed between two knights of the middle ages, extending to an excess of attachment and devotion, which seems marvellous, and almost incredible, to our colder and more calculating minds. Whether a real and formal brotherhood of arms existed between them, I know not; but certainly the attachment of the one to the other was as great as if they had been born of the mother; and yet, strange to say, Ralph de Guador, Earl of Norfolk, was but little acquainted with the family of Roger Fitz-Osborne, Earl of Hereford,—had never seen his mother, and had only met his father, the celebrated favourite of William the Conqueror, on occasions of courtly ceremony or military parade. Such, however, is often the case, at least in a certain degree, at present. Though the deep and devoted attachment implied by the brotherhood of arms in those days no longer exists, yet how often is it that the young choose their dearest friends from circles far remote from that in which heaven placed them? how rarely would father and son agree in regard to the choice of associates? and, alas! how often has the son to regret that he did not use the microscope of experience, which he was fond to fancy had deceived a parent's sight.

These two high lords rode on, chatting gaily as they went; and after a ride of about half an hour, the towers of a tall castle began to appear upon a hill, at some four or five miles distance.

Three centuries ago that castle was a picturesque ruin, now,
the very foundations cannot be traced. At the time of which
I write it was fresh in its first newness; no ivy had ventured to
cling to its walls,—the lichen and the moss had found no footing
on the stone-work,—and the smoke of the cottages below had
hardly shadowed with grey the warm colour of the stone.

The towers were lost and seen, and seen and lost again, as
the party advanced; now rising into view over the tree-tops as
they ascended the hills,—now disappearing amongst the leafy
branches as they rode down into the valleys.

It was at the end of one of the steepest of these descents,
that the young Earl of Hereford reined in his horse, and,
pointing to a small house, superior to the ordinary tenement of
Saxon thrall or ceorl, or of Norman serf or socman, being built
of stone, and not inelegantly ornamented, he said, " There
dwells one of our followers, Norfolk; and, by the glory of the
Virgin, I must even pause and get a draught of wine, for I am
thirsty with the chase. He will have no bad drink, I promise
you, for he is choice in such things: so come, if you are thirsty
—if not, ride on, and I will follow you."

" Nay, let me share the cup," answered his friend; and
turning to the door, they dismounted.

" Here, come you in hither," said Hereford, opening the door.

" Maggy, Maggy, if the old man is out, give me a cup of
wine."

A light step was heard running from an inner chamber, and
the next moment a vision of beauty burst upon the sight of the
young Earl of Norfolk, that seemed to dazzle his eyes, for he
shaded them as if the sun had fallen upon them. The person who
appeared before him was a girl of nineteen or twenty years of
age, not very tall, though somewhat above the middle height.
Every limb was turned in the most exquisite symmetry; the
foot small and delicately shaped, the hand, with the fingers long
rounded, and fair, except where, at the slender tip of each
nature had painted them with the rosy hue of morning.   H
dress was plain, and that of the lower sort of people, which displayed the person to much greater advantage than the long and
flowing robes of the court. The neck, and part of the shoulders,
were exposed; but no russet hue from the warm rays of the sun
dimmed their ivory whiteness. Her eyes and hair were dark,
but yet what could not be called black; and the sparkling
brightness of the former was softened by the peculiar form of

the eyelid, and the sweepiug fringe of long black lashes as well
on the lower as the upper lid. The rest of the features it is
hardly necessary or possible to describe,—suffice it that they
were straight and beautiful; but the mouth, radiant with
smiles, seemed, to the eye of Norfolk at least, as love's own home.

"Well, my good lord," she said, addressing Hereford in gay
and familiar tones, "so you have concluded your hunting earlier
than you thought?"

"Even so, Maggy," answered Hereford, in the same light
way. "And did you see the chase, fair lady?"

"I watched you for about an hour," answered the fair girl,
"but then the wood swallowed you up, and I came down hither."

"Well, then, bring me a cup of wine, sweet one," answered
Hereford, "for we are very thirsty."

"Am I to be your cup-bearer?" demanded the girl, with a
gay toss of the head, glancing her eye at the same time to the
handsome countenance of the Earl of Norfolk.

"Ay, and for my friend here, too," replied the other; "and
be quick, Meg, for we are parched."

"Well, well," she answered, running away, laughing, "you
are all tyrants."

In a moment or two she returned with a large cup, and a
flagon of wine; and first, with a graceful bend of the head, she
presented the goblet to the Earl of Norfolk.

"Nay, fair lady, give it to Lord Hereford," he said; and,
with a smile and a blush, which rendered her fair countenance
more beautiful than ever, she followed the directions she had
received.

But little conversation followed; and the two young noblemen remounted their horses and went upon their way. The
demeanour of one of the party at least was considerably changed
by the brief pause which they had made. Hereford was as gay
and lively as ever, and laughed and talked to his companion,
without noticing apparently the grave and thoughtful manner
which had so suddenly come upon the Earl of Norfolk, who
rode on by his side, striving in vain to keep up the light and
jesting tone commonly assumed amongst themselves by the
conquerors of the Saxon people of England. Now he would
reply with a sharp repartee; now he would join in his friend's
laugh; but almost immediately he fell into thought again, and
remained plunged in what seemed very deep, if not very
pleasant, meditations.

After a time, his altered demeanour seemed to catch the attention of Hereford, who exclaimed in his usual joyous tone, "Why, what has come to thee, Norfolk? Thou art as dull as a crow on a dry day. Have the bright eyes of our fair Maggy struck thee dumb?"

"Not so," replied his friend, "although I will own, Hereford, I think you a very happy man to have such kind looks from such bright eyes."

Hereford laughed aloud. "Thou art in love. Thou art in love with our fair Mag," he cried. "But I am generous: I will give her to thee, if thou wilt. She is a present for a prince."

"But is she not a free woman?" asked Norfolk.

"Oh yes, mighty free, as my ears can witness," replied the other earl. "She takes all liberty, I assure you, if I am over saucy."

Norfolk fell into thought again, for it seemed to him his friend was jesting; and no more was said upon the subject till they reached the castle, which they had seen from time to time as they went upon their way.

Some hours passed in various amusements, during which the Earl of Norfolk gradually shook off his thoughtful mood, and as the hour of supper approached, appeared light and cheerful as ever. The last meal of the day has in almost all ages, and with almost all people, been the brightest and the merriest. Ever since care came into the world, and labour was the work of daylight, it has necessarily been so. For it the two noblemen prepared with some care; for Hereford had informed his guest that they were not to sup alone, as they had dined. Friends were expected to join their party, he said, ay, and some bright ladies too.

Still the beautiful face and the bright eyes which he had seen in the morning haunted Norfolk, even till he entered the lesser hall of the castle, where the guests assembled previous to the meal. There were already ten or twelve persons present, with several pages handing silver basins and water in silver ewers, for the guests who had ridden from a distance to wash their hands before supper. At the farther end of the room— which was not one of the most spacious in the castle—Norfolk beheld the young Earl of Hereford with an elderly lady of a stately and dignified mien by his side; but, somewhat nearer, was a figure full of grace and beauty, with the face turned partly away, and only a part of the cheek and temple shown.

Of faces that please and interest us, however, we mark more than even we ourselves believe; and small particulars, which we do not recollect having noticed, will often reveal to us the presence of a friend, long before we fully see the well-known countenance. There was something in the soft shading of the eyebrow, where it lost itself in the pure white of the temple, in the graceful line of the damask cheek, and the beautiful symmetry of the neck, which sent a thrill of pleasure through the breast of Norfolk; though he could hardly believe that, in the richly apparelled lady before him, he beheld the gay g rl whom he had seen at the vassal's house. He gazed at her eagerly, and then turned his look for an instant to Hereford. The eyes of his friend were fixed upon him with a gay and laughing expression; and the next instant the lady herself turned, and there was no longer any doubt. A smile, light and playful, came upon her face when she beheld the Earl of Norfolk; but, at that moment, Hereford himself crossed towards them, and taking Norfolk by the hand, led him towards the fair stranger, saying, " Let me present you to my sister. Margaret, who lives during my father's absence with my aunt, the Countess of Breteuil, has kindly come over five miles to grace our supper;" and he then added, in a lower voice, " in a different guise from that in which she stole away this morning to witness the hunting."

Right joyous felt the heart of the Earl of Norfolk when he remembered the words of his friend in the morning. " I will give her to thee if thou wilt," he had said; but then came a little trepidation; for there was something in that high and lofty brow, something in that bright and sparkling eye, which, though softened and shaded by a look of feminine gentleness, told him that she was not one to be given, altogether without her own consent; for, even in that age, the convent was almost always a resource against an unwished-for union. He approached, however, though with some agitation; but the kind smile, and the well-pleased look, gave him back his confidence: and, when she laughed gaily over their meeting in the morning, and his unconsciousness of her rank and station, he soon became again, what he usually appeared, one of the most graceful and distinguished of the Norman barons.

I will not pause upon the progress of their love, nor detail all the little incidents, full of interest to them, which occurred to strengthen and encourage it during the space of more than six weeks which Norfolk passed with the Earl of Hereford.

The Countess of Breteuil looked favourably upon the whole; for there was no alliance in the land superior to that of Norfolk. Her gates were always open to the earl; and he had more opportunities than were usually afforded before marriage, of knowing and being known, loving and winning love. He thought he had won it too; and Hereford assured him that it was so: but there was something that still restrained him; and, ere he could permit his friend to write for the consent of his father and the king, he said, "I must hear, from her own lips, that she can be mine with her whole heart."

It was easily arranged that he should have the opportunity of satisfying himself; and, one bright morning of a warm summer's day, he stood by Margaret's side, in a little tapestried room, where before their eyes, beyond the open windows, spread the bright gleaming scenes of nature, and round about hung representations of shady groves, and deer feeding by the side of streams, and hunter-boys peeping forth, with bow in hand and quiver upon shoulder.

The tapestry made a rustling sound as the Countess of Breteuil departed; and Margaret, as she looked round, and found herself alone with Norfolk, became somewhat pale, and turned her eyes towards the ground. She felt that the moment of destiny had arrived; that the weal or woe of life was upon the wings of that hour.

Norfolk lost no time. His words were low, but clear and distinct, full of thrilling passion and devoted love. But Margaret still remained pale till he had done. Then she raised her eyes to his face; and, with strong command over herself, to keep her limbs from trembling, she said, "Norfolk, I know you love me. I have seen it, felt it—and I will not deny that I love you; but I will not promise you my hand till I know *how* you love me. I have seen many a scene of wedded life, which rather than endure, I would shut myself in a convent for ever. Tell me then, tell me, if I become your wife, what am I to become? How are we to live together?"

Norfolk put his hand to his brow, for a moment puzzled by her question; but, the next instant, her meaning flashed upon him, and, with a glad smile, he looked up, and took her hand in his.

"Margaret," he said, "if you do love me, you are mine; for your nature is most noble, and the answer which my heart will give to yours, must satisfy it. If you become my wife, it is not to be the plaything of an hour, a child's toy, cast aside in every moment of weariness or caprice; but it is to be the friend, the companion, the sharer of all my thoughts. It is to be my consolation in adversity, my joy in prosperity, the leading star of all my efforts, the light of all my hopes. This is what you must wish to be, with the man whom you love; and that is what you shall be, I promise you, as noble, knight, and Christian."

Promises are very vain things, and Margaret knew it; but yet, with that answer she was fully satisfied, for it showed her that Norfolk was what she had thought him, and that he was one who could understand her, and could love as she wished to be loved. She felt that he did love her too; and she resolved that he should never have occasion to forget the attachment, which beauty might have first awakened, but higher qualities had confirmed.

Their mutual promise was given; and Hereford joyfully heard that his friend and his sister were pledged to each other. Two couriers were at once sent off—the one to London, to ask the consent of the renowned Fitz-Osborne, the lady's father; the other to Normandy, to crave the king's approbation of the marriage; for in those days, the noble, in his marriage, was as much a thrall as his own serf: and, while waiting for answers, the whole party remained enjoying all the brightest things of life—Love, Friendship, and Hope.

PART II.

Oh, fitful Fortune! The return of the first messenger brought confirmation of their expectations. Fitz-Osborne gladly accepted the alliance of the Earl of Norfolk; and, as he was about to sail at once for Normandy on business that could not be delayed, he furnished his son with full powers to conclude the marriage of Margaret and his friend.

The messenger who had been despatched to William, however, was longer absent. True, the distance was greater—true, the uncertain seas had to be crossed; but still the delay was longer than could be well accounted for; and both Norfolk and Hereford began to ask themselves if William could hesitate. If he should refuse his consent, what then? The very thought well-nigh drove Norfolk mad. To lose his bright and beautiful bride, to see her bestowed upon another, would be worse than death, he thought; and long and earnest were his consultations with Hereford, as day passed by on day, and yet no answer came. They now began, as man ever does when hope gives place to apprehension, to calculate chances against them which they had previously overlooked. They commented freely on William's character; they knew it to be cold, calculating, and cruel. They recapitulated to each other his failings and his faults: they asked themselves, what right he had to lord it so sternly over Norman nobles, to whose swords he owed a crown —he, the son of the tanner's daughter, how came he to have at his disposal the race of Fitz-Osborne? Even his oppression of the Saxons was remembered and spoken of. The two nobles had always pitied them. The famous Waltheof—the greatest man remaining of the Saxon tribes, whose courage, skill, and virtues had raised him so high even in the opinion of the Conqueror, that William had bestowed his niece upon him in marriage—was the intimate friend and companion of both Hereford and Norfolk; and they now expressed to one another their wonder that a leader so well fitted by his powers of mind, by his popularity with his nation, by his military skill, and his indomitable resolution, should have refrained from again raising the Saxon standard against the Norman duke, and waging a war of extermination upon the oppressors of his people.

"It is his religious scruples," said Norfolk. "He has profound reverence for the sanctity of an oath; and you must remember that, when forced to surrender York, he swore never again to wage war against the Norman race."

"Were those the exact terms of his oath?" asked Hereford.

"I believe so," replied Norfolk.

"What would be his conduct, think you, if he saw the Normans divided amongst themselves?" Hereford inquired.

"Ay, that would be a different question," answered Norfolk. "Heaven grant that the time may be far distant!"

Men cannot be expected to submit to tyranny," replied the young Earl of Hereford; and there the conversation dropped: but it was the germ of the most dangerous conspiracy that ever shook the throne of the Norman conqueror.

Three days more passed; and at length the messenger returned. It was to Hereford the letter was addressed; and it was brought to him by his favourite page, young Walter Tyrrel.

"Stay," he said to the boy, while he opened it; "e ay in the
room." With an eager look he broke the seals of the packet,
and with an angry expression of countenance he read the contents. It was a cold refusal to consent to the marriage of Margaret and Norfolk; and, going to the door, he called aloud
upon his friend's name, who was speedily by his side.

"There, read that," said Hereford, "read that; and then let
us consult what is to be done."

The wrath of the lover may be well conceived; but it was
even less than the anger of his young and impetuous friend;
for Norfolk's rage was mingled with grief and a feeling akin to
despair, while Hereford's was the fiery offspring of wounded
pride. Rash, vehement, and fierce were the words spoken;
and, with a terrible oath, Hereford swore that his sister should
still be the bride of his friend, let all the bastards in Normandy
say nay.

"Let us go and see Margaret," he exclaimed. "She will
not refuse her consent where she loves. Once married, you
cannot be unmarried; and if William dare to threaten aught
against us, he may be taught that to our swords he owes his elevation to the throne, and that upon our swords depends his possession of the crown. He cannot trample upon the Norman
nobles as he did upon the Saxon churls; and methinks if
Norfolk and Hereford give their banners to the winds in their
own defence, thousands both of Normans and Saxons will join
them, if they have any desire to preserve even a vestige of their
rights and liberties."

Thus saying, he turned towards the door to seek his sister
Margaret, when his eyes rested upon the boy, Walter Tyrrel.
"Ha, lad," he said, "I forgot that I had bid thee wait; but
thou art trustworthy I know, and would never betray thy
lord's secrets."

"Not to the priest in the confessional, my lord," replied the
lad; and, as he followed the two earls from the room, he murmured to himself, "Were I one of them, I would not wait to
unfurl my banner till it was in my own defence: I would strike
ere I was stricken; but they know best, I suppose."

"Well, what news—what news?" cried the old Countess of
Breteuil, who was sitting with Margaret when the two young
lords entered. "What news from Normandy?"

Margaret asked no questions; but her eyes fixed upon the
face of her brother, and she read there plainly enough the

answer which had been received from William. The ta e was
soon told, and Margaret's warm cheek grew pale.

"Out upon the unthankful hound!" exclaimed the old countess. "What will you now do, my children? Think not to
move him by prayers and entreaties. I know him well. He
is as hard as one of the stones of this castle; harder still—for it
you may hew and fashion, but him you cannot. What will you
do, I say?"

"Go forward, as if his consent had never been asked,"
answered Hereford.

"But there is one consent we must have," said Norfolk;
and, advancing to Margaret, he took her hand and kissed it.
"Sweet lady," he said, "if I lose you, I lose more than life;
and therefore, whatever may be the result to myself, I gain
more than I can lose if you will be mine: but remember, Margaret, ere you answer me in words—for I read the answer
already in those dear eyes—that, if you consent to what we
propose, you may have to share in dangers, troubles, cares,
reverses—many kinds of grief. Have you the heart to bear
them?"

"I will keep my promise, Norfolk," replied Margaret, with
a look full of affection. "What you are ready to risk for me,
surely I ought to be ready to share with you. Nor will I ever
regret, even though a tyrant should cast us into dungeons, and
separate us from each other; I should still know, and feel joy
in knowing, that I had kept my promise, and redeemed my
word to the man I love."

"He will have difficulty in caging us," answered her brother.

"He may mew a hawk, but not an eagle; and he shall find
that I was not born to strike his prey for him and then have
my wings clipped, lest I should soar beyond his call."

So was it determined; but both the young lords knew that
their course was perilous, and that the only chance—if indeed
there were a chance—of inducing William to bear their dis-
obedience patiently, was to show so formidable a front as to
render it dangerous to assail them. This was all that was proposed at first; and they bestirred themselves to gather together
friends from every side, and to form alliances with the other
great nobles of the land—not for the purpose, at least so they
expressed themselves, of waging war against the crown, but
merely to be ready to guard their own rights if they should be
assailed. It was especially an object to gain the celebrated

Waltheof, the famous defender of York—the last, the most noble, and the wisest of all the Saxon thanes, the only one for whom William had shown any admiration and regard.

"Leave him to me," said Hereford; "there is great friendship between us; and I will bring him over, notwithstanding his marriage with, and devotion to, that base faithless wench, Judith, William's niece. We must take him by surprise, however, nor let him know anything of our design till it be complete. He feels the wrongs of his people, although he bears them; and he will soon be led on to snatch at the first feasible scheme for avenging them."

"Were it not better to open his eyes to Judith's conduct?" asked Norfolk. "By so doing we should destroy her influence. And it has often grieved me to see so noble and so good a man thus basely deceived by his false wife."

"No, no," answered Hereford, with a laugh; "he would not believe me. He is a lover, my good friend; and lovers never believe. But hie thee away to thine own country, and prepare everything for the joyful day. I, and my good aunt, and Margaret, will join thee with all speed; and I will give thee her hand, let who will forbid."

* * *

PART III.

THE chapel of the castle of Inningham or Ixningeham, not far from Newmarket, was crowded with nobles of the land. Ladies and lords from every part of England were present to honour the marriage of Ralph de Guador, Earl of Norfolk, with Margaret, the lovely daughter of the house of Hereford. There was but one Saxon present: but tall above the rest, almost gigantic in stature, and with unrivalled dignity of grace and mien, towered Waltheof, the last of the great Saxon chiefs. The words, the irrevocable words were spoken; the blush with which she had uttered them was still on Margaret's cheek; the joyful light of love with which Norfolk had pronounced the vow was beaming in his eyes; and the benediction of the priest was given. He took her by the hand, now his wife, and led her from the altar to the great hall, where the marriage-feast had been prepared. Lords and ladies sat down together; and mirth and revelry reigned around. Every delicacy that France or England could produce was placed upon the board; and the

M

richest wines of Gascony and Poitou flowed in abundance round.
After a short time the ladies rose, and left the table, gathering
round the bride; but, with the men who were left, the revel
proceeded for many an hour. Some drank deep, and some
drank little; but the stream of conversation flowed more rapidly
as the wine circulated. Men's spirits rose; hopes and expectations that were dim grew bright; indignation at wrongs and
oppression became keen and found a tongue; difficulties and
dangers were forgotten, and obstacles were overlooked; till, at
length, Hereford rising with a jewelled cup in his hand, lifted
it on high, and exclaimed, "Death to all tyrants!"

He drank down the wine, and resumed his seat; but there
was not one man there present who, in the excitement of the
moment, did not follow his example, and, "Death to all tyrants!"
ran round and round the table.

Before another cup was filled, Norfolk was gone; but the
words which had been spoken were like a spark to a mass of
dry branches. Eagerly and fiercely, abuse was poured upon
the absent monarch; each noble had something to complain
of; and, under the influence of wine, each grief was told and
exaggerated. Hard words and coarse were applied to the
Conqueror; and determinations were formed in a state of excitement, which cooler thoughts would have shown to be rash
or impracticable. One only remained silent—Waltheof the
Saxon: and to him Hereford's eyes were often turned with
doubt and anxiety. It was not alone that the great Saxon
noble combined in his own person the earldoms of Huntingdon,
Northampton, and Northumberland, but it was because he was
universally recognised as the leader and representative of the
Saxon people of England. He sat silent; but Hereford remarked
that, according to the evil custom of his nation, he drank deep
—deeper than any other there present; and when the young
earl saw the wine had taken some effect, he pressed the subject
on him.

"My lord," said Waltheof aloud, "I owe William, Duke of
Normandy, much. He spared my life when I was his prisoner;
he has loaded me with honours and benefits, when he knew me
to be an enemy; and he has trusted no other of my race. You
cannot expect me to raise my hand against one who has taken
these means of converting an adversary into a friend."

Well, noble lord," replied Hereford, "each man must
..ge for himself; and we Normans hold that two men, as you

and I, may be good friends at the festal board one day, though they know they may have to meet in arms the next. Pledge me a loving cup to my sweet sister's health. Here, lords and gentlemen, is to Margaret, Countess of Norfolk. Joy be with her and her noble lord."

Waltheof filled his golden cup to the brim, and drained it to the dregs; but Hereford, more prudently, after having tasted his, set it down by his side; and then, as he saw the wine working its effect on Waltheof's brain, he plied him hard with many an argument, to prove that it was the duty of a Saxon nobleman to cast all personal considerations aside, and to aim boldly at the deliverance of his countrymen. He represented to him that both the Saxons and the Normans stood as conquerors of England, and that they might very well, when they had freed themselves from the tyranny of William and his favourites, live amicably together as a united people, dividing the lands by fair and equal portions amongst them. He represented in strong and glowing language all the evils which William had inflicted upon the Saxon race, and all the wrongs he had done them. His grinding oppression, his overwhelming taxation, his barbarous spoilation of a peaceful and submissive people, he dwelt upon: he represented that he had excited rebellions merely for the purpose of suppressing them, and making them a pretext for confiscation, if not extermination. He painted a terrible picture too of the cruelties which the Conqueror had perpetrated, of the executions, the massacres, the mutilations which he had commanded, till Waltheof's blood began to boil at this recapitulation of the wrongs of his people; and he, too, uttered rash and ill-considered words, which seemed to pledge him to the conspiracy.

At length, the young earl rose, saying, " Now, noble lords, we are all agreed that this can be borne no longer. Let each man hasten to make his preparation against danger; and, when the time comes, each shall hear from me where we will meet in arms. From that moment, we must throw from us every consideration but one,—that of how we may best secure the liberties and the rights of all."

The party broke up; and each man wended homeward on his way with vague and ill-defined visions of greatness, and freedom, and revenge. Even Waltheof pondered, with a sort of gloomy joy, the hopes of emancipation held out to his people.

But such dreams lasted not long with him ; and on the following morning he woke, languid, heated, dejected, with the consciousness of having given at least a tacit approval to a conspiracy that was hopeless against a man to whom he was deeply indebted. His heart smote him, and the more because he felt an intimate conviction that no peril on his part could produce any beneficial effect to his people, but that every forward step, in the course which had been set before him, would only tend to bring down further oppression and persecution on their heads. In this mood he rode forth, dark, gloomy, repentant ; and the more he thought, the more sad his heart became.

Fair, and false, and faithless, the Countess of Huntingdon was seated in her chamber when her husband returned to his dwelling ; and as soon as he approached her, she employed all her arts, and they were many, to wring from him the secret of the gloom which she very well perceived. At first she did so somewhat timidly, fancying that Waltheof might have discovered her infidelity ; but his tenderness soon banished that apprehension, and she went on more boldly. By persuasions, by entreaties, by caresses, even by tears, she succeeded at length in bending him to her will. He told her all ; and then added, " but I repent that I even listened so far ; and I will take care to frustrate this plot against the king, if I can but discover how I may prevent it without incurring the charge of faithlessness. Would to Heaven I could have some good advice ! but I can consult no one but thee, dear lady, without betraying my noble friends."

Judith would give him no counsel. It was not her object to do so ; and Waltheof left her to meditate over his future conduct alone. At nightfall, however, a messenger, bearing a sealed packet, left the dwelling of the Saxon secretly, and stopped not night or day till he had reached Normandy, and presented himself at the court of the Conqueror. He would give the packet into the hand of none but William himself ; and as he did so, he said, " From your niece, the lady Judith, mighty prince."

William opened it, and read ; and a flush passed across his brow, as if a flame had shone upon it.

A day or two after, Lanfranc, Archbishop of Canterbury, was seated in his large chair in his own private oratory. Beside him kneeled the noble form of the Earl of Huntingdon ; and the eye of the prelate rested upon him with an expression of tender pity and affection.

" Your secret, my son," he said, "is safe under the seal of confession ; and, some time soon, I will appoint you such penance as the Church is accustomed to require. But, in the meantime, if you will take the advice of a mere mortal friend, as well as the counsel of a spiritual father, you will, without an instant's delay, hasten hence to Normandy, cast yourself at the king's feet, and entreat him to pardon your fault, making atonement by a full confession of the whole.

Waltheof rose from his knees ; and giving the prelate his hand, he said, " Father, I will obey you to the letter. I feel that it is the only atonement I can make ; and if it lead me to the block, I will make it."

Within five days from that time he was at the feet of William ; and the whole tale was told. The monarch showed neither surprise nor anger, but raised the earl with his own hand, and said, " My lord, you have done well. I will take instant order that this empty plot of some idle boys shall be frustrated. In the meantime, you must, I fear, remain in some sort a prisoner, though in no very strict confinement. William of Morteville, we give him into your ward. Be answerable for him with your head."

PART IV.

UNDER the shade of an old oak, on whose wide and rugged arms, which in their young freshness had probably stretched over the mysterious rites of the Druids, still grew their holy mistletoe, were seated Ralph de Guador and his fair Margaret His arm was round her waist ; her hand was clasped in his ; her head leaned upon his shoulder ; all sterner thoughts were laid aside ; it was the hour of tenderness and love. They thought not of strife and battle ; they thought not of difficulty and danger ; they only thought that in spite of all they were each other's, and that nought but death could dissolve the bond between them. The honeymoon was half run out ; but yet not a drop of its sweetness seemed exhausted. Nought of bitter had risen up in the fountain of their love ; and Margaret felt that she was more happy than even the dear voice of hope had promised.

From the foot of the oak descended a gentle hill ; and from

the foot of the hill stretched away a glade, beyond which, and a low copse that cut it at the end of about half a mile, were seen rising the tall towers of Framlingham.

What Ralph de Guador said, and what Margaret answered, matters not much here. The words of love—of happy love—vary them how you will, are almost always common-place. All precious things are simple. The diamond is all of one nature.

But presently a figure was seen to emerge from behind the coppice, and ride rapidly up the glade. "Who can that be?" said Margaret. "It is none of our own people;" and she dwelt with pleasure on the words, "our own."

"It seems a boy or a dwarf," said her husband; and then as the horseman came nearer, he exclaimed, "young Walter Tyrrel, on my life! news from your noble brother, dearest Margaret. God send that they be good!"

A slight flush crossed his cheek as he spoke; for the Earl of Norfolk recollected the perils in which he and his friends stood, and thought with some feeling of shame that, lying in the silken lap of love, he had forgotten the sterner business of the hour, or at best had not given it that attention which it needed.

"My noble lord," said young Walter Tyrrel, springing to the ground and approaching, "I am sent by my great master, the Earl of Hereford, to warn you that Waltheof, the Saxon Earl of Huntingdon and Northumberland, has gone to carry his own head to King William, who will doubtless take the offering; and my noble lord further says that no time is to be lost, but preparation must be made immediately. He does entreat you, therefore, to raise all the force you can, and to provide your castles for a war. He will advance upon Shrewsbury, if you will come in the same direction as soon as your levies are in the field. You can meet, he thinks, midway between this and Herefordshire, perhaps near Coventry. But he begs you particularly to secure and fortify one of your ports for the auxiliaries to land, for whom he has sent to Denmark."

The boy delivered his message with graceful freedom; and Norfolk, starting up from the ground, exclaimed, "I have been remiss. I have been very much remiss. But I will make up for lost time; and now I will show what deeds I can do for your love, my lady dear. Back to the castle, Walter, as fast as your horse can go, and bid them have twelve horses saddled, twelve messengers ready to depart instantly."

The boy sprang on his horse's back, and darted away like an

arrow from a bow. Norfolk drew Margaret's arm through his own, and led her on towards Framlingham, saying, " Days so bright, dear girl, are in our cloudy climate ever followed by a storm ; and now, perchance, when you find the tempest howling around us, you may regret you listened to Norfolk's suit, and wedded him against a tyrant's will."

"Never, my knight," answered Margaret. " If I know my own nature, I was born to be the bride of such as thee. With my own hands I will buckle on thy spurs ; I will hang the shield about thy neck, dear Ralph ; I will send thee to the battle with a tear and a prayer ; but I will not set me idly down and weep when thou art gone. Thy spirit shall be with Margaret in thine absence ; and I'll move thy rich earldom from end to end to strengthen thy power against the tyrant's force. I'll ask mothers for their sons, wives for their husbands, to swell the ranks of my noble lord, and diligently and busily will I prepare, that, in case of reverse, you may have strength to fall back upon. Oh, that I could don the hauberk, too, and ride to the field by the side of him I love ! But what woman can do, will I do ; and thou shalt never in thy life have cause to regret that thou didst peril all for the love of Margaret of Breteuil."

The instant they reached the castle, twelve letters were written and despatched by the messengers. Each contained but six words, " To arms at Framlingham, for Norfolk ; " and by the end of the second day, a gallant force of many hundred spears, and a large band of archers, were ready at the castle for the march. During those two days numerous other messengers had been despatched to more distant places. The letters which they bore contained more detailed directions and commands to the vavasors and tenants of the earl. His line of march was pointed out, the halting places named ; and to all, strict charge was given to make no delay, but to join him on the march.

Messengers, however, arrived as well as departed ; but the news they brought was anything but pleasant to the ear. Odo, Bishop of Bayeux, the Conqueror's brother, and Regent of the kingdom, so the tidings ran, was already in the field with a large force ; while the Bishop of Worcester, the Abbot of Avesham, and the Sheriff of Worcestershire, at the head of a powerful army, were marching to oppose the Earl of Hereford, wherever he might attempt to cross the Severn.

This intelligence took Norfolk by surprise ; for the treacherous diligence of Judith, anxious to destroy her husband, was not known for many an after year; and no one could divine how the Regent and the other officers of the crown could be so suddenly prepared to oppose the insurrection.

Nothing daunted, however, the bridegroom parted from his bride, and, at the head of about five thousand men, commenced his march. Margaret, for her part, would add no weight to the pain which pressed upon his heart. She was calm, though grave; and though, at the last embrace, a glittering drop swam for a moment in her eyes, she would not suffer it to run over, but crushed it between the long eyelashes as it trembled on the lids. With streaming banners, and trumpets sounding, the young earl marched on; and from time to time his scouts brought back intelligence of what was passing in the country around. They thought the news was joyful when they carried the tidings that no force was in sight, and the country profoundly quiet. Nor did the countenance of Norfolk undeceive them, though the tale was not that which he wished to hear. He had expected that risings would take place in every part of England, that the Saxon people would start up and make some effort to break their chains, that the lesser Norman barons would take the first opportunity of resisting, armed, a haughty rule which galled their proud spirits. He knew not how tamely a nation can bear oppression to a certain point. All was still.

At length, on the morning of the fourth day's march, a scout came in, in breathless haste, to tell, that just three miles in advance, a large body of men, which he calculated at ten thousand, was coming rapidly forward.

"Then we will fight them," said Norfolk boldly. "Our good cause more than doubles our numbers;" and he marched on. But ere he had gone half a mile, news was brought that a considerable force was seen upon his right; and from the left, too, tidings came of large bodies of light horse scouring the flat country on the side of Cambridge.

The prospect was not pleasant, certainly. To fall back seemed impossible; and yet the odds were somewhat fearful. Norfolk thought of Margaret; but that thought did not sink his heart, or oppress his energies. "I will do great deeds for her love," he said; "then, if I live or die, she will love me still;" and, advancing a little, till he reached a slightly rising ground which he had seen before him, he took possession of the summit, and made the best preparations he could against the attack of a superior force. Calling the inferior barons and leaders around him, in a few brief words he told them that they must now each man prepare to do his best, and make valour supply the place of numbers.

" We have seen battles won," he said, " against much greater disparity than is here. Remember, where there is the more risk there is the more glory, and that one battle gained in such circumstances is more than ten victories with a superior force."

His final dispositions were hardly complete when he saw the lines of the light troops begin to appear, the *Genetaires* of a Norman army; and then, with banner and flag and pennon displayed, came on the overwhelming force of the Regent. The hearts of some of Norfolk's followers sank when they saw the long array of spears, and the green masses of the bowmen, deploying in line, and far overlapping the wings of their own little force on either side. Still they did not attempt to fly, and bore the first brunt of the battle bravely; but, at length, after a fierce and fiery struggle of at least an hour's duration, a body of the Regent's horse contrived to break through a thick hedge which defended Norfolk's archers on the left, and poured suddenly in amongst them. A panic seized the men, and, recoiling in broken masses on their own cavalry, they first carried confusion into the other ranks, and then fled amain, communicating their own terror as they went. In vain Norfolk strove to rally them on, to restore order amongst his cavalry. In vain he exposed himself to every danger. In vain he gathered together a body of two hundred of his stoutest men-at-arms, and endeavoured to stem the progress of the enemy, while others attempted to restore order in the rear. The disarray and terror were too great and too general to be remedied; and the only choice left for him was to remain and become a captive, or to make an energetic effort for escape. Three words explained his meaning to those around him; and marking out a part of the enemy's line, which seemed the weakest, on the left, the small body of about two hundred men, with levelled lances, made a furious dash at that point, broke through the opposing force, and issued forth into the fields and meadows. Orders for pursuit were given at once; and for twenty miles the chase was followed; but, by that time, the pursuers had become few in number; and

Norfolk, wheeling his small force, met them in full career, and drove them back with loss.

From time to time he was rejoined by a fugitive from his own force; and from them he learned, that they had been turned from the direct way to Framlingham by the appearance of some large parties of the royal troops between them and the castle; and it became instantly necessary to decide what was to be done, as the whole forces of the earl were directing their flight towards Framlingham.

"I will cut my way through, or perish," said the young earl, thinking of Margaret; but one of the barons who came from the borders of Norfolk and Suffolk, judging rightly the cause of his lord's desire to force his way into Framlingham, suggested another course.

"To Norwich, to Norwich, my lord," he said. "There were several thousands collected in the neighbourhood, well-nigh ready to march when I came away. I could not wait for them; but you will find them all in arms. Others from the field we have unfortunately lost will come in every hour, while the enemy's force will diminish; and I will stake my life that, within four-and-twenty hours, you will be able to march to the relief of Framlingham, should it be attacked. At present you would but lose your own life and your lady too. What can two hundred men do against a host?"

The counsel seemed wise. Indeed, it pointed out the only course which promised success. It was attended, however, with a result which Norfolk himself did not anticipate. He rode all night; and, early on the following morning, Norwich, then comparatively a small town, with the battlements of the castle rising on the hill above, was before his eyes. He looked up, and saw that the walls were covered with men; and that banners were displayed which he knew right well. The gates, too, were thronged with people, some going in, some coming out, and all in arms.

"Ay, this looks well," he said; and onward he spurred his jaded horse till it was under the gateway of the barbican. Then—oh, what joy and peace to his heart! There, on the draw-bridge beyond, stood Margaret herself, no longer surrounded by women, but in the midst of armed men and captains.

She sprang to meet him, with all a woman's love in her bright eyes. "Welcome, welcome, my dear lord!" she cried. "I sent out men to warn you to keep from Framlingham, at the first news of your disaster, which reached me from an uncertain source at midnight. Have they met with you? But that matters not. You are here, and safe from this bloody fray. And now forgive your Margaret for playing the earl in your absence. I learned that there were many more assembled here not knowing when to march or where; and I came hither with all speed with the small guard you left me. Doubting that you might be outnumbered in the field, and finding the castle unprepared for resistance, I have gathered together stores, and ammunitions, and men; and Norwich Castle can stand out a siege as long as Troy, or at least till my dear brother Hereford comes to relieve it. You forgive me, do you not, for taking such command upon me?"

"And thank thee deeply, dearest," answered Norfolk, embracing her tenderly. "Here, in my good castle of Norwich, methinks I can well set the tyrant at defiance till the people of the land wake from their long trance."

"Let us come in," said Margaret, gravely. "You are hungry, and must have food; you are weary, and must have rest. See to these good lords and nobles, seneschal. The earl will break his fast in his lady's bower."

Her look was firm and confident; her heart seemed resolved and high; but when she was alone with him she loved, she cast herself upon his breast and wept.

"Nay, Margaret," he said, pressing her in his steel-covered arms, "do not grieve, dear girl. Norfolk has lost a battle, but no honour. Fighting against four times his number, he has failed; but what man could do, he has done."

"'Tis not for that I grieve," said Margaret; "but I have news to tell that strike at the root of hope. The instant that the tidings of this disaster came, terror spread amongst the cowards here assembled. Five hundred have left the castle since midnight. Others are taking their resolution more slowly; but they are dropping off one by one."

"We shall still have enough of brave men left," answered the earl. "I brought two hundred with me who will hold out to the last. There must be more of the same nature in the castle; and with them will I keep these walls till the forces of Hereford——"

Margaret shook her head with a melancholy look. "Hereford has no forces," she said. "They are all dispersed.—Hush! they are bringing in the meal."

It was a very melancholy one; but Norfolk's resolution was soon taken. Shortly after noon, he assembled the whole forces within the place, in the great court of the castle; and, standing on the steps of the donjon, he addressed them in a loud clear voice :—

"My friends and fellow-soldiers," he said, "reverses have befallen our arms—reverses produced by the fears of a small number amongst us spreading confusion and disarray amongst the rest. In a few hours the troops of the Regent will be beneath these walls. I would not have any one stay who may bring doubt and hesitation into our councils. Let every man who fears to remain, take his departure at once; but there are those who, like myself, have no chance of pardon or peace from that oppressive lord whom our swords helped to raise to the throne, and who now repays us with ingratitude and wrong. Their only chance is to remain within these walls, and, by a gallant defence, to gain terms of peace from our enemy. He is unjust and tyrannical; but he will not break a sworn capitulation with brave men. Nevertheless, I ask no one to remain. Let every one go, and go at once, who pleases."

The defection was terrible. Within two hours, each man had shown himself in his true colours; and between three and four hundred were all that remained to defend the castle against the forces of the Regent. Nor were those forces long in appearing; for, just as the sun was setting in his glory, dark lines of lances and armed men appeared against the glowing sky, and ere the next morning dawned, the castle was invested.

Margaret and Norfolk stood on the battlements of the keep, and gazed around them. It was a sight to make the heart sink indeed. There lay, on one side, the fair town of Norwich, spread out beneath their feet on the banks of the Yare; and there, hemming them in, appeared the camp of Odo of Bayeux, with the army drawn up in front of the tents, ready to advance to the assault. Margaret's heart did sink; but it was with fears for him she loved.

Before the attack commenced, however, a herald came forward from the bishop's tent, and summoned the place to surrender, proclaiming aloud that Odo, Regent of the Realm, was ready to grant good terms to every one but the traitor Earl of Norfolk.

The reply was to warn the herald back, lest he should be shot nt from the walls, for endeavouring to seduce the vassals from their duty to their lord.

Then the attack commenced; and wild and terrible was the scene. Large blocks of stone were hurled with tremendous force against the walls, the flights of arrows darkened the sky; ladders were raised; and the instruments of siege, as in that day practised, were pushed closer and closer to the ditch.

Margaret sat alone and prayed, while Norfolk, incessant in exertion, and in the front of every danger, animated his men to fight, and succeeded in repelling every effort of the enemy. Night fell; and no progress had been made against the castle. The troops of the Regent withdrew to their camp; but again, as the sun set, a herald appeared, and offered once more good terms to all who would submit, except Ralph de Guador, the arch traitor.

Norfolk, at that moment, stood upon one of the towers of the barbican; and, raising his voice, he demanded, "What does the bishop offer to Ralph de Guador himself, if he should surrender the castle into his hands?"

"Death, on the edge of the ditch, by the headsman's axe!" replied the herald, and withdrew.

<hr>

PART V.

ANOTHER day's hard fighting had passed over, and still the enemy had made no progress. The strong walls resisted every effort. The garrison repelled every assault. The troops of the Bishop of Bayeux had retired to their tents; and those soldiers of Norfolk, who during the day of strife had reposed on the unassailed side of the castle, now manned the parts which had been so gallantly defended for those twelve long hours of daylight.

Wearied and exhausted, with his casque thrown aside, and the hood of chain-mail cast back, Norfolk lay upon the floor of Margaret's small cabinet, with his head resting on her knee, and her fair fingers twined fondly in the curls of his deep black hair. She bent her head over him, and, though the tears glistened in her eyes, yet she spoke words of hope and comfort.

"Those who grasp too earnestly at happiness, dear Ralph," she said, "must ever undergo a period of ruth. The eager bargainers with destiny ever purchase dear the good they covet; but still, when the price is paid, they have it: and methinks much more will not be exacted at our hands. God is merciful; and even out of the dark evils which have befallen us, I feel as if there was a light springing up."

"Alas, alas," answered Norfolk with a sigh, "all is darkness to me! I have brought sorrow and destruction on you, my beloved, and that through your love for me. Hark! there are heavy steps in the gallery. What may that mean?" and he raised himself upon his elbow.

The next instant there was a tap at the door; and Norfolk exclaimed, "Come in."

The door opened; and, to his surprise, he beheld Brian Fitz-Hugh, one of his principal leaders and friends, followed by eight or ten of the most faithful of his captains.

A sensation of dread that he was about to be forsaken by those whom he most trusted, passed through his breast, and that of Margaret too; and, raising himself at once, he stood with his arms crossed upon his breast, gazing in surprise at his unexpected visitors. The lady bent her beautiful face upon her hands, but uttered no word; and after a momentary silence Fitz-Hugh addressed the earl in a firm but somewhat melancholy tone.

"My lord," he said, "my noble lord, we cannot hold out this castle long. The men are becoming exhausted with fatigue; and though perhaps we may resist for three days longer, yet, by the end of the third, these walls will be in possession of the enemy. I have taken counsel with your best friends, here present; each man is ready to die for you——"

"And I am ready to die for them, if it be necessary," answered Norfolk. "Remember, Brian, my noble friend, it was you yourself who bade the herald back; it was you yourself who swore last night that you would not purchase pardon and oblivion by the necessary sacrifice of your friend. I told you then I was ready; I tell you I am so now. Speak boldly, and speak truly, your wishes."

"I will drive no such bargain, noble lord," replied Fitz-Hugh; "'tis not for that we come."

"Then for what—for what?" cried Margaret stretching forth her hands towards him imploringly.

"But for this, dear lady," said Fitz-Hugh, "to tell this noble lord that he must fly. When he is gone, we can deal more freely with this proud Regent. We can embrace the proffered mercy, and insure our lives, though we may be bitterly mulcted in our estates."

"But fly!" exclaimed the earl; "how can I fly?"

"More easily than you think, replied Fitz-Hugh. 'Last night I foresaw this; and I determined to see what could be done, and to prove whether a single man could not pass unobserved from the castle, and return. Thus I was enabled to make sure of the possibility of success, to arrange completely for your flight, and to gain intelligence of the enemy's dispositions this night. The lad Tyrrel, who was sent here a day or two ago from the Earl of Hereford, undertook the office, went down to the mouth of the Yare, arranged for a small vessel to carry you away, and returned unperceived ere daybreak this morning. An hour after midnight a small boat with one rower will be brought as near the castle as possible. The seneschal has shown me the way by which you can issue forth, as you, my lord, well know, within but a very short distance of the river's bank. The enemy's line touches the river two bow-shots above; but the bank is unguarded, because they know that no boats are there, and because their captain in the town keeps any from passing by day. The night is dark; and seated quietly, without the sound of oars, you can drop slowly down with the current till you are past all danger."

"But if they should see him?" cried Margaret.

"They have no boats to follow," said Fitz-Hugh; "all the rest are at the other end of the town; and ere they could reach them he would be far enough. But, moreover, we will watch well on the battlements in arms; and one blast upon his horn, in case of pursuit, shall set Norwich in such a flame, that, on my life, the soldiers to whom the townsfolk have given admission shall have something else to think of than following a single fugitive. Better we all die, even if the worst befall us, than be forced to capitulate and fall by the axe, or be slaughtered here like a badger in his hole."

'True, true," said the lady. "You are right, Fitz-Hugh."

Norfolk mused for a few moments, and then replied, in a thoughtful tone, "I doubt much, my friend, that your plan will not succeed in that particular, without insuring which it were base cowardice in me to leave you. When we are gone, no such terms will be offered. The prey they seek will have escaped their hands; and they will take vengeance on those

that remain. Moreover, your proposal to capitulate will lead to
suspicion. I may be followed to the mouth of the Yare. Ships
must wait for winds and tides; and thus you will lose your
lives without saving me. Better, far better, that to-morrow at
dawn I sound a parley, make the best terms for you that I can,
and then yield myself to my fate."

"Oh, Heaven forbid!" cried Margaret. "No, Ralph, no.
You shall go. I am but a woman; but yet listen to me. We will
not let them know that you are gone. For three days you
say, my Lord Fitz-Hugh, you can defend this castle. Let us
defend it then for two, as if my noble lord were here. I, with my
woman's hand, will lead you on, and my life for it, they shall
never know that Norfolk is not here."

"You, Margaret, you!" exclaimed the earl, with a faint
smile. "No, dear one, no. You must go with me. You
must not risk the peril of falling into this harsh prelate's
hands."

"Forgive me if I disobey," said Margaret firmly, but tenderly. "Remember, Norfolk, the words that were spoken
between us when you asked my hand. Show that you hold me
as you promised then you would, not as a pretty painted toy,
but as your friend indeed; and let Margaret do her duty, as
her heart tells her that duty should be done. You must go
alone, my beloved husband; and, as for danger, I fear none.
We will conceal your absence, and defend the place till you are
safe away; and we will then make terms as best we may.
What! think you he would slay me? Oh, if he dared, he
would light up a flame in Norman hearts that soon would
scorch stern William on his throne. But it is in vain. There
is no man on earth dare hurt a lady for compassing her husband's safety. Say I not right, my Lord Fitz-Hugh, that he
must go alone?"

"He must indeed, dear lady," replied the baron; " else 'tis
no use that he should go at all. The boat will but hold two
men; for 'tis a mere cockle-shell, a painted toy, that skims
along the water like a bird, and will not bear much weight.
Besides, the more, the greater danger. I thank you, lady, for
speaking plainly that which I had no voice to say. It was
resolved beforehand that he must go alone. If he will stay, let
him not try to make a composition with the enemy; for we will
hear of none when he is sacrificed, and are resolved to die
within these walls. If the foe break in, we shall all perish—he

and you, and all of us. His only way to save us is to fly, and
fly alone."

" Then it must be so," answered Norfolk, sadly ; " but remember, Brian, to you I trust the only treasure left me. For pity's
sake resist not long. Measure your strength ; and, oh, take
every heed that you capitulate in time. Heaven, and Heaven's
Lord ! the thought would drive me mad, if I could deem you
would be rash enough to let the place fall by assault, when you
have the power to get good terms."

" Fear not, fear not, my lord," replied Fitz-Hugh ; " this lady
shall soon rejoin you in safety. Of that I pledge my word.
Else we will fight to the death, or slay ourselves—and her."

It was a rude speech ; but it was a generous one, according
to the notions of the day; and Margaret thanked him in her
heart for words which might have seemed to others as a
threat.*

Hours passed rapidly for Norfolk and his bride; for theirs
was one of those cases with which " time runs active." Oh,
how rapidly they flew till the moment of parting came. Then
the earl, disrobed of his armour and lightly clad, with nought
but his good sword and dagger by his side, passed down the
low-browed passage which led to the most secret and least
known sallyport of the castle. No one accompanied him but
his seneschal ; and the good soldier turned the key in the lock,
drew quietly back the bolts, and went out first himself to listen.
All was quiet in the town and camp ; but above on the castle
walls was the tramp of men, and the sentinels calling to each
other to ascertain that sleep oppressed not any of the watchers
on the battlements of the beleaguered place. In a moment
after, he returned, and, with tender reverence, kissed his young
lord's hand.

Norfolk passed forth from his stronghold solitary and alone ;
and the door closed behind him almost without sound.

He was alone in body, but another heart went with him.
Quietly, near the gate leading to the town, more than one body
of the little garrison had been assembled in arms. Their
leaders were on the two towers above, which looked towards
the water. Margaret was in a watch turret alone ; for she
would have none to witness her emotions. She strained her
eyes upon the darkness, to catch one look of him she loved ;
yet she thanked Heaven that she could see nought through the

* See a curious incident of a very similar nature in Joinville.

black veil of night. She bent her ear to catch a sound of his progress; yet her heart beat gladly when no sound reached her ear.

"He must have reached the water," she thought. "Hark! Was it a whisper of the wind, or the ripple of a boat?"

She could not tell; but she still watched and listened. Still all was silent. Oh, blessed silence! Had there been a voice, a call, a trumpet-sound, her heart had burst at that moment with its intense emotions. All was still for well-nigh an hour; and then Margaret heard distinctly the march of the party who relieved the sentinels in the town, and the challenge of the watch. "He is safe! Thank God, he is safe!" she said; and, descending from the turret, she sought her solitary chamber, and wept bitterly.

PART VI.

THERE were no tears in Margaret's eyes when, the next day, by the rising of the sun, she appeared upon the walls amongst her husband's soldiers. High soul and courageous energy were on her face; and ere she left the battlements the arrows of the enemy were falling round her. Neither then was she long away; for many a time throughout the day she returned, whenever she thought the spirits of the troops might wax faint; and, covering her silk attire with a plain hauberk, she passed round *apparently* as fearless as the oldest soldier there. With smiles, and praises, and thanks, and words of high encouragement, she animated all hearts; and not a man but would have died for that sweet lady with a right good will. Proudly, eagerly, they fought, and laboured under her eye. The bow-string twanged with deadlier aim, the mangonel was sprung with more terrible effect when she was present. She mastered all her woman's fears, though she felt them; and even when an arrow glanced upon her hauberk she started not, nor drew aside.

An old soldier, standing by, saw the shaft fly, and the firm, unblanched look; and, catching the hand of the dauntless girl, he kissed it, exclaiming, " God bless thee, noble lady, take care of your precious life! Were ill to happen to you, all our hearts would die."

The enemy near the walls beheld the old man's actions; and one of William's officers, standing by the Bishop of Bayeux, remarked, "There must be the earl himself. The man kisses his hand. With such affection round him as that, we shall not easily win the place."

"Pour me a plump of arrows on that spot," said Odo. "I do not think it is the earl. He is taller by the head than that stripling hauberk bearer. Yet 'tis no harm to give him a shaft or two."

But, unconscious, Margaret moved away, and, passing through one of the towers, escaped the fate intended for her. Night fell, and still the banner of Norfolk waved upon the walls of the castle; but sooth to say its defenders had hardly strength to wing a shaft, or hurl back a ladder, by the time that the sun set.

Yet Margaret passed one half the night in prayer.

"I would, indeed, essay them again," said Robert Fitzurse to the bishop, as they sat in Odo's tent an hour before sunrise. "We have lost three hundred men already beneath these walls; and if they are determined to die rather than yield their earl to death, you must mitigate the strictness of your first message."

"I dare not," said the bishop. "The king's commands are peremptory, not to promise life to Norfolk."

"Nay, it can be done without that," answered the other; "when men fight with the courage of despair, hope, be it ever so slight, will soon curdle resolution. Reserve the earl a prisoner for the king's disposal,—nay, even promise to entreat for him."

The bishop smiled, for he knew his brother well; but he said, "Be it so," and a herald was called, and despatched once more to the gates.

He undertook the task with some fear, and showed it: but still he went, and was absent well-nigh an hour.

"What say the garrison?" asked the bishop, when at length he returned.

"It is the Earl of Norfolk speaks, mighty and reverend sir," replied the herald. "He says, 'Go and tell the brave and noble Bishop of Bayeux, that Norfolk has not yet wiped off his armour the stains received by a fall from the bishop in a wrestling match near Cambridge. To-morrow, perchance, his hauberk will be clean; and then he will do aught that may be, to show his reverence for the king and honour to the bishop.'

"So he can jest!" said Odo. "Well, we will clean his armour for him. Bid the men advance, and tell them, if they win not the wal's ere night, I shall hold them cowards and recreants."

His words were without avail. Another day closed, and the banner of Norfolk still waved over the towers of Norwich Cast.e.

"I must win this place, or I am disgraced," said the Regent to himself, as he looked over a list on the following morning early; "so great a desertion during the night speaks ill of the soldiers' hopes. Ho! call the herald hither. Go ask if they accept our terms," he said, when that officer appeared. "Say, 'tis the last time they will be proffered; and mark them well: life, liberty, and arms, to all men within the walls, except the Earl of Norfolk. To him, a fair appeal to the king's clemency, which I myself undertake to entreat for him. Stay, I will go with you for a part of the way."

The herald once more advanced to the gates, while the troops, drawn up in line, ready for the renewed attack, waited anxiously for the result, well knowing from experience that the lives of many hung upon that moment.

After a brief conversation with some armed men upon the barbican, the herald returned with a more cheerful countenance. "They are mighty bold in words, my lord," he said, "yet will they accept the terms, on the addition of one slight condition, which methinks you will easily grant."

"I will grant no more!" said Odo, fiercely.

"Then they bid you begin the attack at once," said the herald; "and if you do win, 'twill be a bloody victory. Yet hear the condition, mighty lord."

"Well, speak it!" answered the Regent.

"They say," replied the herald, "that you offer life and liberty to every *man* within the walls except the earl; but you say nought of the women. They demand the same assurance for the countess and her maids, and that you will not by any means, direct or indirect, endeavour to separate her from her husband."

"Granted, granted!" cried the prelate with a laugh, "I do not fight with ladies. Back to your tents and sports, good soldiers! The place capitulates, and we shall soon march merrily back to London."

"They must have a charter under your hand and seal, my lord," said the herald, "with that condition clear

"So be it," said the Regent; and, retiring to his tent with a scribe, the terms were soon set down at full, subscribed, and sealed.

By the tenour of these conditions, the nobles and knights, ever with the exception of Ralph de Guador, Earl of Norfolk, were to march out of Norwich Castle at noon; and the castle, with all its stores, ammunition, and arms, except the personal arms and money of the garrison, was to be surrendered to the Regent; and as the sun neared the meridian, Odo of Bayeux approached the gates, with a large train, to receive possession.

Exactly at the hour appointed, the gate of the barbican was thrown open; and in regular order the train issued forth. First came the archers, two by two, in their steel caps and light shirts of mail, and then the horsemen one by one. They were barefaced; and each paused for an instant before the princely prelate, and turned towards him and his train with an inclination of the head, to let him see that the earl did not pass unnoticed amongst them. When they had proceeded about a hundred yards beyond the bishop, both bodies drew up in array; and then appeared a page, leading a war-horse fully caparisoned. Then came a bevy of terrified girls on horseback, with their veils thrown back and their faces shown; and, at last, on foot, fully armed, leading the horse of the Countess Margaret, appeared Brian Fitz-Hugh. Margaret's beautiful face was somewhat pale; and still she wore the light gabardine of chain mail which she assumed after her husband's departure. In her hands she bore the keys of the castle; and, slowly approaching the bishop, she offered them to him, as he gazed upon her exceeding beauty with admiration and surprise.

"My lord," she said, "I bring you the keys of Norwich Castle, which I have boldly defended for my husband, its lord. I beseech you to pardon me that I have resisted your power thus long, which I have done only out of duty towards him whom I am bound to love and respect."

"Lady, lady, what is this?" exclaimed the bishop. "You defend the castle! Where is the lord, your husband?"

"I trust at his castle of Dol, in Brittany," replied Margaret; "but perhaps you know better. I have not seen him for some days."

"Out upon it—this is treachery!" exclaimed Odo of Bayeux. "I have a mind to call up the troops, and make every one prisoner."

"Nay, for your honour and good faith," answered Margaret, —the look of high courage coming into her face again,—"keep your plighted word with a woman."

"But it was gained from us treacherously," exclaimed the bishop; "or, more likely still, you have taken advantage of our easy trust, and passed him forth from the castle since the treaty was signed."

"No, on my honour," answered Margaret. "He has not been within these walls for several days. 'Tis I who have defended them. I have commanded. I have shared the soldiers' danger. Had your eyes been sharp, you might have seen me on the battlements; for I saw you right well. But there is no mistaking Odo of Bayeux," she added; "me, in my littleness, your eyes might well pass over."

"I do remember, I do remember," said the bishop thoughtfully. "I saw a slight form, like a woman's, on the walls, and a soldier kiss her hand."

"Well, then," continued Margaret, "as you are noble, gentleman, prelate, and Christian prince, keep faith with that woman, and own she has done well in using her small power to cover her lord's retreat. You will find, within those walls, I have kept faith with you. I have left all, and everything, except that which is merely needful for my journey. Arms, stores which would have held out the place for many a week, jewels, and plate, and money,—all are there. So help me Heaven, as I would not in the least violate the convention to which we both have pledged ourselves. Do you keep it too, my lord, and bring no dishonour on your noble name."

"Well, be it so," replied the bishop. "For my own part, lady, I would fain keep you with me, and show you to the world as a marvel of true love and faithfulness. But I will do no wrong to Fitz-Osborne's daughter; although, in truth, I fear my good, stern brother will look somewhat askance at me, when he hears I have let Norfolk slip out of my grasp."

As he spoke, he advanced on foot to the side of her horse, and gallantly kissed her hand. "Wait yet one moment," he said, "I will mount and escort you past our lines; and I beseech you, tell your lord, that were I not wedded to the Church, I should envy him his earthly bride."

The colour mounted into Margaret's cheek; but she merely bowed her head in silence, and then, accompanied by the bishop and his train on horseback, passed on her way till she was two miles from Norwich.

There Odo took his leave; and Margaret and her little band rode forward.

PART VII.

Some months had passed since the fall of Norwich Castle, when, at the small town of St. Hilaire, on the confines of Brittany and Normandy, a lady sat alone and wept. A few minutes after, a nun entered the room with a beaming face.

"Weep not, dear lady, weep not," she exclaimed, "there are better tidings. Your noble lord may yet be saved."

"Indeed!" exclaimed Margaret, starting up, and brushing the tears from her eyes; "indeed!" but then she shook her head, and in a sorrowful tone added, "It is impossible. Has not the tyrant sworn, that he will leave his bones beneath the walls of Dol, or have the blood of my dear husband?"

"True, true," said the nun; "but man strives in vain against God's will. The King of France is marching with a mighty power. The Duke of Brittany is in arms likewise. This news is three days òld, déar lady; and ere now——"

"A battle may have been fought, and my poor Norfolk lost!" replied Margaret sadly.

"Think not so, think not so," said the nun. "Put your trust in God, and he will deliver you."

"I have no other trust," answered Margaret. "I do beseech you, good sister, send out one of my people to gather news. 'Tis strange we are so near, and tidings come so tardily.— Hark! what is that?"

"Horse galloping through the streets!" cried the nun. "I will go up into the tower above the gates and see.—Joy, joy, lady!" cried the nun, returning after a short absence; "Dol is delivered! the siege is raised! Yesterday at noon the King of France appeared; and William instantly commenced his retreat. The earl, they say, came forth with all his troops, fell on his rear, and took his camp and baggage."

Margaret clasped her hands, and raised her eyes to heaven. "Now God send us peace at last!" she said. "If I know Norfolk well, he will be moderate in victory. Now, good

sister, I will to the chapel, and pray to God to grant me the
spirit of peace, although I fear this stern King of England, who
by war has risen and thriven, will still keep the sword undrawn.
Oh, how many woes there are in ambition!"

Margaret knelt and prayed; and before the altar she remained more than an hour; and her whole heart was with her
prayers. So much so, that she noticed not the sounds without.
Yet there was noise enough in the small town; for every moment arrived fresh troops from before Dol, though the trumpet
sounded not, and the voice of the clarion was still.

At length she was roused by a ringing step upon the pavement of the chapel. It was firm and equal but very slow; and,
turning round, she beheld a noble looking man covered with a
steel hauberk, but with his head bare. On his heels were
gilded spurs, or goads as they ought rather to be called, for the
place of rowels was supplied by a long sharp point; and his
sword, unbuckled, was in his hand, with the cross pressed upon
his breast. His air was very grave, and his features were
stern and sharp. His eyes were fixed upon her; and he said,
as he approached, "Let me not interrupt your devotions, lady;
I, too, come to pray."

"May your devotions be blessed," replied Margaret, with a
feeling of dread, she knew not well why.

"How know you what my prayer may be?" said the
stranger.

"Because I would fain believe," replied Margaret, "that
there is not one man on earth so impious as to bring to this
holy place, and to offer to the throne of God, a criminal desire
or unjust petition."

"Indeed!" said the stranger, gazing at her, "Have your
prayers, too, been so high and holy, that the all-seeing Eye—
which pierces through the veil of mortal selfishness, and sees the
naked passions of man's heart—can look well pleased into your
bosom and grant its utmost desires?"

"I humbly trust so," answered Margaret, overawed by the
stern, bold man before her. "My prayers have been for peace
—for peace through the Lord of peace. I have prayed that God
would so turn the hearts of men and kings, that they should
lay aside hate and animosity, pride and vengeance, and, remem-
bering that they are brothers, seek that which was the essence
of good tidings from on High, when angels proclaimed to the
shepherds the coming of the King of Glory *to bring peace*."

"And did no other aspiration mingle with your prayers?" demanded the stranger. "Did you not ask triumph for a husband's arms, the downfall and reverse of tyrants, and vengeance for loss and wrong?"

"No; God forbid," cried Margaret, earnestly, "that I should insult God's glory by such prayers as that! Strange sir, I know not who you are that venture thus to question me; but all I asked was—peace."

"Stay," cried the stranger, as she was turning away. "Your prayer is granted, lady   Mine might have been of a less holy nature, had I not met an angel to show a better way.—Ho! without there. Bring in the treaty they proffer! Give me a pen. Here, on this holy altar, will I sign the peace which I just now refused; and God so help me as I keep it well."

A number of attendants poured into the chapel at his call, and one bore a large parchment, which he spread upon the altar. Another held an ink-glass; and the stranger, bending one knee upon the step, wrote in a bold free hand the one word—

" William."

Then, taking the parchment, he held it towards Margaret, saying, "Take it, lady! Bear it to your husband and his allies, and tell them that your virtues have wrung from William of England that which he had refused even to their successful arms. You were the first cause of war between us—you be the messenger of peace; for, now that I have seen and known you, I can well believe a man would peril life and fortune, his own repose, and a kingdom's safety, sooner than lose your hand." *

* The defeat of William before Dol, and his subsequent treaty of peace with the Count of Anjou, the Duke of Brittany, the King of France, and Ralph de Guador, are mentioned by almost all historians. The Earldom of Norfolk was never restored; but, by this treaty, Ralph was secured in possession of all his continental lordships, and the plunder of William's camp was estimated at the value of £15,000—an enormous sum in those days.

THE WILL.

BY MISS PARDOE

CHAPTER I.

It was a sweet summer night. Earth and air were alike still,
but it was a stillness which did not amount to silence; for the
song of the bird, the sigh of the wind, and the quivering sound
of the leaves as they were stirred by the low breeze, came
soothingly to the ear, and kept the mind awake to the sympathies of nature. Existence is in itself a blessing at such an
hour, to all who are capable of appreciating its purer enjoy-
ments. Wherever flowers were scattered over the earth, the
air was full of perfume; and the long lines of moonlight which
chequered the landscape, lay broad and pale, as though tempered in their brightness by the calm solemnity of the scene.

Nowhere were the flowers sweeter, the landscape fairer, or
the night birds more full of music, than around Greville Lodge,
at the particular moment of which we are about to write.
Without the house, all was calm and beautiful. The picture
within was somewhat less tranquil, less spirit-stirring. But the
fault did not lie in the locality itself; for nothing could be more
luxurious or more elegant in its arrangements than the chamber
in which our narrative commences. It was easy to see that
wealth and taste had gone hand-in-hand in its adornment,
and that neither had been spared. The lofty bed was hung
with silken draperies of pale blue damask, and the high bayed
window, which was flung widely open to admit the cooling
breeze, was similarly sheltered. Sofas and couches, of the most

fantastic variety of texture and form, were dispersed over the yielding carpet; bijouterie of every description crowded the dressing-table and mantelpiece of black marble; and more than one mirror of costly dimensions, panelled into the walls, gave to the room rather the appearance of an apartment prepared for the reception of guests, than a chamber destined to repose.

Such as it was, however, all its elaborate luxury was on that summer night subject of self-reproach rather than of enjoyment to the principal occupant; for upon the bed, whose silken curtains were flung back, and whose tasseled ropes were knotted recklessly together, to compress their voluminous folds into a still smaller compass, that no breath of wind might be impeded in its passage to the sufferer, lay stretched the dying form of Charles Greville, the coxcomb, the epicurean, the sybarite, and the sensualist—Charles Greville, once the Beau Nash of the ball-room, the Brummel of the banquet. There were neither sighs nor tears to disturb his last moments; and yet about his bed stood three fair women—pale, anxious, and terror-stricken, it is true, but displaying none of that beautiful devotion, that graceful self-abnegation, that holy energy, which women of all stations, and of all countries, occasionally exhibit, to an extent which may well put to the blush the colder and more calculating feelings of the other sex; and which they seldom fail to exert in a marked degree, even where their sympathies are coldly met, and their exertions grudgingly acknowledged. Here, however, it was not so. Mrs. Greville and her daughters surrounded the bed of death with one general terror at their hearts, one general question in their minds, " How are we to exist when he is gone ?"

Taken in one of its phases, the inquiry would have been pious, dutiful, and full of an overflowing love, which saw earth once more resolved into chaos, by the evanishment of the poor spirit that was even now struggling feebly to retain its hold upon the pain-tossed frame it was so soon to quit; but this was by no means the sense in which it was made by the fair trio in the death room. Each and all were thinking of the noble income which must expire with the selfish being who had sacrificed their future prospects to his own egotism; by whom the mother had been first deluded into marriage against the will of her family, who, in consequence, rejected her; and subsequently abandoned, with her infant girls, almost to penury, because her presence, and the knowledge that he was a *married man*, trammelled her husband in certain circles, and embarrassed him in all.

For long and weary years the mother and her children had been aliens from their home; and it is very doubtful that they would ever again have found themselves domesticated beneath the patrician roof of Mr. Greville, had he not in one of his periodical penances to advance the paltry stipend he allowed his wife—a duty, and about the only one that he entailed upon himself twice a year, because he did not think proper to entrust even his most confidential friends with the retreat of his family, lest the fact of their existence should be thus kept alive, and perhaps obtruded upon him at some unfortunate moment—had he not, we say, upon one of these occasions, despite his long-enduring indifference to everything relating to "the women of Hertfordshire," been irresistibly struck by the extreme beauty of the two sisters, who, at the respective ages of fifteen and seventeen, might have sat as models—the one for Hebe, the other for Diana.

As the fact forced itself upon him, *the Honourable* Charles Greville withdrew his eyes from his daughters, and fastened them, with all the cold fastidiousness of a virtuoso, upon his wife. The survey was perfectly satisfactory. Mrs. Greville had never been remarkable for a hyper-degree of refinement, but there was a decided air of fashion about her. The connoisseur under whose particular and scrutinising notice she had now fallen, took in at a glance that, although her dress was made of inferior materials (he could possibly have accounted readily for the circumstance), it was, nevertheless, remarkably well put together; in short, that she was what, with her fine eyes, her well-preserved teeth, her small hands and feet, her slight and symmetrical figure, her beautiful hair, and her careful toilette, a very showy, creditable, and sufficient person to place at the head of his table, to acknowledge as the mother of his girls, and to address as Mistress Greville in the hearing of his associates.

So far all was well. The exterior of the whole party was everything that he could have wished; but the recollection (for the first time painful) of the amount of Mrs. Greville's allowance during her eleven years of exile, forbade all hope that the minds of the young ladies could bear comparison with their faces. He saw at a glance that their fine hair was dressed with almost German skill and precision; that their pretty feet were *chaussés* with exemplary care; and that no exertion had been spared to

make their peculiar attractions *tell*, by either of the fair sisters;
but a shudder of anticipatory disgust came over him as he
reflected on the probable consequences of encouraging them to
talk! for hitherto he had never heard their voices, save in
monosyllabic replies to his arriving and departing courtesies.
which, sooth to say, were cold and brief enough.

Mr. Greville, however, in this instance as in many others, did
injustice to the innate cleverness of his wife. He had so long
accustomed himself to think only of one person who must be
considered at Greville Lodge—the dear self who was the alpha
and the omega of his own interests—that he entirely overlooked
the existence of that other probable instinct and intellect which
might, had it only a chance of asserting itself, be even a match
for his own, although perchance by a broader and less refined
method of demonstration. How could the unapproachable
Charles Greville speculate upon such a contingency? Poor
Mrs. Greville had been struggling upon £150 a year, deserted
by her family, and despised by her husband, who, so far from
esteeming her an object of pity, frequently asked himself, in a
moment of reflection, whether he were not over-indulgent in
permitting to her the use of a name which, in a paroxysm of
stupid passion, he had bestowed upon her; and with great
readiness permitting himself to be convinced of the fact. It
was, however, fortunate for the peace of all parties, that the
honourable egotist did not endeavour to act upon this conviction; for the lady, whose wits had been sharpened by poverty,
and whose naturally stirring nature was excited to still greater
energy by the necessities of her position, soon became aware of
the full value of the fragment of aristocracy which adorned her
name; and often did she boast to her girls, when they grew old
enough to understand her, that "the Honourable" had been
worth more than a hundred a year to them. And she was
right. We are a nation of tuft-hunters. Here and there a
nose may be curled, or a lip may be raised in scorn of rank;
but this sublime contempt is only affected by the saints and the
radicals, and no one quite believes it to be genuine even in
them. Deny it who dare, I again boldly assert the fact: we
are a nation of tuft-hunters. The folly is bad enough in
London, although it must be confessed, that, of late years, what
should have proved a most effectual cure has been copiously
provided in the persons of about as many foreign title-holders
as there are hours in the year :—

> " Strongenoff, and Strokonoff ;
> Meknop, Serge Lwdw, Arsoniew of modern Greece ;
> And Tschitsshakoff, and Rognenoff, and Chokenoff,
> And others of twelve consonants a piece."

Not to mention Poles, Prussians, Frenchmen, and Italians, or the family party of North American Indians, who some time since arrived in town to display their ring-nosed aristocracy and scarlet blankets to the admiration of civilised England.

What, however, is mere folly in London deepens into positive vice in the country. A baronet is a great card in a post town, and an honourable is a standing trump in a village. A knight's widow, or a relict of a town mayor, dubbed during his mayoralty, is not to be despised ; and no party can be complete without these local patricians. The handle to their names is lodging and provision to them. Let their impertinence only equal their necessities, and they are quite secure ; for no one would venture to be the first among the little people to incur the coolness of "the title." Mrs. Greville had soon become abundantly aware of this amiable weakness in the few visitable inhabitants of the pretty, shady, picturesque inland village, in which it had been the will and pleasure of her husband to establish herself and her daughters in a small "cottage of gentility," which he had inherited from a godfather; nay, so cleverly did she turn her advantage to account, that it not only secured to her the Welsh mutton and sherry dinners of her party-giving neighbours, but the cider, poultry, and eggs of the less distinguished parishioners, who, following the lead of the gentry, were ever ready to sacrifice a trifle in order to secure the passing recognition of the lady of quality.

To Mrs. Walker, the curate's wife, and Mrs. Parsons, the lawyer's lady, it was a great delight, during their periodical visits to their relatives, to talk of their "sweet friends, the Honourable Mrs. Greville and the two Honourable Miss Grevilles ;" for the worthy gentlewomen had never studied the peerage, and they consequently extended the distinction to the whole family without hesitation or misgiving; and had they ventured to resent sundry little insolences and over-reachings on the part of their dignified acquaintance, they must have forfeited this charming privilege ; a fact of which they were so well aware, that they did not even venture to admit to their better halves, in the security of a fireside *tête-à-tête*, that the mistress of Rose Cottage made them occasionally pay a high price for the honour of their countenance; nay, they virtuously endeavoured to convict themselves of injustice, for they felt that they could not forego the gratification of "pulling down the pride" of distant aunts, cousins, and nieces, who sometimes, upon the strength of a yearly trip to London, and an introduction to some third-rate milliner, endeavoured to overwhelm them with "the last new fashions," by assuring the triumphant possessors of the finery that they had been most shamefully treated, for that the Honourable Arabella Greville had worn one precisely similar two years previously, and that the Honourable Miss Blanche had declared that she was positive to having seen the same thing upon Lady Somebody Something, a cousin-german of hers, the season before.

Luxuries like these must be paid for. Poverty had added to Mrs. Greville's natural shrewdness. She was too clever a tactician not to make the discovery, and to profit by it; and thus it was that she condescendingly permitted Arabella to share the singing lesson of the two Miss Walkers, and Blanche to study the harp under the auspices of pretty little Mrs. Peters, the apothecary's bride. Then the five Parsons girls had a French governess, the wife of an *emigré* who died in the village, and who had imbibed the local passion for the Grevilles, because they reminded her of the *bon vieux temps* when she was herself *Madame la Comtesse de Ribedout*, and frequented the Tuileries, before *ce coquin de Buonaparté* revolutionised the capital of the world, and made a fine art *Mont de Piété* of the Louvre; and assuredly, nothing could be much more pleasant than to hear the *ci-devant* Countess and the helpless Honourable talking together in a tone of condescending regret of the joys and triumphs of high blood and exalted station; the one wiping away the scattered snuff from her lap with a well-darned *mouchoir*, edged with cotton lace, and the other ostentatiously spreading forth the scanty folds of her turned sarsenet. But even Madame Ribbedout, as she was familiarly called in the neighbourhood, did not enjoy this honour gratuitously; for it was soon gently hinted to her that while she was giving her lesson, it would cost her but little more trouble to include the Miss Grevilles, in which case she would be welcome to the tea-table at Rose Cottage whenever she could be spared from the lawyer's school room: and this arrangement, while it greatly benefited Arabella and Blanche, afforded a proud theme of gratification to good Mrs. Parsons, who talked largely of her

girls being educated with the Honourable Miss Grevilles, and
obtained for their mother the reputation of an exceeding
condescension, which she contrived to turn to account in a
variety of ways.

For all this maternal manœuvring, the husband and father
was, of course, by no means prepared; and thus, when upon
venturing to touch very delicately on the subject of the Miss
Grevilles' educational deficiencies, his lady blandly informed
him that Arabella had a superb voice, which required only a
little more training to render it almost too perfect for a private
room; that Blanche touched the harp like a tenth muse; and
that both sisters spoke French with an accent known only in
the Fauborg St. Germain. The Honourable Charles opened
his large drowsy eyes, and turned them in astonished admiration on his long-neglected helpmate. How had she contrived
all this upon the same income which he paid to his cook? He
quite longed to ask her; but he remembered his own dignity,
and he forebore.

Nevertheless, Mrs. Greville had gained an immense triumph
over the lethargic mind of her husband at the moment in which
he made the discovery, and she was by no means a woman to
lose her vantage-ground. The selfish voluptuary rapidly ran
over in thought certain recent twinges of the gout, an increasing obesity of girth, and diminution of calf—in short, the
ci-devant man of fashion felt a conviction that his reign was
almost over—that he must soon abdicate or be dethroned; that
he began to require to be nursed, and amused, and cosseted;
that, in short, he might as well make a home, by recalling his
wife and children to his house, to be the breakwaters for his
temper, and the slaves of his will; and accordingly he hinted
something of the sort to Mrs. Greville, who only sighed, and
remarked that she had now become so thoroughly reconciled to
a village life, and felt that her dear girls were so safe away
from the great world, and all its temptations, that with an
additional hundred a year, which the increasing expenses of
their daughters now rendered almost imperative, she thought
that perhaps, all things considered, they had better remain
where they were, at least for a time.

Mrs. Greville was decidedly a very clever woman. Her heart
was almost bursting with alarm lest he should take her at her
word; for long-endured poverty had only tended to make her
attach an overweening importance to money. She remembered

her manifold deprivations, and shifts, and expedients; and she had also glorious reminiscences of the pomp and profusion of Greville Lodge, with its powdered lacqueys, its well-appointed equipages, and its luxuriant table; but she had tact enough to feel that any appearance of eagerness on her part to close with the proposal of her narrow-hearted husband, would tend to make him hesitate; while, on the contrary, her well-assumed air of reluctance only confirmed him in his new resolution. It will be easily understood that when once the well-acted hesitation of the lady had given place to a meek and resigned declaration of her determination to act in all things as the will of her husband might dictate, the consequent arrangements were by no means difficult or intricate, although every preparation made by Mrs. Greville was accompanied by the expression of her reluctance to change the tenor of her existence, and her apprehension that she should prove unequal to the cares of a large establishment, after the limited nature of her experience.

The girls were by no means deceived, however, by the bearing of their mother; they were accustomed to her peculiarly involved system of action; nor did they lack penetration, even slight as their knowledge of their honourable father had hitherto been, to discover at once that thenceforward the egotist would be as thoroughly "managed" as they had themselves been. They had wit enough, also, to still the beatings of their own hearts, and to assume, under the schooling of their mother, an appearance of placid indifference very foreign to their real sensations.

All this was wonderfully agreeable to Mr. Greville. *He was obeyed*, and, he believed, at some cost; for he, worthy man! had so long been accustomed to be clothed in the "purple and fine linen" of the world, and to revel amid the "fleshpots of Egypt," that it never struck him how great their attraction must necessarily be to those who had hitherto known them only by hearsay; and that it was little probable that three handsome women, who had for years blushed unseen in a country village, should prefer the roses and clematis of their own small and inconvenient cottage, to the marble floors and velvet draperies of Greville Lodge.

Great was the pomp of the leave-taking when Mrs. Greville and her daughters were at length about to quit their little nook in Hertfordshire. The Honourable Charles had departed, after having assured himself that his orders would meet no further opposition; and a round of dinners were given to the mother and daughters, which were the more keenly relished by the former, as she felt that to these, at least, no return *could* be expected. But of all who wept, or appeared to weep their approaching loss, there was no mourner so sincere, and so sad, as the poor Frenchwoman. She could have said in her heart—" Ichabod, thy glory is departed," for she felt that the patrician tea-table at Rose Cottage was no more, and that for her there was no longer any world save that of the school-room; no memories, save those of regret and humiliation. Nothing could be more *à propos* than the violent attack of gout under which Mr. Greville was suffering when the fair trio reached their new home; and nothing could be more characteristic than the manner in which their transit was effected. They left the village in the solitary stage-coach by which it was traversed three times a week; and as the Walkers, the Parsonses, the Joneses, and the Peterses declared, it was quite delightful to see how snug and comfortable they were, with the whole inside to themselves, and picked up at their very door! At a town upon their line of road, they found a post-chaise awaiting them, into which they packed themselves and their slender wardrobes with considerable exultation; but within two stages of their destination, they were met by the roomy, well-hung, thickly-stuffed family coach, fitted up with as many imperials, cap-boxes, carriage-trunks, and sword-cases, as would have sufficed to contain all the contents of Rose Cottage, furniture inclusive.

Here they were requested by a tall footman, all powder and precision, to halt for the night, in order that they might make a new and more graceful distribution of their luggage, which they accordingly scattered through the multitudinous conveniences by which their several apartments were encumbered, as widely as possible; and, on the following morning, to their immense delectation, they found themselves rattling along behind four post-horses, with a couple of servants in the rumble. Arabella looked exultingly at her mother; and Blanche burst into tears. Poor things! All the three were too much bewildered by this unexpected turn in their fortunes to remark the fine and beautiful gradations by which, without one consideration for their comfort, the relative to whom they were now hastening, had saved at once his pocket and his pride. Human nature is a magnificent anomaly!

But to recur to Mr. Greville's gout. When the ladies arrived at the lodge, they found him seated in his morning room, in the " deep obscure " of a purple morocco lounging chair, with his right leg, swathed in flannel, resting upon a regent. Above the fire-place hung a full-length portrait of himself, by Lawrence, in a hunting dress, leaning upon a favourite horse. Beside his chair was suspended a miniature in a chased gold frame, covered with plate glass, of himself, in an evening costume ; there was a marble bust of himself in Roman drapery, standing upon a pedestal of *verd antique* between the windows ; and in a large panel above the door was an imitation bas-relief of himself in infancy, as " Cupid stealing an apple from a sleeping Nymph."

Despite his gout, Mr. Greville had every appearance of being " at home " in his own house.

The reception of the mother and daughters was coolly courteous ; but the elder lady had not been in the room half an hour before the egotist began to wonder how he had ever done without her. She understood him exactly. She dismissed the worn-out valet who was renewing the cold fomentation, and applied the saturated cloths herself with so light a touch, that the attention of the invalid was irresistibly attracted to the fair and dimpled little hand which passed over his shrinking limb like a breath of air ; and he internally chuckled as he remarked that the solitary ring which adorned it was her marriage ring—the badge of her social servitude ! Come what might, he had secured an admirable nurse, who could not " give him warning," as half a score of others had done ; and thus the bargain could not be a bad one ultimately,

Now, our friend Charles Greville had a little weakness, which is, however, as we are taught to believe, by no means peculiar to himself, but shared by many other gouty gentlemen. He was inordinately attached to what are called " the good things of this life ; " and when he should have applied " patience and water-gruel " he obstinate insisted on substituting turtle and champagne. His " fool of an apothecary," and his " bore of a nurse," had expostulated in vain. Who could possibly know what was good for him better than that idol of his existence—himself ! He despised patience ; and as to water-gruel —faugh ! it was the diet of the parish-unions. Turtle was at least the substitute—a poor one, it is true, but still the substitute for something recognised : champagne was a light, laughing, lovable beverage ; a liquid fit for gentlemen—it

could do no harm to those with whose blood it could blend
without discrepancy; *ergo*, it was the most meet and fitting
libation for the Honourable Charles Greville, with confirmed
and obstinate gout in his left foot, and certain flying twinges
on a voyage of discovery previous to location. Mrs. Greville
did not venture on contradiction. Her amiable husband dined,
on the very day of her arrival, upon stewed eels, curried game,
and lemon-cheesecakes—not one of which the affectionate and
excellent lady had ever heard denounced as unwholesome. The
gentleman was delighted: he had "for once," he said, "been
suffered to take his food in peace;" and, although he confined
his comments to that circumstance, he was possessed of sufficient
taste to feel that his table not only looked better, but was more
comfortable, with three fine women seated about it, than when
his solitary cover was laid at one of its extremities, and his only
companions were the supercilious and silent personages who
wore his livery.

It was pleasant to reflect also, that, like everything else by
which he was surrounded, the said ladies were *his own*, whom
he was at liberty to snub and twit as he pleased, and who were
dependent upon his sovereign will for all that they possessed.
The girls played their parts admirably. They did not venture
to call him "papa;" such a reminder constantly dropping into
his ears, would have recalled to the memory of the failing
voluptuary that another generation had grown up to push him
from his stool; whereas the smiling but punctilious "sir" of
his beautiful daughters, and the shrinking diffidence with which
they permitted, rather than encouraged, his occasional caresses,
flattered his vanity, and threw his thoughts back upon a thousand agreeable passages in his past life. Let it not be lightly
inferred, however, that any of his reminiscences brought with
them visions of self-sacrifice, even for the fair beings whom it
had occasionally been his good pleasure temporarily to idolize.
We have record that the Duke de Richelieu ordered his
servants to burn one of his carriages, because Mademoiselle de
Saint Amaranthe, of whom he was at the moment enamoured,
refused to allow him to set her home from a party where they
met; that the Prince de Conti caused a diamond which he
had offered to the Comtesse de Blot, and which she declined
to accept, to be ground to powder, and then made use of it to
dry the ink of the note which he wrote to reproach her with
her cruelty; and that the Fermier-General Bouret fed a cow

upon green peas at 150 francs the measure, in order that an opera-dancer, to whom he was devoted, and whom the faculty had placed upon milk-diet, should have her lactean draught in perfection. Our home-experience, although not quite so exaggerated, would nevertheless afford us some reasonable illustrations in the same style; but, after the three foregoing they are unnecessary. We are merely anxious that our readers should not do the Honourable Charles Greville the injustice to believe that he had ever been guilty of any such enormities. On the contrary, he had carefully eschewed all follies of the sort : he considered them as beneath his dignity; and, in the present instance, with regard to his daughters, the sentiment as usual began and ended in self. He wondered how he had hitherto contrived to exist without them; and therefore it was that, ere a month had elapsed, masters were secured at an immense expense, to perfect them in their several accomplishments, and that the toilettes of all the party revealed their Parisian origin.

The outlay was most judicious. Mrs. Greville in her point-lace cap and dress of rich satin, and the Miss Grevilles in all the elegant prettinesses of the existing fashion, were sufficiently distinguished-looking to satisfy even the fastidious selfishness of their exacting owner; and when the magnificent voice of Arabella, and the exquisite harping of Blanche, made eloquent music where all had before been silence, Mr. Greville began to reconcile himself to the fact of being not only that object of his former terror—a married man—but even the father of two grown-up daughters. Skilfully, while he was in this suave mood of mind, did the clever lady whom he had just reinstated in her rights, lead him occasionally to glance into the future. She knew full well that the sensual egotist to whom she had linked her destinies, had, when for the second time he was disappointed in his expectation of an heir, made such a disposition of the family property as to secure luxury to himself during his life, and to leave the unfortunate girls, who were unable to perpetuate his name, to elbow their way through the rough world as they might. But she was also aware that there was a great accumulation of ready money at his banker's, which he had been literally unable to convert into additional personal enjoyment; a fact which she had ascertained when, during one of his sharp paroxysms of gout, she had acted as his amanuensis. This was the golden egg over which Mrs. Greville brooded day and night. She had not the slightest dependence upon either the justice or the stability of her husband; nay, for aught that she knew, he might, as she told the girls, turn pious in his last moments, and bequeath this coveted hoard to schools and hospitals—and then, where were they? The matter was important. Mr. Greville was by no means a man with whom it was safe to trifle. The greatest delicacy and circumspection were requisite, for in mooting the subject, she was hinting at the possibility of his death, and, invalid though he was, he had the greatest possible objection to die at all. The point must, nevertheless, be carried. She had served a bitter apprenticeship to poverty, and had no idea of "setting up" on her own account, if either wit or determination could afford her a better establishment.

Not a word, however, turn, coil, and twine as she might, could poor Mrs. Greville extort from her husband on this all-important subject. When, newspaper in hand, as she was daily reading aloud to the languid voluptuary, who was too indolent to encounter its mighty columns for himself, she found some case of luxury transformed to want, from which she thought that anything like a parallel might be drawn, in vain did she eloquently sigh over the hard fate of the victims, and paint in glowing colours, broadened and deepened from past experience, the misery of such a fate, the refined habits marred, the fine feelings quenched, the noble aspirations annihilated,—at the termination of each tirade, even although it occasionally cost the lady tears as well as words, the Honourable Charles was either asleep, or feigned to be so; which, as far as regarded the purpose of his wife, came precisely to the same thing. In vain, when noble bridegrooms were united to rich heiresses, did she pathetically remark upon the all-sufficient power of wealth, and the utter impossibility of well-born young women, be their personal endowments what they might, "getting-off" in an advantageous manner, and doing credit to themselves or *their families* by forming high and honourable connections. When she paused for breath, Mr Greville either yawned or took snuff, or, if in unusual good humour, nodded his head in acquiescent indifference. The lady was very clever; but she was, on great points, no match for the egotist after all.

And so time went on; and Mr. Greville fasted upon Severn salmon, and Ascension turtle, and Strasbourg pâté; and the gout went on also. Now a pang, and now a pause; now a twinge, and now a truce; until it gradually made good its quarters, and commenced its final attack. From the toes it travelled to the ankles, from the ankles to the knees—then came shooting pangs, commencing the patient knew not precisely where, but ending everywhere; and still the toast and water was rendered "decently palatable" with pale sherry, and the gruel "flavoured" with cognac, and the barley-water "relieved" by Madeira; the worst feature of the case being, that the Honourable Mr. Greville was not, in the meantime, relieved by anything; and ultimately even he, obtuse as he was, both by nature and principle, on this particular point, even he began to think it just possible, when he felt beyond all stretch of further self-deception, that the enemy was actually invading the region of the stomach, that he *might not* recover.

And thus we have travelled back to the luxurious sick-room of which we sketched the interior some pages ago.

Truly, wealth is a fine thing, so long as, with his "purple and fine linen," the Dives of the world commands also sound health and wholesome appetite. Then, indeed, he may, in his selfish soul, laugh the sons of misery to scorn, and sicken at the rags and black bread of poverty and toil. He possesses all their riches, but they have none of his! There is no parallel between them; no, not one.

Peace, peace, repining starveling! who would find added bitterness in thine own scanty lot, from this conviction. Thou art revenged in the sick-room, in the death hour, at the grave's mouth, ay, amply, fully, wondrously convicted of thine error. Sickness to the labourer brings at least respite from toil; to him even the vapid diet of the hospital is a variety; death robs him of no worldly vanities. It wrenches asunder, it is true, alike with him and with his tyrant, the holiest bonds of affection, the closest links of humanity; the freeman and the slave for one hour bear the same agony; but unlike those of the voluptuary and the sensualist, the poor man's woes end with those natural pangs. He leaves not behind him the objects of his life-long idolatry, that they may pass to other hands— the stately mirrors in which he has so often gazed admiringly upon his own reflection; the hangings of silk and velvet, which have at one time sheltered him from the sunlight of summer, and at another screened him from the draughts of winter; the coins of gold and silver whose very sound and touch were luxury; the jewels and the raiment which told his tale of

prosperity and power to all by whom he was approached ; the
" harps, and lutes, and dulcimers " which had made music for
his idleness, though they often failed to soothe the evil spirit,
and the troubled Saul found no David among his minstrels ;
the tables at which he had feasted ; the goblets from which he
has drunk ; " the chariots and the horsemen " by which he has
been surrounded. The poor man, at the " supreme moment,"
is spared the struggle of expiring vanity and selfishness. He
leaves no worldly wealth behind to be cavilled for by eager
relatives, talked of by the idle and the interested, and distributed by the law. When he has rendered up " his great
account," the books of the world are closed upon him, and his
name is forgotten, save where it was registered in loving hearts
and lingering memories—and in the grave! Would the poor
man repine, even although he knew too well beforehand that
he will be laid there at the close of a pauper funeral? Nay,
nay, he hath no need to do so. Let him leave to the GREAT
their grim damp vaults, where shelved and lettered coffins
are ranged in ghastly rows; and relatives who have borne
deadly feud, or silent hate, the one towards the other throughout their lives, are piled up side by side in a wanton mockery
of kindred and affection, to curdle and decay together, and to
make one common feast for the same foul reptiles! Let him
leave to the RICH their tall and iron-guarded tombs, even
although thereon, deep graven into the stone, be set forth the
pompous enumeration of the many gifts and virtues, for the
first time freely and ungrudgingly admitted by the survivors.
Let not the POOR envy these. Upon their less assuming graves
the summer sun shines down blithely; the summer breeze
wanders lovingly; the wild blossoms and the wild bee are to
be found nestled amid the fresh grass that covers them like a
garment; the gentle rains of spring, and the silvery snows
of winter, come to them pure from heaven; and there is nothing
of man or of man's vanity, left to separate the creature from its
Creator. Let them remember, and find a hallowed and a holy
comfort in the conviction, that

> The stately tomb which shrouds the great,
> 　Leaves to the grassy sod
> The dearer blessing that its dead
> 　Are nearer to their God!

Mr. Greville was indeed a Dives. He had much from which
to part reluctantly in this world and thus, as he writhed in

agony upon his bed, his eyes wandered rapidly, and **f**r the
first time greedily, over the luxurious appliances of his apartment. He had never before felt their value, for he had never
before been conscious how very soon they would cease to
minister to his egotism. Everything had been done to lessen
the shock, as well as the suffering, of sickness, to the querulous
and exacting invalid. His medicines had been administered in
goblets of delicately-tinted Bohemian glass, and his "slops"
in cups of Sèvres or Dresden china; perfumes and essences
were scattered in every direction, in every variety of *flacon* and
sachet invented by modern folly; books, pamphlets, caricatures,
and journals crowded the sofas; forced fruits and exotic flowers
covered the tables; while washes, dyes, soaps, and powders,
and all the thousand puerilites for which we have not time to
find a name, but which are essential to the "making up" of a
ci-devant jeune homme, cumbered the ample *toilette*, as if in
mockery of the human pangs which were leaving wrinkle upon
wrinkle, and making of life an agony.

"Why do you all stand staring about me, as though you
expected me to die with every breath that I draw?" vehemently and suddenly exclaimed Mr. Greville, as after having
completed their survey of the apartment, his eyes wandered
over the pale faces of his wife and daughters: "Can you do
nothing for me, but look as if I had become an object of terror
to you all? Has not your boasted affection the power to save
me from one of these accursed pangs?" and even as the words
were uttered, he set his teeth hard, and clenched the eider-down
quilt in his convulsed fingers, while a cold damp started upon
his brow, as he cast himself back upon his pillows in a fresh
paroxysm of pain.

"My *dear* Mr. Greville," said his wife, in the accent of
gentle and timid expostulation, which she never attempted save
when she had some important point to carry, "do not reproach
us for our deep and anxious sympathy. Are you not everything to us? And yet, now I think of it," continued the lady,
as if struck by a sudden conviction, "the sight of *so many* sad
faces congregated about you may well affect your spirits.
Leave us, my dear girls, until Mr. Greville shall himself sum-
mon you. He is too well assured of your devoted affection,
for your absence from his side to imply neglect."

The young ladies, awaiting no second bidding, but inclining
their heads silently and gracefully to their dying parent, glided

out of the room. Mr. Greville looked after them as they dis‑
appeared, and, for the first time in his life, a sigh, which was
not for his own sorrows, rose to his lips. "What is to become
of them?" he murmured to himself, while the eager ear of his
wife caught up his low and tremulous words. "They are hand‑
some, very handsome; and if I have, perhaps "——Again the
sharp agony passed over his frame, and warned him that he
had to do only with the present; Mrs. Greville wiped the
clammy moisture from his brow with a handkerchief like a cob‑
web, and a touch as light as a gossamer; and once more the
wretched man subsided into comparative ease.

"It is too late now—too late—too late. It is useless to
torment myself upon the subject," were his next articulate
mutterings; "they must do the best they can. Marry—ay,
some men have a fancy for wives—they had better marry.

"Alas!" whispered the lady, in a tone of sentiment admir‑
ably suited to the occasion, as she affected to suppose that the
remarks of the invalid were addressed to herself; "*that*, my
dear sir, is *quite* impossible, unless you are good enough to
make a suitable provision for them; in which case there could
be no doubt of their success; for with a tolerable fortune, great
beauty, and the name of Greville, they would be very desirable
matches. But if you leave them penniless there is no hope.
They must then content themselves with a life of toil, and
mortification, and hardship." And again the embroidered
handkerchief was applied to the fine eyes of the speaker.

"Curse the gout!" shouted Mr. Greville, furiously, as a con‑
vulsion of keener pain than he had yet experienced shook his
whole frame, and distorted his still handsome features; "were
my limbs given to me only to be made the sport of devils!—
Don't whine to me, madam!"—he pursued still more violently,
as soon as he had recovered the power of speech. "Let them
work——can their labour entail on them such agony as mine?
Can the poverty to which they have been all their lives accus‑
tomed bring such mortification as mine, in thus seeing myself
chained down to this infernal bed, surrounded by a parcel of
puling women? Can any hardship be equal to living upon slops,
and swallowing the filth vomited by the foul shops of chemists,
and the surgeries of dirt-compounding apothecaries? What is
the use of talking in such a strain to *me?* Are you not well
aware that I sank all my property in a life-annuity? Do you
suppose me to be such an idiot as to have left anything to

chance in these days of failures and bankruptcies? You might as sensibly have suspected me of living upon boiled mutton and Cape Madeira! Spare me your reproaches, however, Mrs. Greville," he pursued, as he perceived that a sudden fire flashed from the eyes of the lady, and that she was about to speak, in perhaps somewhat less a subdued strain than was her wont: "I was assuredly a fool to marry, as I did, for a pretty face, when I was warned against it by every friend I had in the world, all of whom knew that marriage was the ruin of a man of my *caste.* I see it well enough now, and have done so for years; but where there is no remedy, it avails nothing to shatter one's nerves with regrets and repinings. I did it, and the thing can't be undone. I have little to find fault with since I summoned you home—I feel that I should miss you, if you were not here; and so I have considered it right."

The lady leant eagerly forward. Her breath came quick and short, and her heart beat rapidly. Mr. Greville had paused to give way to one of those long, convulsive yawns which are so universally the accompaniments of sharp and fitful bodily pain; and at its close, his own selfish annoyances were once more uppermost. "It is very extraordinary, Mrs. Greville," he remarked bitterly, "that you can remain so quietly and comfortably seated when you must see that the moonlight is streaming in through that window at your back, upon the foot-curtains of my bed, and producing an effect that besides wearying my own eyes, must make me look in those of others like one of the demons in Der Freischutz!"

Poor Mrs. Greville! She rose, and excluded the offending moonlight by drawing over a portion of the open casement a fold of the silken curtains. She had never been guilty of a poetic tendency, although during the period of her village residence she had entertained a certain respect for the moon, as it had occasionally enabled her to defer for an hour or two, upon that lady-like pretext, the expense of candles; but at that moment she would gladly have consigned all its beams to the bottom of a coal-pit! It was the first time that Mr. Greville had even been betrayed into a hint concerning the future,—he lived only in the present,—and she was shrewd enough to feel that it would require most able management to bring him back to the subject which he had so abruptly abandoned. The genius of Mrs. Greville was, however, equal to all exigencies; and she was by no means destitute, as has been already shown, of the same impulse of self-consideration which had throughout life distinguished her amiable lord; although in her case it had assumed a modified and less repulsive character. It was also certain that she could not, as the Honourable Charles had done, rid herself of all domestic anxieties by pensioning off her daughters with an allowance of £150 a year. Nay—the miserable woman knew not whether, when the painwrung and rapidly-sinking invalid before her should have ceased to suffer, she might not be left destitute with her two orphan girls; and it was therefore not surprising that her naturally quick wit was sharpened to its extremest power at such a crisis. Hitherto, since their reunion, not the slightest demonstration of attachment had been ventured upon by either party. Mr. Greville had once or twice, when she was about to head his table in an unusually becoming dress, and was looking more than commonly fashionable and distinguished, condescendingly testified his sense of the fact by touching her brow or her hand with his lips, as Sir Charles Grandison may be supposed to have saluted Miss Harriet Byron at the termination of their seven years of courtship; and Mrs. Greville, who had too much at stake to run the risk of offending by any unwelcome advance or innovation, had sometimes bestowed the same favour upon her husband on the receipt of a trifling figured bank-note, or the payment of a heavy bill for millinery; but beyond such courtesy she had never ventured.

She remembered the fact at the very critical moment; and with it came the conviction that she had now exhausted upon the self-centered being before her, every other care, and deference, and attention which it was in her power to exert; she had been to him, since her return to Greville Lodge, at once a companion, a secretary, and a nurse; she had never rebelled against his caprices, never disputed his tastes, never controlled his appetites; and what had she gained beyond present **luxury?** Positively nothing. She at once felt that she had **but one** winning card left in her hand, and that the time had indeed come to risk it. So convinced, she did not hesitate for a moment to act upon the conviction; and although it has taken a long time and many words to tell, Mrs. Greville had thought, and felt, and resolved all this during the few seconds in which she was engaged in shutting out the moonlight; and accordingly, when her office was completed, instead of returning to her seat, she moved noiselessly to the pillow of the invalid, and pressed her lips against his cheek.

The intense surprise painted in the eyes of Mr. Greville it would be difficult to describe, but there was no shade of displeasure mingled with the astonishment. It was a novelty for any one to act for themselves, in anything in which he was concerned; and to the *blasé* man of the world any novelty was welcome. They were alone, too; for the attendants were snugly established in the ante-room, profiting by the relief afforded by the administrations of their mistress in the sick-room; and thus there was no one by to remark his weakness in permitting the tenderness of his own wife. The lady saw her advantage at once, and felt that the ice was broken.

"My beloved Charles!" she murmured, as she laid her small cool hand upon his burning brow; "why cannot I, by supporting a portion of this torture, relieve you of at least a few of those sharp pangs? But you are surely better, just now, love! You are more composed—more tranquil. Is it not so?"

Mr. Greville was still half-bewildered, and did not immediately reply.

"Endeavour to rally, Charles," pursued the lady, as she sank down gently to her knees, beside the bed, without removing her hand; "think how much depends upon your life—your health—the happiness of myself and our dear girls! And they are lovely girls—are they not, Greville?—girls to be proud of, to be ambitious for, doing credit to their name and to their blood. Both, both beautiful! but Arabella incomparably the most lovely."

"Sir John Shepperton, when he dined here last month, thought Arabella very like me," said the invalid, fairly off his guard.

"Sir John has the eye of a painter as well as a critic," replied Mrs. Greville in the same low quiet murmur; "he could not fail to be struck with the resemblance. And our fair Blanche is perfect, too, in her peculiar style."

"' *Bionda testa, occhi azurri, e bruno ciglio,*'" whispered out Mr Greville; "a far more common class of beauty, but still beauty, I admit. Enough of them for the moment, however. I feel easier just now, and I would talk of yourself. Not that I have an idea that this attack will prove fatal. Dr. Phillimore looked as though he wished me to ask him *his* opinion, but I am not one to be hood-winked by the professional prejudices and jargon of a physician. I have no idea of paying a man for attempting to frighten me out of the world " (Mr. Greville had once more forgotten his wife in himself); "and as their absurdity about this, that, and the other thing driving the gout into my stomach—things, too, to which I have been accustomed all my life—it's sheer humbug, and, I verily believe, done purely to torment me."

Mrs. Greville bent down her head upon the thin, white hand which rested on the coverlet, and this movement brought back the thoughts of the patient to herself. "*You* have been more rational, Ellen, than any one about me. I owe you that confession, and you shall find that I have not been ungrateful. Shepperton volunteered to take all the trouble off my hands, and so I authorised him to purchase an annuity with the money that was lying at my bankers. I can do nothing for the girls; I have no means; but you will have £1,400 a year for life."

Mrs. Greville felt as though she should choke, but tears fortunately came to her relief, and they fell upon the hand of the invalid. "Spare me a scene, Mrs. Greville," he said coldly; "I am too weak to contend with violent emotions; and, moreover, I never had a taste for them; they are unnecessary and unlady-like."

"How shall I thank you?" commenced his companion.

"By giving me a tumbler of that claret—the last brought up; and by doing so without comment or hesitation. Had you been less prompt in complying with my wishes during your domestication here, I should never have racked my head, at such a time, about your annuity."

The lady obeyed in silence; and the voluptuary swallowed another accessory to the fatal disease which had now progressed sufficiently towards a vital part, to leave him without pain. The wine gave him a temporary energy, under whose influence he said suddenly, "Open that bureau, Ellen; the key is on my dressing-table. My cursed Will lies there—there, just in front, ready to be signed; and I will do it now, when I feel it to be a piece of unnecessary humbug, for I am better than I have been for the last month; and the thing will be off my mind. Call in four of the servants to witness it, and then Inkpen will, I suppose, leave me in peace."

As Mrs. Greville held the precious document in her hand, and prepared, as usual, to obey, without remonstrance, the orders of her husband, happy as she felt in the consciousness of her own future security, the conviction that her children were utterly without provision rendered her desperate. She had long ceased

to be scrupulous when she had a point to carry; and a thousand wild and impossible fancies swept across her busy brain.
Suddenly she started; her resolve was taken. She placed the
Will once more within the bureau; and gliding to the window,
closed it, without noise, and drew the curtain over it, as if to
prevent all interruption from without. Then approaching the
bed once more, she was about to address her husband, when he
exclaimed impatiently, "What is the meaning of this mummery?
Are you going to make a scene for a melo-drama out of the
signing of a sheet of parchment, which I shall, very probably,
destroy the next time I sort my papers; and only trouble
myself about to-night, because I have been worried upon the
subject until I am anxious to get rid of it altogether?"

"Bear with me one moment, my dear Charles," said the lady,
preserving all her self-possession for the great work which she
had in hand, and not suffering the impetuous ill-temper of the
invalid to ruffle her for an instant. "I will not try your patience
long. You say that I have been useful to you; that I have
been submissive and obedient, and have saved you from the
perpetual and annoying contradictions of others. I am glad,
most glad, that I have been thus enabled to perform my duty;
for I am as well aware as you can desire me to be that I have
done no more. And now will you forgive me, my dear Charles,
if I remind you that I have never yet ventured to make a
request of you? You may tell me, and you will be right, that
you have, since my return home, left me little or nothing to
desire. I am fully conscious of that fact also; but still I do not
think that you will refuse the first petition that I have ever
made to you, and I am about to risk it now."

"If it be anything reasonable," said Mr. Greville impatiently,
"it is quite possible that I may not; but pray let us get it
over at once, for I am beginning to be weary of all this circum-
locuti n."

"I would ask you, then, my dear love," murmured his wife,
as she again bent her knee beside his pillow, "I would ask you
not to leave your daughters penniless."

"Mistress Greville," said the invalid, in an accent of suppressed rage, gnashing his teeth as he spoke, "is it your pleasure to mock me on my sick-bed? I have already told you,
madam, that I have made suitable provision for my widow, and
that I can do no more."

"But indeed, indeed, you can do more, much more—all you

please, dear love, if you will only be guided this once by me.
I do not ask you for money, Mr. Greville. You have already
provided nobly for me, nor can the girls want while I live;
but, should I die——"

"It is not so easy to send people out of the world as doctors
and nurses would fain have us believe," growled the only half
appeased patient, curious, in spite of himself, to learn the
meaning of a mystery that he could not fathom. "Phillimore
wanted to kill me off ten days ago; and here I am, more likely
to live than I was five years back, although I have refused to
listen to his cursed croaking, or to follow his unpalatable advice.
I *am* better to-night, I am sure I am—and, therefore, if all
this rhodomontade is in any way connected with my Will Mrs.
Greville, tell me what you have to say at once, for I repeat that
it will soon be no better than waste paper; as, since I have
felt so wonderfully better, I have remembered that it contains
half-a-dozen things which I shall alter."

"Then, if so, my love," said the lady, coaxingly, "I am sure
you will not hesitate to indulge me in my caprice, and I shall
explain it without further hesitation. I do not think that I
need waste more words upon the subject. I want you simply
to make a codicil to that Will, and to leave our dear girls
£30,000 each."

"You are assuredly deranged, Mrs. Greville!" said the invalid, as he attempted to raise himself upon his elbow to look at
her more closely; but fell back again from excessive weakness.
"You are most assuredly deranged! Have I not told you,
till I am weary of repeating the same words, that I have nothing save my personals to bequeath? and yet you persist in
asking me to give my girls the fortunes of a duke's daughters'"

"Not to give them fortunes, my dear Mr. Greville, only to
append a codicil to your Will. Do you think it seemly or
fitting that *your* daughters should appear to be left portionless ?"

"But the money, madam; where is the money to come from
with which you wish the young ladies to be endowed ?"

"Nay, nay, dear Charles, all this war of words is sheer folly,
let me have my way in this whim; and surely you will do it
without further reluctance, when you remember that you have
declared the very Will itself will not, in all probability, be long
in existence.'

We will not intrude further on this matrimonial *tête-à-tête*

Let it suffice that Mr. Greville's Will was duly signed and witnessed, and before ten o'clock that evening; and that, mortification having succeeded to the violent pangs by which he had been previously assailed, the testator, after declaring once every five minutes that he felt better and easier than he had done for months, was a corpse within eight-and-forty hours afterwards.

Sir John Shepperton, as the most intimate friend and associate of the deceased, was summoned from town at the request of the widow; and it was with great but silent astonishment, that he found himself enabled to congratulate the Honourable Mrs. Greville on the fact, that her departed husband had compensated nobly for his early neglect of his family, by securing to herself a suitable provision for life, and by bequeathing to his daughters, each the ample portion of £30,000.

CHAPTER II.

IT was with considerably more pleasure than that afforded by the contemplation of the *fortunes* of her daughters, that Mrs. Greville found herself, by the will of her deceased husband, the sole proprietrix of all his " personals."   This at least was real and tangible; and as she moved, in all the solemn mockery of woe, through the gorgeous apartments of Greville Lodge, she found great consolation for the fact that she was compelled to vacate the premises within three months of Mr. Greville's death, in the consciousness that although house and grounds had ceased to be her own, the " furniture and effects " could not fail to realise a considerable sum, when consigned to the ivory hammer of the auctioneer; even without taking into consideration the miscellaneous articles of taste and value which she might deem it expedient to reserve, as certificates of the past, and resources for the future.   There was the miniature of the deceased in its chased gold frame—the likeness was undeniable, a little flattered perhaps, but the frame was beautiful.   The widow could not necessarily part from so very precious a relic of all that she had lost.   The family plate was what Mrs. Greville denominated in her own pet phraseology, "a capital nest egg;" the family coach was essential; the horses were sold off at once; and after satisfying herself that her weekly outlay was unnecessarily great at the Lodge, and that by leaving at once she might, to quote

herself once more, "kill two birds with one stone," she decided,
at the close of her first month of widowhood, upon writing to the
proprietor of the house, and at once resigning its possession :
upon the plea of her reluctance to prevent his occupancy of the
premises, should such be his intention, and her desire that he
should have the opportunity (still only supposing that he might
be glad to do so) of securing such of the "fittings-up" of the
house and offices as he might wish to retain.

Nothing could possibly have been more civil, proper, and ex·
pedient on both sides.   Mr. Adams, on the receipt of the lady's
letter, hastened to pay his respects, and to tender his thanks in
person ; for, being a moneyed man, and about to bring a bride to
the Lodge, he was naturally anxious that it should be spared the
profanation of a public sale.   Mrs. Greville understood his position at once ; and so did the clever agent who was called in on
her side to arrange the valuation of the property : a fact which
by no means injured the interests of the lady, who, after removing the thousand and one articles of *vertu* and nicknackery which
she decided on retaining, found herself in possession of the
gross sum of £3,000, realised by the remaining " personals "
and the well-stocked cellar of wine.

The next care was to discharge all the servants save her own
maid, the French *suivante* of her daughter, and the under-
butler.   Mr. Greville had not burthened his last Will and Testament with any legacies ; even his favourite valet was discharged
with a month's wages in perspective : and then Mrs. Greville
had, as she remarked to her daughters, " washed her hands of
the whole concern ; " and three days subsequently the family
coach was again upon the road, furnished with all its travelling
appliances of trunks, boots, and imperials, infinitely better and
more closely packed than when it had conveyed the fair trio
upon their first journey.

Great was the internal exultation of the party when their four
smoking posters were suddenly checked before the Imperial
Hotel at Cheltenham ; and " the Honourable Mrs. Greville,"
her daughters, Mdlle. Justine, Mrs. Buskbody, and the staid-
looking Mr. Jenkins, alighted, amid the obsequious greetings
and officious services of half-a-dozen waiters, headed by the
bowing host, and his smiling wife.   Nothing could be better.
The lozenge upon the carriage panels, the deep mourning of
the whole party, the trim-looking, pretty little *soubrette*, and
the perfectly respectable middle-aged air of the English servants,

sufficed at once to convince all present of the excellent position of the widow and her beautiful daughters; and ere they had thoroughly settled themselves in the handsome suite of apartments selected by the admirable tact of the elder lady, Mrs. Greville had already begun to congratulate herself upon the wisdom of her arrangements.

They had evidently created " a sensation;" that was a great object—for first impressions are always important. She had selected Cheltenham in preference to any other husband-promising place, because, although still teeming with very eligible invalids and valetudinary nabobs, she was aware that, as far as regards fashion, Cheltenham had been shelved for some time, and was consequently no whit too gay or diss'pated for her recent state of widowhood; and that the girls would have a fair chance of getting off, without any risk of reflection either upon her prudence, or the glaring unfitness of a frequented watering-place.

To the young ladies themselves all places were necessarily equally agreeable, if we except only the village in Hertfordshire which had so long been their home; and of which they retained certain memories by no means consonant to their present tastes and pretensions. It is true that the widow once more impressed upon them the necessity of prudence and economy—words which during her sojourn at Greville Lodge she had suffered to fall into utter disuse; but the fair listeners were well aware that even these obnoxious terms no longer bore the same meaning in which they had originally been presented to their attention; and they consequently only smiled and nodded, and smoothed down their glossy hair, and arranged their mourning collars, and looked pretty and placid. Nevertheless, Mrs. Greville was serious. She had, as she rejoiced to reflect, plenty of ready money for the moment; but hotels, and marriageable daughters, and second tables, are all expensive things; and if neither of the girls *should* marry during the " golden age," she remembered that they must all ultimately fall back upon the fourteen hundred a year—*her own* fourteen hundred a year; or—and this reflection was worse than the first—if she herself should see fit to run the risk of matrimony a second time (and who could believe that the opportunity would be wanting to a fine-looking, well-dowried widow of forty-five ?) the explanations which must inevitably ensue could scarcely fail to ruin her prospects.

Principle is a plain word, but its decided meaning is by no means so tangible. Mrs. Greville piqued herself, as she said, upon "always acting on principle;" and such being the case she commenced her operations for the forthcoming campaign, by desiring her daughters, on any and every occasion, to declare that they were (as they knew only too well was indeed the case) wholly dependent upon their mother. "Do not shrink from this confession, my dears," she said, in conclusion, after impressing upon them the expediency of the line of conduct; "rather, on the contrary, make a parade of it on every occasion; for by so doing you not only preserve your own veracity and dignity intact, but you disarm the anger of those who, self-deceived, may feel it their interest to affect to yield credence to your words, when, in point of fact, they only imagine that you make the assertion from a romantic fancy of being loved for your own sake, and not married for your money. That there are individuals who are weak enough to act in this way I well know; but in such cases the fault will not be ours, if they find themselves disappointed. At all events, *our* path is plain, I have explained to you what is clearly your duty, and what I beg also to assure you is most undeniably your interest. It now remains for you to obey me, and to do your best to provide for yourselves, while I still possess the power to keep up an appearance calculated to assist your views. For the present I cannot, of course, go into any society, nor indeed venture into public at all, save in the pump-room, where my weak health will explain my presence; but as it is by no means a part of my plan to shut you up in an hotel drawing-room, where you can neither see nor be seen, you must take a quiet walk every day under the escort of Jenkins and Buskbody; and I trust that I need not remind you of your deep mourning. More than this, it will be impossible for us to do at present; so we must live on the hope that, in some way or other, we may make one or two eligible acquaintances, under whose chaperonage I may safely permit you, before many weeks are over, to enter into the gaieties of the place, until I am myself able to become your companion."

The acute reader will now perfectly comprehend the whole scope and nature of Mrs. Greville's tactics. The effect which was produced by the foregoing harangue upon the minds and feelings of her daughters, it would be worse than idle to explain. They knew that they were handsome · their worldly mother had made them early acquainted with the fact, and had impressed upon them all its importance. They had been flattered and pleased at the idea of passing for rich heiresses—for they had not been deceived for a moment into the belief that .hey were really such; but they at once felt that their mother was right, and promised obedience the more readily, that they were well-inclined to trust to the power of that beauty which they had heard so much and so constantly extolled.

As Mrs. Greville sank back luxuriously in her well-cushioned *bergère*, and spread abroad the folds of her crape-covered bombazeen, she indulged unreservedly in a self-approving reverie. She had acted upon principle! No one could accuse her of attempting unworthily to deceive. The fortunate suitor who, having won the fair hand of either of her girls, received, on his application for the £30,000 bequeathed by the Will of Mr. Greville, a reply of "no effects," could not blame *her!* Would he not have been told over and over again, both by herself and her children, that they had no fortune? And could *she* be answerable for his unbelief? The good lady smiled triumphantly to herself, however, as she remembered that her servants were not undeceived—it was no part of her policy that they should be so; and really, if people *would* question waiting-maids and servingmen, they deserved to receive false information. And thus the affair was mentally arranged between Mrs. Greville and her conscieuce; and having eased her mind of the burthen which had oppressed it, the worthy lady yielded to an inclination which was frequently her " custom i' the afternoon," and soon slept the sleep of the virtuous.

There is a trite, old apophthegm, which assures us that Fortune favours the bold; and, assuredly, our friend, Mrs. Greville, proved no exception to the rule. How, indeed, could she fail, when all had been so admirably arranged? The widowed and handsome mother, seen only transiently when her sable veil was lifted for an instant in the pump-room, or as her well-appointed carriage passed along the street; the two beautiful sisters, looking only the more lovely from the interest inspired by their deep mourning dresses, walking pensively along, arm in arm, followed by the grave footman, and guarded by the starched and somewhat sour-looking duenna. No effort was made by any of the party to form acquaintance, or to mingle in the frivolities of the butterfly-crowd about them. What could be more undeniably correct or desirable? And then, when the position of Mrs. Greville, and the beauty and fortune of her daughters were considered — for Buskbody and Jenkins had exchanged all the family secrets for sundry savoury suppers and social cups of tea, shared, indifferently, with the head servants of the other hotel guests—who could desire more eligible acquaintance ?

"And did the man positively assert, from his own know'edge, that these Miss Grevilles were rich heiresses, Collins ?" asked Lady Dampmore, of her woman, as she sat before her toilette-glass, putting the last touch of rouge to a cheek already out-blooming nature. "I always receive such reports with great reservation."

"I can assure you, my lady," was the rejoinder, "that Mr. Jenkins can't in no way be mistaken, for all the upper servants were by to hear the poor gentleman's Will read; and although Mr. Jenkins is only the Honourable Mrs. Greville's own man here, he was under-butler at the Lodge, and so was present himself when the lawyer gave it out, as plain as I'm a-telling it to your ladyship. The widow got a good fortune of so much a year, with thousands of pounds ready money, and heaps of pictures and silver; and the young ladies £30,000 a piece, all independent like of their mamma."

"They are very handsome girls, at all events," half-soliloquized the lady, settling her turban a little further back, to give better effect to a cluster of glossy curls, which did Isidore infinite credit; "it is really a pity that they should be shut out from everything on account of their mother's mourning. I have a great mind to call upon them. I must take it into consideration. Is the carriage round, Collins ?"

"Yes, my lady; and here is your ladyship's gloves and fan."

And Lady Dampmore hastened where her rubber awaited her.

By some strange fatality, the respectable person whose acquaintance we have so abruptly made, was, upon the evening in question, singularly absent. She was certainly, if not the most scientific, at least the most successful whist-player, generally speaking, at that period sojourning in the card-loving town of Cheltenham ; yet, on this occasion, she trumped her partner's best card, misdealt, and finally revoked. It was enormously vexatious, as she herself declared, and as the unfortunate gentleman who was her *vis-à-vis* had all along been thinking. It is a melancholy truth, however, that *neque semper arcum tendit Apollo ;* and even so the well-practised Lady Dampmore in her turn failed. She was more collected when, on her return from the rooms, she seated herself at her desk, and, before she prepared for rest, wrote and sealed a letter, which bore the address of—

"SIR FREDERIC DAMPMORE, BART.,
Albany, London ;"

and which ran as follows :—

"MY DEAR FRED,—You well know that I am always alive to your interests ; and well it is for you that I am so, or you would not now be in chambers at the Albany. However, your debts are paid, and you have promised not to game again : so I will not aggravate old grievances. We are going on much as usual. Two of our best hands have left ; but we are always sure of tolerable players at the crown table. My last month's gains did not quite pay my bill here, but I cannot complain, upon the whole. I am convinced that I could not do better anywhere else. And now to business. Among our latest arrivals in the house, are a widow with her two daughters ; sprigs of nobility, but all *solid* and *satisfactory.* The girls are uncommonly handsome, and have fine fortunes : £30,000 a piece, their servants say, but this is, I have no doubt. an exaggeration ; if it should be only £20,000, however, situated as you are, it would answer the purpose very well. You had better run down, *unexpectedly*, and look about you ; but don't come for two or three days, by which time I shall have made their acquaintance. At present they know nobody ; so I shall make my residence in the same house with them an excuse for calling. Take my advice, and don't let this chance slip through your fingers.

"Your affectionate mother,

"DORCAS DAMPMORE

"Imperial Hotel, Cheltenham."

It was with no slight satisfaction, that on the morning after this maternal epistle was written, Mrs. Greville received the gracious and gratifying visit of the amiable Lady Dampmore ; who, could she have read the heart of the widow, might have spared herself two-thirds of the elaboration of excuse and explanation with which she accompanied her advent. Never was guest more welcome. Mrs. Greville was beginning to weary sadly of her solitary state; and as Buskbody had received a hint from her new friend and fellow-abigail Collins, that *her* lady was about to call upon *her* mistress, nothing could be better arranged than the drawing-room of the mourning recluse. Lady Damp-more was positively dazzled by the waste of luxury around her, amid which was not forgotten the precious miniature in its frame of filigreed gold. They were both clever women, but the baronet's mother was no match for her new acquaintance. Lady Dampmore had all the courage of Mrs. Greville, but she handled her speculations roughly, and wanted the delicate tact and touch of the new-made relict. Had they exchanged *rôles*, for example, Mrs. Greville would never have mentioned, during her first visit, the existence of her son; while Lady Dampmore, on the contrary, expatiated on his numerous excellencies, and lamented over her hard fate that she never could induce him to give her any of his company, and must not venture to expect even a glimpse of him during her stay at Cheltenham: a place of which she declared he detested the very mention. Mrs. Greville most kindly condoled with her upon the privation, and almost before her visitor left the room, was busied in marvelling within herself how many days would probably pass before the young baronet arrived, and which of the girls he would prefer. The war of wits was by no means equal.

Meanwhile the Miss Grevilles sat by in graceful silence. Arabella was sorting silks, and looking occupied behind an embroidery-frame, wherein was stretched an elaborate piece of laborious idleness, admirably executed by one of the young people of Mrs. Wilks's establishment, which passed for an undeniable evidence of her own taste and industry; while Blanche, seated under the shadow of her harp, might have passed for a modern St. Cecilia. Altogether, the effect produced upon Lady Dampmore was everything that could be wished; and as she traversed the gallery to regain her own apartment, she gave herself considerable credit for the promptitude which had led her to secure so tempting an opportunity of retrieving the shattered fortunes of her *roué* son.

The habits of the Greville family were now completely changed. Nothing could be more considerate and obliging than Lady Dampmore; she sat an hour or two every day with her new friends; and it was amusing to see with what perseverance each lady sought to draw the other out, and how skilfully Mrs. Greville confined all her communications to her period of luxury and splendour. These confidential communions afforded her, moreover, the opportunity for which she had long watched, of lamenting that her poor girls had been reared in habits of expense which, under *existing circumstances*, they ought not to indulge. Lady Dampmore was at first a little startled ; but the remark had been made with such a happy, tranquil, satisfied smile, that she answered it by another equally unembarrassed, and merely replied that if every one thought like herself, the Miss Grevilles would have nothing to desire. Then there were always a couple of seats in her carriage at the service of her " young friends ;" and on the fifth morning of their happy intimacy, she actually carried them off to a concert, despite the well-acted reluctance and disclaimers of their mother, who entreated "dear Lady Dampmore" not to inoculate her poor girls with a love of dissipation.

And thus a week passed by, and both the elder ladies, each in the recesses of her own breast, began to wonder at the protracted absence of the much-desired baronet. On the eighth morning he terminated all doubts and fears by his presence, but, much to the dismay and dissatisfaction of his lady-mother, he did not come alone ; and, as if to annoy her still further, his companion was the handsome Charles Lorraine, a young barrister of family and talent, likely to turn the heads of half the young ladies in Cheltenham.

" Don't look so black, Lady D.," was the first salutation of the affectionate son, as the friends shook hands with the discomfited manœuvrer : " Didn't you write word that there were two of them ? Surely you never meant me to marry them both ! so I thought it only fair to give a friend a chance ; and if we can't agree about the choice, we can have a cast of the dice, and decide it in a business-like manner."

" Dampmore is as hare-brained as ever, you see, my dear madam," remarked Lorraine, as he watched the deepening frown upon the brow of the lady. " Do not, however, indulge him by putting a moment's faith in his rhodomontade. My errand in Cheltenham is not to marry a wife, but to visit a sick friend ; and as your son was also purposing a run down here, he good-naturedly postponed his journey for a couple of days in order that we might travel together."

This piece of information did not by any means tend towards

the restoration of Lady Dampmore's placidity. What mischief might not the absence of those two days have done! And then, as she also reflected, the sick friend could not absorb all Mr. Lorraine's time; and what chance would her sallow, attenuated, sickly-looking son have against such a rival? It was really too bad! Remedy, however, there was none; the evil was done; and thus her good genius soon whispered that she had better make the best of the matter, and not irritate Sir Frederic into opposition—a feat very easily accomplished—by any exhibition of displeasure.

Then, again, what her son had remarked was certainly a fact, he *could not* marry them both; and his title was something of a set-off against Lorraine's handsome face; a second flirtation might also cause a diversion, and prevent the attention of Mrs. Greville from being too exclusively fixed upon the movements of the baronet, and her mind from dwelling undividedly upon his circumstances, a study which would inevitably, as Lady Dampmore believed, induce some very inconvenient inquiries from the mother of the co-heiresses; and in all probability break off the match. Poor Lady Dampmore, however, clever as she was, did not understand Mrs. Greville. The latter lady was by no means disposed to be categorical or curious upon such points; she simply " acted up to her principles," and was as anxious as Lady Dampmore herself to avoid all unnecessary explanation.

An affectionate little note from the happy mother of a newly-arrived and unexpected son was soon dispatched to the widow and her daughters, entreating them to take their coffee in Lady Dampmore's drawing-room, quite *en famille*; and was accompanied by the assurance that Sir Frederic, even upon the mere description of her new friends, was most eager to make their acquaintance; and would, had she encouraged him in so ultra a measure, have already called to pay his respects. In conclusion, Lady Dampmore declared herself to be so very, very happy, that she required only the presence of dear Mrs. Greville and her sweet girls, to complete her satisfaction: and in this, at least, she was sincere, for " the Duke " himself never longed more ardently for the moment when he could exclaim " Up, boys, and at them!" than did Lady Dampmore for that in which she should salute one of the young beauties as her daughter. " Dear Mrs. Greville " was, however, quite aware that both she and " her sweet girls " were seen to much greater advantage in her own apartments, surrounded by the luxurious elegances of the dismantled Lodge, than they could possibly be elsewhere. At home they were a family group set in a costly frame; abroad they were still attractive, it is true, but they lost the advantage of all the silent implications of wealth which helped forward her projects better than words; and, such being the case, she replied by disclaiming the possibility of even visiting "dear Lady Dampmore" at so early a period of her widowhood; and requesting that, waiving all ceremony, the party would do her the favour to meet in her rooms, instead of attempting to lure her from what she felt to be her duty.

No hesitation to comply with so agreeable and reasonable a request was even affected; and accordingly, at nine o'clock, Sir Frederic and his friend were introduced, and most gracefully and cordially received by the widow and her daughters. Arabella and Blanche did their duty admirably, for they both looked beautiful; and Mr. Lorraine was soon ten fathoms deep in love with the majestic person and delicious voice of the elder sister. He was himself an excellent musician, with a voice rarely equalled in amateur life; and while Sir Frederic lounged listlessly on the sofa, keeping up what he denominated a conversation with Mrs. Greville, and occasionally addressing a sleepy remark to the other members of the party, his friend was singing duets with Arabella, and promising to forward to her, on his return to town, as much new music as would occupy her for the next six months. The mother bit her lips, and tried to look unconcerned; but the annoyance of Lady Dampmore was beyond all concealment.

Little, however, availed all her generalship; the signals were disregarded. The long lank limbs of her amiable son were stretched comfortably across the carpet, his mouth was close to the ear of Mrs. Greville, and the only perceptible symptom which he gave of enacting the *rôle* of a modern Cœlebs, was the occasional distension of his large, light, meaningless eyes, as he turned them upon Miss Greville and his friend. He seemed to envy their rapid advances towards intimacy, although he was too indolent to emulate them; nor did he show the slightest animation until his excellent mother hinted something about *écarté* (at which patrician amusement, *soit dit en passant,* she contrived, before the party broke up, to ease her hostess of five guineas), when he suddenly awoke as if touched by an enchanter's wand, and proposed to try his fortune against Blanche.

Poor pretty Blanche! Inexperienced as she was, she was quite conscious, from the comments of her mother on the receipt of the note which had collected together their impromptu circle, that it was an experimental meeting; and although she had, with the natural instinct of a free fresh nature, turned with admiration to the beauty of Mr. Lorraine, she had nevertheless been tutored in the school of expediency sufficiently long, to be quite aware that Sir Frederic was " a great catch," in spite of his saucer eyes, his sallow complexion, and his indifferent and almost insolent *insouciance*. Nay, so well do we understand the humour of women, even the youngest and the fairest, that we are not quite satisfied that the last negative quality quoted, was not the surest triumph of the baronet. In courtesy and manner he could not compete with his friend more successfully than in mind and person ; and the very attempt at rivalry would consequently have been premeditated failure : whereas, a woman considers it a triumph to her beauty when she succeeds in making a mass of inert matter, like Lady Dampmore's son, give signs of life ; and accordingly Blanche very wisely did not pause to consider whether it was herself, or the cards, which had awakened the gentleman from his trance, but very meekly rang the bell, which he suffered her to do without changing his position, and prepared to administer to his amusement in his own way.

It is possible that some young beauties might have felt disposed to rebel in so extreme a case ; but it must be remembered that Miss Blanche Greville had served a very stringent and effective apprenticeship under her honourable and egotistical papa, when she had imbibed very magnificent notions of the privileges of the other sex ; and that she had, moreover, certain very disagreeable reminiscences of the *nature* of her expectations : therefore, all things considered, she comported herself in a very prudent and praiseworthy manner, and proved herself quite worthy of the admirable tuition of her exemplary mother. So well, indeed, did she act upon the instructions which she had received, that she commenced her gambling campaign by objecting to the points proposed by her adversary, who, anxious not to lose his time entirely, even in the society of a beautiful girl, who *might* hereafter become his wife,—for he had as yet by no means decided that he cared which of the fair sisters he might honour with his hand, provided he secured the fortune of one of them,—thought it as well to win a few pounds by way of keep-

Ing himself awake, especially where money was so evidently no object; nor did she confine herself to a simple objection, for she very heroically accounted for her reluctance by saying that she considered it a point of principle that girls without fortune should not indulge in high play. The little expletive fell innoxious, however, for Lady Dampmore had already mentioned to her son this "peculiarity of the Greville girls, and their evident inclination to be loved for their own sakes." So Sir Frederic only smiled one of his inane and languid smiles, and left the points to her own discretion.

When the party broke up, the effects of this delicate policy were highly favourable to Blanche; for the gentleman was, contrary to all his calculations, a considerable loser. *Ecarté* had been one of the valetudinary amusements of Mr. Greville, and by dint of practice the ladies of his family were great proficients in the game. Their mamma had judged it expedient to lose to Lady Dampmore; for she felt that the five guineas which she disbursed were by no means thrown away; but Blanche, with the natural enthusiam of her age, threw all her energies into her occupation; nor could she have played her cards better under the circumstances,—we beg it to be distinctly understood that in using this expression we do not even mean to imply a pun,— for the astonishment of Sir Frederic at the skill of his fair antagonist was so great, that it enhanced immensely his respect for her intellect. Such a wife, properly managed, as he promptly reflected, would be a fortune in herself. As she won game after game, he looked at her more attentively, and remarked that her eyes were "darkly, deeply, beautifully blue," that her hair was like threads of gold, and encircled her calm, fair brow like a glory; that her arms and her hands were faultless; and that, in short, her £30,000 thrown into the balance, she was the very wife suited to him.

Lorraine, meanwhile, had entirely forgotten that Arabella was an heiress; he did not even heed her disclaimer when some allusion was made to the subject of money: he was dazzled and entranced. She was so very lovely, so very graceful, so very musical; he almost wished that he had known her as many months as hours, that he might have flung himself at her feet, and poured out all his passion.

A happy woman was Mrs. Greville when she sought her pillow that night. To be sure, Arabella *should* have captivated the baronet, but who could control destiny; and it was decidedly

a great stroke of good fortune that they had each secured a suitor
at once; for that the gentlemen *were* both caught, she did not
permit herself to doubt.   A few awkward misgivings as to the
final result of her policy did indeed somewhat damp the self-
gratulation of the lady, but she put them aside.   Sufficient for
the day was the evil thereof; and the girls had behaved
admirably!

The reflections of the rest of the party were less satisfactory.
With all her anxiety for her son, and the natural tendency of a
mother to overlook his defects, Lady Dampmore could not conceal from herself that neither in person nor manner was he
worthy of either of the elegant, and accomplished, and beautiful
Miss Grevilles.   He was ruined, too; his estate heavily mortgaged, and his word pledged for debts which he could not pay
off for years.   Had the fair sisters passed only one season in
town, the case would have been altogether hopeless, for they
must have heard much which by no means redounded to his
credit.   It was in their ignorance only that she had trust; and
she felt, moreover, that if Sir Frederic's suit was to be brought
to a happy issue, it must be principally through her own
agency, for that he was far too indolent to exert himself, even
in so extreme a case as this.   She remembered the different
bearing of Lorraine; the undisguised admiration which had
brought a flush to the cheek of Arabella, and given a tremor to
her voice; and she sighed to think that *his* success, at least,
was beyond doubt.   Despite all difficulties, however, Lady
Dampmore felt that the affair must be brought to a conclusion
with all possible and decent speed; some busy London friend
might warn Mrs. Greville before her daughter was committed,
and then all her exertion and anxiety would have been vain :—

> "Happy's the wooing
> That's not long a-doing,"

murmured the unfortunate lady to herself; "and assuredly if
this is long 'a-doing,' it will never be done; so I must refuse
Sir Frederic money the next time he asks for it, and that will
put him on the *qui vive*, and settle the matter at once."

"So much for running down to Cheltenham!" mused Lorraine, as he flung himself into a chair in his dressing-room; "I
have certainly taken leave of my reason.   How can I hope
that such an angel as Miss Greville" (N.B.—Women are all
angels with men in love) "would bestow herself on me?—I

have family, it is true, but her blood is as good as iL.z ;—talents, they tell me, but she is all mind—it breathes in every note of her sweet and exquisite voice ;—my career is scarcely yet commenced, my income is limited, and she is enshrined, as indeed she ought to be, in indulgence and luxury—and then, her money—ay, that vile money! That at once overthrow.. every hope :—Mrs. Greville is a woman of the world ; she will never listen to me, even should Arabella be induced to do so. I will leave Cheltenham to-morrow. I will see General Spencer in the morning, and start by the mail at night. I will go back to my solitary chambers, and——forget her!"

"Devilish deal of trouble, this love-making!" muttered Sir Frederic Dampmore, as, with his hands thrust into his trousers pockets, he paced up and down his room, pausing at intervals to swallow a draught of hot brandy-and-water, from a large tumbler which stood upon his dressing-table ; "Bore, too, staying at this confounded place, where there's nothing rational to do. I'd give her up at once, if it wasn't for the £30,000. Not but the girl's devilish pretty—and clever, too, in her way. Mighty quick at the cards. Egad, she's nearly cleaned me out ; and Lady D. isn't pleased after all. Says I didn't exert myself; after sitting quietly for two hours, and losing my money like a pigeon. There's no satisfying some people. However, I must try what I can do, and Lorraine must speak a good word for me ; that's only fair, as I brought him down."

And so Sir Frederic Dampmore went to bed.

"Well, Arabella, what think you of our new friends?" asked Miss Blanche Greville of her sister as soon as the two beautiful girls found themselves *tête-à-tête* in their own apartment.

"Nay, Blanche ; what think *you* of them?" equivocally retorted her sister; "you are the person who engrossed the coveted baronet. This friend, you know, was a mere supernumerary, whom we *may* never see again."

Blanche laughed and pouted, as she replied, carelessly, "Well, then, if you ask my opinion, I consider the coveted baronet a stick ; and, moreover, a very ugly one. As rough as an Irishman's shillelagh, as stiff as a marshal's baton, and as unwieldly as the staff of a drum-major. A mass of ill-compounded matter, as inferior to his dear, delightful, lovable mother as one human being can possibly be to another. I like Mr. Lorraine a thousand times better."

Arabella blushed; and her fine brows contracted with an expression very like annoyance.

"Do not be angry, Arry, dear," pursued the younger sister; "you have most decidedly made a conquest, and I congratulate you—but, as for *my* Cimon ——" and she shrugged her pretty shoulders; "I don't really think that, even all things considered, I shall be able to make up my mind to it."

"You are jumping very hastily at a conclusion, Blanche," said her sister; "neither of the gentlemen in question may have an idea of *us*."

"Perhaps not," said the young beauty, as carelessly as before; "and if they have not, I shall be sorry for you, Arry—I should have been sorry for myself if I had attracted the young barrister, for I should not think that there can be many Lorraines in the world; but, as far as regards myself, I am heart-whole."

"And I, Blanche? do you mean to imply that I am not equally so?"

"I imply nothing, fair sister; only I cannot forget that this is the first occasion on which either of us has been an exclusive object of attention to the other sex; and I am quite sure that had I been in your position this evening, I should not have come unscathed from the trial."

Arabella was silent.

"Heigho!" resumed Blanche, as she removed the comb from her magnificent hair, which fell like a cloud of gold almost to her knees; "they say that we are very pretty girls, Arabella; and it is well that it is so, as it is our only chance of being commonly comfortable in our marriage state; for it is certain that the men who marry us will most decidedly burn their fingers."

"We have now come to the point, my dear Blanche," said Miss Greville, in a tone of deep and unaffected feeling, throwing herself back into her chair, and pressing her small hand heavily upon her forehead; "I have thought, for the first time, during this eventful evening most seriously of our position, and I feel it to be an ignoble one, Blanche; mean and unworthy; an existence of acted falsehood and systematic deceit."

"What *can* you possibly be talking of, Arabella?"

"Of ourselves, my dear sister—of Mrs. Greville's husband-hunting daughters. Do not be angry, Blanche; but listen to me patiently. I am not about to speak harshly of our mother,

We will hope that she is doing what she conceives to be her duty; but the last few hours have taught me that she has mistaken her path; *your* eyes are not yet opened, for neither your heart nor your imagination are touched. I will confess to you that such is not my own case; nor will I longer affect blindness to the effect which I produced to-night upon Mr. Lorraine. Blanche, he *shall not* be deceived! I already feel that I would rather never see him again."

"How very absurd!" said the younger sister, pettishly; "I presume that you followed mamma's instructions, and told him that we had no money."

"I did—but do you, in your heart, imagine that he believed the statement, Blanche? Can you conscientiously say, that when we were so instructed, it was intended that we *should* be believed?"

"I am no casuist, Arabella; I only know that if we **are** not married while the ready money lasts, and are condemned to become pensioners on mamma, we shall lead a most miserable life: so, *vogue la galère*, say I; I am not responsible for the consequences of a policy which I did not originate."

"I would fain hear you reason differently, my dear Blanche," was the subdued reply; "as for myself, my resolution is taken. I shall seriously and positively undeceive Mr. Lorraine, before I suffer his attentions to become more marked. As yet he is not committed, nor shall he be made the victim of my unhappy position."

"Mamma will never forgive you, and you will ruin me."

"Do not say so, Blanche; I am convinced that I shall, on the contrary, save you. Mamma's displeasure I must support as I best can; but my resolution is irrevocable."

"We had better say good night, at once, Arabella," broke in Blanche; "my temper will not hold out much longer against your folly:" and the first cold kiss that had ever passed between the sisters, was given and returned.

Poor Miss Greville wept herself to sleep. She believed that her tears were caused by the effort which she was about to make in opposing her mother for the first time; she was not herself aware how deeply the handsome person and devoted attentions of Lorraine had touched her heart. Her only consolation arose from the conviction that her decision was a proper one; and she strove to believe that all might yet end well. Blanche, meanwhile, fell asleep, half ashamed of her own arguments, and half angry with her sister for raising the doubt by which they had been caused. Could their mother have over-heard their dialogue, she would not have closed her eyes throughout the night.

The next day was one of gaiety; in the morning, the party drove out in Lady Dampmore's barouche; when, despite all the entreaties of the two elder ladies, Sir Frederic insisted on mounting the box, and exhibiting his skill as a whip; upon which Mr. Lorraine, true to his prudential resolve of the pre-vious night, volunteered to bear him company. The servants then mounted the rumble; and, greatly to the annoyance of Lady Dampmore, this expedition, for all the purposes which it had been intended to further, was a decided failure.

A late dinner had just been brought to a conclusion when, greatly to the surprise of all assembled, Mr. Lorraine rose, and apologising for his abruptness, announced his departure by the mail, which was about to start in ten minutes, and he had still some arrangements to make. Mrs. Greville bit her lips with mortification; Lady Dampmore smiled her regrets; and Blanche glanced furtively towards her sister; Sir Frederic uttered something very like an oath, and rousing himself into energy, began to remonstrate vehemently with his friend; and, mean-while, Miss Greville sat by, calm, pale, and apparently unmoved; but she was, nevertheless, smitten to the heart. She felt, even although she had known him only for a few hours, that Lorraine had trifled with her; and the natural dignity of her sex prevented all betrayal of the internal struggle.

All the baronet's arguments, if, indeed, his wordy objections deserve to be so denominated, produced no effect upon his friend; Lorraine believed that he was acting honourably towards Arabella, while he was securing his own safety, and accord-ingly, making his leave-taking as brief as courtesy would permit, he hurried from the apartment, and, by a violent effort, tore himself away from the presence of the only woman whom he had ever felt disposed to love.

The field was now left free to Sir Frederic; and nothing could have served him better with Mrs. Greville than the departure of his friend. She became so nervous lest he should follow the erratic example, that she petted and praised him, until he began seriously to ponder within himself whether the mother, " with her hundreds a year, and thousands in ready money, with silver, wine. and pictures" might not be a better speculation than one of the daughters with £30,000. "The widow," as he told Lady Dampmore, to her extreme consternation, "was still a very fine animal, and knew the world better than the girls; nor did he believe, from what he had seen of her, that she would stick at a thing or two, which, all circumstances considered, might be quite as well."

Lady Dampmore had no alternative but to praise the grace of Arabella and the beauty of Blanche, and to remind him that whoever married Mrs. Greville before her daughters were disposed of, would be saddled with them as a matter of course, until they at least were of age; which, accustomed as they were to every description of luxury, would be by no means a trifling deduction from the lady's income. "Remember, too, Frederic," she concluded, "that, pressed as you are, it is ready money that you want; a wife's income, handsome though it might be, would not save you from a gaol. My advice to you therefore is, not to trifle with your luck, but to secure one of the girls, no matter which. I shall be happy to welcome either as Lady Dampmore, and to accept my dowagership with a good grace."

The maternal reasoning was unanswerable, and Sir Frederic did accordingly seriously incline towards the thought of immediate matrimony; but, judging from the urbane and affectionate *empressement* of Mrs. Greville that both the young ladies were equally at his service, he could not decidedly make up what *he* called his mind. One day he lounged beside the piano, while Arabella, with a full heart, but steady voice, tried over some of the songs which had, according to his promise, duly arrived from town, inscribed with Mr. Lorraine's compliments; and the next he spent hours stretched along a sofa beside the harp of Blanche, half asleep, and believing that he was making infinite progress in his courtship by the very fact of his presence; without having as yet given either sister reason to conjecture to whom he should ultimately throw the handkerchief. Thus, to the terror of Mrs. Greville and the mortification of Lady Dampmore, did matters stagnate for a whole month; when one morning, as the suitor had given his hair the last twist before the drawing-room mirror, and was about, as usual, to betake himself to Mrs. Greville's apartments, in order to ascertain, or rather to arrange, what he termed "the order of the day," he turned suddenly towards his mother, as if a new light had just broken upon his obtuse brain.

"Lady D.," he asked somewhat sententiously, "are you quite

sure that we are not playing a devilish shallow game here?
On what authority have you put forward your statement as to
the fortunes of these two Greville girls? Who told you that
they were heiresses? Who knew them before they came
here?"

"How many more absurd questions in the same breath, Sir
Frederic?" asked his mother in her turn. "I *am* quite sure
of my game. I had my intelligence from the best authority—
the very best in a case of this description—it was the news of
the second table. The butler of Mrs. Greville told Collins in a
fit of gossipry, without an idea that it would ever come to my
ears, that he was present at the reading of Mr. Greville's Will,
when all was bequeathed as I have already told you."

Sir Frederic's reply was a fit of contemptuous laughter. "So
far," he exclaimed at last, "nothing can be more satisfactory.
And now to my second query: Who knew them before they
came here?"

"Dear me, how can I undertake to say?" replied Lady
Dampmore, startled in spite of herself by her son's objections.
"You may depend upon it that, if they had made a very general
acquaintance elsewhere, you would not now have the opportunity of patching your broken fortunes with the money of either
of them. But there—I wash my hands of the whole affair; do
as you please. I have been very weak in believing that you
would now take my advice for the first time in your life. I
have said all that I mean to say upon the subject."

"In that case, with your kind permission, I will act," said
the gentleman; "and I shall commence operations by writing
to Lorraine, and starting him to Doctors' Commons, to look at
the Will. No pig-in-a-poke work for me, Lady D. I may be
glad to bite, but I'll take devilish good care not to be bitten."
And with a smile of satisfied self-appreciation the enlightened
young baronet drew a writing-table towards him, and forthwith
indited the threatened epistle to his friend.

The result will be, of course, anticipated. Lady Dampmore
could not repress a shudder of dread as she saw her son receive
the answer of Lorraine, which arrived by return of post; but
doubt and misgiving vanished at the "All right!" with which
he terminated its perusal. The young barrister had lost no time
in complying with the request of his friend. He had been to
Doctors' Commons, had duly paid his shilling for the privilege,
and had then read the Will, wherein the Honourable Charles

Greville had bequeathed to each of his daughters, on the day of her marriage, or her majority, the sum of £30,000.

It was now Lady Dampmore's turn to triumph. She was surprised that Sir Frederic should have degraded himself by believing, for an instant, that any deceit were possible. She felt personally hurt that *her* friends should have been classed with the sharpers and swindlers, to whose contact he was only too much accustomed ; and she trusted that, in future, he would do her the justice to place a little more faith in her penetration. Her amiable son only replied by inquiring which of the girls she would advise him to have, as he declared that, to himself, it was a matter of perfect indifference ; when Lady Dampmore immediately named Arabella : she thought her the most manageable. And Sir Frederic, with Lorraine's letter in his pocket as a certificate of safety, forthwith proceeded to offer himself and his debts to the acceptance of Miss Greville.

He had not, however, reached the extremity of the gallery, when he remembered the terms in which his mother had recommended the elder sister ; and with the cunning of persons of his stamp, he muttered to himself—" So, so ; ' the most manageable,' is she, Lady D. ?   You want to manage my wife as you try to manage me ; but I'll take you in for once, for, egad ! I'" ask Blanche."

By what he considered a fortunate fatality, he found the young lady alone, stringing her harp ; an occupation from which, however, she immediately desisted, in order to do the honours of her mother's drawing-room. We feel no inclination to weary either our readers or ourself by detailing the advances of Sir Frederic. That he did his spiriting gently we are bound to believe, as Miss Blanche Greville, the beautiful and the accomplished, did not disdain to listen ; and only replied to his verbal professions by calmly remarking—" You are aware, of course, Sir Frederic, that I am utterly without fortune ?"

" Devilish glad of it, Miss Blanche," was the prompt response, as the gentleman pressed the letter of Lorraine closer to his person to assure himself that its existence was not a dream ; " want a fine woman at Dampmore Hall to displace the dowager, and needn't look farther."

" But are you quite sure that you shall not repent marrying a wife without money ?"

A smile of the most liberal and benevolent impression radiated the heavy features of the baronet as he replied playfully—·" Don't

you be afraid, my dear girl, we'll manage to make the pot boil.
And now, what say you ?   We'll talk no more about ways and
means.   Will you have me ?"

" Really, Sir Frederic," said Blanche, with well-acted coquetry,
" you have quite taken me by surprise.   What do you expect
me to say ?   I can venture on no decision without mamma's
consent."

" And if the old lady says ' Yes ?' "

" Why then, perhaps," laughed Blanche, " I may consider
of it."

And of course Mrs. Greville did say " Yes," only warning Sir
Frederic to look well into his own heart before he allied himself to her " penniless girl ;" equally, of course, he told her that
he had done so, and that without Blanche he should be miserable.
The last argument was unanswerable ; so the two matrons exchanged a sisterly embrace.   Arabella shook hands with her
intended brother-in-law, quite unconscious how near he had
been proposing himself as her own bridegroom ; and all was
harmony and good-humour.

But, desirous as Mrs. Greville herself was to see the marriage
fairly over, and Blanche definitely disposed of " for better, for
worse," she was by no means prepared for the ardour with which
Lady Dampmore (prompted as she declared by her son) hurried
forward every preparation for the happy union.   She would
not listen to the bride elect when she talked of entrusting her
trousseau to a town milliner ; the craft abounded, as she declared,
in Cheltenham, and the future Lady Dampmore ought rather
to aspire to lead the fashion than to follow it.   And when Mrs.
Greville faintly remarked something about collecting their
connections around them upon so interesting an occasion, she
laughed her out of what she termed her antiquated notions, and
cited twenty instances in which personal friends of her own, of
high rank and enormous wealth, had left London just before
the ceremony, expressly to rid themselves of the crowd by
which they must, otherwise, have been inevitably surrounded.
Mrs. Greville made some feeble resistance, and she had reasons
of her own for neither insisting too pertinaciously, nor too
strongly ; and accordingly, after a few days' hesitation and
well-acted reluctance on the part of Blanche, the time for the
marriage was named, greatly to the relief of the two principal
parties, who were both tired to death of the farce which they
were severally enacting.

This important point decided, Lady Dampmore procceded to suggest that the ceremony should be conducted as privately as possible, and that Blanche should have no attendant at the altar save her sister; while Sir Frederic, on his side, should be accompanied only by a single friend; in w]ich case there could be no impropriety in herself and dear Mrs. Greville being of the party to church, and having the happiness of seeing their beloved children united. Nothing could be more affectionate and endearing; and as both the elder ladies shed tears, while discussing the subject, it was, of course, arranged according to their desire: upon which Sir Frederic declared that he should make a groomsman of Lorraine, for that it would be devilish hard, as he was by when they were turned off, that he should not be in at the death.

The heart of Arabella gave one wild boun?' as she heard the decision of the baronet; but she compressed her lips tightly, and no one remarked her emotion, and so a week rolled by. The satins and blondes, the Brussels lace veils, and chip bonnets were all duly trimmed; and at length the eve of the marriage-day found the party assembled as usual round the tea-table of Mrs. Greville, with the addition of Mr. Lorraine, who had been deposited at the door of the hotel just as the *promessi sposi* and their affectionate relatives were terminating their dessert.

Blanche looked uncommonly pretty; there was a triumphant expression in her deep blue eye and about her small mouth, which Lorraine had never previously seen there, but which he took no trouble to understand. Mrs. Greville, too, was radiant, and her joy circled like a halo round her weeds; nor did the young barrister fail to perceive how much it was increased by his own presence. Lady Dampmore was calm, stately, and somewhat dictatorial; like one desirous to enjoy to the full the success of her exertions. Sir Frederic, a shade more lethargic and more uncouth than ever. His work was done: "all the love-making,' as he took an early opportunity of observing, with great self-gratulation, to his friend, "being happily over."

From his rapid examination of these several individuals, Lorraine ultimately turned, with an expression strongly bordering upon disgust, to remark Arabella. She had placed her chair slightly behind the circle, and beyond the glare of the lights, and he fancied that an emotion of deep pain contracted her fine features at intervals. Amid the strife of tongues she alone was silent; but it was not the silence of sullenness. To all the puerile questions which were from time to time addressed to her, she answered promptly, and with a smile; but Lorraine felt that the heart was sick from which that smile was forced; and, be it from what cause it might, he watched her narrowly.

Could he have detected, in the look or manner of Blanche, one sign or symptom of reluctance at the sacrifice which she was about to make—could he have seen anything in the bearing of his so-called friend which implied anything more worthy than the quiet triumph of a selfish nature, there is no guessing how that evening would have terminated. As it was he remained passive; the two *écarté* tables were formed as usual, and he found himself once more *tête-à-tête* with Arabella at the piano.

Once or twice Sir Frederic shouted across the room, from the sofa upon which he was lounging at full length, opposite his beautiful betrothed, to know " why the devil they sat gossiping there, instead of giving them some music;" and, with the most meek humility, on each occasion they complied with the implied request, and poured forth a flood of melody which might have liberated another Eurydice : but the song, whatever it might be, once terminated, the conversation was resumed; and one who had watched them might have seen the bosom of Arabella heave, and the tear stand in her fine dark eyes, as she spoke rapidly but impressively, and the gentleman laughed away her asseverations, as if in disbelief. Blanche kept a careful eye upon them; and, as the best method of diverting the attention of Sir Frederic from what she believed to be a very important dialogue, she played carelessly, and suffered him to win; a manœuvre by which she succeeded in wholly riveting his attention upon the game. To Lady Dampmore the quiet flirtation, as she termed it, was now altogether a matter of indifference. Her son had secured his prize; he had selected the sister he preferred, and the other *must marry some one*; therefore, as well Sir Frederic's friend as any other; while Mrs. Greville looked upon the extraordinary understanding which had evidently grown up between her daughter and the rising young barrister as, what Oliver Cromwell called the battle of Worcester, her " crowning mercy."

The morrow came; and at half-past ten precisely the marriage party drove from the door of the Imperial Hotel, amid bows and smiles of all the household functionaries; and, after twenty minutes passed in the church, and sundry autographs deposited in the vestry, Sir Frederic and Lady Dampmore drove back to breakfast, followed by their bridal train. As they entered, the bridegroom arranged his lank hair with his equally lank fingers, and hurried his lovely wife through the crowd, which had collected about the steps and in the hall, so rapidly, that she had scarcely time to return the courtesies, or to receive the bouquets, that were offered to her; and the last carriage had not driven from the door when he rang for tea and coffee, and warned Blanche " not to be all day changing her toggery, as he wanted to be off." The new Lady Dampmore turned upon him the prettiest look of contempt imaginable; and had it not been for the memory of *certain circumstances*, it is probable that she would not have contented herself with a look. As it was, how-ever, she only threw herself on a sofa, and desired " Frederic " to ring for her maid.

The breakfast passed off heavily enough. Mrs. Greville was highly nervous, and took far too much trouble in explaining to Mr. Lorraine that she was overcome by the idea of parting with her sweet Blanche. Mr. Lorraine himself was thoughtful, even to absence; and appeared to be infected by the same malady. Arabella was drowned in tears, far more bitter than a temporary separation, even from an only sister, should have called forth; while Blanche and her bridegroom listened to the unceasing *bavardage* of the triumphant Lady Dampmore with as much composure and indifference as though they had no interest in the event which had so palpably affected all round them.

The breakfast was no sooner over than Sir Frederic and his mother suggested to Mrs. Greville that, previous to the departure of the newly-married pair, whose four greys were already mar-shalled before their house, and whose respective wardrobes were in process of arrangement on and about their travelling carriage, it might be as well to have half an hour's explanatory con-versation on matters of business; and as this desire was inti-mated, Mrs. Greville gracefully bowed her assent; and, with a heart whose beatings threatened to burst through her sable bombazeen, she p:ceded them to her private room. Blanche had already retired to her apartment to put on her travelling dress, and once more Arabella and Lorraine were left alone.

Had they been less in love than they actually were, they must have been lost in amazement at the length of time which was consumed in that private conversation; and even as it was, Arabella once or twice glanced towards the French clock upon the console. Soon, however, she forgot even to wonder: for

Lorraine was urging her, with all the impetuosity of a sincere and long pent-up passion, to be his—his, ere some happier man stepped in, and robbed him of her heart.

Arabella, trembling with mingled happiness and shame, could only falter out—"You do not credit what I told you last night, Mr. Lorraine? Alas! alas! how should you? How should your frank and open nature yield credence to anything so unworthy? But here, here on my knees—" and she sank down before him as she sobbed out the words—"here, in this abject posture, do I swear to you, by all that woman holds most dear, that the tale of deceit and shame is true. Let us part, then, Mr. Lorraine—let us never meet again. For my sake—for both our sakes—only promise me, promise me on your honour as a man, that you will acquit me of all share in this most weak and wicked stratagem!" And as she faltered out the prayer she seized the hands of her companion, and gazed imploringly into his face.

For a moment Lorraine did not attempt to raise her: she looked so beautiful, so graceful in her tears; her love for him shone so vividly through her desire not to forfeit his respect; there was so holy an abandonment in her whole expression and attitude, that he could not break the thrall in which his admiration held him; but suddenly he withdrew his hands from hers, and lifting her from the floor, he pressed her to his heart as he murmured fondly—"I will promise anything, everything, if you, Arabella, in your turn, will promise to be mine—my fond and faithful wife—my friend through all the trials of my coming life—the partner alike of my joys and of my sorrows."

"Alas! alas!" exclaimed Arabella, struggling to free herself from his embrace; "you do not yet believe me!"

"Listen to me, dear girl," said Lorraine, soothingly; "we may be interrupted. Mine has been a delicate and a difficult position. Dampmore, startled by the frequent disclaimers of your mother and sister, wrote to me three weeks back to examine your father's Will; I did so, and by the following post acquainted him with the result."

Arabella covered her face with her hands, to hide the crimson blush that had mantled over her brow and bosom.

"After I had dispatched my letter," pursued Lorraine, "a lawyer-like misgiving came upon me. I remembered that it was not specified from whence the funds were to proceed for the payment of your respective fortunes. It is probable that, after having complied with Dampmore's request, I should nave dismissed the subject from my thoughts; but short as had been our acquaintance, I had learned to love you, Arabella; anc. I was anxious to comprehend all its bearings and details for my own sake."

"And you found——" sobbed Miss Greville.

"I found, dear love, that the inheritance which I feared would cause your worldly mother—for I had soon discovered that your mother *was* worldly, Arabella—to deny my suit and separate us for ever, was a mere fable; that your father had sunk all the remnant of his property in a life-annuity for your mother, and that yourself and your sister were penniless. I made the discovery fully and perfectly, only on the day previous to my return here, and I need not explain to you the peculiarity of my position. Dampmore was a fellow-collegian—could I suffer him to be——" Lorraine paused, the word which had risen to his lips was one which he could not bring himself to utter to Arabella; but despite his caution, the pause was to the full as bitter to the shrinking girl. He felt that it was, and hurriedly resumed.

"It was too late to interfere to save either party; for I regret to tell you that Blanche has wedded herself to ruin. Dampmore is steeped in debt; his estate is mortgaged; and he is now chiefly dependent on the jointure of his mother."

Miss Greville's tears flowed still faster.

"And now, dear Arabella—for so you must indeed suffer me to call you—let us speak and think only of ourselves. I cannot offer you luxury; I may not be enabled to do so for years to come; but I can secure to you a home of love and comfort, worthy of your truth and principle. How say you, then, will you make my happiness, and entrust me with your own?"

Miss Greville only replied by hiding her face upon his shoulder.

They had forgotten the event which brought them together—they had forgotten the purpose for which they had been left so long *tête-à-tête*, they had forgotten that Blanche, whom *bienséance* forbade to leave her chamber until she was summoned thence by her bridegroom, must long ago have expected the companionship of Arabella—they had, in short, forgotten all save themselves and their affection, when they were startled by the violent opening of the door, and the sudden apparition of Sir Frederic Dampmore.

"What are you two about here?" he exclaimed with a

convulsive laugh; his usually leaden eye burning with a fierce light, and his thin lip quivering with agitation, as he rushed to the breakfast-table, and poured out a tumbler of champagne, which he emptied at a draught; "Love-making, eh? All right, old fellow! I'm off with my handsome heiress; and advise you to make sure of the sister. Don't lose time either, or some rascal or another may step in and spoil your chance. I should like you to share my luck. Curse all monopolies; I don't want to be the only happy man on this auspicious day. All right, you know, eh? you saw it with your own eyes, so there can be no mistake. Why don't you pluck up a spirit, and offer yourself to Arabella and her £30,000?"

"I have done so," replied Lorraine, quietly, "and Miss Greville has honoured me by accepting my hand."

"I'm devilish glad to hear it!" said the baronet with another yell of laughter, as he gave his friend a violent blow between the shoulders, and then tossed off a second bumper of champagne. "Here's to your happy bridal, old boy! But I hope you'll be prudent when you come into your property, and not make ducks and drakes of it, as I have done. Where's Blanche? Where's my heiress? She must come and salute her new brother-in-law. But your sure you're serious, Lorraine? that you're not humbugging?—I'm a little hard of belief this morning."

"I am quite serious," said Lorraine, in a constrained tone; "I should not venture to trifle with Miss Greville."

There was something in this assertion which struck the half-intoxicated baronet as so eminently ridiculous, that he threw himself down upon his favourite sofa, in order to laugh more at his ease; and the paroxysm had not yet abated, when the door once more opened, and admitted the elder Lady Dampmore and Mrs. Greville. The brow of the dowager was as black as night; her cheeks were flushed, and her breath came quick and hard, like that of one who has not yet mastered some violent emotion. Her companion, on the contrary, was as pale and as calm as a piece of statuary: her look was somewhat troubled, indeed, as her eye first fell upon Lorraine, but she conquered the weakness in a moment, and sailed towards the upper end of the room with a cold, hard smile upon her lips

"Give me leave, my good mother-in-law," said Sir Frederic when he became somewhat more composed, raising himself upon his elbows as he spoke; "give me leave to present to you, and to back by my best recommendation, Mr. Charles Lorraine, who is a candidate for your other heiress. You will not, I suppose, forbid his addresses; and I invite myself to the wedding."

"You are, I trust and hope, aware, sir," said Mrs. Greville, turning composedly towards the new suitor, "that my daughters are portionless?"

"Perfectly, madam," replied Lorraine, as he looked steadily towards her; "I am aware that Mr. Greville, after a career of egotistical indulgence, converted the remainder of his property into a life annuity for yourself; and that, in the partial aberration of his last moments, he was induced to make a parchment bequest to his daughters, with what intention I have too much respect for Miss Greville to inquire."

As Lorraine spoke, Mrs. Greville sank speechless and aghast into a chair near which she had been standing; while the baronet sprang from the sofa in a blustering attitude, and approached him evidently with a hostile attention.

"Hear me out, Dampmore," said the barrister, as he waved him off with quiet dignity, which produced an instant effect upon the mystified senses of Sir Frederic; "for until you are told it was only two days ago that I learned this, you have some reason to believe that you have cause of complaint against me. I now beg to explain that fact, and also to remind you that there were circumstances connected with your own affairs which would have rendered any interference on my part unnecessary and absurd, as well as impertinent."

The baronet skulked silently and sullenly back to his sofa.

"Come, come, Dampmore," persisted Lorraine, "let us eschew all malice. Are we not to be brothers-in-law? and that, I trust, not many weeks hence; and have you not already invited yourself to our wedding? And after all, what are you, my dear fellow, but the biter bitten? The world is full of such mistakes as yours; and, moreover, have you forgotten that you have married one of the prettiest women in England, and that she has had on her travelling-bonnet for the last hour?"

"Mr. Lorraine is quite right, Sir Frederic," said Mrs. Greville, rallying her spirits; "you are, indeed, a laggard bridegroom. Pray do not, by your own childish folly, expose to all the inmates of the hotel, that, after all the asseverations of myself and my daughters, you have been the dupe of your own disbelief, that there *were* persons in the world possessed of sufficient moral courage to act up to their principles."

" Spare your sententiousness, madam," said Lady Dampmore, as she motioned her son from the room. "I would advise you to take leave of your able assistant, my estimable daughter-in-law, before her departure, which will take place in ten minutes, as I shall be careful that you never meet again."

Sir Frederic gave one general nod : his head was too heavy with the fumes of the wine to prompt him to a wordy leave-taking ; but as he reached the door he muttered, almost audibly, " Devilish bore of Lady Dampmore to interpose. If I'd done as I liked, I should have married the mother, and been all right."

Mrs. Greville had already vanished. She was taking leave of her beautiful and unfortunate daughter Blanche ; but Arabella made no effort to follow her; she was so bowed down by grief, shame, and mortification, that she could only weep upon her lover's bosom, and beseech him, again and again, to promise that he would never, when she became his wife, drive the iron into her soul, by any allusion to the period when she moved and was known as one of the co-heiresses under her father's " WILL."

KING VERIC:

A SCENE OF THE ROMANS IN BRITAIN.

BY MARTIN F. TUPPER, D.C.L., F.R.S.

PROEM.

A FEW months ago, during some antiquarian researches at
Farley Heath, near Guildford (unusually prolific in coins, urns,
ornaments, and other ancient remains, which generous old
Rome so kindly threw away for our cabinets), it chanced that
one day the labourers found nothing at all—except one little
gold coin. Contrary, however, to all rustic estimation, that
morsel of gold was a treasure, alone worth all the toil of all the
many weeks of excavation : not for the mere gold's sake, still
less only for its antiquity, but because it bore obversely the
name of Veric the King, the son of Comius. To say that the
coin is worth a hundred times its weight in gold is not to say
enough, for it is unique ; and whenever two or three numismatic maniacs may at some time future be got together at an
auction to struggle for its possession, keen indeed will be the
strife, and bold indeed the biddings, before one or another shall
be the fortunate possessor of our little coin. On a previous
day, a mite of silver, bearing a youthful head and the legend
of Mepati, was scarcely less interesting as a discovery, or less
valuable for rarity. Here, however, we leave the mere anti-
quarianism of these sweet suggestive morsels to be discussed in
drier places ; and referring the more learned reader to certain
numismatic chronicles and archæological journals for duller disquisition on such matters, let me now tell you shortly how true
a tale, and yet how new, mine eyes have read herefrom anent
King Veric and young Prince Mepati.

POEM.

It is just nineteen hundred years ago, some forty or fifty before
the Sun of Righteousness arose with healing in his wings.
Taranis the Thunderer was then chief god of Britain; and
Hæsus the bloody, thrice-great Teutates, with a legion of other
names—dark spots now shone away into oblivion by the noon-
tide lustre of truth—shared with him dominion over wood, and
stream, and hill, and valley—over winds, and waves, and fire.
And now this day—this very day of our story—not few had
been the fair-haired maids whose life-blood had been shed in
sacrifice to such, beneath the curved poniards of the green-clad
Ovates; and loudly had the sacred bards, in flowing robes of
blue, struck from their harps the spirit-stirring hymn that called
the patriot Briton to combat his invader—spirit-stirring, indeed,
for the cords of those black-oak harps had once been the heart-
strings of princes and magicians in old time : now they seemed
to wail for the dead, now to shout for revenge on the living ;
anon, with ghastly energy, the sentient string would thrill with
warlike ardour—anon would die away with tones of saddest
pathos. And wherefore had the victims bled, and the sacred
harps been tuned ? Why had the fleshy mound been heaped
with its huge burnt-offering on the unhewn footstool of Taranis?
What had the oak-tiaraed Druid noticed in the Adder's Stone ?
How had the hoary seers read the stars, that this unwonted stir
should have vexed the shadowy vale of Coed Andred ?

Do ye know Coed Andred ? I trow, many who shall read
these lines know it full well; and may be glad for a while to
linger with me in the wildest forest-track of ancient Surrey,
whilst, I try to conjure up, in a resurrection of to-day, how
the hundred of Blackheath must have looked in those primeval
ages.

Changeless since the Deluge, changeless as now and to the
end of time, stood the chief feature in the landscape, a heaven-
kissing hill : in those days known as Moel Mawr, or the High
Mount—later, more mournfully, and yet more triumphantly
celebrated as Martyrs' Hill, where some early witnesses to Jesus
and the Resurrection sealed their testimony with their blood ;
and later still, in this our luke-warm day, corrupted into the
familiar name, St. Martha's. On its summit was built the
Beacon, whose nightly fires had melted into one mass of vitri-
fication the rude iron sandstone of which it was roughly heaped :

studded about within the fosse-and-mound enclosure, which lined
the hill on all sides, were the snug round kraals of our native
ancestors, built of chalk, with wattled doors, and a hole at top
for light, air, and an exit to the thin blue smoke of the logs
always left smouldering on their pebbled floors. Two circles
— still visible on the south side of the hill—marked spots
devoted to the comparatively pure idolatry of Druidism ; and
on the eastern shoulder, that most accessible to an enemy, were
successive ridges of ditch and band—at this day well-nigh (but
not quite) filled in and levelled. This then was one of the chief
strongholds of Britons nineteen centuries ago: behind them, to
the north and east, were the sacred groves and avenues of yew,
consecrated to religious meditation ; and, except a few bare
spots, appearing like islands in the ocean of surrounding forest,
all round for miles and miles to the horizon, was a tangled,
pathless, marshy, and pestiferous wilderness of trees. There,
fallen across the streams—the same so pleasant now, so well
defined, and full of leaping trout—the rotting ash and beeches
dammed the currents, and on all sides converted our sparkling
Tillingbourn and our peaceful Wey, into the wide-spreading
dangerous morass. Where now fair Albury reposes in its cul-
tured vale, where the sheep-bell is heard upon the downs, and
the wains creak beneath the harvest riches of the farmer—then,
in his inaccessible solitudes, roamed the elk or the bear ; then
the wild boar grunted as he ground his beech-mast; and the
pack of hungry wolves sagaciously watched the gluttonous
monster till he flung him down to sleep among the brambles.
Instead of the tame and sweet-breathed cows, going home at
eventide with well-filled udders, there roamed among the coarse
patches of pasturage, herds of sheeted cattle, maned like lions,
with short horns and long stag-like faces, fierce, yet timorous.
Now and then, the red-deer would nobly stand against the sky
on some commanding height, as at Holmbury, or at Ewhurst
in the Hurtwood there abounded ptarmigan and black-game
(still, indeed, plentiful there), enamoured of the dark blue
berries and, as a natural consequence, there also abounded the
wild cat and the fox. All around St. Martha's, at evening,
after some sultry summer's day, arose a dense pestilential vapour
from the dank foliage rotting and sweltering below ; and, excepting for the far-seen stranger's settlement, on the bare heigh'
of Fairlee, the panorama was one of rank, unwholesome, gloomy
jungle   R

But—why had the virgin-victims bled within those magic circles? wherefore was the beacon a smoke by day and a flame by night? what means this gathering of the woad-stained clans, coming in by twos and threes, with their dew-lapped bull-dogs, their targe and spear, and bow and hammer—converging, from the eastern heights, from the Hog's Back on the west, from Coed Andred, and from distant Leith? Incessant is the clang of their shields, loud the clamour of their tongues; and furiously they look upon each other, as men betrayed would look upon a doubtful, a suspected friend. And still, in their rude language their cry is the same—" Why lingers King Veric? why comes he not from Leith to lead us to the battle? Has he brought the Roman here—not for us to plunder, as he promised, but to conquer us, hemmed in our fastness, while we sit down idly here to starve? Whose was that too true voice, shouting —' Veric is a traitor?'"

Slowly emerging from the wood, a war-chariot is seen approaching. Up the sandy steep, with strenuous effort, the foam-covered stallions plough their violent way: and look! pallid and haggard, on his iron-bound chariot, stands the British king.

Look on him! even now, while the clamorous crowds are circling round to ask the same terrible question,—look! with what majesty and firmness he comes to quell the storm. Arrayed in his royal robes of the seven rainbow colours, with a fillet of gold and pearls around his massive brow, and the torque upon his neck, he is here in his scythed car, to lead the remnant of his host for one last desperate charge against the invincible Roman.

Oh, with what bitterness of spirit did the conscience-stricken king now repent his feeble, his treacherous, though, originally, patriotic policy! He had come to his inheritance as one of the stock of imperial Comius, full of good hope, and zealous for his people; but the multitude of petty factions, arraying chieftain against chieftain, sept against sept, loosened the bands of government, divided the strength of the country, and seemed to be opening an easy way for the domination of those iron strangers. Already had the Roman settled down in force at Clausentum and at Venta—our Southampton and Winchester; already had they ravaged all the coast, and pushed their outposts far into the interior; but all their discipline and hardihood could have availed little against the natural impenetrability of this part

of Veric's dominions, had he not himself paved the way to
their success, by the fault and the folly of a double-handed
treachery!

This was his plan. By secret emissaries to invite the legate,
Aulus Plautius, to render him assistance as against domestic
foes; thus, by the sword of Rome, to cut down the mutiny and
disaffection which now had for a long time paralysed his army,
and threatened to throw his ancestral realm into anarchy and
ruin, thus also, as he fondly hoped, to weaken, by a war against
each other, the rebels at home and the invaders from abroad, too
surely waiting for the results of discord, to pounce upon himself as their prey; and thus, in fine, as his subtle policy had
suggested to the well-affected councillors around him, to " cut
down his foes by Rome, and Rome by his own good celt."

But Aulus Plautius, that prudent consular, at a glance divined
the scheme; and the wily barbarian found himself out-generalled
by the plainer and more honest courage of his inconvenient
ally. It is true that, under the guidance of King Veric's
messengers, Aulus Plautius had safely threaded, with a well-
selected band, the perilous morass of Coed Andred, and had
hewn down, in fair fight, a multitude of the unruly patriots,
whom Veric stood aside to see fall beneath the Roman sword;
but it is also true, that the astute Aulus had kept open his
communications in the rear, and that every hour brought up
detachments of sturdy legionaries, with " elephants, and other
new terrors of war," which had easily and safely wound their
labyrinthine way from distant Venta to the promontory of
Fairlee. Accordingly, when the fight, so seemingly politic,
was over—and King Veric, with his loyal followers, felt well-
enough disposed to thank the Roman in kind, for the help of
his bloody lances—behold! the orderly and well-disciplined
array of iron soldiery whom Plautius quietly reviewed in the
field of battle, after its laurels had been reaped, speedily convinced Veric that he had made the ruinous mistake of placing
his deadliest foe on the vantage-ground due only to a patriot
monarch's truest friend. There, in the heart of his dominions,
stood the imperial standards, invincible, implacable—and yet,
as invited by himself, in all the seeming friendliness and confidence of good alliance. Oh, how often is the crafty taken in
his own net, and the shrewdness of political economy shown to
be remarkably short-sighted!

What was now to be done? Notwithstanding the studied

honours rendered to the king, and in spite of the frank friendliness accorded to the man, it was perfectly manifest to all that Veric was, in fact, the prisoner of the astute Plautius. Pre cisely as Pizarro in after ages proved the most inconvenient friend to the Mca Manco that it could be possible to find, so it now fared with Plautius and his overreached inviter. Many a chuckle did the stout prætorians indulge in at their host's expense, and many a joke passed about the veritas of Vericus among the gay young centurions over their Falernian. It grew intolerable. Every day, by dint of galleys from Gallia to Clausentum, and thence by forced marches to Fairlee height, Rome stood stronger in his camp, and Veric waxed weaker in his kingdom. What was to be done?

It was high time, indeed, for poor King Veric to be up and stirring, for he was fast losing all the loyal hearts he once loved, as well as was already quit of those, perhaps equally patriotic, whom he lately feared. Such are the fruits of double-dealing: beware, ye far-seeing Machiavellis!—"honesty," after all, "is the best policy;" and, by way of pressing into our service another time-honoured adage, poor King Veric found to his cost that the Roman sword was far too "sharp-edged a tool" to be trifled with.

One night, being that just before this day on which we have seen the furious and doubtful Britons converging on St. Martha's Hill—(and if any one wishes to know the exact date, I can assure him it was the 17th of March, A.U.C. 710, just forty-three years before our era)—one dark night, after certain games and a carouse wherewith the Roman general had indulged his troops, King Veric escaped, alone and disguised; as thus :— the whole day had been devoted to festivities; for it was not only that of the general's nativity, but they had, as a settled colony, inaugurated on that same morning a "*temenos*," or consecrated site, to Apollo on the highest point of Fairlee : accordingly, Phœbus expected all his true votaries on that occasion to relax the stern demands of discipline, and to get "fou" upon imported Falernian and indigenous mead, on the well-recognised principle of "*neque semper arcum tendit Apollo*." Here, at least, Veric outwitted his guards: for, having lulled their watchfulness by a simulated intoxication early in the evening, and fallen fast asleep *off* the triclinium, it is small wonder that, later in the night, wrapped in the scarlet chlamys of his neighbour—a stout but slumbering tribune—he crept away, passed the sentinels, and stood once more in real freedom on Fairlee Heath!

All that night, painfully and dangerously, he forced his difficult way, by paths well remembered as a child, through the tangled Hurtwood, by Ewhurst and Holmbury to his ancient palace at Leith. On the way he had grappled with a prowling bear, and more than once had heard the wolves on his track· but a sharp sword and a stout heart, and a stern purpose of revenge upon Aulus for his hated hospitalities, made the monarch and the man invincible to mere brute force. And, early this morning had he entered his own stronghold—alone, a fugitive but still a British king.

His first act was, by messengers, and beacons on every height, to raise his subject clans; and the place of meeting, as we know, is yonder heaven-kissing hill—well named "heaven-kissing," ever since a martyr sanctified it with his blood, and pious Newark gave the rude old ironstone choir, with its keyless arch, a Gothic nave and transepts;—well named, since even as now, after evil dilapidations within these ten years, our recent zeal restores it to the Lord—a fair tabernacle for His service.

See! how they crowd around the king. See! how many throng to kiss his chariot-wheels. See! too, how many stand aloof, and doubt him as the traitor, but that no one save a patriot dare stand alone upon that hill among the fiercest clans of Comius.

On the northern edge of the upper sacred circle stands Oreddlyn the Druid. His robes and beard are white, but his eyes are bleared with rheum, age, and tears, and his palsied hands are ruddy with blood. A green pall covers the victim: Maachal, the daughter of King Veric, in her country's darkest hour, has offered herself a spotless sacrifice to appease the gods of Britain. Well knew the king in his inmost soul (though none had dared to tell him) *who* lay beneath that pall—*whose* heart trembled in that golden vessel—*whose* blood Oreddlyn came to sprinkle upon *him*, to consecrate his arms to victory! And the king stood like a statue, white, firm, breathless; and the king calmly looked round him on the rude and hurrying multitude, and, as he spoke, the words seemed to come from some image of his former self, some clay model made to imitate life. And the king said, "Britons—my children, my free, my fearless children—look not on me so! By my Maachal's dear blood—by the thunder of Taranis—by mine own honour—and by the sacred fillet which I wear, Veric is no tra'tor! Hoping to secure your peace and welfare in the stability of your lawful monarch's throne, my folly welcomed to these shores that dangerous ally, the Roman : my councillors and I had looked for other issues; and well are we rewarded for having imitated Celtic Gaul! for having laid aside the frankness, the honour, the fair spirit of a Briton, and tried to compass by duplicity what valour only should have won. I repent—O Maachal! my Maachal, I repent! My people, here am I, to lead you on at once against yonder smooth invader. Let this night—whereon our silver queen, kindly for us, shines not upon the Roman, but trims her newborn crescent as our sign—witness his utter destruction on the heights of Fairlee!"

Loudly, too loudly—for the watchful clarions echoed it at Fairlee — the British thousands clanged their brass-bound shields; and earnestly, with all the good feeling indigenous to England's soil, did many a heart there reproach itself for having doubted Veric. Then did they throng around him; and he felt himself once more a British king—but alas, for Maachal, sweet Maachal!—and the father fell like a corpse upon that fearfully defined green and bloody pall.

All is now preparation at St. Martha's; and, owing to the diaphanous nature of barbarian tactics, all was equally preparation at the colony at Fairlee. If young Mepati, the eldest son of Veric, was busy with his painted peers in chiselling flints into arrow-heads, and fixing them to the feathered reeds, Flavius and Candens, stout lieutenants of the general, were ready with their iron cohort, secured at every part against the night attack. All the outposts upon Blackheath, Wonersh Hill, and Shimley Green had been called in; the suttlers and camp followers had left their wooden huts, and crowded for security within the diagonal walls of Fairlee : scouts were posted on every eminence around to give notice of the foe's approach, and Plautius with his legion felt never more happy than when he saw that the poor betrayed traitor was falling into the snare prepared for him at Fairlee.

Red, and robed in lowering clouds, down sank the sun behind the hill of Waverley. There Oxana, the witch, had brewed a magic potion in her caldron, whereby, as by a cordial elixir, Veric had been made invincible by man : there, from her gloomy cell had she uttered out the oracle—

> "Unscathed, unbesieged, in his own royal home,
> Veric shall die when his hour is come!"

This distich, bruited through the gathering host, gave a confidence to the Britons which dangerously bordered on contempt for the handful of invaders pent within their rubble walls at Fairlee. Who had ever known Oxana's prophecies to fail? for ninety years the bleared and wrinkled hag had forecast every coming shadow, and well could read the quivering entrails, reeking from the hands of the Ovate; while the blood of the gentle Maachal, martyr in her country's cause, had insured the patriot bands a leader and a king whom hand of mortal man should never wound or slaughter.

And now the night was glooming on apace—moonless, chill, and gusty: and, leaving the beacon well heaped, with the old men and the children gathered round, to show as if the multitude still rested on the hill-top—down by several paths in many bands, converging upon Fairlee Camp, slowly, and in single files, crept on the host of Britons. One band, headed by the young Mepati, passing what we now call Chilworth and Tangley, skirted Wonersh Hill, and meditated their attack from the west; another, down by the marshy track of Postford, debouched upon Blackheath, to take the enemy on its northern side; a third, winding along the hanger, surmounted the Weston height and Birkett Wood, so getting to the eastern flank by way of Blackheath Lane; and a fourth, marching over Albury Heath and Farley Green, were to make a detour to the south, and attack the camp by way of Wood Hill.

The new moon, which was to rise at one in the morning, was agreed to be the sacred signal for a simultaneous attack: so soon as ever her lower horn topped the old larches upon Albinger mound, the Britons were to rush from the woody ambuscades, and destroy the slumbering hive of Romans upon bare Fairlee.

Cleverly, before their advancing bands, the scouts of Plautius noiselessly receded—and all the camp, in deep silence, were awaiting the attack behind their mounds and ramparts, when the crescent slowly rose blood-red upon the eastern sky. With breathless expectation the legionaries stood to arms—for it needed no magician to suggest to them that Veric would fight beneath his favouring planet, and must wait her rising. Hush! hush!—not a sword-chain jingled at the wrist—not a war-horse

neighed—not a light was seen—not a leaf stirred.   All around
seemed innocently sleeping nature.

Suddenly, from every side at once, rushed, with loud shouts,
and torches hastily rubbed alight, and flint-topped spears, and
heavy celts, and heralded by a shower of sling-stones, the
swarming masses of barbarian Britain!   And now the clarion
sounds, the standards are reared, and the flare of suttlers' huts,
lighted by the patriot torches, reveal the orderly steel-clad
cohorts in their battle-array.   On one side all is a chaos of
wild ungovernable energies; on the other all is placid order,
the quiet lion's strength of skill and discipline.   Nevertheless,
through all that fearful night, by turns on every side, the weary
Romans charged among the mass in column, or routed the thick-
coming waves of frantic warriors with the serried line of spear
and buckler; or, falling on their flanks and rear with the heavy
turmæ of horsemen, swept away, as by the besom of destruction,
the ant-like swarm of patriots.   Yea, till the morning's dreary
dawn, the fight still waxed more furious, more dubious; everywhere was Veric, slaughtering, unscathed; everywhere was
Mepati, leading on fresh bands to the attack, and firing from
all points the wooden huts of the invaders; everywhere, like a
hive of wasps attacking an eagle, the brave barbarians hope-
lessly renewed the fight.   But, when morning's dawn revealed
the slaughter—and showed their own thinned and wasted band
of tumultuaries, in hopeless contrast with the unbroken ranks of
Rome—then, pell-mell, as if their courage had indeed been all
due to the favouring influence of the queen of night, beneath
whose screen they had fought, fled in all directions the skin-
clad British host;—all was ruin, all was confusion—and the
fortunes of King Veric were utterly lost!   Mepati alone, and a
small band of nobles round him, battled to the end; and—the
last scene has been sung by me in stanzas: so, then, by way of
a change, bear, in congenial verse, the end of this prose poem,
and see how truly spake the prophetess, that Veric should die
at Leith, in his own home, unscathed and unbesieged.

Veric, the king, in his chariot of war,
  Like a statue straight upstood,
As his scythed wheels flashed fast and far,
  Smear'd with the Roman's blood;
His huge bronze celt was crimson with gore,
  And, round his unkempt head,
The golden fillet his fathers wore
  Was dabbled with drops of red!

And rage in the monarch's eye blazed bright,
  And his cheek was deadly pale,
For Plautius Aulus had won the fight
  With his mighty men in mail:
The carross of hide and the wicker targe
  Were riddled far and near;
And terrible was the prætorian charge,
  And keen the cohort's spear.

And over the Hurtwood and over the heath,
  Alone—alive he fled,
For the car bore straight to his stronghold of Leith
  The living—and the dead!
Young Mepati lay at his father's feet,
  Hewed by the ruthless foe;
And the bloodhound may track on the trickling peat
  The pathless way they go!

Young Mepati—well had he borne him then,
  On Fairlee's fatal day,
He boasted that ten of those bearded men
  Had vanished from the fray:
His flint-head shafts went merrily home
  As four hard hearts had felt;
And six of the stalwart guards of Rome
  Had bowed to the stripling's celt!

Young Mepati, come of the Comian stock,—
  Ha! look! they hem him round,
And down is he hurl'd in the battle-shock,
  And trampled to the ground:
But Veric has seen with his lightning eye,
  And, struck as the bolt, goodsooth!
Like thundering Thor with his hammer on high,
  He has saved the gallant youth!

But woe! for the foe had smitten him sore;
  And eight deep wounds in his front,
With red lips swore how well the boy bore
  That hideous battle-brunt!
Proudly the monarch smiled on the child,
  In his rescuing arms upborne;
But—all of his son that Veric has won
  Is a corpse by the tigers torn!

Then, deep as the ocean's distant roar,
  The father gave a groan—
And the Attrebate king by his gods he swore
  He should not die alone;
Back on their haunches swift he stopped
  Those untamed fiery steeds,
As an eagle down on the dovecote dropped,
  Or a whirlwind in the reeds!

And, was it then that the monarch's life
 By the Waverley witch was charm'd ?
The javelin sleet of that stern strife
 Around him flew unharm'd !
And weary he cleft with his wedge of war
 The hundredth foreign brow,
Before he would flee in his iron car,
 As he is fleeing now !

For lo ! to that false foe ho had lost
 All that a king can lose ;
His veteran chiefs, his patriot host,
 Scattered as early dews :
Treason had winked at the stranger's gold,
 And faithless friends had fled,—
And Mepati's self—his darling bold—
 Alas ! that he is dead !

He flies, as only a king may fly,
 To fight yet once agen,—
On his hill-top high like a lion to die
 At bay in his own den !
And lo ! the black horses are white with foam
 Strong straining up the steep ;
To carry the king to his ancient home,—
 Yon far-seen castle keep !

But—woe upon woe ! for the wily foe
 Hath been before him there,
And, while the lion was prowling below,
 Hath spoiled the lion's lair :
Dead, dead, and stark, and smear'd with gore,
 Beneath a smouldering heap,
Wife, daughters, and sons, and the grandsire hoar,
 On death's red ashes sleep !

Then burst in agony, rage, and pain,
 That noble broken heart ;
And under his beetled brows like rain,
 The spouting tears did start ;
And down like a poll-axed bull he drops,
 And weak on the threshold lies,
The wellspring of life freezes and stops—
 He dies—the hero dies !

But, look ! a light on his royal brow
 A strange prophetic flame—
The spirit of Vola over him now
 In solemn calmness came !
He saw the Gael at the gates of Roma,
 And carnage on the track,
And Britain's spoilers hurrying home
 To drive the terror back.

He saw in the midst of his native plains
  Fairlee's polluted hill,—
Where Rome so long should forge her chains
  To bind the Briton still,—
He saw it ruin'd, and burnt, and bare;
  And—from one mite of gold,
He saw a Saxon stranger there
  Read off this tale of old!

And I wot not that either Dion Cassius or Gabriel Brotier, or even Beale Poste himself, can tell of King Veric more, or more truly, than, reader, is recorded here.

THE LAST IN THE LEASE

BY MRS. S. C. HALL.

"Why, then, Grace, where was the good of all the larning I gave you, girl darlint, if you won't read us what's on the paper? sure it's pleasant at times to hear the news."

"Uncle, dear, sure it's all the pleasure in life I'd have in accommodating you," replied Grace, still continuing to twirl her wheel; "only that, you see, I can't read and spin at the same time."

"What news you tell us," persisted Corney Burnett, or, as he was commonly called, "Black Burnett;" "what news youtell us. Whoever expected you to read and spin at the same time? And indeed, dear Grace, it's glad of an excuse I'd be, set aside the reading, to get you from your wheel; the bur and the twirl of it's never out of my eyes nor ears."

"It's eager to make the linen I am, to keep us clean and comfortable,—and you above all, uncle; to see you comfortable, sure, is the pride of my life, to say nothing of the blessing."

"Thank you, Grace; I believe it from my heart. And why shouldn't I? since the day I promised my poor brother (God be good to him!) to be a father to the both of you, I never had a care on _your_ account anyhow."

"Nor on account of poor Michael, either, uncle. Poor Michael, for the sense God has left in him, is as good a boy as is to be found in a month of Sundays."

"Ay," replied Burnett, sorrowfully; "but it's very mournful to see him sitting there, staring into the turf-fire, and seeming to care for nothing on the living earth but that cur of a dog."

"Snap loves him dearly: it's wonderful, so it is, to see how he watches every turn Michael takes; the poor baste's eye is never tired looking at him, nor his ear never shut to his voice," said Grace, putting aside her wheel and unfolding the remnants of a tattered newspaper.

"Read the news—read the news," reiterated the half-idiot boy, who had been, as his uncle truly said, staring into the turf-fire, his dog curled round his feet, and his long bony fingers clasped over his knees. "Read the news, Grace. What you see wrong in others, mend in yourself,—what you see wrong in others, mend in yourself:—is that the news, Grace?"

Grace could hardly forbear smiling at the rapidity with which he pronounced and repeated a sentence that had obtained for him the *soubriquet* of "Preaching Michael;" and she replied, "I think, Mick, honey, it would be news if people did so."

"Ay," repeated the idiot, "what you see wrong in others, mend in yourself."

"Hold your whisht,* will you?" exclaimed Black Burnett. "What name's to the paper you've got, Grace?"

"That's more than I can tell you, uncle dear," replied the gentle girl; "for the name's clean tore off: but sure it's no matter for the name; one paper's as good as another."

"Oh! be quiet, now; don't you mind that some papers are for one side, and some for t'other,—and both can't be right, that's an impossibility. How ould is it?"

"I can't tell that either, uncle; but it can't be very ould, tor just down here it says that small bonnets are all the thing, and the last time Mrs. Hays, of the big house, was past here, she had a hat like a griddle: so, as she's tip-top, she'd have tip-top fashions—why not? So I'm sure the paper's not over a fortnight printed, any way."

"Well, read what they're after saying in the big houses of parliament; read every word, not as you did the last loan of a paper I had: Barney Doolen told me twice as much out of it as you read, Grace."

"Barney made it, then," exclaimed Grace, nevertheless colouring deeply—for she knew the charge was not altogether unfounded, as she was in the habit of skipping a great deal. "Barney made the news, I say, uncle; for I read it from top to bottom,—and then again, and again,—and most of it backwards to plaze you: it took me as long as I'd spin a pound of flax—so it did."

* Keep silence.

"I wish I knew if that paper was one of the right sort," said Burnett, without heeding her observation.

"I'm sure it is," she replied; "for at the very top it begins with ' Father Mulvaney's Sarmon.' "

" A priest's sarmon put on the paper," repeated the good old man, rubbing his hands gleesomely, and drawing his " creepie " closer to the fire; "let's have it, Grace. Now show your fine larning, my girl;—but aisy, there,—first let me light my *doodeen*.* Augh!" he continued, after screwing up his tobacco in a piece of dirty brown paper and thrusting it into a hole in the wall " for safety." " Augh! Grady's tobacco isn't worth a farthing a pound—he always keeps it in paper."

" What you see wrong in others, mend in yourself," exclaimed the natural.

" He has you there," laughed pretty Grace, as she glanced at the paper-ends sticking out of the wall.

" Read the sarmon,—one at a time, if you plaze, Miss Grace," said Burnett, looking serious; but Grace, before she did her uncle's bidding, sprung up, and kissed his wrinkled cheek affectionately, whispering, " You are not angry with your own poor Grace?" The seriousness passed from the old man's brow, and Grace commenced showing her "larning." She had not finished the first sentence, however, when she stopped, and said, " Uncle, it's very strange, but this sarmon is spelt quare—not in good English."

" A mighty fine judge you are, to be sure," replied Burnett, again roused to the " short passing anger." " A mighty fine scholar you must be to faut a priest's sarmon and the printing of a newspaper! I suppose you'll be for preaching and printing yourself."

Grace recommenced :—

" ' Boys and girls—but most particularly boys—we must all die! Ay, indeed die,—as sure as grass grows or wather runs. Now you see that the great min of *ould* times are all dead! Not a mortial sowl of thim all alive.' Uncle," said Grace, pausing, " do you think that's true ?"

" True!" repeated Black Burnett, not looking in the mildest manner from under the deep and shaggy brows which had gained him his cognomen; " to be sure; and to all reason it's true. Show me one of the people of ould times that's alive."

' Molly Myran, of Crag's-pass, near Carrickburn, 's above a

* Pipe.

hundred," replied Grace, who feared, she hardly knew why, that the sermon was a sort of quiz upon the priesthood, though she dared not say so.

"Molly Myran!" again repeated her uncle, contemptuously. "Heaven help the child! Sure no one's worth talking of amongst the rale ancients that's less than a thousand or two! Go on with the sarmon."

Grace continued—

"'There was Julus Sasar, and twelve of them there was—*mortus est*—he's dead!'"

"Morty who?" inquired Burnett, sharply.

"*Mortus est!*—M-O-R," continued poor Grace, reading, and then spelling the letters.

"I hope you are reading what's on the paper," persisted her uncle, doubtingly.

"As true as Gospel," she replied, "that is what I'm reading. 'There was the great Cleopathra, an Egyptian, and a grate warrior; he used to dhrink *purls* for *wather*—*mortus est*—he's dead, too! There was Mark Antony, a great frind and co-adjuthor of Cleopathra's, he had a grate turn for boating and the like—*mortus est*—he's dead, too! There was Charleymange, a grate Frinchman of larning and tongues, and with all his larning—*mortus est!*—he's dead, too! There was the grate Alexandre, the gineral of the whole wide world—'"

"Lord save us!" ejaculated the old man, as he knocked the ashes out of his pipe against a stone which projected from the back of the chimney.

"'The whole wide world!'" repeated Grace; "'he used to roar and bawl whenever he couldn't set a faction fight a-foot; and it isn't at that he'd stop, if he had his own way, for it was all fun to him—*mortus est*—he's dead, too! There was the grate Cicero, a mighty fine preacher, like myself—*mortus est*—he's dead, too. There was the wonderful Arkimedays, he was a great magician, an admiral, and a navigator; he used to set ships o' fire by just looking at them through a spy-glass; he had an eye, boys, like a process—*mortus est*—he's dead, too!——'"

"Grace," interrupted the old man, "I believe, after all, you're right. I wish I had the name of the paper. I don't think it's of the true sort, so I'll *roul* it up, put it into my pocket, show it to his reverence at the 'station' on Friday, and ask him if the sarmon's a right one."

"Just let me go over it a bit first," said Grace, intending

doubtless to refer to the paragraphs on fashion, as all girls in Ireland and out of Ireland invariably do. "Sure, I'm not so fond of spending my time at anything of the sort." She continued looking over column after column, until at last she came to a name she thought she had heard her uncle speak of.

"Didn't you know one James Kenneth, uncle?"

"To be sure I did, Grace. What has honest Jemmy been after, to be put on the paper?"

"He's dead, uncle."

"The Lord be good to us!" ejaculated the old man; " James Kenneth was fifteen years to the good younger than me!—My poor Grace!"

"Why, what had I to do with him?" inquired the girl, astonished at her uncle's earnestness.

"Not much, to be sure,—and yet you had, Grace, as a body may say."

"But what's very strange, uncle, is, that just under his death, is the death of his son Thomas,—a young man in his seventeenth year!"

Grace was so intent on the paragraph, for people are always touched by the deaths of those who are nearly their own age, that she kept her eyes fixed on the paper, and it was some minutes before she perceived that a death-like pallor had overspread her uncle's countenance. She sprang from her seat when she perceived it, and flinging her arms round his neck, inquired if he was ill.

I have observed the manifestations of joy and grief in the inhabitants of many lands. The Scotch are wisely taught from infancy to subdue their feelings; they bring them at an early period of life under a quaker-like subjection, which, though decidedly advantageous to themselves, throws a coldness upon the feelings of others. The expressions of English sympathy or anxiety, though the sincerest in the world, are blunt and ungraceful. You feel that those of French tenderness are tricked and garlanded with a view to effect; their tears are shed after a form—their sorrow is made picturesque. But the anxiety, earnestness, the truthfulness of Irish sympathy, sorrow, or tenderness, burst uncontrolled from the heart,—the *young* heart, I should say, for *old* hearts learn how to regulate their feelings, and it is well they do, for otherwise they would go wounded and tortured to their graves. To one accustomed only to the well-bred habits of modern society, the earnest and gushing sympathy with which an Irish girl enters into the joys, griefs, hopes, and fears, of those she loves, presents quite a new and delightful reading of human nature,—it is most beautiful and eloquent in its character.   She loses all consideration of self—she weeps— she laughs—because those she loves weep or laugh.   She forgets that she is a separate creation—and feels as if created for her friends—friends!—the word is all too cold to express her devotion, it must be seen to be understood—excited, or it can never be appreciated as it deserves.   Grace Burnett was a creature of smiles and tears—a sunbeam or a shadow.   She had never been seen to frown, though she was often sad, because her uncle was at times moody, even to ill-temper—the neighbours said they sometimes pitied her ; had they understood the happiness she felt in soothing his irritations, they would have envied her her delight when saying—" No one can please my dear uncle half as well as I."   Grace was proud of the influence her affectionate gentleness had gained over Black Burnett.   And now, when she hung round him and inquired so earnestly if he was ill, and what troubled him, she thought her heart would break at his continued silence : even her idiot brother seemed to sympathise with her—he fidgeted on his seat, looked at her, shuffled his fingers through his hair, and at last came and stood by her side.

"Something's come entirely over him that I've no skill in," said she at last despairingly, " Mick, speak to him, Mick—he'll mind you, maybe."

" What you see wrong in others, mend in yourself," muttered the idiot.

" Ay, Grace—my poor Grace—and that's it, sure enough," said her uncle, recovering from his stupor—"that's it!—the sarm'n that poor natural preaches was evermore in my ear, and maybe that was the reason it did not reach my heart—' What you see wrong in others, mend in yourself.'   Wasn't I constant at Mr. Hanway, of Mount Grove, to get a lease of years, instead of lives, for his farm ?—didn't I worry Mr. Maguire till he had his lease properly drawn ?—and when forty acres of the best arable land in the county went clean out of the hands of Nicholas Cruise, who passed so many censures on his carelessness as Black Burnett ?"

" What you see wrong in others, mend in yourself," again said Michael.

" By the blessed saints !" exclaimed Burnett, his agitated

feelings taking another turn, and glad of escape by words or violence, " if you repeat that to me again, you poor tantalising ill-featured fool! I'll find if there's any brains in your sknll!— It's a purty thing for you to be reproaching me, that nursed you since you came out of your shell." Michael and Snap paired off into the chimney-corner, and Grace burst into tears.

" Ay, cry;—you may well cry, Grace, but it's no use. I'm ould, and almost helpless—and God only knows," continued the farmer, as he paced up and down the spacious kitchen, which his father and grandfather had trod before him, " God only knows how long I may be in the land of the living ; and then, Grace, then what's to become of you ?"

" Me, uncle ?"

" Ay, you, uncle ! — why you're growing as great an *omadawn** as your brother !"

Grace feared to ask a question, but still the tears rained down her cheeks.

" Hav'n't you heard me say that I had three lives in the new lease of this place—James Kenneth, and his son Thomas— Thomas, who was born the same year as you, my poor Grace —and—but the Lord forgive me, what an ould sinner I am!— Tom Kenneth, cut off, as a body may say, in the very bud of his youth—the same age as you, Gracy—within a week the same age—yet he is taken—a fine, strong, healthy boy— he is taken—and you, a delicate, weakly girl, but the delight and treasure of your uncle's heart—you are left upon the earth, and in my own house, to bless it, as you have always done. God forgive me my sins !—but I was always a passionate man —hot and hasty—you'll forgive me, my child!"

The old man kissed the daughter of his heart and his adoption; and at once the sorrow passed from her lovely face—quicker than she could wipe away the tears.

" Sure, thanks be to God, I've heard you say that your own life's in the lease, and sure that's to the good still, and will be, please the Almighty, for many a long day to come. And, uncle dear, maybe the landlord will still renew it, upon years; —and even if he didn't, don't fret on our account, for—— "

Before she could finish her sentence there was a loud knock at the cottage-door. Snap, in his eagerness to investigate the character and demands of the visitor, overturned the wheel, and

---

* Fool.

without heeding the mischief he had done, poked his snub nose through an aperture in the post, and growled angrily.

The visitor opened the door at which he knocked before Burnett had time to raise the latch; but Grace, as her uncle turned to do so, made time enough to whisper Michael, "If you'll be a good boy, and not repeat what vexed uncle just now, for three days, I'll give you a rosy-cheeked apple, and butter to the potatoes for a week." Mick laughed with delight, and Grace finished her speech just in time to say, "Kindly welcome," illustrated by a pretty curtsey to the muffled-up stranger, who was now standing in the midst of the apartment. He was a stout, thick-set man, whose blue great-coat, strong brogues, and well-fitting beaver, told of his belonging to the " warmer ' portion of the commonalty;—his " shillelah " was more carved than as it is usually seen in a countryman's hand, and when he politely removed his hat, his brown clustering hair curled around a handsome, yet disagreeable countenance;—at least so Grace considered it—she thought of the simile in the mock sermon she had just read, of " a look being as bad as a process;" and after dusting a chair with her apron, and pushing it towards him, she waited, expecting that he would speak in reply to the friendly greetings he had already received. He stood, however, in his old position, looking alternately at Burnett, at Grace, at Michael, and then investigating, with curious eye, every article of furniture in the kitchen—the delft neatly arranged upon the dresser—the three deal chairs—the stools and " bosses "—the noggins—the settle—the wheel; that most unusual piece of furniture in an Irish cottage—a small work-table, and a neat book-shelf " facing the dresser,"—all were scrutinised—until at last Burnett became annoyed at his visitor's rudeness, and in a rough tone said, " he hoped he liked all he saw, for he would be sure to know them again."

" Ay," replied the man ; " like, to be sure I do—everything here is to be liked—and——" his eye glanced familiarly at Grace—" loved, for the matter of that; but——" he paused, and looked round again—and again.

" It's a wild night, and I'm thinking you'd better take an air of the fire," said Burnett.

" Thank ye, so I will; it feels very comfortable," said the stranger, walking under the shadow of the wide chimney, and spreading out his hands to the heat, which Grace had increased by the addition of some " sods " of turf. " The boy—a natural

—the dog," he continued, talking aloud, and yet as if to himself—"the dog, the pretty girl—everything exactly as I saw it.
It is very strange!"

"May I make so bould as to ask what is so strange?" inquired Burnett.

"Everything—everything here," he replied, turning his back
to the fire, and again surveying the apartment.

"Nothing out of the common, sir, barring Grace's little work-
table—a compliment from the carpenter," observed the simple-
minded man, while Grace blushed at the allusion to her—(truth
will out)—her lover!

"Stranger and stranger still," resumed the traveller; "and
that *that* young lady's name should be Grace!"

"Young lady!" repeated Burnett; "she's an honest man's
daughter, and a good little girl, but no lady."

"She's your niece, and that poor fellow's your nephew, and
that dog's name is Snap, and your name is Corney Burnett,
commonly called Black Corney, or Black Burnett."

"Holy Mary defend us!" ejaculated Grace, crossing herself;
even Mick opened his large brown eyes; while their uncle said,
"Why, then, it's known you must be among the neighbours,
though you're strange to me, and your tongue's not of this
country."

"I have walked seventeen miles since I entered a house—I
was never in this part of the world before—and I was born in
foreign parts; and yet I am as much at home here as if I had
lived in the parish all my life! Every stick of your furniture
I feel as used to as if it had been my own!"

Black Burnett crossed himself as he turned to look round his
cottage, and Grace slid slily out of the kitchen into her little
chamber, and dipping her fingers in the vase of holy water that
hung at the head of her humble bed, sprinkled herself with it;
wetting her fingers again, so that on her return to the kitchen
she might convey a few drops to her brother's person: her
uncle wore a scapular, so she considered *him* safe.

"Why, then, may I ask again how you gained your information," questioned Burnet, as he seated himself opposite his
mystifying guest, who, on Grace's return, was seated also.

"Indeed, you may," he replied, "and, what's not always the
case, I'll answer you--*I dreamt it!*" Upon this there was a
loud exclamation, and a general crossing succeeded. Their
visitor looked round and smiled. "Do not be ashamed of your

religion, my good friends; I have been in many countries, and one religion's as good as another, if acted up to; that's my belief. Cross yourself again, my pretty maid, and you, too, Master Burnett, and I will tell you how it was; but first let me ask, is there not a deep line of sand-pits near this, a little way off the road leading to the left?"

" There is!" replied the uncle and niece together.

" And—now mark me!—is there not a very large elm-.ree a few perches farther on?"

" There is!" responded the same voices.

" And when you pass that, you descend a steep, green valley?"

" You do!"

" At the foot of the valley runs a bright clear stream, with a bridge over it?"

" There *did* run a stream there," said Burnett; " but Peter Pike turned it into his mill-dam, as I told him, contrary to nature and Act of Parliament; so that now there's a bridge without any water under it."

The traveller's countenance fell, but it brightened immediately, and he continued: " And farther down that stream are the ruins of an old abbey; and under the south window of that abbey stands a broad, flat, marble stone?"

" Ay, true enough," said Burnett; " I've pegged my top on it many a time when I was a boy."

" Peter Pike, then, has not turned that stone into his mill-dam," persisted the stranger, smiling; " and as it remains there —why, my friend, our fortune's made—that's all!"

" I don't see—I don't understand—you've not insensed * me into it yet," said Burnett.

" The time's not come for telling all. I have said enough to prove to you that, without ever having been here before, I knew exactly what I have told, and more too, which, when I have had some refreshment, you shall know."

What the Irish peasant has to give he gives freely, be it much or little. Hospitality has been called the virtue of savage life: be it so; its exercise is delightful to the wayfarer. As the even ng advanced, it was evident that, notwithstanding Grace's desire to hear all the stranger had to communicate, he was not disposed to gratify her curiosity, and she and her brother were soon dismissed to their beds. There was a half-

* Enlightened.

finished closet inside Grace Burnett's little room, which served (if truth must be told) as the nursing-chamber of a pet calf, which she was rearing with more than ordinary care; for the creature was milk-white, devoid of spot or blemish, and consequently regarded with superstitious tenderness. As the stranger was to occupy Mick's bed, the poor natural was content to share the calf's straw; but when his sister went to cover him with a supernumerary blanket, she found him sitting, his arms enfolding the neck of his favourite dog, and his eyes staring with the expression of one who listens attentively.

" Go to sleep, Michael."

" Whisht !" exclaimed the boy, holding up his finger.

" What's ails you, Astore ?"

" Whisht !" he again repeated.

" Lie down, Michael."

" No, no! I saw—whisht!—I saw what Lanty Pike kills the birdeens with, peepin', peepin' in the strange man's breast—I saw the muzzle of it—he! he! Uncle's the fool, if uncle trusts him—whisht !"

The astonishment occasioned by the stranger's story at once faded from Grace's mind; but if it did, her first impressions returned with tenfold strength. How was her uncle to make his fortune? What connection could he have with the traveller's dream, or the broad, flat stone in the old grey abbey? Her spirit sank within her. A tythe-proctor had been murdered about two years before, and thrown into the gravel-pit. Her heart beat feebly within her bosom, and half creeping, half staggering, to the door of her chamber, she put her eye close to the latch-hole, and saw, to her astonishment, her uncle evidently preparing to accompany the stranger out, though the night was dark and stormy; the traveller was already equipped, and Black Burnett was putting on his " big coat." Nor did it escape the girl's observation, that the whisky bottle was nearly empty, and that, though the stranger was perfectly sober, her uncle's cheek was flushed, and his step unsteady. She was about to let them see that she was not gone to bed, and to entreat her uncle not to go forth that night, when she remembered that their cottage was " a good step" from any other dwelling, and that if their mysterious guest intended violence, he could easily overpower a half-drunken man and a feeble girl; poor Michael was always counted as nothing. She saw her uncle take up his spade from out the corner, and, notwithstanding the stranger's entreaties to be permitted to carry it, she was pleased to observe he persisted in his determination to bear it himself. A tremor she could not account for came over her, and as they closed the outer door, she nearly fainted.

Black Burnett and his visitor proceeded on their way in the direction of the gravel-pits.

"You're sure of the road?" inquired the stranger.

"Am I sure that this is my own hand?" replied Burnett; "first the gravel-pits—then the bridge—no, then the elm—then the bridge—then the ould abbey—then the flat stone! Ah! what will the neighbours say, when Grace flourishes off to mass on a side-saddle? and to think of your bringing me such news just as I'd got into the doldrums about the lease. Three days—three nights, I mean—since you dreamt of the goold?"

"Three, exactly."

"Under the flat stone?"

"Ay! do let me carry the spade; and see, as we seem to be on the edge of the gravel-pit, had you not better walk next to it? you know it, and I don't."

"I thought you said you war up to every turn of the crag, through the drame?"

"Ay, to be sure; but give me the spade."

"I tell you I won't; hav'n't you the bag that's to carry home the red goold? Lord, how they will all stare! Grace shan't put off ould uncle then with a bottle of whisky; I'll have a whole cask! Whir, man alive! can't you walk straight, as I do? you almost had me over the edge of the pit, and there's good six feet wather in the bottom of it. There, just where the moon shines, is the elm-tree, and———"

In all human probability the word would have been his last, for the murderer's grasp was on the arm of his intended victim, but that Michael—the half-idiot Michael—with a whoop and a halloo, bearing a lighted stick in his hand, rushed so closely by them that the sparks of his wild brand starred the stranger's coat; while Snap, hearing his master's voice, barked either in glee or anger.

"Hurroo! hurroo! Uncle, uncle, here's the light for your's or the devil's pipe! Hurroo! night-rovers — ill-gatherers! hurroo! hurroo!" and shouting and jumping, Michael kept before his uncle, now tossing his torch into the air, and then whirling it round his head.

"Send the cub to his den," said the stranger, in so fierce a tone of voice, that the inebriated Burnett noted the change, and turned to look at his companion.

"Send the idiot home," he continued, "or by the Lord I'll send him somewhere else!" and, as he spoke, he drew a pistol from his vest.

The sight of the weapon sobered the old man in a moment "Stop! stop!" he exclaimed, "if you hurt a hair of that boy's head, you'll pay for it—that's all. You're no true man to draw a pistol on such a natural as that;—besides, what use have you for the fire-arms?"

"Use!" repeated the traveller; "why, you know your country has not the reputation of being the quietest in the world. So, for my own personal safety—— "

"Quietest!" repeated Burnett; "I'll trouble you not to say anything against the country. I'm thinking you're not the sort I took you for—to offer to fire at a poor natural, whom every man in the parish would fight to purtect; and then to abuse Ould Ireland!"

"My good friend," interrupted the stranger, "let me beg of you to send that boy home; to trust our secret with an idiot would be absurd in the extreme."

"As to getting Michael in, when Michael would rather be out, I might as well tie a rat with a sugan.* There's no use in gainsaying the poor natural. So I'm thinking the night is so wild, and that crathur so bent upon watching what I'm after, that we'd better go back;—to-morrow night will do as well."

"If you'd just let me frighten him with a flash in the pan, it would send him to bed as gentle as a fawn."

"Flash in the pan! God help you, man alive!—the whisper of a pistol even would send Michael over the town-land before you could say Bannachar; and he'd have a crowd round us that would beat a priest's funeral to nothing. No, no; all we've for it to-night, is to back and be aisy."

Burnett was determined, and his companion was compelled to submit, after trying in vain to impress upon the farmer's mind that as it was the third night after the dream, it was particularly favourable for such an adventure.

"Sure the goold is there, and if it has stayed there for maybe a hundred or two years, what's to take it away now, or before to-morrow night?" argued Black Burnett; but I much doubt if the idea would have influenced him, had not the sight of the

* Straw rope.

pistol awoke his suspicions, or, as he said himself, if something had not "come over him" that turned him homeward.

The next morning the stranger lingered about the cottage, making himself familiar with every winding path in the vicinity, and trying, as it is called, to "make friends" with Michael Michael, however, was true to his first feelings, and eyed the stranger as a shy dog may often be observed to regard a person who has treated him secretly with harshness, and yet would wish to be on outward terms of civility. He offered him gingerbread—Michael threw it in the fire; nuts—he flung them back into his lap. In the favour of Grace, he made no progress either. His compliments were unregarded; and to complete his mortification, the favoured carpenter came to stay there for a day or two. He could not help thinking that the carpenter had been sent for, either by Grace or Michael, as a spy upon his actions. He saw that every movement he made, every word he spoke, was watched, and whatever plan of action he had formed was evidently frustrated for the present. Black Burnett talked to his guest eagerly of the anticipated treasure; whatever suspicions or fears had been awakened in his mind had passed away with the darkness of night, and his habitual incaution and natural obstinacy tended to make him as easy a prey as a murderer could desire. The next night it blew a perfect hurricane—the sort of storm which a strong man cannot stand in—and the thunder and the lightning sported in their fierceness with the winds and rain. The door of the cottage was forced in more than once; and as the fire gleamed upon the stranger's face (for he had gathered himself up, silent moody, and disappointed, in Burnett's chimney-corner), Grace could hardly forbear thinking him the incarnation of an evil spirit. If superstition detracts from our wisdom, it adds to our poetry; it is the high-priest of a poetic mind, and I much doubt if a vivid imagination could exist without it. There is often more genuine poetry in the mind of an Irish peasant than critics would deem possible. The weather was such that no one dared venture out; and the more terrific the storm, the more Michael rejoiced. He leaped—he clapped his hands; he seemed to his sister as if under the impression that his uncle owed his safety to the war of elements, which shook to the foundation their humble dwelling. At intervals the visitor and his host would look out upon the night, but it was only to return with discomfited aspects to their seats.

"Uncle," said Grace, drawing him gently aside, "uncle, darlint, I want to spake a word to ye ; it's about the lase, uncle. Matthew (her lover) has tould me that the landlcid himself will be passing through Ross to-morrow, and he doesn't want any of us to know it, because he's always bothered about leases and the like ; and you are sensible* no Irish gentleman in the world likes to be tormented about business of any kind—he'd rather let it take its own course without toil ; but Matthew says, uncle, that maybe, as my mother nursed him, and poor Mike—weak though he is—is his own foster-brother, if I watched and could get a glimpse of him, he'd spake to me anyhow."

"I wouldn't be under a compliment to him for the lase," replied Burnett, proudly. "Maybe, Grace, it's more than himself I'll have one of these days."

"Sure it's no compliment, if we pay the same as another ; and you were never a gale† behindhand in your life. And, uncle, honey ! if it's trusting to drames you are——"

"You're not going to prache to me, are you ?" said the impatient man, interrupting her.

"No, not prache, only there's a look betwixt yon man's two eyes that has no mercy in it. Uncle, a-cushla—take care of him !"

"You're a little fool—a worse natural than Mike—that's what you are !"

"But you'll take care—and about the lase ?"

"Let me alone, will you ? Grace, you're a spiled girl—that's what you are—and it's myself spiled you," replied Burnett, turning again to look out on the night, which, fortunately for him, was worse than ever. It was long past two before the family retired to rest ; but Grace's head was too full to sleep. She was up with the lark ; a calm and beautiful morning had succeeded the storm. Matthew, her handsome lover, was soor roused from his light slumbers in the barn, and she counselled with him long and earnestly upon her plans.

"The terror of that strange man leaves my heart when the daylight comes," said the innocent girl, "and yet I don't like to quit him alone with Mike and uncle. Mike thinks he'd have pitched uncle into the gravel-pits, Thursday night, but for him ; to be sure, there's no minding what Mike says."

Matthew thought differently ; he said he had observed that, at times, her brother evinced much intelligence.

* Aware.   † Quarter's rent.

"The landlord will be in Ross about eleven, you say; and it's a long walk from this. A-weary on the drames! But for the dramer, uncle himself would go, I know;—and yet there's truth in them at times—and it was wonderful how he knew us all."

Matthew smiled.

"Can't I go myself, and you stay here?" she continued.

No; Matthew would not do that. What, let her go *alone*, as if no one cared for her, to meet her young a id handsome landlord!—he didn't care about the lease—not he—but to suffer her to go alone! If she thought it would make her mind easy, his brother Brien, the stonemason, should go to work at the New Pier "forenent" the house, and he would be a safeguard.

That was a pleasant proposal; and in her eager desire to obtain a promise from the landlord that he would grant her uncle a lease of years, she more than half persuaded herself that her fears were imaginary. "At all events," she argued, "no harm can happen him in the bames of the blessed sun. I'll be back before night; and if I do but bring the promise—the written promise from the landlord—uncle will be in a good humour; and then, maybe—maybe—I'd coax him over to give up the drame, and take a fresh oath against the whisky!"

Poor, poor Grace!

She wakened Michael, and telling him to take care of his uncle, promised him some fresh gingerbread if he was a good boy, and kept his pledge; and having first left the breakfast ready, set off on her adventure, escorted by as true a lover, and as sensible a friend, as ever fell to the lot of a country girl.

Matthew is a perfect jewel in his way—sober, attentive, and industrious;—fond of his nome—of his wife, and children;—worthy to be held up as a pattern to all the married men in his country, whether poor or rich. I honour Matthew, and think him—(and that is saying a great deal)—as good as any English husband of my acquaintance.

When Black Burnett got up, he was not a little annoyed at finding that pretty Grace had disappeared, contrary to his desire; and though he well knew the cause of her absence, for once he had the prudence to keep his own counsel, saying only to his guest that she had gone to Ross. During the early part of the day the visitor walked about as he had done before; but at noon the mason saw a strange boy give him a piece of paper—a note or parcel—he could not tell which, it was so "*squeeged*" between their hands; but something of that sort it certainly was.

After dinner, the stranger proposed that he should accompany Black Burnett a little way on the Ross road, to meet Grace on her return; nor did he object to poor Michael bearing them company. The stonemason (honest Brien) thought, after a little time, he would follow in the distance; though from the earliness of the hour, and the road being much frequented, he had no apprehension of anything wrong; keeping, however, his eye on the man he had been cautioned by his brother and his intended sister to watch till their return. The two went, to all appearance, cheerfully, on their way: the stranger was one who had seen many countries; he could make himself very entertaining, and nobody loved a jest or a good story better than poor Burnett. Michael stopped occasionally to gather blackberries, to speak "to a neighbour's child," to "hurrish" the pigs, or to throw stones at the crows which congregated in the fresh-ploughed fields. The brilliant morning had sobered down into the fine, tranquil autumn day; the broad-leaved coltsfoot (almost as destructive to the cultivator of Irish ground as the super-abundant "rag-weed") turned the silver lining of its light-green leaves to the declining sunbeams, and the hedges were gaily decked with rich clusters of the red-ripe hawthorn-berry.

"I cannot get on any further without something to drink," said the stranger, stopping opposite a wayside public-house, which was adorned by the O'Connell arms, and a most unlike likeness of the "Agitator." "You have treated me; now I must treat you."

"I have no objection to a glass of '*rale* Cork,'" replied Burnett; "but I must not taste more than one, or Grace, the slut, will haul me over the griddle for it."

"I tell you what; have some of Cherry's excellent ale, and if that doesn't warm you, you can have something *short* afterwards."

"Something what?" inquired his companion, unaccustomed to English slang.

"Strong, you know. Come, my pretty mistress, a quart of Cherry's best!"

The clear and beautiful ale sparkled as, after he received it, he poured a portion into a measure, and turned towards the fire with the remainder, inquiring of his companion, "Shall I warm it for you? Would you like it warmed with some sugar and spice, as we do in Wales?"

"No, no, do not put it on the fire; I would rather have it as it is," replied Burnett; "Cherry's ale wants nothing but the drinking."

"You see," said the stranger, turning to the landlady, "*you see he would not let me put anything in it.*"

In an instant the draught was at Burnett's lips; he had walked far, and the heat and exercise had overpowered him. Another moment, and his destiny on this side the grave would have been decided; but his time was not yet come. Michael rushed into the room, and seizing the cup from his uncle's uplifted hand, drank it nearly to the dregs.

"Sorrow catch you for an ill——" but ere Burnett could finish the sentence, his eye rested upon the changed and changing countenance of the stranger. Disappointment, rage, anger, and hatred were painted upon his distorted features; painted so vividly, that both the landlady and the intended victim exclaimed at the same moment, "*It is poisoned!*"

What has taken some time to write, was the transaction of less than a minute; the villain seized the measure, and attempted to throw what remained of the contents into the fire, but the arm of a strong serving-maiden prevented this purpose. He then rushed to the door; but here again he was interrupted by the stonemason, who had quickly followed their steps, and poor Mike, who, with the strong animal instinct of hatred, clung to his legs to impede his progress.

"Fool! idiot! cursed fool!" exclaimed the ruffian, endeavouring to draw a pistol from his vest.

This recalled Burnett to his senses. "My boy! my poor Michael!" he exclaimed; "lay not a finger near him; for if you do, this hour—this moment—shall be your last!"

"Why do you hold me—what have I done?" inquired the stranger, as his presence of mind returned. "Who talked of poison? if there *was* poison in the ale, *the landlady saw that he would not let me put anything in it.*"

It happened to be fair-day in one of the neighbouring villages, and a crowd soon collected round and in the house. Amongst them—hurried forward by others, without knowing the cause of the excitement, but accompanied by her lover—came Grace Burnett; on seeing her uncle she could not resist throwing herself into his arms, and whispering, "I've seen his honour—I've got the promise, and his honour's own self's coming this way—run out and make your *obedience* to him."

"He's a magistrate, thank God!" exclaimed Burnett, rushing to the door. "Grace, for the love of God, look to Michael!"

"Michael, what ails you, honey?" said the affectionate girl, turning to her brother.

" Nothing, nothing, nothing ails me—they're all foolish—nothing ails Mick—nothing ails Mick," he replied, jumping and tossing his arms.

"Keep aisy—keep aisy," said the landlord. "Sure the doctor's sent for, and will tell us what to do presently."

When Burnett's landlord left his carriage, and entered the public-house, the look of assurance which the stranger had assumed changed to one of fixed despair—he seemed like one for whom there is no redemption. "What you, Lawler!—you accused of such a crime? Your brother told me you were in Dublin."

"My brother ought to have done his own business himself," growled the fellow; "but no one can say I meant to hurt the boy."

The rest is soon told. A favourite steward had induced Burnett's landlord to promise him, that when the *last life in the lease* dropped, he should have the farm upon which his heart was set. By bribes and entreaties, he prevailed upon his brother—a man of wild and reckless habits—to undertake the getting Burnett out of the way. His first plan was to decoy him from home, and precipitate him into the gravel-pits: this failed, by the providential interposition of poor Michael, whose idiotcy was strongly mingled with shrewdness. The villain waited another opportunity, knowing he had a strong hold upon Burnett's superstition and his love of wealth; but that very morning he received intimation from his brother that it must be done quickly, as the landlord himself was talking of passing through and about his farms, and if once the Burnetts "got speech of him," it would be "all up." He at once decided on using poison, and we have seen how it was prevented from taking effect upon his intended victim. Had any evidence been wanting, the remains of arsenic found in a paper on his person —his brother's letter, which the stonemason had seen him receive—the contents of the beer when analysed by a neighbouring doctor, who unhappily did not arrive until poor Michael had felt that something more than usual "ailed" him—were all proofs of his guilt. But it is impossible to imagine anything more vehement, more terrible, than the excitement which prevailed amongst the country-people, while the poor idiot was suffering the agonies of death. It was difficult to prevent their tearing the culprit to pieces. The fact of his wanting to take land over another man's head would have been enough to rouse their indignation; but when they saw the simple inoffensive creature, whose gentle words, and good-natured though witless offices, had endeared him to every cottager, their wrath knew no bounds.

"It's a lesson to the landlord to see after his tenants himself, that I hope he'll not forget," said one. "Sure the God of heaven, if he lifts the dews from the earth, sends it back again in rain; but everything is took from poor Paddy, and nothing returned!"

"Lift me to the air, Gracy," whispered the dying boy to his sister: "I know I'll be waked soon; but let poor Snap have the butter and gingerbread you promised me, for I never preached my sarmon since to vex you, Gracy." The hardest and sternest wept when they saw the poor faithful dog lick his master's purple lips, and saw that master's dying efforts to push from him the thing he certainly loved best in the world, murmuring, "Maybe t'would hurt him—maybe t'would hurt him!"

Dread and fearful was the hope of exterminating vengeance which Black Burnett swore against the stranger Lawler and his brother, over the body of the dead idiot; but it was not needed —the one paid the forfeit of his crime, and was executed within a month after its committal—the other disappeared, and wa never again seen or heard of in the country. Black Burnett abandoned whisky, and grew rich; but never could bear to hear of people finding money under flat stones.

Matthew and Grace still inhabit the dwelling, though it is far more comfortable than it was; and Snap's descendant cannot find a hole in the door-post to poke his nose through, though he is quite as cross and curious as his grandsire.

[There are persons now living who remember well the excitement produced in the county in which it occurred by the appalling event that has formed the groundwork of this story. It was related to me by a clergyman who, under the name of "Martin Doyle," has published a variety of little works upon rural and domestic economy, the value of which, to the Irish farmer and cottager, is greater than pure gold.]

A VERY WOMAN;

BY MISS M. B. SMEDLEY.

"FERTILE in expedients!" said Clara Capel to herself, as she stood alone at the breakfast-table with a spoon filled with tea-leaves carefully poised in her hand on its way from the caddy to the teapot. The life of Sully lay open on the table beside her, and was the immediate cause of her soliloquy. "Fertile in expedients!" thought she, "it is always the same. All great men are so, whether statesmen, or generals, or authors. They don't make a handsome, tidy, comfortable theory in their own minds, and then throw away everything they meet with because it does not exactly suit the place they have got ready for it; but they take the world as they find it, and having got their materials, they improve here and correct there; they invent this, and beautify that, and combine all, till at last they have built up a great edifice to the glory of God; and the irregularity and variety, the dreamy lights and doubtful shadows, are, in fact, the beauty of it." (Clara was pleased with her illustration, and so paused to polish it a little ere she proceeded.) "To give up labouring because the persons or the systems by whom and under which you have to labour are not ideally perfect, is very much as if an artist were to give up painting because his oil-colours didn't smell of otto of roses, and were apt to soil his fingers. 'Make the best of it!'—that is the motto of all practical greatness—and what a *best* it is sometimes How infinitely and wonderfully the result transcends the means. Well, and the same sort of mind which, when the proportions are large, is fit to rule the world, must be necessary, though with small proportions, for the guidance of a family, or a course of every-day duties. Of that I am quite sure. And this is a woman's business, not to sit down as I do, and grieve inwardly because she cannot do what she would, but to do what she can, and that cheerfully. Goethe says, 'It is well for a woman when no work seems too hard for her, or too small; when she is able to forget herself and to live entirely in others.' Why am not I thus? I *can* be, and by God's help I *will* be. Unselfishness and energy, these are the great secrets, and these are within everybody's reach. I may be, if I choose, the life and centre of this home of mine—the one who helps all, the one to whom all appeal. I may bring order and even elegance out of all this confusion, by descending to details, and going to work heartily. Why should I be ashamed to do so? The heroine of a Swedish novel goes into the kitchen to dress beef-steaks for her husband's dinner, and yet is capable of diffusing æsthetics in a manner that few Englishwomen could equal. One would not be less liked and admired "—(here it must be confessed that a particular person was in Clara's thoughts, though she gave mental utterance to no name)—" for such exertions, but rather more. Men, especially, never think so highly of a woman as when she contributes to the comfort of others; and how *can* she contribute to the comfort of others, if her most active bodily exertion is to dance the polka? But this must be all *real.* It must be *done*, not thought about; and the disagreeables and the failures which one must needs encounter, must be laughed at and overcome. Then how charming it will be when I see my work, and feel that I hold the family together, and that they all look to me, and have recourse to me; and that by sacrificing my own particular wishes and tastes I am able to sustain them all, and to make them all happy!"

Clara clasped her hands together in the enthusiasm awakened by this idea, and the contents of the teaspoon went fluttering over the white tablecloth, not omitting to sprinkle the open butter-dish which stood near.

"Isn't my mistress's breakfast ready yet, Miss Clara?" asked a somewhat untidy-looking maid, as she entered the room, carrying an empty tray, and followed by the master of the house and sundry other members of the family; "she has been waiting for it this quarter of an hour."

Clara looked bewildered at this sudden summons from her castle in the air.

"Why, the tea isn't even made!" cried Mr. Capel, indignantly. "Really, Clara, it is very tiresome. Books," w.th a wrathful glance at the volume of Sully, "are exceedingly well in their way; but it is one of the worst characteristics of a regular blue-stocking to be dreaming over a book when she ought to be making herself useful. Half-past nine o'clock, too, and the children's breakfast not ready yet. If this goes on, I shall have Julia installed as housekeeper in future; she may, perhaps, be better, and it's quite certain she couldn't be worse!"

"I am very sorry, papa," said Clara, meekly, the ready tears gathering in her eyes.

"Oh! it's easy to be very sorry," returned her father, as he sat down and began cutting bread and butter with great vehemence; "but the fact is, you don't care for such things— you never think about them—your head is full of other matters; and as long as you have your German and your music, it's nothing to you that your mother has to wait for her breakfast. If you gave one-twentieth part of the thought which you bestow on a sonata by Beethoven to the comfort of your family, it would be better for all of us!"

How unjust we are to each other! and yet scarcely to be condemned, for the action is all we can see; and when the action belies the thought, how can we form a right judgment? And who is there so perfectly disciplined that his habitual actions do indeed represent his inward aspirations?

Clara was naturally timid; she attempted no self-defence, but hurriedly and nervously proceeded with the business of breakfast. She made tea, conscious that the water had ceased to boil, but afraid to expose the fact by ringing the bell for a fresh supply. Quietly and silently she provided the children with their bread-and-milk, distributed the steaming cups to her elder brother and sister, and finally placed the strongest beside her father, who vouchsafed no acknowledgment of the attention, his temper not being improved by the discovery that he was spreading tea-leaves upon the bread with his butter. Then, while the servant and tray still waited, she was hurrying out into the garden, leaving her own meal untasted, when her brother stopped her: "Where, in the name of wonder, are you going, Clara?"

"Only to gather a nosegay, to send up with mamma's breakfast," replied she, apologetically, as she paused on the threshold.

"A nosegay!" cried Mr. Capel, with an indescribable mixture of wrath and contempt, while George and Julia could not restrain their laughter, and the younger members of the family observed that restrained and awkward silence natural to children when a disturbance is going on among their elders. "A Nose gay!" upon my word and honour, Clara, you are too provoking. Just come back and sit down, will you? I hate this confused uncomfortable way of having one's breakfast—it is wretched—it puts me out for the whole day. And your mother waiting all this while! She would much rather have a cup of tea than all the nosegays in the world. It will be time enough to think of the *graces* of life when you have learned a little better to fulfil the commonest *duties*."

This closing sarcasm was quite too much for poor Clara; and as she resumed her seat and her occupation, her tears fell fast. She tried hard to restrain them, and cautiously screened them from her father's observation behind the urn. Then followed sundry of those small, quiet kindnesses, which are always forthcoming when any member of an affectionate family is in trouble, however deserved. George and Julia exerted themselves to maintain a forced conversation, and the former kept vigilant watch over the sugaring and creaming of his father's cup, in order to repair any oversight, without drawing attention to it; Emily silently supplied her sister's plate with bread and butter; and little Annie, who understood nothing except that Clara was crying about flowers, stole round to her side with a rosebud, just gathered from her own garden, soft and fresh as her own smiling lips, and quietly slipped the offering into Clara's hand.

Mr. Capel was angry enough to feel his indignation **rather** increased than abated by the evident distress of the culprit; it seemed to reproach him for a severity which justice had entirely demanded, and by aggravating his discomfort, aggravated also his ire. He pushed his plate from him, saying, in a kind of *finale* tone of intense disgust, "A wretched breakfast, indeed!" then sharply rebuked Emily for spilling her bread-and-milk on the carpet, and trod hard on the toes of the family spaniel, who spent his life in an abortive attempt to commit suicide by thrusting himself under the feet of each member of the household in succession, but who, being a favourite, was generally praised and petted for this, as though the natural place of dogs was wherever human feet were about to be planted; and if the dog escaped being trampled on, and the human being escaped a fall, it was a wonderful exercise of skill and affection on the part of the former, and he deserved high commendation for it. Ponto howled aloud; and Emily, who was very tender-hearted, and whose nerves were somewhat affected by the preceding scene, burst into a violent flood of tears; little Annie, as a matter of course, roaring, with all her might, for sympathy.

The Capels were universally pronounced a very happy family; nevertheless, this specimen of their domestic felicity was by no means solitary of its kind.

Mr. Capel could scarcely be blamed for seizing his hat, and rushing forth to his office in a passion; however, he was by no means a fundamentally ill-natured man, only a little hot-tempered and fussy; so he came back again in five minutes, and made his peace with Clara, kissing her, and telling her " only to be a little more thoughtful in future, and these unpleasant scenes wouldn't happen." He then patted Emily's head, and bade her not to be such a little goose; neither did he omit to stroke Ponto, as he passed out for the second time. Poor Clara, with swollen eyes and aching forehead, betook herself, work in hand, to her mother's bedside, there to reflect upon this first specimen of her powers as leader and life of a family.

I suppose it will be thought that my heroine was a very weak, inconsistent, and self-indulgent young lady, whose good resolutions evaporated in soliloquies, or had just solidity enough for the construction of a castle in the air. We must, therefore, endeavour to give an idea of her character and position, which, as generally happens, were, in the first instance, peculiarly unsuited to each other: whether she ever succeeded in solving the great problem how to bring them into harmony, remains to be seen. She was nineteen years old, and the eldest of seven children: her mother was a confirmed invalid, who never left her bed till noon, and then only to be moved to a sofa; a gentle, uncomplaining sufferer she was, somewhat weak both in will and intellect, but full of tenderness, and beloved by all who knew her. Mr. Capel was, as we have seen, a good kind of man, hot-headed and warm-hearted, deficient in cultivation, but not in natural capacity, a rigid disciplinarian by fits and starts, and, consequently, the man of all others, to produce utter confusion in his household. Seven children and a sickly wife taxed to the utmost the moderate income which he made as a lawyer in a country town, and the perpetual struggle of a naturally liberal disposition compelled to live and make live upon insufficient means, was quite enough, when not converted by self-discipline into a means of improvement, to account for the growing irritability of his character. George, a promising youth of eighteen, and the delight of his elder sister's heart, was intended for holy orders; he was amiable and clever, even elegant in mind, but somewhat irresolute: there was about him a feminine want of self-dependence, combined with an occasiona obstinacy of purpose, so sudden and disproportionate that it seemed to arise from a secret suspicion of his particular defect, and a desire to prove to himself that it had no real existence. As it often happens in such cases, he was apt to overdo the cure, and to apply it at wrong times; he was like a person who coddles himself all the summer when he is quite well, and goes out without a hat on the first frosty morning. Of course he catches so violent a cold that he must needs stay in-doors for the next six months. Julia was a pretty, good-humoured, common-place girl of sixteen, very ready with small-talk, and passionately fond of partners. She was popular wherever she went, and was just the sort of person to be habitually quoted by gentlemen as an example, to prove that it was quite unnecessary for a woman to have a mind.

The two little boys, Frank and Hugh, had rosy smiling faces hands never clean, and shoe-strings never tied. They got on very well at the day-school, thought it great fun to call their master "Dick" when he was quite out of hearing; invariably slammed the doors in summer, and left them wide open in winter; and always had in their pockets a knife, a piece of string, six marbles, two broken slips of wood, a rusty nail, the leaf of a Latin grammar, an ounce of toffy, some crumbs of bread and cheese, a hard ball, and an apple. Emily was a rather self-sufficient lady of nine years, who thought it great promotion to put back her hair with combs and wear worked collars. She was a vigorous stickler for the rights of woman, which she not unfrequently attempted to obtain from her brothers by personal violence, being always ready with the true English sentiment, "How cowardly to touch a girl!" if the smallest retort were attempted. To say the truth, the two schoolboys suffered many an instance of grievous tyranny at her hands, which they bore the better because they had not yet opened their eyes to the fact. Little Annie, with her earnest blue eyes, sweet shy manners, and pretty loving ways, was the pet, the plaything, and the sunshine of the whole household. Cla herself was the genius of the family, and as inoffensive a genius us it would be possible to find anywhere. She had been a precocious child, having learned all her letters before she was two years old, and composed a decided rhyme before she was four; neither had her talents evaporated as she grew up. She played very well, and sang with much feeling; she had a great aptitude for languages, was fond of reading, fonder of thinking, fondest of dreaming. She was very shy, and did not please in general society; she was uncomfortably conscious that her abilities were overrated, and believed herself to be destitute of those attractions which perhaps most women covet more than ability. In person she was interesting rather than pretty, having much intelligence and sweetness of countenance without regularity of feature, so she believed herself ugly, and tried to persuade herself that she was careless of admiration; yet she had much grace of manner, a musical voice, and a captivating smile, and if she had not often made herself repulsive out of the fear of being so, she might have been as popular as her sister. She had a most warm, loving, tender heart; a gentle, timid temper; a strong, though quiet will; great natural reserve; great anxiety to be loved; boundless aspirations after excellence. She was at once enthusiastic and indolent, sadly deficient in continuous energy, yet never slothful. She felt herself useless, and despised herself for being so, and was almost ashamed to set about curing herself of the faults peculiar to what is called a "woman of genius," because she was not certain that she was one. She had all kinds of ideal pictures before her eyes which she was impatient to realise; but she was obliged to be architect and mason in one, and she did not know the simplest rules of construction. She was the person of all others most likely to be misjudged by those who did not thoroughly understand her; for, with an original and striking character, keen thoughts, and decided opinions, she had so little natural presence of mind, that she often appeared to have no character at all, and she was so self-distrustful that she sometimes disclaimed an opinion almost in the moment of uttering it, lest it should turn out to be wrong. She saw all the evils around her with a perception almost morbidly acute: and she was too busy with self-contempt for the sorry part she had played in the family drama, to think for a moment of criticising her fellow-actors. Suddenly she had waked up to the consciousness of all this, having hitherto lived, half-studiously, half-dreamily, indulged in all her inclinations both by the love of her parents and the pride which they felt in her talents; and while frequently regretting and feeling teased by the civil disorders of the little commonwealth, ontenting herself with the notion that she never could amend them, as it was useless for her to try to be practical. This, however, was but a vague half-expressed thought, although it was very decidedly acted upon, and the evils were perpetually growing, and at last her eyes opened. Sorrowfully and earnestly her heart accused itself before God, and then took refuge from its own reproaches in the intensity of a fresh resolution. No one suspected what was going on in her mind, and numberless were the little difficulties unconsciously thrown in her way; not a few, also, were the helps lent to her as unconsciously. Indeed she began to think that it only depended upon herself to turn every difficulty into a help; the steeper the path the sooner you reach the summit, if only you have strength and breath for the ascent. Clara thought she *had* strength and breath; and should they fail her, she knew where and how to renew them. Her purpose burned within her with a fervour almost with a passion, which those only can understand who are in the habit of feeling much which they never betray, and who, believing with all their hearts that the will *has* power over life and circumstance and soul, are yet conscious, even to agony, of its practical impotence. The words "conquer self!" were ringing in her ears, throbbing in her heart and brain, blinding and deafening her for the time to all outward sights and sounds. With an almost terrified hope that she should ensure their fulfilment, she repeated them inwardly as she knelt at the altar on the following Sunday, her whole spirit being (so to speak) in the attitude of a vow, though her lips pronounced no deliberate pledge. And afterwards, during the evening luxury of a walk with the children, when they, bounding away in all directions, left her to solitary meditation, she calmly reviewed and sealed her resolution. How strange and how happy is the effect of even the most transient intercourse with nature upon a heart, wounded and erring, and yet desirous of good! How it soothes agitation and softens pain, and creates life afresh, and in a nobler mould! And this work is done not merely by gorgeous skies or lovely moonlights, by bright waters looking up like children into the solemn faces of mountains, or sleeping under the shadowy guardianship of overhanging woods, by the glory and the beauty of earth; it is done likewise by her simplest and quietest pictures, by her cheapest and most unpretending gifts. The sight of one dark-leaved tree rocking slowly against a dim heaven; the mere aspect of one green field is often enough to change and subdue the whole course of thought. Is it not, perhaps, because these creations are fresh and unmarred from God's hands that they so speedily affect us; because in this they transcend man, in whom there is so much of personal and of evil that the workmanship of God is, as it were, disguised, and only to be discovered by careful search. The blade of grass which we pluck is what its Creator intended it to be; who shall dare say so much as this of himself, or of any other?

Clara was very happy so long as she was busy with reveries of the future, and generalisations of duty; but she was far too much in earnest to rest in these, and on the Monday morning she determined to begin her new work heartily. She asked herself the question " how ?" and the sublime of thought instantly became the ridiculous of action. She would superintend their very indifferent cook in the preparation of dinner, and she would make herself a gown! Her mother had presented her with one on her last birthday, which lay useless in a drawer because she had not yet been able to save enough out of her scanty allowance to pay the dressmaker. How easy it is to look upon life as a whole—how *very* difficult to encounter its details! Clara got up three hours earlier than usual; and when the housemaid descended to her morning toils, she found the field preoccupied with shapeless segments of calico and unmeaning strips of silk, and a vast array of variously contorted wisps of paper which were afflicted with a mental hallucination, and believed themselves to be patterns. Her young mistress stood in the midst, considerably flushed and somewhat despondent, having as yet achieved no visible end but the scattering of an immense multitude of minute pieces of thread and sewing-silk upon the surface of the drugget. She now submitted, with rather an ill grace, to be hunted from room to room by the much-worried domestic, being finally dispossessed of the parlour only just in time to gather up her museum of materials with all haste, and thrust them at random into a closet, to make way for breakfast. After that meal she resumed her labours, varying them by an occasional excursion into the kitchen, which so amazed the cook that she had not self-possession enough to organise any immediate plan of resistance. The confusion of the party was at its height, when a knock at the door announced a visitor, and Mr. Archer entered. This was a gentleman who had been known to the Capel family for some years. He was good, clever, agreeable, and slightly satirical: at thirty-six a confirmed old bachelor in all his ways and thoughts; everywhere much liked, and everywhere a little feared; a great admirer of Julia with whom he flirted in the easy, frank, comfortable way peculiar to his class, but by no means so fond of Clara, who was afraid of him, and whom he had never aken .he trouble to know. In person he was gentlemanlike and pleasing, without being handsome; but he was afflicted with lameness, in consequence of a fall from his horse in college days. He assumed complete indifference to this defect, spoke of it openly, nay, even jested upon it, but in reality, and in secret, he was conscious of it, even to painfulness, believed himself (absurdly enough) unacceptable to any woman by reason of it, and, though he never betrayed, by look or manner, the slightest sensitiveness when any allusion was made to it, and though his own freedom of expression rather encouraged such allusions in persons of coarse feeling, yet there can be no doubt that all such words inflicted their wounds, and that the delicacy which avoided them was among the surest claims to his regard. When a man speaks of himself, except it be in the close and holy confidence of a true friendship, wherein falsehood is impossible and disguise absurd—distrust him! Either consciously or unconsciously, be sure that he is only throwing aside a veil to put on a mask.

"Well, Sappho!" cried Mr. Archer, as he entered the room, and came to a dead halt, in front of a mysterious coil of pink ribbon, upon which Clara had some vague, undeveloped designs: "in the name of wonder, what does this portend? Private theatricals, of course?—and you are mistress of the robes? What costume will you provide for me?"

There is no saying how much good Mr. Archer might have done Clara if he had discarded that objectionable habit of calling her Sappho. As it was, in every conversation which took place between them, there was an unhappy little basis of irritation on her part to begin with, which caused her to consider nis most innocent remarks sarcastic, and, not unnaturally, disposed him to think unfavourably of her temper. She now answered him as gravely as if no joke had ever been made since the Deluge: "Mamma does not approve of private theatricals. I am only making a dress."

He assumed a demure expression of countenance. "I beg your ladyship's pardon," said he, with a profound bow, and then turned to Julia, who came forward with laughing cordiality, holding a book up before his eyes, and assuring him that she had "read it *all* through—every word of it!"

Mr. Archer was in the habit of lending Julia books, which she read, or professed to read, chiefly with the object of discussing them afterwards with him. To say the truth her reading was a very desultory kind of skimming; but as Clara always studied them in good earnest, her sister generally contrived to pick up enough knowledge about them to carry her effectively through a conversation, as readers of reviews are often known to pass for proficients in the literature of the day. The present volume had not, however, taxed her powers of endurance very heavily—it was Tennyson's poems.

He took it from her hand, and turned the leaves: "And which is your favourite?" asked he, "'Locksley Hall,' of course—everybody chooses 'Locksley Hall' on a first reading. What a colourist he is! The Venetian of poets."

"But I like this very much," said Julia, looking over his shoulder, and laying her finger upon the name, "Love and Duty."

He read it—at first carelessly, and as if about to pass from it again; but the passionate music laid strong hold upon him, and he could not leave it unfinished:—

> "Far furrowing into light the mounded rack
> Beyond the fair green field and eastern sea."

He closed the book, uttering the two last lines aloud as he did so with a prolonged emphasis, just a little exaggerated, in order to save himself from being laughed at by making it look as if he were half in joke. "Just a glimpse of light at the end," said he; "a promise of dawn—giving one a faint hope that this most unlucky couple might, perhaps, be happy after all. Do you know, Miss Julia, I should not have expected you to choose this poem for a favourite."

"Why not?" inquired the young lady.

He looked doubtfully at her. "It is so *very* sentimental," said he with a half-smile.

"I think *I* am very sentimental," answered Julia, a little affronted.

"Besides," pursued Mr. Archer, "don't you think the verses are wrongly named 'Love and *Duty?*' Would it not have been more in accordance with duty if the young man had held his tongue about his love, seeing that, for some reason or other, the obstacles to its prevailing were insurmountable?"

Julia did not very well know what to say, so she gave him a bright look and a smile which implied that she had a vast deal in her mind on the subject, but thought it better not to express it. Clara answered bluntly, "That is a masculine view of duty, and therefore, of course, selfish."

"How so?" asked Mr. Archer. Some specia. interference of his good genius prevented him from saying Sappho, and consequently Clara, forgetting her shyness in her feeling for the poem, replied without hesitation—"Because she could feel no security that she was beloved till she was actually told so; no woman could: and not to give her that security would be to deprive her of her only comfort in the after desolation."

Julia looked up once more with her expressive smile: "That is exactly what I think," said she. Mr. Archer answered *her*, not Clara—thinking the smile a great deal more eloquent than the speech, and giving it full credit for the substance of all that it shadowed forth. "You are perfectly right," said he, "but it is a new view to me." Then he opened the book once more, and read the lines half unconsciously—

> "Was it not well
> *Once* to have spoken?—it could not but be well!"

"Come, I shall retort upon you. Isn't this a feminine view of duty, and therefore, of course, loquacious? All women think that it cannot but be well to speak under any circumstances."

"What a shame!" exclaimed Julia. Clara went quietly back to her work with a look of contempt. She had not the gift of trifling. Presently, however, she looked up with a brightening face. A new visitor had arrived—Mr. Dacre. (We will inform the reader, in confidence, that we have some reason for supposing Dacre to be the name which was left blank in Clara's opening soliloquy.) He was also one among the family intimates, and moreover Clara's especial friend, though there was nothing between them partaking of the nature of a *flirtation*. They had the same tastes, generally the same opinions; he had considerable genius, which she indisputably overrated; he was elegant in his modes of thinking, feeling, and speaking, and liked few things better than a conversation with her. As to his *character*, that is, the combination of will, temper, heart, and habits which are somewhat more important than mere intellect, it lacked stability, and was without that nameless ascendancy which seems to be the special mark of a high manly nature, and by virtue of which it stands erect, guiding and subduing those whose merely intellectual gifts may perhaps be superior to its own. This deficiency, however, Clara did not feel; perhaps she was scarcely aware of it : we do not criticise most strictly those to whom we stand the nearest. Clara could speak, and speak freely, to Mr. Dacre of subjects on which, in her own family circle, and among her other acquaintance, silence was practically enforced upon her, not by want of comprehension, perhaps, but by want of sympathy. The shyest and most reserved nature is precisely that which most enjoys the rare privilege of speaking—rare to it because it needs so peculiar a combination of outward circumstance and inward disposition to induce, or rather to enable it to do so. So slight a coldness, so small a sneer, is enough to repulse it, and shut it up for a long while to come. These characters are often boundlessly unjust in their feeling towards others, if not in their judgment about them; but it is very difficult for them to help it. It may be because we are so *very* thin-skinned that a touch has wounded us : but while the wound still smarts freshly, we can scarcely be chidden for avoiding a repetition of the touch.

I am sorry to record that no further progress was made in the construction of the gown that morning.

In her evening self-examination Clara did not by any means spare her own feebleness of purpose. The next day, and the next, and for many succeeding days, she renewed her efforts with unflagging vigour. "*To be practical;*" this was the sentence inscribed upon every thought, and prompting it to immediate action. Very troublesome she was, there can be no doubt of it, in the first fever of her undisciplined usefulness She wore a stern aspect, she was grievously and unnecessarily punctual, painfully energetic, and so abrupt in some of her resolves that it was more than ordinary nerves could endure. She would call in all the bills at unheard-of times of year to the great discomfiture of tradesmen, and introduce an unexpected charwoman to clean the drawing-room, in the midst of a morning visit. But these natural exaggerations — like the painter's first.efforts at art, which, if he have true genius, are often caricatures, o'erstepping, not falling short of, the modesty of nature, exuberant rather than deficient—gradually softened down, as a habit grew out of a succession of impulses. Her many failures became so many lessons to teach gentleness; her perseverance was too strenuously vigilant of its own defects to degenerate into obstinacy. She imposed one law upon herself which she never broke, and which perhaps more than anything else tended to her improvement; namely, that whenever any service, duty, or business was needful in the family life which was of a disagreeable kind, or in any way repugnant to her own taste, she volunteered to perform it. She resolutely ignored, so to speak, the peculiarities of her own character, doing violence to them with a promptitude and energy which was the surest test of the reality of her intentions. No confession of disinclination—no look of reluctance appealed to the unselfishness of those about her; and it gradually began to be taken for granted that Clara " *did not mind*" doing a hundred things which she did cheerfully, but which perhaps she would have given worlds to avoid. They still called her, with good-humoured bantering, the " genius," the " blue-stocking," the " unpractical lady," but somehow or other they did not *act* upon the notion which was too permanently established in their language to be uprooted.

"News, Clara, news!" cried Julia, as, squired by Messrs. Archer and Dacre, she entered the room, full of glee and glowing with the exercise of a country ramble.

Clara looked up; she was teaching Annie her lessons, and Annie was wilful, and by consequence slow to learn, and Clara had the headache.

" Oh, we must not disturb Miss Capel," said Mr. Archer, with assumed deference; " that is one of the awful duties with which our frivolous conversation must not interfere for a moment. If we were to be compassing the queen's death, our treason would not check that running accompaniment. ' I, n, in—s, t, r, u, c, struc—t, i, o, n, instruction.' Have I divided those syllables correctly, you poor little victim?" and he pulled the unreluctant Annie upon his knee, and began to play with her long curls.

" I don't know," replied Annie; " I have not got into four syllables."

" That's a pleasure to come," answered her friend; and opening her writing-book, he volunteered to provide her next copy, and solemnly set down in huge text-hand the words, " Heaven preserve me from four syllables."

Clara laughed; but it was somewhat languidly. " There,

there, we will release you this once, Annie," said she. "And pray tell me your news, for I am all curiosity."

Her eye wandered to Mr. Dacre and Julia, who were whispering together in the background; but they did not respond to the look, and Mr. Archer answered her, "Mr. Middleton is going to be married."

Clara was as much excited as any news-teller in the world could wish. Her wonder and interest were great. Mr. Middleton was the vicar of the parish, a sensible, agreeable, middle-aged man, indefatigable in his duties, and supposed by all his friends to be a confirmed old bachelor. She inquired eagerly concerning the lady.

"To begin with the most important part, said Mr. Archer, "she is very pretty, and she is twenty-five years younger than her husband."

"Have you seen her?" exclaimed Clara, "and what sort of person is she? Will she make a good clergyman's wife? Oh, how anxious the poor will be about her!"

"She will make a perfect wife," said Mr. Archer; "she will always look handsome and good-humoured, she will be active and affectionate, and she will never require the smallest mental exertion on her husband's part. It will be a very easy life for him; so long as he is satisfied with himself, he may feel quite sure that she is satisfied with him."

"Mr. Middleton deserves something more than that," observed Clara with quiet disdain.

"*Deserves?* Perhaps; but what if he doesn't *want* it? A hard-working man like Middleton doesn't want a spur for his times of leisure—he wants a pillow."

"And you think a wife is only meant for times of leisure?" said Clara.

"And times of sickness," replied Mr. Archer; "she may nurse him if he is ill, and I think Mrs. Middleton will make a very good nurse."

Clara's lips curled as she asked, "Will she be a *companion* for him?"

"She is the companion he has chosen," answered Mr. Archer, leaning back in his chair and laughing. "A woman's notion of a wife is so different from a man's! Let her be handsome good-tempered, warm-hearted, and well-principled, and she is a fit companion for the greatest man that ever was born, always supposing she is devoted to him."

" Without either refinement or intellect?" inquired Clara.

" Certainly without intellect," replied he; "intellect in a wife gives one so much trouble. It is rather in the way than otherwise. Let her be positively stupid, dull, slow of perception, if only she looks handsome, and flatters one's vanity, by seeming to be fond of one, you will find a clever man talk to her and busy himself about her for hours together without being weary. And as to refinement, that too may be very easily dispensed with; one grows accustomed to its absence, and so forgets to miss it. After habitual intercourse with a mind that is *not* refined, one's whole estimate alters, and a mind that *is* so, seems prudish, affected, oppressive to us."

" Of course you are not in earnest," said Clara; "you cannot *really* mean that the very highest and closest union of which human creatures are capable should—— but why do I argue about it? It is very absurd."

"I am not talking about *theories*," he answered, "such as young ladies cherish in the deep recesses of their hearts; but about plain matters-of-fact. It may be very shocking that it should be thus; nevertheless, thus it is, and it is useless to attempt to conceal it. But I should like very much to hear your notion of what a wife ought to be, though I think I pretty well know it without asking."

" Tell me, and I will tell you if you are right," replied Clara.

Mr. Archer heaved a deep sigh, cast up his eyes, and answered in a low, agitated voice: "She should live only for him; be his in every word, thought, and feeling; cling to him with the most submissive devotedness; and have her own way in everything."

Mr. Dacre and Julia, who had joined the disputants, laughed heartily at this definition, but Clara looked cross. " After this," observed she, " I can hardly be expected to state my theory."

" Oh," cried Mr. Archer, " I wasn't talking about theories, but about practice. Very few people would like the look of their practice if it was exhibited to them in the shape of a theory."

" Clara, how *can* you look so grave?" exclaimed Julia; " we all know Mr. Archer is not in earnest."

" Indeed I am," persisted he; " I never joke. My witticisms are as lame as my leg. When I introduce Mrs. Archer to you, you will all discover that my theory, at least, suits my practice."

Six weeks after this conversation, Clara and Julia paid their bridal visit at the vicarage, and were introduced to Mrs. Middleton. She was very pretty, with lively, open manners, and but little of the bashfulness which is generally supposed to be indispensable to a bride. She made the girls feel quite at their ease, walked round the grounds with them to exhibit the improvements, and dwelt particularly on the charms of a certain new bay-window, which "Mr. Middleton had built for her, to her own little sitting-room." The apartment in question had been a mere closet, but was now the prettiest in the vicarage, with its delicately-tinted walls and white muslin curtains, its flower-strewn carpet, luxurious couch, and low embroidered chairs, its prints, and its books, and, above all, its delicious, half-solitary, half-social window, with a charming view of lawn, and ornamental flower-baskets, and winding walks, and cool, shadowy trees in the background. It looked the very temple of pleasant study, dreamy leisure, or intimate *causerie*.

"What a boudoir!" cried Julia, as they walked home. "It is perfection. I declare, I think I could marry Mr. Middleton for the sake of such a room as that!"

"And how exactly the lady suits the room!" rejoined George, who had accompanied his sisters; "she is much better-looking than I expected. She has more elegance of person, if not of manners, than Mr. Archer led one to imagine. How blue her eyes are! I do admire blue eyes!"

"Talking of the bride, of course?" said Mr. Dacre, joining himself to the group.

"Yes," answered Clara; "what do you think of her?"

"She is exquisite!" exclaimed Mr. Dacre; "and so naïve and girlish; she is like one of Murillo's pictures."

"She is very pretty and pleasant," said Clara; "but I do wish she had not made Mr. Middleton build that bay-window."

There was a general outcry, what could she mean? Was it possible she could not admire it? It was the greatest improvement conceivable, &c. &c.

"Well," said Clara, "I think it is a great improvement in one sense, but not in another. Mr. Middleton used to spend all he could save from his income in charity; and I think a clergyman's wife ought to help her husband in his self-denials, not encourage him to relax them."

"Oh, dreadful! my dear Miss Capel," cried Mr. Dacre; "the

poor clergyman has trials enough out of doors. Do, for pity's sake! let him find comfort and indulgence at home."

Clara thought it perfectly necessary that he should do so; but she did not think that the wife's devotion to her husband's comfort implied the necessity of leading him into expense for mere luxuries, and so she said. She said it, moreover, in a very unpleasant tone of voice, shortly and sternly, as if she were sentencing Mrs. Middleton to the galleys, and feeling that she deserved it.

"My dear Clara," observed George, "I think this is uncommonly like judging one's neighbours."

Clara felt rebuked. She was never cross to anybody except Mr. Archer; so, after reflecting a moment, she looked up at George with a frank bright smile, and replied, "It must be *very* like indeed, George, for I suspect it is the thing itself; and as that is a much worse offence than building unnecessary bay-windows, I will let poor Mrs. Middleton alone."

"Yes, pray leave her to enjoy her sweet little boudoir unmolested," said Mr. Dacre. "All the bloom and fragrance would be crushed out of life, if duty held it in so iron and perpetual a grasp. A woman's greatest charm, after all, is that she is—a woman! and that charm Mrs. Middleton possesses in the highest degree."

He turned to Julia as he finished, and the rest of the walk he spent in wrangling with her about the colour of her ribbons, and commenting upon the curls of her glossy dark hair, apparently quite as much to his own satisfaction as to hers. He followed them into the house to ask Clara's opinion upon a difficult German passage, discussed it with her for about a quarter of an hour, in a steady, business-like manner, and then took his leave.

Shall we admit the reader to another soliloquy of Clara's, as in one of her rare half-hours of idleness she stood at the tabl arranging some freshly-gathered flowers to decorate her mother' bed-room. "Charm!" she repeated slowly to herself, "that is what I have not. Mrs. Middleton is captivating; she may do what she pleases; she has the gift, the mysterious, enviable gift, of winning that interest and admiration which are sure to ripen into love. Julia, too—it is no matter what she *does* or *says*—she fascinates by what she *is*. But I?—people esteem me, and make use of me, and are very much obliged to me, and value me, and so forth; but for me, for my own self, they care nothing. It is the book I discuss, or the sonata I play, or the service I perform, about which they think; the *person* who discusses, or plays, or does what they want, has no interest for them except as a vehicle. Those whom I best love miss me in absence because of what I did for them, not because of what I was to them. I have no gift—I have no charm." Poor Clara! was she not a very woman? I am ashamed to confess it; but I suspect she would gladly have changed places with Julia at that moment, for the sake of possessing Julia's mysterious power of attraction. I am afraid that she would rather have been teased about ribbons than consulted about German. Then she resorted to Mrs. Middleton and her bay-window, and condemned herself for censoriousness; but after all could not manage to bring herself into a right state of feeling about it. Surely it was, without doubt, a deliberate act of self-indulgence, and it was difficult for Clara to be lenient to deliberate acts of self-indulgence in others, when they were just the very things against which she was making so vehement a crusade in herself. It is so hard to avoid self-consciousness in the voluntary and independent pursuit of duty.

Clara went up-stairs with her flowers, but was stopped in the dressing-room by little Annie, who came to meet her on tiptoe, and with her finger at her lips. "Mamma is asleep," whispered she; "I have been sitting to watch her, and she is quite fast asleep now. I gave mamma her dinner. She said, when you came in, I was to be sure and tell you that she wants a new book from the library, and that there was rather too much salt in the broth. I was to tell *you*—not Julia, because Julia never remembers. I have been hemming a pocket-handkerchief for mamma. Oh, Clara, how happy it is to be useful!"

The little girl's face was radiant with innocent pride and glee; and she looked up into her sister's eyes for approval and sympathy. "Do you think," asked she, "when I grow up, I can ever be as useful as you are?" Clara kissed her, without speaking; and they went out together to procure the new book for Mrs. Capel. It was quite an expedition for Annie to go to the library, and she was in the highest exultation. As they passed through the garden, they came upon a most busy and tumultuous scene. The next day was Mr. Capel's birthday, and the children were to surprise him with a feast in the summer-house. Emily and the boys had just completed their preparations, wreathing the pillars and pediment with green leaves, and bringing their choicest geraniums to stand on either side of the entrance; they were contemplating their finished work with the highest satisfaction. Poor Annie! She was to have helped in the arrangements, but she had been forgotten. True, they had called her, but she did not answer, for she was in her mother's room; so they went merrily to work, and never thought of her again.. She stood still, tears of anger and grief gathering in her eyes. Some slight sense of wrong they had certainly, but after once saying they were sorry, and it was a pity, they went back to their chaplets, quite at ease, Emily expressing a consolatory hope that she "wouldn't be such a baby as to cry about it." Poor Annie! She had not even been missed, and the gathering tears began to fall.

"Stay and help them, darling," said the sympathising Clara; "you may fetch the pink gladioles from my garden—and, hark! don't say anything about it, but I will send for a parcel from the town, of something good for the feast!"

O, how quickly the tears changed into sparkling smiles! O, how eagerly the little labourer hurried to her welcome toil! no sense of slight or sorrow remaining, working with all her might among the others, overflowing with gratitude and happiness.

And as Clara went forth on her solitary walk, her conscience said to her, "The kingdom of heaven is of little children."

A year passed away—another note was struck in the scale of life, as it rose towards its final cadence. Who notices enough those solemn sounds—those lonely strikings upon the bell which tolls and then is silent?—who takes heed whether the note be higher or lower than the last utterance of that grave music, or whether it be unchanged? Our years, for the most part, are like poor Beau Brummell's valet, who, whensoever his master went forth to a party, remained behind to gather up the "failures" strewn about his dressing-room, in the shape of some dozen cravats, rejected because the wearer had been unable to attain due perfection of tie. Only the parallel must not be carried too far—for, alas! we very often strew the floor of time with our failures, and go forth uncravated, after all.

"Julia, dear what is the matter? Won't you tell me? Why are you crying?—are you unhappy about anything?"

Clara's arms were around the waist of her sister, who wept

silently upon her shoulder. After a while she looked up, smiling through her tears, one of those bright, unmistakable smiles which tell of warmth, life, and light, as truly as sunshine does when it falls upon rippling waters, or woos spring flowers to unfold themselves.

"It is very silly to cry when I am so happy," answered she, after the fashion of Miranda; "can you guess what has happened?"

Clara looked earnestly into her face. "Yes," said she, "I think I can. Dearest Julia! I have long expected it. Tell me everything as soon as you can speak."

Clara's tears were flowing nearly as fast a' her sister's. It is the way which women have of watering al. the young, tender plants of happiness which spring up new in the garden of life, to make them grow.

"He spoke this morning," said Julia, still hiding her blushing face. "And will you tell mamma? for I shall never find courage. Oh, Clara! it seems so strange—and I never thought he was in love with me."

"But everybody else thought so," replied Clara. "His manner has shown it for a long time—only, I know it is a matter-of-course that these things are discovered by the lookers-on, and not by the persons whom they most concern. I dare-say you thought he was quite indifferent to you, and rather wondered that he did not pay you more attention."

"Yes, indeed!" murmured Julia; "I always thought he liked *you* the best!"

Clara felt greatly astonished, for such a blunder as this outdid the ordinary mistakes of young ladies in Julia's situation. "Like *me* the best!" repeated she. "What! Mr. Archer!"

"Mr. Archer!" exclaimed Julia, kindling into an articulate-ness and decision scarcely to be expected of her, "who was thinking of Mr. Archer?"

Clara looked at her without speaking. "It is Mr. Dacre," added Julia, holding down her face and relapsing into bash-fulness.

There was a silence of some minutes, and then Clara warmly renewed her congratulations, and went to tell the news with all possible tenderness to her mother. How did she feel? It is difficult to say. There was immense astonishment and a momentary pang of something that was neither disappoint-ment nor jealousy, and yet there *was* a pang, vehemently and

Instantly chidden into quietness, with a sensation of terror at its selfishness. And then she talked long and gently with her mother, listening to all her doubts and hopes, sympathising with all, dispelling the one by the earnest assurances with which she encouraged the other. And then she tol' her father, and bore part in the somewhat colder discussion which ensued of ways and means, and future position, times, and seasons, and such like sublunary matters, of which it would have been profane to breathe a word in Julia's presence. And then she went out for a quiet walk with George, and listened and responded to his unmixed delight—all brothers are so pleased when their sisters marry—with a very good grace. And each one of the three with whom she discussed the great event wound up the conversation by saying, " Do you know it is *such* a surprise to me! I fancied he liked *you*." And to each one she answered laughing, " Oh, how could you dream of such a thing ?"

Her vanity was a little mortified—so she told herself in her subsequent deliberations on the matter. Mr. Dacre had belonged to her, and it was not perfectly pleasant to see him appropriated by another. He had from the first courted her friendship, and she was unused to be preferred, and she felt that her belief in her own incapacity for winning affection was strongly confirmed. She could not escape sundry far from agreeable misgivings ; she had supposed him to be liking her best when he was only thinking of Julia. How often must she have bored him by her conversation when he wanted to be talking to her sister. Her cheeks burned at the idea, and she inwardly resolved to withdraw more than ever from attention in society ; she must have been vain indeed, far vainer than she had suspected, to have fallen into such an error. She would watch herself strictly for the future.

The real truth was, that Mr. Dacre *had* liked her best originally, but had ceased to do so, partly from natural instability of character, partly from another cause, which may perhaps seem utterly improbable, but which did, nevertheless, exist. Clara's strenuous efforts to be practical and useful had impaired her attractions in his eyes. When he first became acquainted with her she had been exactly the kind of person about whom he could dream to his heart's content; there was no oppressive reality about her; no substance of character. Her time was divided pretty equally between study, music, and conversation—all three very elegant employments, which did not in the slightest degree interfere with the consistency of his idea portraiture of her. But when she took to darning stockings, the ideal began to fade; and when she was heard pronouncing decided opinions on matters of fact—when she was seen not merely hurrying, but absolutely bustling, about her household concerns—when she cut short a disquisition on æsthetics to go and assist in putting up the drawing-room curtains—and was too busy settling accounts to come and play Beethoven, he quietly gave her up and betook himself to her sister. It may sound paradoxical, but the truth is, that Julia's uselessness was her great attraction in his eyes. Of course he was unconscious of it, but so it was. In the first place, it enabled her to be always at his beck and call; no imperative duty thrust itself between them. As she had nothing particular to do, she might just as well be making herself agreeable to him. Moreover, she was never pre-occupied—a great charm to man's vanity— because, in fact, she was never occupied at all except when he occupied her. And the very absence of all that was definite or interesting in her character, while it ensured placidity of temper, gave his restless imagination free play. She was nothing at all, and therefore he might fancy her to be just whatsoever he pleased. There are certain smooth tablets on which you may write whatever you like; it needs but a wet sponge to efface the whole inscription. It is said that these tablets are made of the skin of an ass, but I would not for the world make an un- civil use of this fact in natural history.

Clara's next feeling was compassion for Mr. Archer. She was quite sure that he was disappointed, and, in fact, he had reason so to feel. Even a man so free from vanity as he was might have been led to believe himself preferred by Julia's manner. She wondered how he would take it, but could not help laughing when she caught herself devising gentle means of breaking it to him. Soon afterwards he drank tea with the Capels, his congratulations were cold, decidedly cold; Clara was certain that it cost him much to offer them at all. She exerted herself to talk to him, and though he was in a more than ordinarily sarcastic humour, she did not lose her patience, for it seemed to her quite natural. Subsequently she prevailed on her father to forego his intention of asking Mr. Archer to the wedding, and reflected with pleasure that she had at least spared him that pain. As a matter of fact, Mr. Archer, being wholly unconscious of the special kindness which dictated his exclusion, was a good deal hurt by it, which Clara, happily, never discovered.

And the wedding came and passed—a commonplace wedding enough. The bride, of course, had never looked so pretty, and the bridegroom behaved admirably. I never yet heard of a wedding at which it was not expressly stated that the bridegroom behaved admirably. Sometimes I cannot help wondering what it can be that bridegrooms are so strongly tempted to do that resisting the temptation is enough to entitle them to such extravagant praise. The bridegroom on the present occasion looked at least as well as he behaved, being, by good luck, an unusually handsome man, tall and distinguished in figure. There was a great deal of white lace, and a great many tears, and a crowd of people staring at the bride, and prophetically calling her " poor dear " at every third word, and a quantity of flowers to walk upon, which performed their symbolism to perfection, looking bright and fresh when the bride set her fairy feet upon them, but getting crushed and decidedly shabby by the time that the other members of the procession followed; and there was a priest in white, saying solemn words, and two faint voices slowly faltering their responses, speaking, in fact, with their hearts, which seems to be almost as difficult as reading with the back of one's neck; and there was a cluster of faces in the little vestry looking like rain-clouds at sunset, so glowing and yet so tearful; and there was a small collection of autographs made by trembling hands for the benefit of the parish; and there was hurrying back to the sound of a perfect steeplechase of bells; and there was a breakfast which was a dinner in a stage disguise which deceived nobody, but just enabled people to call it by a wrong name; and there were a few desperate struggles at small talk made and then abandoned; and there were healths drunk and speeches grotesquely pathetic delivered, and a band outside playing " Hearts of Oak," with a vague idea that it was appropriate to the occasion; and an agitated toilette, in which it seemed wonderful that the lady's stockings did not get upon her hands, or her bonnet upon her feet; and a rushing down stairs, and sundry close embraces in the hall, silent and sobbing, as though the form thus passionately grasped were just about to be committed to the executioner; and four horses galloping as fast as four horses ought to do when they are carrying joy away from sorrow: and it was all over.

Clara felt very lonely—not that Julia had been a companion

to her in the highest sense of the word—nevertheless, it seemed as though a completer kind of solitude than heretofore were come upon her life. She had no one but George to whom she could now speak of what she felt, and to him she clung with a fervour of affection absolutely passionate. This was in truth the greatest fault of her character, and it may be described in a single phrase—*the need of idolising*. That a woman must needs lean and love, who will deny? But that she should lean helplessly and love immoderately is the evil. Yet never was there a woman in the world, of true woman-nature, to whom this was not a danger narrowly escaped, an obstacle scarcely surmounted, if indeed escaped or surmounted at all! Clara followed her brother's college career with proud and joyful devotion; in a very agony of hope she watched through each crisis of the course, and language is powerless indeed to express the rapture of her thankfulness when the final trial was passed, and the honours of the first class won. With her whole heart she believed that the world had never before owned such a genius as George's. She associated herself in all his pursuits, tastes, troubles, and pleasures, with a touching mixture of reverence and tenderness, and so made him her all, that she could scarcely be satisfied to be less than all to him. The incredulous scorn with which she turned away from sundry intrusive whispers, that he was not quite so steady as he might have been, was too lofty to be otherwise than calm. It is little to say that she would have given her life *for* him. An every-day affection could do thus much out of mere shame, if the alternative were distinctly set before it; but she gave her life *to* him, and that is far more.

His college course was now over, and, in one of those fits of enthusiasm natural to a character of his stamp, he announced his intention of devoting a year to retirement and study, preparatory to his examination for deacon's orders. He talked and felt beautifully concerning the responsibility about to come upon him; and his sister's warm heart bowed itself before him as he talked, grateful to him for thus realising its highest ideal. There was a painful struggle in her mind when he asked her if she would come with him to the cottage which he had chosen in a retired village on the sea-coast. At first she believed that her duty forbade her this great happiness, and that she must needs stay at home to uphold the system of domestic comfort which she had constructed; but she was overruled in her own favour by her parents. They did not tell her all the motives which determined them upon sending her with George, for many reasons; but the fact was that their experience had by no means encouraged them to a perfect reliance upon his steadiness, and they had so grown into the habit of looking to Clara in all trials, of seeing her arrange all difficulties, endure all annoyances, and bring order and comfort out of all confusions, that they felt, as though by establishing her under her brother's roof, they were setting a guardian angel to watch over him, and keep him from going astray. Circumstances, unfortunately, prevented this plan from being put into practice according to their original intention. Little Annie was ill, and Clara was obliged to stay at home to nurse her. George had been more than four months in his solitary abode when his sister set forth to join him. Long enough to commence to waver in, and to forsake his original resolution,—or to persevere in it till he made a habit of it.

Clara had never in her life felt so perfectly happy as she did when her brother's arms received her on alighting from the —— stage-coach. The solitary journey, always a nervous business, was over; the warm welcome so long looked forward to was actually being received. She was now with him, in five minutes more she was making tea for him. How comfortable the little room looked in her eyes, with its soiled carpet, gaudy paper, straight-backed chairs, and narrow horse-hair sofa! How delicious was the tea, made with water guiltless of having ever boiled; and surely never before was such a dainty tasted as the under-done mutton-chop which the good offices of the hostess had provided for the refreshment of the traveller! If she noticed anything amiss, it was only with the agreeable anticipation of reforming it, and so making him more comfortable than he could possibly have been without her. And she looked greedily at the well-filled book-shelf, and thought how she should make extracts and look out passages for him, and sit by his side while he worked, holding her breath lest she might disturb him; and how delightful it would be when he should look up for a moment to read a striking sentence, or discuss a doubtful argument! He looked a little pale, he had certainly overworked himself. Now *she* was come, that could never happen again; she would beguile him into the refreshment of a walk, or the luxury of a little chat; she could help him in all his labours, and ensure his not overdoing them.

"You look tired, dear!" was her observation, her eyes fondly fixed upon his face.

"I was up late last night," he replied; "and I have a little headache."

"You will have no more headaches now *I* am come," said she. "When I think bed-time has arrived, I shall take away the books, and put out the candles. I have no notion of letting you work so hard in the present as to impair your power of working for the future."

He laughed. "Oh," answered he; "I was not working *last* night. Wonderful to relate, I was at a party. Three old college friends of mine have taken a shooting-box in the neighbourhood, and I dined with them, and we kept it up rather late. They are capital fellows."

"I am *so* glad!" cried Clara; "I was afraid you had no society or amusement at all here, and that must be bad for anybody. You know, love, you mustn't think of me; I am used to be alone, and rather like it. So I hope you will spend as much time with your friends as you did before I came. Are *they* studying, too?—how lucky it was that you met them here!"

"Not exactly. Very lucky!" replied George, with a slightly embarrassed manner; and the next minute he began to talk of home, and they separated for rest, after one of the most delightful evenings that Clara had ever spent. The next morning after a happy *tête-à-tête* breakfast, she fetched her work, and sat quietly down, anxious not to be troublesome or officious in her offers of service, but ready to work, to wait, to talk, to be silent, to sympathise, with alacrity, as she might find she was wanted. George produced his books and papers, and took his seat, with a desultory yawn. The length of time that it cost him to find his place, the vague, aimless manner in which he went to work, the parade of new pens and clean paper, might have caused a more suspicious person than Clara to guess that, at the very least, he was resuming an interrupted habit. He had not been employed above an hour, when a note was brought him, and he started up eagerly. "I am going out, Clara, dear,—I shall be back to dinner;" and he was gone, without further explanation. That day he *did* return to dinner; but the compliment to his sister was not often repeated. Gradually, even her loving credulity was forced to confess that he was idle—even her faith in him, which could have removed mountains, began to waver. He was scarcely conscious him-self how far he had departed from his own determinations; he was so resolutely blind to his own defects, that it would have needed a stronger hand than poor Clara's, who, alas! was only anxious to be blind with him, to open his eyes. Moreover, he *did* work by fits and starts; and she remembered each day of work with a vigilance more eager than his own, and added it scrupulously to the account, and tried to persuade herself that his relaxations were only necessary, as long as she could. Her sense of her own inferiority to him was so strong, that it was long indeed before she ventured on a remonstrance, and what she suffered, ere she did so venture, can scarcely be described. It was about three weeks after her arrival—he had been out all day, and she was sitting up for him. He came at about one o'clock in the morning, and she heard his voice in the passage, calling vehemently for tea, before he would go to bed. She hurried out to him: "George, dear! come in—nobody is up—I will get you some tea directly."

He came in—his manner was strange and abrupt—he looked vacantly at her—uttered an oath, the first she had ever heard from his lips—threw himself on to a sofa, and before she could complete her hasty and trembling preparations, was breathing hard, in sudden, heavy sleep. Even Clara's inexperience could not mistake the symptoms, and, instead of making tea, she sat down and cried—*how* bitterly, none but those can tell who have believed in, and doated upon, and worshipped an imaginary divinity, and then suddenly discovered it to be weaker than ordinary human weakness. To Clara's pure and gentle eyes, this was grievous sin—and, with the painful charity of disappointed affection, she began to devise excuses for what she could not refuse to see; but, oh! the bitterness of the new, terrible truth, which made those excuses necessary!

When George awoke on the following morning, he was still on the sofa, and his sister still watching beside him. It was some time before he thoroughly comprehended what had passed, and then, half-ashamed, half-angry, he made an awkward explanation; he had been out all day in the open air, had returned quite exhausted, and a glass or two of wine more than his habit had been too much for him—he was afraid he had frightened her—what a simpleton she was not to have gone to bed, &c. &c. And poor Clara took this scanty balm to her aching heart, and tried to be satisfied with

George was by no means very bad, only Clara had fancied him so very good that it was hard to be undeceived. Her influence, patiently, tenderly, trustfully exerted, was not without its effect. And bitter as was her disappointment, she lived through it; the path which seems perpendicular when you gaze at it from a distance, may toilsomely be climbed when your feet are actually set upon it. Some half-dozen times, in the course of Clara's sojourn with him, the scene which had so bitterly afflicted her was repeated; but, on the whole, he improved. He tried to work more regularly; occasionally he refused an invitation; sometimes he laid out a plan for the distribution of his time, and once he kept to it for a whole week. Clara learned to rejoice in things which, three months before, she would have disdained to believe. It is wonderful what love will bear—how perfect is its theory, yet with what a beautiful hypocrisy that theory will accommodate itself to facts, and strive to seem unaltered. The union between this brother and sister was never disturbed: she never spoke harshly to him; indeed, she was too timid to speak as freely as she ought. But gradually the reproving silence of her quiet sorrow did its work, and the last month that they spent together, resembled, in some faint degree, the portrait of her imagination; and the time for returning home arrived.

"Yes, there it is! That *is* the church tower, George; how kind of the moon to appear for a moment, and show it me! We are almost at home. In five minutes more, the horses' feet will be upon the stones."

Their heads were put eagerly out of the carriage windows as they drove up the street, and turned the well-known corner. Soon, by the light of the wayside lamps, they distinguished the small, formal-looking, red-brick house, with its green door and trellised porch, its miniature front garden, some thirty feet square, with a straight gravel walk up the middle, and a circular border on each side, in the centre of a plot of grass. The upper and lower windows of the house were dark, though it was already two hours after sunset; suddenly the gleam of a candle was seen; it passed rapidly from one window to another; then the door of the house was thrown violently open, and a female servant, without bonnet or cloak, rushed out, and ran at full speed up the street, scarcely a second ere the carriage stopped before the swinging gate. Quick, speechless terror came upon

George and Clara, and the former was out of the carriage almost before it had ceased to move—sick at heart with nameless fear, his sister followed him into the house. There was no one in the hall. From above-stairs came the sound of hurrying footsteps, interrupted by a low moaning and sobbing, as of some one in great agitation, but unable to give it free vent. Clara stood still, appalled. She would have given worlds to know, either at once or never, what was happening. She felt tempted to turn and run away, as if she could so escape what was about to come upon her. In another moment, the loud, unrestrained cry of childish sorrow burst upon her ears, and little Annie came running down-stairs, weeping bitterly, and covering her face with her handkerchief. The brief paralysis which had rendered Clara incapable of thinking or acting, passed away in an instant; taking the child in her arms, she asked, in low, hasty accents, "What is it, Annie?—what is it?"

"Papa, papa!" sobbed the little girl; "he has had a fit—he is dying!"

They stood together, a moment, in the dark hall, closely folded in each other's arms, but unable to see each other's faces. Then Clara hurried up-stairs—but ere she joined the ghastly and troubled group who stood around the bed, all was over, and she was an orphan.

The course of the great sorrow is common-place enough, a thing of every day. There is the wild incredulity and the unreal composure, half stupor, half excitement; there is the struggle, more or less vehement, of the will against the adverse power which is labouring to subdue it; the defeat and the victory, the brave effort, the helpless surrender. There are prayers, such as that prayer which was once wrung from the agony of a great heart, and which is the voice of a new grief for all time. "Lord! thou hast permitted it, therefore I submit with all my strength."* There is the heavy weariness, and the aching resignation, and the utter weakness, and the deep solemn calm, and the holy strength, and the melancholy peace so sweet in the midst of bitterness, when the vision of heaven dawns upon those eyes which are too blind with tears

* This was the ejaculation repeatedly uttered by the unhappy Henrietta Maria, when she began to recover from the stupor into which she was thrown by the news of her royal husband's murder.

to see any longer the beauty of earth; there is the slow, painful return to old habits and ways, the endeavour, now feeble,
now vigorous, the gradual interrupted success, the shuddering
recurrence of familiar images and associated sounds,—and the
final closing up of a memory into the heart's inmost temple,
where it dwells and lives for ever, which the world calls forget-
fulness, or at least recovery. And the mourner goes back
again to the outer world and common life, like one who has
had a fever and is in health again, though somewhat wan and
feeble, and needing more than heretofore to be cared for and
considered. Sorrows are the pulses of spiritual life; after each
beat we pause only that we may gather strength for the next.

Mr. Capel's affairs were found to be in great confusion. It
often happens that the men whom we have believed to be most
cautious and least sanguine are the very men to engage in
some sudden rash speculation which results in ruin. Such
was the case now. He had embarked what little principal he
possessed in a new railroad; the scheme failed, and his family
found themselves literally penniless. The poor widow and
little Annie were taken by Mrs. Dacre, whose very moderate
income was taxed to its utmost to maintain them. A situation
as pupil-teacher in a considerable school was found for Emily;
Clara and George were, for the present, received at the vicarage. Mrs. Middleton was throughout Clara's chief support;
her warm unselfish kindness amply atoned for any little
deficiency in refinement. She insisted upon taking the poor
dejected girl to her own home till a suitable position as
governess could be found for her, and she interested herself
most earnestly in the preliminary negotiations, taking special
care that Clara should not "throw herself away in a hurry,
which would be perfectly absurd, as the vicarage was open to
her for any length of time, and she would not suffer her to
leave it unless the prospect were thoroughly satisfactory." As
Clara witnessed her life of busy charity and honest self-denial,
she forgave her the bay-window, and reproached herself not a
little for her former censorious judgment. Every comfort
and help came from or through Mrs. Middleton; it was she
who found the situation for Emily, and assisted Clara in
arranging and carrying through the whole affair; it was she
too who cheered George when his heart was heavy and his
hopes were low, as giving up, of course, his intention of taking
orders, he began the wearisome task of looking for employment.

Aided by her, Clara began gradually to rally from her extreme depression, and to exert herself as heretofore. Her greatest present difficulty, the maintenance and destination of her two younger brothers, was relieved in an unlooked-for and mysterious manner. In the midst of her first despondency arrived a letter from the master with whom the boys were placed, acknowledging the receipt of a year's payment in advance for his pupils. On inquiry it was found that the sum had been sent in Mr. Capel's name; but all exertions to discover the source from which it came proved utterly futile. This bounty, come whence it might, came like manna in the desert; yet poor Clara was nearly as much inclined to murmur at it as were the Israelites of old. There was in her character a strength of natural pride, hitherto unsuspected by herself, mingling a bitterness with her gratitude, of which she felt deeply ashamed. The discipline which she was now undergoing was specially needful to her, and therefore, of course, specially painful; she had so loved to be all-sufficient in her family, to know secretly, however little she presumed upon it outwardly that she *was* the prop, the guide, the guardian of them all. Now she found herself helpless, powerless, useless; one whom she had well-nigh despised was her supporter, one unknown was her benefactor. She herself was—nothing!

It was Clara's birthday; no one ventured to congratulate her, and she herself shrank from any allusion to the subject. When we are in much affliction it seems natural to put out the lights. They can but show others what we suffer, or force us to contemplate their tears. At breakfast, Clara received a note from a lady in the neighbourhood, a stranger to her, who required a governess for her children, and requested an interview with Miss Capel. Twelve was the hour appointed, and the writer's residence was two miles distant from the vicarage. With many a good wish and many a salutary caution from Mrs. Middleton, who failed not to remind her again and again, that she had *promised* not to *conclude* an engagement without previous consultation, Clara set forth on her solitary walk. As she went, she thought anxiously about George; he was trying for a situation as mathematical tutor in a scholastic establishment, which had just been founded under somewhat peculiar circumstances. The founder was a man of large fortune, and eccentric habits; he had reserved to himself alone the selection and appointment of the various professors, and it was said that he tried the patience of the applicants not a little, in the course of his investigation of their claims, moral, intellectual, and theological. George's college honours had been much in his favour, and Clara's hopes had been high till a few days before, when he eceived a letter which appeared to annoy him, and which he did not show her He was a long while composing his reply, and after he had despatched it, he seemed more than usually low-spirited, and evaded all discussion of the subject with his anxious and vigilant sister. It was not possible to her nature to seek the confidence even of those she most loved, when they withheld it, so she wondered and grieved in silence; and many a fear, and many a prayer, passed through her heart, in the hours when her aching head rested on a pillow now unfamiliar with sleep. Thus, more than commonly anxious, and with the bitter memory of former birthdays stirring within her, she knocked at Mrs. Bouverie's door, and was admitted into that lady's presence.

Clara felt too sorrowful to be shy, otherwise the exceeding coldness of her reception might have daunted her a little. Mrs. Bouverie, a tall, lean, hard-featured woman, of fifty-six, with keen eyes, thin lips, and a general dryness of expression perfectly indescribable, slightly bowed, and, without rising, motioned her visitor to a seat. She uttered two civil sentences, which she had learnt by rote, about its being a fine day, and a long walk; and then proceeded at once to business. She was one of those people who are as chary of small talk as though they were capable of conversation, and as niggard of courtesies as though they were ready with secret kindnesses. Now it is all very well to be reserved when you have got something to hide, but it is really too provoking to see people so careful to lock up empty caskets, and seal blank envelopes. It is an imposition upon society, and ought not to be tolerated.

We will not weary the reader with the oft-repeated scene of hiring a governess. Suffice it to say, that Mrs. Bouverie having inquired into Clara's qualifications, and examined her testimonials with apparent satisfaction, proceeded to sum up her own requisitions in the following manner :—

"You will have six pupils, Miss Capel, between the ages of seven and fourteen; you will have the exclusive charge of their education in English and French, and the two elder girls will learn German. The music-master attends once a week, and you will be present at the lessons, and will very carefully watch—I am particular about this—the practising of each of your pupils daily. Drawing and fancy-work you will of course teach yourself. You will breakfast and dine early with your pupils, and walk with them for two hours a day ; and at eight o'clock, when the younger girls go to bed, I shall expect the pleasure of your company at my tea-table. I always like musc c in the evening, and shall hope to hear you play and sing with your pupils. You will have perfect freedom, and I hope you will be very comfortable. My housekeeper will settle the pecuniary arrangements with you." *

Miserable as Clara was, she yet shrank from the future indicated by these words. She remembered at a little fishing village on the sea-coast to have seen a mule employed in carrying sand and sea-weed ; the animal had a kind of wooden saddle fitted upon its back, and was sent to and fro between the carts waiting to be loaded and the water's edge, a distance of some eight hundred yards. To and fro, across this measured melancholy space, it trudged doggedly and patiently, pausing at the one end of its journey to receive its burden, and at the other end to be relieved of it, and pausing for nothing else. Clara thought of the mule when Mrs. Bouverie described her governess's day, and felt glad that she had pledged herself not to decide. She replied quietly and courteously that she would send a definite answer in the evening, as she was bound to consult a friend ere she finally determined. Mrs. Bouverie drew herself up, and Clara became aware that it was possible for her manners to assume an additional coldness—a fact which the strongest imagination could scarcely have conceived before experiencing it. However, Mrs. Bouverie piqued herself upon being always considerate, so she said with grim civility, " You will do what you think best, Miss Capel ; and now I need detain you no longer."

When Clara re-entered the drawing-room at the vicarage, she found George alone. His face was flushed, and his manner perturbed ; he started up, as she came in, with a nervous eagerness very unusual in him. Not a question did he ask as to the result of her expedition ; he began at once upon a totally different topic. " My dearest Clara, I am so glad you are returned. This is a matter of the greatest importance. Read

---

* This trait is from life.

this letter : you will soon learn how much depends upon you; and I am happy, indeed, that it is upon you it depends." He placed an open letter in her hands as he spoke, and Clara read as follows :—

"*Brampton, April* 17.

"DEAR SIR,—I am most anxious, in circumstances which it must be allowed are somewhat difficult, to act with all the consideration towards yourself which is compatible with justice, and with a strict adherence to that determination with which I have already acquainted you. Common fairness requires that you should be the first person to learn the steps I may resolve upon taking. I have, therefore, to inform you that, not considering your explanation of the very painful reports alluded to in my last perfectly satisfactory, I have written to Mr. Middleton (who, besides being the clergyman of your parish, is an old and highly respected acquaintance of my own), to say that if he is ready to vouch for your freedom from this pernicious habit, I am ready on my part to appoint you to the vacant professorship. I have the honour to remain, yours sincerely,

"RICHARD BROOKES."

Clara looked up wonderingly and full of inquiry. Her brother had scarcely patience to wait till she had finished the letter. "Now, Clara," exclaimed he, "it all depends upon you. Mr. Middleton's conscience, it seems, is very squeamish in these matters; he heartily wishes to serve me, I do believe, but it seems he has made a rule of never becoming responsible for any man on his own assertion merely. But if *you* will assure him that during the time you kept house for me, you had no reason to believe—in short, I suppose you guess what these confounded reports are. Old Brookes has been told that I drank, and it seems he has a vow not to give one of his professorships to any man on whom such an imputation rests. You have only to free me from it, and I am secure. These miserable reports refer to the time that we were together; and Mr. Middleton says that he will pledge himself for me, if you will give him your assurance that he may do so. He is in his study. Go to him directly, there's a good girl, for it only wants an hour of post time."

The words were poured forth breathlessly; but Clara stood immovable, clasping her hands together with a look of misery. Then she ran to George's chair, and folding her arms about his neck, covered his face with tears and kisses, as if to atone for the pain she was about to inflict. He half pushed her away, saying impatiently, "Come, come, what does this mean?"

"I cannot do it," murmured the sobbing girl; "you *know* I cannot. Oh, my dearest brother, what will become of me!"

George was furious; he affected incredulity, he tried entreaties, protestations, menaces, ridicule. She *could* not be in earnest. Would she ruin her own brother, because some once or twice she had seen him when he had been a little imprudent? And when he said this, he positively believed that it was but once or twice, and that her scruples were as absurd as they were unkind. Clara wept to agony, but never wavered. It was, indeed, a martyrdom which had more than the bitterness of death. And this idolised brother parted from her at last with words which burned indelible traces upon her heart—she did not love him—she was his enemy—she had ruined his prospects for ever. She felt that she had alienated from her the only heart which she had believed to be entirely her own. She sat down in a kind of desperation, and wrote to Mrs. Bouverie, accepting the situation, and offering to come to her immediately. She did not like to send a servant with the note; she feared to be prevented from sending it at all if she delayed, and yet she felt that it was the only thing to be done. Inaction seemed impossible, and she hurried out with it herself. How she walked those two miles she did not know. Her head ached to distraction, and her thoughts were all bewildered; but she left the note, sealed her own fate, and then· set forth again to the vicarage. "I shall be very unhappy, always, all my life," said she to herself; "but George will not care! George will not care!" and the words seemed to strike heavily against her brain, and ring dizzily in her ears. She held her forehead with her hand, and stood still, wondering if any woe could go beyond what she then felt, and feeling certain that if there were any such sorrow she should be called upon to endure it. She longed for death, for imbecility, for madness—for anything that should obliterate consciousness and destroy the capacity for suffering.

"May I speak to you, dear Miss Capel?" said a gentle voice at her side; "I have so long wished to see you. Surely so old a friend as myself has some privilege." And Mr. Archer took her trembling hand in his, and then drew it within his arm, looking earnestly into her face, and adding, "You are ill--is anything fresh amiss? Can I serve you? *Pray* tell me."

Clara burst into an agony of weeping; and, as soon as she could speak, tried to put aside his questions, but he was not so to be baffled. He persevered till he had drawn from her the history of what had occurred, which she gave wi h the less reluctance that she knew him to be already aware of George's misconduct. Indeed, it was a hint received from Mr. Archer which had induced Mr. Capel to send Clara to his son. Incoherent and interrupted were her words, but her listener speedily apprehended their meaning. He soothed her with the utmost tenderness, and once more put hope into her desolate heart. He knew Mr. Brookes well, and had, indeed, recommended George to him; he would speak to George, and if he found him properly disposed (of which he felt no doubt), he would himself see Mr. Brookes, and endeavour to induce him to accept his (Mr. Archer's) surety for George's future steadiness and good conduct. He entertained no fears. Above all, never let Clara for one moment regret that she had done right in circumstances so painful. She had probably saved her brother, for this lesson would be one that he never could forget. Clara could scarcely express her gratitude. They walked together for some time in silence, her tears flowing quietly and relieving her over-strained nerves. At last he spoke again: "Do you remember a conversation we had some years ago about Tennyson's 'Love and Duty?'"

She looked up in surprise. Yes, she had not forgotten it.

"You said then," he pursued, "that no woman could feel sure that she was beloved till she was actually told it; and that it was selfishness in a man to keep silence, because, in order to avoid the possible humiliation of a refusal, or the pain of a scene of parting if separation were necessary, he *might* be depriving her (mark, I only say *might*) of a certainty which— she *might* wish to possess. Clara . .　 ! all this while I have loved you !"

There was again a silence—Clara's face hidden in her hands. And so, not absolutely discouraged, Mr. Archer told his story. He had loved her all this while—for her charms, for her faults, for her noble struggle against those faults, for her self-conquest, for *herself*. He believed it impossible that she should love him; he had never meant to speak of it. But those words of hers had remained unforgotten; and at last, he was doing what, perhaps, he might ever afterwards repent. *Did* he repent it ? He spoke of his defect, he accused himself of presumption, he was ashamed, afraid of what he had doɪe. Reader, did he repent it ?

Oh, how often did Clara Archer, the happy idolised wife, recur to those days of self-deception when, out o.' the bitterness of her mortification, in believing that he did not like her, she persuaded herself that she disliked him! How did she delight to trace the marks of her secret, unsuspected, unacknowledged love, in her irritability towards him, her shyness in his presence, her unsatisfied and morbid cravings after affection, which were, in truth, so many witnesses to that inner sense which was awake indeed, but unconscious and ungrateful. How did she, who had so gloried in her self-dependence, glory now, in owing all to him! Yes, all! Her happiness, the comfort of her family (for I need scarcely say that *he* was the anonymous benefactor), the complete reformation of George, who distinguished himself to her heart's content as mathematical professor; and the impɪ vement in her own character, which she verily believed to hav been caused, though unconsciously at the time, by her contemɪlation of his. In her happiners as in her bitter grief, in her weakness as in her strength, in he.' faults as in her noble qualities, she remained from first to last—

A VERY WOMAN.

"THE TRUST,'

BY MRS. BURBURY

"How little is the happiness
  That will content a child ;
A favourite dog, a sunny fruit,
  A blossom growing wild.

"A word will fill the little heart
  With pleasure and with pride
It is a harsh, a cruel thing
  That such should be denied.

"And yet how many weary hours
  These joyous creatures know ;
How much of sorrow and restraint
  They to their elders owe."

L. E. L.

"Alas ! alas !
Why, all the souls that were, were forfeit once ;
And He, that might the vantage best have took,
Found out the remedy : How would you be,
If He, which is the top of judgment, should
But judge you as you are ?   Oh, think on that ;
And mercy then will breathe within your lips."

Measure for Measure.

ONE of those terrible commercial panics which now and then occur in this country, shaking the credit of the wealthiest houses, and utterly destroying that of others, took place, as is too well remembered, in the autumn and winter of the year before last. Many were the homes destroyed and hearts broken ; and much as English pity goes abroad to look for objects of compassion, there could have been found in the sufferers and victims of this home affliction, quite as deserving, and almost as romanti ; sufferers, as were ever sent forth by Poland or France :

but it is only with one out of many of these cases we have now
to deal

Mr. Neville was a mercnant; one of those who, trading
largely with toreign houses, have most of their capital invested
either in goods in their possession, or in vessels upon the sea.
He was a young man of noble disposition and unsullied integrity;
but somewhat proud and obstinate, so that when he had once
decided upon any course, it was a matter of great difficulty to
alter or divert his intentions. This decision of character was
especially seen in his marriage; for, regardless of the violent
opposition of his family, he chose and wedded a young woman
without any earthly recommendation, but high principle, good
birth, and some talent. She had not only no fortune, but when
he married her was working laboriously as a governess for the
support of her family, who after her marriage became, of course,
dependent upon her husband. The Nevilles, who were a rich
and money-loving race, never forgave either Harry or his
wife, and for some time would not receive her; though at last a
hollow peace was made up by the means of Harry's youngest
sister — a loving-hearted girl of eighteen: and Mrs. Harry
Neville, eager for her husband's sake to conciliate his family,
accepted the advances which they made, and gladly came forward with the hand of friendship. But she was not a person
with whom such people as the Nevilles could ever be really
friendly, for she was too courteous to the poor, too unbending
in spirit, and too bitter in her reprobation of mean thoughts
and time-serving actions, to render her society greatly coveted
by those who were in all things her opposite. Still they kept
up a show of affection towards her; and when the blow came
that shattered Harry's fortune, and left him penniless, his wife,
judging of his relations by her own heart, and feeling what in
a similar case would be her conduct, never doubted but that
they would so far assist him as to place him in a position to
battle with the storm, and rise again. But she was mistaken;
not only was Harry arrested and thrown into prison, but she
was left with two young children, penniless, in a strange place,
without receiving a single line of sympathy or pity from one of
them. In vain did she write to urge upon them the necessity
for assistance, and the cruelty of withholding it; in vain did
she represent the absolute need for immediate relief: all her
appeals were unheeded. At last Beatrice Neville (her husband's youngest sister, who was in France) heard of her brother

Harry's misfortunes, and wrote to her eldest brother, entreating that for her sake something might be done for Harry's children. She also wrote to their mother, lamenting her inability to offer (until she was of age) any help that might be of real use, and advising her to let her little ones, Blanche and Jessie, go to Mr. Edward Neville's house, where they might be tenderly cared for until something effectual could be done. The same post brought a letter from Mr. Edward Neville, mentioning his sister's wish, and requesting that the two little girls might be sent to him.

Oh, that poor mother! who, but the God who watched over her, can tell the intense agony of that hour! When first she read the letters her heart trembled, then seemed to stand still, then beat till its fierce pulsation nearly choked her. She returned to them again and again, to see if there was any hope for relief without this horrible separation, or any shadow of invitation to herself. But no! all spoke the same hard words as before, save that now she saw a postscript which in her haste she had quite overlooked. It was, that, relieved of the *burden* of her two children, she might return to her mother, and, doubtless, could earn her living easily in some respectable way.

She read it over and over again; her brain was surely wandering. It could not be! her husband in a London prison, herself miles, miles away in a country village, and their children separated from both!—she could not agree to it—she would die rather! Her darlings so tenderly nurtured, so fondly loved, with their warm hearts and generous natures, how could she bear to send them from her, to be at the mercy of those hard, cold spirits who could so forget all human love as to propose such a separation? Even if Beatrice had been there it would have been different; for she was gentle, merciful, and good, loving God with all her heart, and faithfully following his holy laws. But she was far away, and could not watch over her nieces. No, no! they should not go. But what was to be done? her purse was nearly empty, and she saw no prospect of its being replenished. She sat down, and supporting her head between both her hands, tried to think. What a chaos was her mind! how one wild thought drove out another! and visionary schemes and delusive hopes followed each other in rapid succession, but all were vain; upon none could she rely for help. Where were all her friends—those who had eaten and drunk at her table, and been flattered

by her notice?   As well ask where is the gossamer which this
morning, with its multitude of borrowed pearls, glittered in the
sunshine, but now, since the summer storm, has vanished?
She ran over their names: there was not one on whom she
dared venture to depend.   What could she do?   Her health,
which was very delicate, unfitted her for active employment, even
if she could have procured any.   How was she to obtain bread
and the shelter of a house for her children?   Alas! alas! she
knew not.   Their merry voices sounded on the stairs, and she
covered her ears with her hands, and crushed them violently
that she might not hear their laughter; for it seemed to her
that if the tones reached her brain she must go mad.   She
dreaded lest they should come in—those darling children whom
she loved better than her heart's life!   She feared to see them;
but they turned away, some fresh trifle had caught their fancy,
and they passed the door.   Then there was a silence, and she
listened with painful and straining earnestness to catch a sound
of their voices—something to assure her that they were still
near her.   This horrid stillness was a foretaste of that lasting
bereavement which threatened her.   At last a shout of joy
broke the silence, and she sank back in her seat, exhausted
with conflicting emotions.

The children had no idea of the cause of their father's
absence, and still less imagined why their fare was altered and
their comforts curtailed: for it was the bright, gay spring-
time; and so that they could wander in the country lanes,
gathering violets, and making round cowslip balls, and had
at home their mother's smile and sympathy, they cared
very little for the change.   Tenderness and love, the willing
kiss and ready interest in their joys and sorrows, were more
to them than the costliest house and most luxurious table.
Children love the *people* they live with, not the *appliances*
around them; a stately house and splendid wardrobe are no
compensations to them for the unloving eye and careless voice
This very ignorance and innocence rendered the proposed step
more difficult to accomplish; for how could their mother chill
their warm young hearts by prison tales: and if *she* did not
tell them, how could she ensure that the terrible truth would
be gently spoken, and that their spirits might not be crushed
by the knowledge?   No, no; they should not go; and so, for
this day, she comforted herself.   But the next, and the next,
brought the harrowing details of poverty still closer; and she

knew that not only would it be impossible to keep the frightful truth from her darlings, but that her power to provide even their frugal means would soon be at an end.

Could she bear to see them want food?—and to that it was coming faster and faster. Had she a right to keep them from the comfortable home offered by their uncle, to starve with her? Both alternatives were horrible! God help her! what should she do? There was another thought, too; this offer had evidently been made, presuming upon her well-known motherly devotion; they knew, or thought they knew, that she would never consent to part with her children, and the fact of her having thus declined their charity, would afford an excellent plea for refusing to assist Harry. God forgive the hearts that could thus speculate upon a mother's agony!

It were a weary task to tell all the misery which Mary Neville endured, before she gave up the charge of those whose life and happiness were dearer to her than her own. But the day at last came when they were to leave her. She had determined to tell them nothing, and let them go as if for a visit. How glad little Jessie was!—children love a change—and she remembered the large garden and gorgeous peacocks at her uncle's, and the last huge piece of cake he had given her, and her cousins' playthings, and she was wild with glee to see them all again. But Blanche was older by three years, and her mother's pallid face and choked voice, and the intense gaze of agony that the child often caught fixed upon herself, struck her as something strange and wrong; and the promised visit lost its charms, for, without knowing or guessing why, the child's instinct of danger told her that some sorrow was at hand.

Beatrice had enclosed a note to Mary for the expense of the journey with the children, and she had therefore determined to take them herself to their uncle. The day was fixed; and the night before, Jessie, who had tired herself with running about, went early to bed; but Blanche petitioned "to sit up a little longer, she would be so good and quiet, and not disturb mamma a bit." So Mary and the child sat together in the twilight till evening deepened into night, and the heaven was bright with stars. The mother's heart was breaking; there was a long, heavy silence; for even Blanche's young spirit trembled at the stealthy approach of evil, which is ever most terrible when, as to her, neither its shape nor form is known, and we only learn from what quarter the blow is coming, when it has been struck. At last Mary said, in a voice which sounded strange to the child, for it had, till lately, been singularly sweet and cheerful—" Blanche, my child, listen to what I say, and try always to remember it. You and Jessie are going to your uncle's to-morrow. I shall not be able to stay with you, but I hope you will be as good as if I were always present—pray remember this, because your happiness will greatly depend on your conduct. Never disobey your uncle or aunt, be affec tionate and friendly with your cousins, and never, never forget to pray night and morning to God. Pray to *Him*, Blanche," she said, with a terrible earnestness, fixing her eyes, in the pale star-light, upon the child, "for He is your true and only friend : in sorrow or trouble go to Him ; pour out your heart, and He will hear you. He will be always near, though I am away. And dear little Jessie ; Blanche, Blanche, will you——"

The sentence was unfinished ; for, overcome with the intensity of her feelings, Mary fell senseless from her chair, and the little girl who had hitherto, in similar attacks, seen her mother attended by numerous and loving hands, now knelt by her *alone*.

The next day, at four o'clock, the chaise which conveyed Mary Neville and her children from the railway, stopped at Mr. Edward Neville's door, and he himself appeared to receive them. He kissed each of the girls, and handing out his sister-in-law, left her to enter his house alone, while he debated with the driver about an extra sixpence.

Mrs. Edward Neville was the exact reverse of Mary ; she had possessed a large fortune, was of *parvenu* extraction, and though by no means ignorant, was certainly not a well-educated woman. She had, during Mary's prosperity, been rather afraid of her ; had envied her ease and repose in society, and the higher tone of everything about her, for, try as she would, she could never attain Mary's perfect quietness of manner.

Her dinners were as good, often, as far as quantity was concerned, better ; but somehow they never went off so well, because from her love of money struggling with her love of show, she had always inexperienced servants, who, on " party days," were running over one another all about the house, looking for queer things in queer places, and causing the well-drilled waiters and cooks, hired for the occasion, the utmost perplexity ; while their mistress, who had quite sense enough to see that something was wrong, fidgeted and fussed, tried to talk to her guests while she directed the whereabouts of dishes with her eye ; stopped suddenly in the midst of a conversation to listen (as she thought unobserved) to whether the next cover was coming, and tormented herself, and perplexed everybody until, what should have been a pleasant social meeting, was to *her* a toil and a heartburning, and to her guests either a source of sly amusement or of pity. All this mortified her, because she saw that, with a smaller house and fewer attendants, the dinners and evening parties over which Mary presided, not only were conducted so quietly that the awkward machinery of the thing was never displayed, but that the hostess while tendering her hospitality (not forcing it) upon her friends, was as gay and free from anxiety and care, as the merriest person in the room. It was acknowledged by their mutual acquaintance, that while nothing could be better than Mrs. Harry Neville's parties, nothing could be much worse than Mrs. Edward's.

This was all remembered now, and though she was not wicked enough to rejoice in Mary's misfortunes, yet the idea of patronising one who had been the object of her secret envy, was certainly very pleasing to her self-love. In accordance with this feeling, she only rose from her chair and made two steps forward to meet Mary and her children, as they entered. But in Mary's sad face and eyes there was something so beseeching and sorrow-stricken, that her stateliness gave way, and she came quickly from her place, and shook hands with her sister-in-law cordially ; while Mr. Neville, who had saved the sixpence by out-talking the coachman, now entered in high glee, and gave the children a very hearty, though not very elegant, welcome.

Dinner was soon served, and as it happened to be Mrs. Neville's birthday, all the children dined with their parents. Oh, how anxiously did Mary watch her darlings, lest they should do or say anything which might offend ! Gaiety, even in childhood, and a preference for one dish or taste over another, is a sin and presumption in the poor ; but Jessie was habitually too well behaved, and Blanche watched her mother's eyes too narrowly, to permit them to do very wrong. And when the cloth was withdrawn there had not been a single particle of gravy spilled upon the spotless damask, nor an atom of potatoe left upon either plate, to call a frown to the face of

their aunt, who, though indifferent, to a most lamentable degree,
respecting all such things when "they were alone," was pain·
fully particular "before people."

The hour was drawing near for Mary to depart, and she
sought an interview with Mr. and Mrs. Edward Neville alone.
She had so much to say to them, so much to deprecate and
beseech. And the children having left them, Mr. Neville said,
filling his glass—

"Well, Mrs. Harry, and what does your husband mean to
do when he gets out? With my family and expenses, and
now in addition the charge of his two children, I can do
nothing more to help him, of course. He can't expect it."

"I hope you will see Harry——"

"Oh, no, quite impossible. I went once, you know, but the
place is so horribly uncomfortable. I could not go again; it
could do no good."

"Yes, it might; because I cannot but hope that if you were
to see him now, something might be proposed which would
answer for you both."

"Answer for us both! My dear lady, you never were much
of a calculator,—how could you be, seeing that until you
married you had never overmuch to calculate,—but surely you
must have learned enough now to know, that an insolvent means
a man without a shilling, and how any connection with such
a man can answer to another, I confess I don't see."

Oh, what unwelcome words of stern and bitter truth were
gathering upon Mary's lips! But she thought of her children,
and was silent. He went on :—

"I am out of patience with Harry; but it is just what one
might have expected, living in the extravagant way he did,
and holding himself so high and mighty. It won't do, Mrs.
Harry, especially when other people have to be at the expense.
I suppose he thinks nothing of the cost of these little girls, but
takes it all for granted, as if money was to be picked up in the
streets."

Mary's lips quivered, and but that she remembered the Scrip·
ture precept, "A soft answer turneth away wrath," she would
have uttered, with indignant and contemptuous eloquence, such
terribly unanswerable truths, as would have silenced, if not
shamed him. Fast upon her memory came those words of
God's apostle,—"If a man say, I love God, and hateth his
brother he is a liar. And this commandment have we from him,

that he who loveth God, love his brother also." And again,
—"Whosoever hateth his brother is a murderer, and ye know
that no murderer hath eternal life abiding in him; but whoso
seeth his brother have need, and shutteth up his bowels of
compassion from him, how dwelleth the love of God in him?"
All this flashed vividly before her spirit's eye, and trembled
on her tongue, but for the sake of Harry and those dear
children, she resolutely held her lips closed, and was silent.
And at last her reward came, as, charmed with the impression
he fancied his eloquence had produced, and having exhausted
all his brotherly invective, he became silent too, and for awhile
neither spoke.

But time wore on, and the latest train by which Mary could
return, would, she knew, start in two hours; therefore she was
compelled at last to break the heavy silence, though in a voice
so husky with the tears she tried to suppress, that her words
were nearly inarticulate.

"You will write to me very often—once a week—will you
not?"

"Oh, yes, if I have time; but there can be nothing to say:
I hope you won't fidget yourself," replied Mrs. Edward.

"Oh, sister!" exclaimed poor Mary, using that sacred name
for the first time, "my children are my life, I would die for
their sakes, and this separation has all the bitterness of death;
but I hope it is for their good—I trust in God that it is!"
and she looked up in agony, to heaven, "and, therefore, for
them I bear it; but if I am not to hear of them, at least,
weekly, I *cannot* bear it: I shall then surely die; we have
never been separated. Oh, think what I shall suffer, alone, my
husband in a prison, my children away; and, for God's sake,
as you are a wife and mother, do as I implore you!"

"Really, Mrs. Harry, this is very strange, you are so ex-
citable; it is such a serious thing to promise. I might be out,
or busy, or ill, or——"

"Nonsense, Kitty!" interrupted her husband, who was
touched by the mute agony of the mother's face; "you shall
hear every Sunday—no, I can't write on Saturday; but I will
on Sunday—every Monday you will have a letter; so if my
wife can't write, I will."

"God bless you!" exclaimed Mary, clasping her hands.
"You will tell me everything, every little ailment or sorrow?
It may seem troublesome; but you will have pity upon my

anxiety. Think of your own children, and act by me, as you would have me, in a similar case, do by you. And, oh! be kind to them, consider how young they are; and if they offend or displease you, be gentle and tender to their infancy, remember that they are motherless. You have sought THE TRUST—oh, fulfil it faithfully, as you will answer to God at the last, terrible day; for if they come to harm, either of body or of soul, while in your hands, I can never forgive you while I live, and, dying, I will appeal to God for vengeance! You have sought the TRUST, I say again; and for your own soul's sake, look well to its performance. But if, in brotherly love and holy Christian charity to my children and their father, you have undertaken it, may all the blessings of God be on you and yours for ever; and for every happy hour, every joy your care gives to these orphans—for what else are they—may years of happiness be repaid to you here, and endless bliss hereafter."

She had risen, and now fixed her large, blue eyes upon the face of her brother-in-law, who gazed, half indignant, half pity-ing, and entirely puzzled, upon this unlooked-for energy in the thin, fragile creature before him.

"I really don't know what you mean, Mrs. Harry; I offered to take the children to please Beatrice, and because I wished to relieve you from the burden."

"*Burden!*—my children a burden!—what burden are the flowers to the earth?" exclaimed Mary, impetuously.

"Well, well! I did not mean that; but you are so hasty, you do not give me a chance. What I intend is this—to take Blanche and Jessie off your hands, so that you and Harry may be free to take situations, or do what you think best for yourselves; they shall fare the same as my own children, and be brought up in the same way" (he did not add, that Beatrice had promised to repay him when she came of age). "I always liked them, and they shall have as kind a home as I can make them; and beyond this I can promise no more. I think what you said in your letter about the children not knowing of their father's extravagance and imprisonment, is nonsense, because nothing would be so likely to give them a wholesome dread of careless-ness, as to hear of his misery. But still, as it is your whim, why it must e'en be so; and they shall never learn it from me. Are you satisfied?"

"Yes. The promise is now registered in heaven, and God as well as their earthly parents will require at your hands an account of how it has been kept. Therefore look heedfully to your trust; a mother reckoning for her children will be no easy creditor to baffle."

———

Blanche and Jessie had been a year with their uncle, when the reader is next introduced to Mr. Edward Neville's house. With the miserable details of the poverty-stricken life of Harry and Mary during those twelve months, we will not pain him; but pass them over with a sigh that in Christian England, such grief should daily cry to God, for the relief denied to it by man. It was a hot wet day in May, the air was oppressive both with heat and damp, and people could hardly breathe in the close, stifled atmosphere. It was one of those days which make even cheerful hearts gloomy, and gloomy ones desperate. Mr. and Mrs. Edward Neville were standing in the breakfast-room of their handsome mansion, listening with a painful, frightened earnestness, to the carriages as they drove past on the high road. They were fearing an arrival. Every moment they turned a glance upon the costly French clock which ticked upon the chimney-piece, and compared it with their watches, but neither spoke, until Mrs. Edward exclaimed—

"I do so dread her coming; it seems but yesterday that she left them, and warned us of her return. Oh, how I wish we had never taken them! Beatrice, too, is so angry that I am afraid we have lost all her interest for ever."

"Yes, and no wonder. If I had known how things were going on, I should have interfered long ago; but, of course, I thought that you would do all that was right by the children, and I saw them so seldom that I had no opportunity to remark the change. I would not have had it happen for a thousand pounds; what will the world say?" said Mr. Neville, walking angrily about the room.

At this moment the footsteps of the physician were heard descending the stairs, and Mrs. Edward cried—

"Oh, there is Dr. Lewis, do not let him go; she will be here directly, and I dare not meet her; beg him to stay."

Her husband went out to obey these entreaties, and as he was talking to the doctor, a fly drove furiously up, and Mary Neville (Harry was in Wales) sprung out and rushed into the house. The physician, who knew her well, came hastily forward, and throwing open the dining-room door, began—

"My dear Mrs. Neville. pray come——"

"My children, my children!" cried Mary.

"Do come in here for a moment," said Edward, offering his hand to lead her into the room; but spurning it, with a gesture of disgust, she fixed her eyes upon him, and replied—

"I am here, as I told you I would be, to demand a reckoning for your TRUST. God help us both, if it has been betrayed."

"Pray let me speak to you for one instant," said Dr. Lewis, pitying the agitation of Edward, as she uttered these words in a hard, bitter tone. She gazed into his face a moment, and read something there which paralysed her strength; then, glancing through the door to the windows of the room before her, she saw that they were darkened, and with a cry of agony, so utterly desolate and appalling, that even the practised physician shrank back in terror, she fell heavily upon the marble floor. Not long did this happy insensibility befriend her; misery was too busy at her heart to suffer it to remain unconscious long, and in a few minutes she revived; and with a sudden energy sprang up, and seizing Dr. Lewis's arm, said, in a hissing whisper—

"Dead—both dead?"

"No, no."

"Which?" and as she spoke, she shivered from head to foot, while her eyes glared upon the sympathising physician with such a fearful expression that he could not choose but reply—

"Jessie."

A deep, terrible groan answered him, as the painful clasp with which she held his arm was relaxed, and her hands fell listlessly by her side. Then, after a minute, she said in the same shrill unnatural whisper—

"Blanche, where is she?"

"Up-stairs; but I must prepare you to find her very ill." Mary's hands clasped each other convulsively, and her lips opened without a sound; "but you must be calm; pray, do not agitate yourself."

"Calm!" she repeated with a scream; "calm!—my heart is frozen! I am ice!"

"Pray, pray, Mrs. Harry——" began her brother-in-law; but at his voice she started as if stung by a serpent, and exclaimed—

"If you would have me keep my senses, and not go mad before you, be silent. I have not seen my dead and dying children yet, when that is done I will talk to you. Let me go now, Dr. Lewis," and with a bend of her head, and action of her hand, as if to deprecate all further speech, she passed the physician and her brother-in-law, and went out into the hall, in which, listening with a trembling frame and blanched cheek, stood Mrs. Edward Neville. Upon seeing her sister-in-law she would have escaped, had it been possible; but her fears of recognition were needless. Mary never seemed to see her, and crossing the hall without a word, ascended the stairs, followed by the medical man.

When they reached the upper landing, Dr. Lewis passed his companion, and going forward, opened a bedroom-door opposite to them, and in a minute the mother was in the chamber of death. On a little bed, from which was stripped all curtains and drapery, to allow the air to play freely around it, lay Blanche Neville; but so sadly altered that even her mother could scarcely recognise her. Her eyes, round each of which was a frightful circlet of black, were closed, and her breathing was laboured and heavy; she was not asleep, but the stupor of death seemed gathering over her. Mary staggered as the terrible sight met her gaze; but, recovering in a moment, approached the bed. Kneeling by it, and discovering when she raised her face, the grieved features of indignant sorrow, was Beatrice Neville; she rose as Mary came up, and shrinking back she cried—

"Do not hate me, do not hate me! I have travelled day and night since I heard of this; and God knows" (and she raised her eyes to heaven) "I would have saved their lives with my own. Since I came I have never left this room: and this morning, this morning"—but, overcome with the recollection, she turned away, and burst into tears. The sound of voices aroused Blanche, and opening her eyes, they fell upon her mother. In an instant it seemed as if life and health had come back to her, for springing up in bed with a strength of which no one would have thought her capable, she held out her arms to Mary, and cried—

"Mamma! mamma! mamma!"

Before the words were half uttered, mother and child held each other in a close embrace; and after a few minutes, Blanche said, holding her mother's hand between both her own wasted ones—

"You will not leave me here, again, dear mamma?—do not —pray, do not!"

" Never, my darling, *never!* I will stay with you, and when I go, so shall you."

" Mamma, Jessie is dead! we have been so unhappy! oh why did you not come before? And papa, he is not so wicked, is he? Can't *he* come, too?" said Blanche, in a laboured voice, for her breathing was very painful.

" Yes, darling, he will be here soon."

" I thought so, I knew it was not true; Aunt Edward said that he was wicked, and shut up in prison, and that if we were troublesome we should be shut up too."

Beatrice groaned, but Mary clenched her hand until the nails were buried in the palm, and said, quietly—

" Never mind, Blanche, dearest, you shall not be shut up, and papa is now, I dare say, coming to see you; he has only just heard of your illness, so you must try and get well, to see him."

" I shall never be well again," said the child; " I know I never shall: I have been ill so long, and Aunt Edward said it was all fancy; and that you would never come to see us, because we fretted; and she was angry with us, and made us go to school; and told our governess we were obstinate, idle children, and could do our lessons if we chose. And she said we were charity-children, and ungrateful, and wicked; and we should come to want, as you and papa had done."

" Blanche, Blanche!" cried Beatrice, imploringly; but the mother sat, seemingly unmoved, while the child gasped out its tale. Only her eyes spoke, and their language was frightful.

" Are you there, Aunt Beatrice?" said the sufferer: " I love you; if you had come before, we should have been happy. Why did you not come? Oh! how poor Jessie and I used to cry ourselves to sleep, wishing for mamma and you! But it was of no use, you never came, you had forgotten us.'

" My own, my own!" cried Mary, folding her child to her heart.

" Mamma, why did you leave us? Oh! why did you leave us to be so very miserable?"

Mary rose suddenly. She could not breathe; her heart seemed swelling till it threatened suffocation: and Dr. Lewis, eeing the terrible expression of her face, came from the window, where he had stood to conceal his emotion, and said, in a gentle, pitying voice—

" Blanche, darling, if you love your mamma, do not distress her so; see how ill she is: she will not leave you again, if you

are good; but, if you talk in this way, I shall not let her stay
to nurse you."

"Oh! do not go—I will be so good—do not," faltered the
child; and, overcome with the excitement, she fainted.

All that weary day and night, Mary and Beatrice watched
by the bed of the death-stricken child whose piteous delirium,
revealing as it did the miseries of the past year, rendered them
nearly incapable of performing the duties of their agonising
post.

How quiet was that usually noisy house; the very footfall
of the inmates, as they moved about, could not be distinguished
until they had reached you. The muffled bells, and trebly-
carpeted passages, the hushed and whispering voices, alike
betrayed the awe which was upon them all. And well might
they tremble and fear, and still their very hearts, to listen to
the sounds in the sick-room above, for the avenger was at hand:
the awakened and sleepless wrath of the betrayed and bereaved mother, was watching by her child. Good need had
they all to dread the reckoning, if that last one died.

And now, in as few words as will serve to do so, we will give
a sketch of the circumstances which, in a year, had robbed
Mary of her treasure.

Blanche and Jessie were singularly graceful and elegant
children, gentle and refined in manner, and delicate in health.
Not sickly or troublesome, but, like all beautiful things, requiring tenderness and care. In this they were the very oppo-
sites of their cousins, who were noisy and ungovernable, full
of the enjoyment of abundant health and animal spirits; and,
as may be easily supposed, the occupations and games which
gave joy to the one were, invariably, either too tame or too
riotous for the other. Now, this difference in the style of the
children was, in itself, irritating to Mrs. Edward Neville,
especially as people always noticed and encouraged the timid,
retiring, little strangers, much more than their boisterous
cousins; so that she strove to lessen the favourable impression
they made, by telling every one, in a tone of compassion, that
they were "poor Harry's children, and that they had taken
them out of charity; but, really, their mother had so indulged
and spoiled them, bringing them up in all sorts of whims and
extravagancies, that they were a source of continual trouble,
always fancying or refusing something. It was a sad thing, to
be sure; but Mr Edward Neville was so benevolent and good,

that, dreadful as his brother's conduct had been, and sa lly as he had disgraced the family, he had taken his children, and clothed and fed them just as if their father had behaved credit-ably, instead of being such a reprobate."

Indignantly did the hearts of the humbled and insulted children often swell at such words as these, and studio' sly did they try to hide themselves from notice. But Mrs. Edward liked to play the good Samaritan, and parade her unhappy little nieces to the world ; so, day after day, they were exhibited to the visitors, till their altered looks and faded beauty called forth exclamations of pity instead of admiration. Their cousins were far from being ill-natured or cruelly-disposed towards them, and never really intended to distress them ; but they had no sympathy with their delicate health and gentle tastes ; and now, hearing repeatedly from their mother of the worthlessness of uncle Harry, and the extreme charity of their father in giving his daughters shelter, they learned to look upon the sensitive and peace-loving children as interlopers, and butts for their practical jokes. Beatrice, in her frequent letters of inquiry respecting her nieces' welfare, had strongly urged upon her brother the necessity of educating them carefully, with a view to their future independence, promising, upon her coming of age, herself to defray the expenses. At first Mrs. Edward demurred at this ; but Beatrice insisting upon it, she hunted out a cheap day-school at the village, a mile from her house, and thither, in wet weather or dry, in heat or cold, did the poor delicate children walk twice a day. In vain did they complain of fatigue ; in vain did their aunt see, first their appe-tites, and then their bodily energy, failing ; she told herself, and them, that it was perverseness and idleness, and that to yield to their request, that they might stay at home, would only make them more delicate and fanciful.

Who now can tell, but the pitying angels who bore them invisible company in their weary life, the hopeless tears of misery those poor children shed, as, day after day, they rested at short intervals along their walk to school ; and how they wondered why it was they were so desolate and deserted, and if they were, indeed, as their aunt said, quite forgotten ! And often calling to mind their mother's injunctions, Blanche would strive to cheer her darling little Jessie ; and when the poor child sobbed till her heart beat painfully from weakness and grief, she would conjure up bright hopes for the future, joyful visions of their mother's return, and in this way calm for a time the misery which was wearing her young life away. Thus the evils increased, till the sad, frightened little things—those petted darlings of their parents whose earliest years had been unbroken sunshine—became spiritless, heart-crushed, and feeble. At last a low contagious fever broke out in the school, and Blanche and Jessie were soon attacked by it. For the first day or two they were mocked and laughed at, told they were fine ladies and fanciful, and must not play truant; but on the third, Mrs. Edward was startled by seeing a chaise drive slowly up to her door, and her nieces lifted out from it, the youngest in a state of perfect insensibility. The governess, who felt deeply for her gentle, patient, little pupils, had accompanied them home, and now urged, in very indignant terms, that Dr. Lewis, the leading physician in the neighbourhood, should be sent for ; and so much alarmed was Mrs. Edward that she eagerly agreed to the suggestion. He came, and she shrank terrified from his look and tone as he said—

"If these children's parents are alive, and ever wish to see them again on earth, let them be summoned instantly. I have little hope of saving them ; they are so enfeebled and reduced in stamina that there is scarcely a shadow of chance for their lives."

Mr. Neville was immediately summoned from his counting-house, and, though himself far from blameless in the matter, he vehemently upbraided his wife with her cruel and heartless neglect of their sacred charge. Neither of them dared to send for the mother, whose confidence they had so recklessly betrayed ; but they wrote to Beatrice, who had just returned from the Continent, to come to them as speedily as possible, at the same time informing her of the reason for which her presence was required. As soon as Beatrice received this letter she set off, only delaying long enough to write to Mary, begging her to lose no time in joining her at " The Lodge." When she arrived she found Jessie dying. Throwing off her travelling dress, she waited for no interview with her sister-in-law, nor explanation of the cruel scene she was called upon to witness, but at once took her place by the sinking child, and never left her until God, in mercy to her sufferings, sent His angel to put an end to them for ever.

Before she died, Beatrice had the unspeakable joy of seeing her loving eyes rest in recognition upon her, and of receiving from her dying lips a fond message of devoted affection, to be conveyed to her mother. It was fortunate that the patient little sufferer had been so impressed by her aunt, during the last year, with a conviction of the extreme improbability of her ever seeing her parents again, that now, in this desolate hour, she never pined for or expected them. It would have distracted her broken-hearted nurse if that misery had been added to her already overflowing cup; but she was spared it, and Jessie Neville died in her arms, with a smile upon her emaciated face and words of love upon her lips. The death-spirit had breathed softly upon her heart, and its pulse was stilled. No convulsion, no terror or pain, left its impress upon those lovely little features to make them terrible. Quietly, as if to sleep, the sinless soul resigned itself to God; and, as if the answering smile with which it greeted its happy sister-angels lingered still upon its lips, the face which had so long been sorrowful was now brightened with a calm and holy joy.

Morning was breaking heavily over the rain-soddened earth; the birds chirped gloomily, as if the long-continued wet had made them hopeless and sad, and they despaired of seeing the glad sunshine again. Beneath the shrubs the water had washed away the gravel, and laid bare the white stones; and tiny rivers were coursing their way below the grass-raised edge of the lawn, and down the walks, while a warm thick fog, almost palpable to the touch, steamed up from the earth. What a terrible atmosphere was this for fever to riot and thrive in! And Beatrice and Mary knew, when the struggling light, breaking through the thick low clouds, revealed the melancholy prospect, that all hope from the benefit of fresh brisk air and a lightened atmosphere was over for that day.

Very early, long before half even of the busy people of the world were up, Dr. Lewis stood again by his patient. A great change had taken place, and the fever had spent its fury; and as if satisfied with the misery it had wrought, and the beautiful prey it had already seized, seemed playing coyly with the stricken and helpless Blanche. Inflammation, that covert and energetic foe, was subdued; and the sleep into which the child had sunk since daybreak, was more deep and quiet than any which had blessed her with its balm since she had been attacked. Now, for the first time, the physician had hope; and when Mr. Berry, his able and active colleague, joined him for their consultation, they agreed that the case wore a more cheering aspect than it had yet done, and that, if previous to the attack the child's strength had not been most cruelly undermined, she might even now battle successfully for her life. Early in the morning she awoke, and taking the nourishment offered by the trembling hands of the mother, after a few minutes fell off again to sleep, being too much exhausted and too drowsy to talk.

By about midday Harry Neville, to whom Mary had sent Beatrice's enclosure and note, arrived; and the brothers, who had never met since they had dined together on equal terms in the house of the younger, now stood face to face. The insolvent and the *millionaire*, the betrayed and the betrayer.

Not one single word did Harry speak; but there was a stern look in his eyes which made his guilty brother tremble, as his own sank before them. It was the resolute gaze of one who would be fooled no longer, of one who knew his wrong, and was come to punish it. There was no anger, no passion or fury, but a calm determination. The father had come for his children, to reckon for their usage; the trusting and the faithless were at length confronted. For rage, and violence, and upbraiding, Edward Neville was prepared; but this deep, passionless, word-less indignation, was something so unlooked-for, and impossible to escape from, or explain away, that the worldly man, the rich and prosperous merchant, whose banking-book and ledgers were the glory of his heart and the envy of his rivals, cowered like a slave before the gaze of his father's son. And he felt that he would have given all the money of all his race, dearly as he loved it, for the power to stand erect before his fellow-man, and give a fearless account of his trust. But it was in vain; the past was telling its own tale, and its work had to be reckoned for.

When Harry had seen his child, he came down into the room where his brother sat, and walking up to him, said :—" When I was in prison, and *she* was destitute and alone, you induced my wife, in peril of starvation, to yield her children to your care— do not speak," he continued, waving his hand, as he saw Edward about to answer: " Like the generals of old, who starved into subjection the garrisons they could not conquer, you played upon the mother's agony, to rob her of her children; and, with a strange refinement of cruelty, would have separated her from me also, setting at nought those holy laws which are written upon the very hearts of all Christian men. It would seem as if you had all along hated her, and, coward-like, exulted in the misery which brought her so low as to accept charity from you, though, as I know now for the first time, Beatrice had made herself responsible for the food and clothes you only bestowed as her almoner. To gratify *yourself*, you took my children ; had it been to serve me, or with even a *shadow* of the holy charity you feigned, you would have doled out some little pittance to have kept husband and wife, parents and children— placed in such relationship by God—together. But no, that would not have served your purpose ; you would have given joy instead of misery to those you loved to humble, and have lost the daily pleasure of parading your brother's charity children before the eyes of the world. You chose your path, have followed it, and now, at its end, must give up a plain and true account of how you have walked. Two healthy, happy, loving children were given to your care a year ago ; one of them is dead. How ? by what means ? Did God smite her in the midst of joy, and take her from the care of loving hearts ? Or was her life worn away by the slow, unfailing poison of petty cruelty and neglect ? Was not her heart crushed and saddened by being held up as a burden upon your household ? And when at last her tender body sank, was she not even then taunted with her own feebleness and her father's follies ? The blood of Abel, slain by his brother, cried not to God for vengeance more loudly than does that of your victim, and it must be answered.

"Now listen to me : Position, wealth, a fair name, are all and each your idols, and for these you have bartered your soul to the world. But you stand upon a tottering steep ; let but my last child die, and far and wide as the human language is spoken the story of your treachery and hypocrisy shall be told. You shall no longer stand in the sight of God and man the living LIE that you have hitherto appeared ; but by my hand, with my voice, the cloak of seeming shall be torn away, and you shall be proclaimed the heartless, mercenary despiser of God's laws that you are ! If my child lives, though I will never own fellowship with you again, but, *rich* as you are, spurn your friendship as I would that of the loathsomest wretch on earth ; yet, in gratitude for God's mercy, I will spare you. I will recollect that you are my father's son, and that once you were innocent. *I* will remember, though *you* forget, that once we played together ; that the same mother nursed us, and that the same home sheltered us. For my dead mother's sake, for the honour of my father's name, and for the memory of their death-beds, when we were left as children to cling to and cherish each other, your reputation shall escape. But do not believe that, because I am silent, the world will be so. No! your sin will find you out; and from the grave of your tortured victim will rise the spirit which shall whisper in men's ears the crime that lies buried there; and it will be your misery and punishment, on earth, to feel that every man you meet knows you for the heartless brother and faithless guardian that you have proved yourself. And now, until my child's fate is decided, we meet no more."

A few hours after this interview between the brothers Beatrice sought one with Edward, the result of which will presently appear, and then returning to the sick room, resumed the place which for three weeks she had never quitted, except for a brief slumber upon the mattress by the bedside. How much, during those anxious hours, did the sisters-in-law find in each other's heart to love! Watching by the same couch, praying from the same holy book, and resting their hopes in the same Almighty and pitying Father, it is no wonder their former differences were forgotten, and that, purified in the sacred fire of affliction, these fellow-wanderers in a world of trial at last became sisters in love as they had so long been in name.

For many, many days, did Blanche's spirit hover upon the brink of the unseen world; and so calm was the child, so subdued was all the frenzy and delirium of the fever, that one would have thought her soul was even then holding communion with the white-robed angels, who bent their radiant heads to whisper to her of the awful glories and joys of her future home. All was so peaceful, that surely if she were to die, the bitterness of death was past; and from this idea, half pain, half peace, the watchers strove to take comfort. The weather still continued sadly against their patient, for the rain, which fell incessantly, engendered a wet, oppressive atmosphere, most injurious to a weak and fainting invalid; but, contrary to all expectation, after a week's incessant anxiety, they saw Blanche begin visibly to amend. Her progress to health, though very slow, was still constant; and Dr. Lewis told Mary he might now venture to say that, with God's blessing, her child was out of danger.

Of all the glad hearts made so by this announcement, not one experienced the deep thankfulness and joy of Beatrice Neville. Widely different in disposition from both her brothers, thoughtful yet loving, gentle yet firm, careful yet liberal, and gifted with no common intellect, she had seen with grief the unholy selfishness of her eldest brother. And while every sympathy of her woman's heart gathered round the bereaved parents, she dreaded the extreme of unchristian requital into which, if their last child died, their utter desolation and agony might hurry them. For there was no question (so Dr. Lewis told her in confidence) that the death of Jessie—and if she perished, that of Blanche, too—was caused by the unfeeling and injudicious treatment they had experienced; which, by reducing their strength and destroying the energy of life, had first predisposed them to low fever, and then rendered them powerless to struggle against it. Often and often, as she sat by the bed, in the early days of Blanche's illness, she shuddered indignantly at the piteous words the poor child seemed, in her delirium, to be repeating to her sister, and the beseeching tones and plaintive expressions which appeared but too familiar to her lips; and very, very thankful was she to Mary that, when with quivering lips and ghastly face she listened to these cruel evidences of her child's misery, she refrained from upbraiding her with having entreated and forwarded the project which had ended so deplorably.

The day came when Blanche was lifted from her bed and carried into another room ; and, though exhausted by the fatigue, she soon rallied, and smiled eagerly upon the three loving faces—those of her father, mother, and aunt—who stood by her.

It was the 11th of June, St. Barnabas' day ; and the sun, so long a stranger to the earth, broke suddenly through the clouds with majestic glory. From all corners of the rain-wearied earth went up to heaven the songs and incense of praise ; and as the party who were gathered round the sofa gazed out upon the thankful earth, the sweet chiming voice of the holy church-bell, calling the people to the daily prayers, rose cheerily on the air. Surely, surely, God, their Father, sent that sweet tone, and softened their hearts, as, listening to its music, it recalled to their minds the prayers that all over the Christian world were then going up to Him, to be laid upon the mercy-seat of His omnipotence. Blanche's eyes (for she had been sleeping) opened, and she said to Beatrice—

" Dear aunt, say a prayer—the Lord's Prayer ; you are too late for church, so let us pray together here."

They all knelt reverently by the child, and complied with her wish ; and certainly the voices of each lingered over the petition, "Forgive us our trespasses as we forgive them that trespass against us," longer than over any other sentence of the prayer. But, as they rose and resumed their seats, neither spoke on the subject to the others, till at last Beatrice said, gently—

"I have long wished to speak to you, Harry, upon your prospects for the future; and a feeling that I cannot define urges me to do so now, telling me that I shall be successful in obtaining my wishes."

She looked anxiously at her brother, to read, if possible, in his countenance, what impression her words made; but no feeling, except that of surprise, was written there; so she went on:—

"For all that has passed during the last fifteen months, Harry, I dare not offer any excuse; my own heart too loudly tells me that nothing can be pleaded. What is past can never be recalled; and I fear" (here her voice became husky with emotion, while Mary's tears fell fast, and even Harry covered his eyes) "never, never repaired. But the future, or at least the present, is our own; and I am authorised to say, that whatever plan or wishes you may have formed shall be gratefully forwarded, at any sacrifice."

As she spoke Harry sprang from his chair, and a vehement and wrathful ejaculation burst from his lips; but Beatrice rose, too, and laying her trembling hand upon his arm, and gazing into his face, while her own was bedewed with tears, said, beseechingly—

"Mercy, Harry, mercy! Have you forgotten our mother? What would she have said to hear such words from your lips, her darling and best-loved child?"

The angry man cast down his eyes; his mother's name was a spell against which he could not struggle. Beatrice saw her advantage, and continued:—

"Pity and forgive *them*, Harry, as God has pitied and forgiven *you*. You cried to Him for mercy on your child, and He spared her. The other"—and she bent her head upon his shoulder to support her frame, which trembled like one palsied —"is in heaven! Jessie is at rest."

Mary's sobs had now become convulsive, and she could scarcely breathe; while the emotion of her husband was nearly as distressing.

"Forbear to urge me, Beatrice," said he. "Do *you* .iave mercy. Why do you name my poor murdered child—slowly, heartlessly tortured to death by my own brother? Do you think I have forgotten?"

"No! no! God knows *that* is impossible for any of us; bu; you may forgive."

"Never, Beatrice, never! I will leave his house in peace. I will not curse him; but I will shake off the dust from my feet, and see him no more till we stand together before God."

"'Forgive us our trespasses as we forgive them that trespass against us,'" murmured the sweet, low voice of the child. Harry started; the feeble tones seemed unearthly; and in his excited and over-wrought state, a natural occurrence appeared almost a miraculous one. He sat down and wept.

"Dear Harry," pleaded his sister, "listen to the voice of innocence. If you, at the great day of which you speak, will stand in need of mercy, render it now to your offending and guilty brother; and as you do to God's erring creature here, it shall be done to you hereafter."

Mary sprang up, and, throwing herself upon her husband's neck, exclaimed—

"Forgive! forgive! *I* do, with all my heart."

"My wife! my darling Mary!" said Harry, weeping, as he pressed her wasted form close to his heart; "they would have robbed you of both your children—and do you plead for them?"

"God has spared one, and the other is with Him," she said, gasping; "let us bless Him for His mercy, and sacrifice our revenge as a thank-offering. He might have taken both, and yet He had mercy; let us not, then, be harder to soften than our offended Master, lest, in His anger, He turn again and smite us."

"'Father, forgive them,'" murmured Blanche, softly, using unconsciously the holy words of our Redeemer.

She scarcely knew for what she pleaded, but it was something for which her darling mother and aunt were weeping; and her gentle heart went with them in their prayers.

"God help me! this is a hard trial," said Harry.

"For my sake, if you love me," urged Mary.

"Mary, Mary, what would you have me say?"

"That from your heart you forgive your brother!" she replied.

"I DO," he answered, slowly, "for your sake, my wife."

"And for GOD's sake," whispered Mary and Beatrice together as they clung, in tears, to his neck.

For Ease, Strength and Durability,
BRITISH
ARGOSY
BRACES

ARE THE BEST
AND
Most Suitable for Summer Wear.

A Very Serviceable and Elegant Brace.

OF ALL HOSIERS AND DRAPERS THROUGHOUT THE WORLD.

USED IN THE ROYAL NURSERIES.

MATTHEWS'S
PREPARED FULLERS' EARTH

Is invaluable for Protecting the Skin and Preserving the Complexion from Winds, Redness, Roughness, Chaps, etc.

6D. & 1s.   **OF ALL CHEMISTS.**

SPECIALLY PURIFIED FOR THE SKIN.

Is the BEST REMEDY yet Discovered.

It acts like magic in relieving pain and throbbing, and soon cures the worst Corns and Bunions. It is especially useful for reducing Enlarged Great Toe Joints, which so mar the symmetry of the feet.

THOUSANDS HAVE BEEN CURED,

some of whom have *suffered for fifty years without being able to get relief* from any other remedy. A trial of a box is earnestly solicited, as Immediate Relief is Sure. Boxes 1s. 1½d., of all Chemists; free for 14 stamps, from the Sole Makers:

M. BEETHAM & SON, ⬥⬥⬥ ⬥⬥⬥ ⬥⬥⬥ **⬥ENHAM.**

For all	**From the Laboratory of** **THOMAS JACKSON** **Strangeways, MANCHESTER.**	the Year Round.
H.R.H. PRINCE **ALBERT'S** **CACHOUX.**	**DAINTY MORSELS IN THE FORM** **OF TINY SILVER BULLETS,** **WHICH DISSOLVE IN THE MOUTH,** **AND SURRENDER** **TO THE BREATH THEIR HIDDEN** **FRAGRANCE.**	**At 6d.,** Or by Post, **for 7d.**
JACKSON'S **BENZINE** **RECT.**	For taking out GREASE, OIL, PAINT, &c., from Carpets, Curtains, Clothes, Drapery, Dresses, be the material Cotton, Linen, Silk, or Wool, the texture Fine or Coarse. It cleans admirably Kid Gloves and Satin Slippers, Furs, Feathers, Books, Cards, Manu-scripts. It may be freely used to rinse and wash Frail or Gilt Trifles, to which water would be destructive.	At 6d., 1s., and 2s. 6d. Parcel Post, 3d. extra.
JACKSON'S **CHINESE** **DIAMOND** **CEMENT**	REGISTERED — TRADE MARK. **FOR MENDING EVERY ARTICLE OF ORNAMENT OR FURNITURE, CHINA, GLASS, EARTHENWARE, &c.** It surpasses in neatness, in strength, and cheapness, and retains its virtues in all climates. It has stood the test of time, and in all quarters of the globe.	*Sold* *in Bottles at* **6d. & 1s.** *Or by* *Inland Post* **1s. 2d.**
WANSBROUGH'S **METALLIC** **NIPPLE** **SHIELDS**	**FOR LADIES NURSING.**—By wearing the WANSBROUGH Shields in ordinary, whilst the nipples are healthy, they screen from all external sources of irritation. They are easy to wear, holding on like Limpets. Sore Nipples heal whilst reposing in the bath of milk secreted within the Shields, which give at the same time both Comfort and Protection. *Every box is labelled Wansbrough's Shields. Made by* Tho. Jackson	**At** 1s. per Pair, or by Inland Post, 1s. 2d.
JACKSON'S **RUSMA.**	For the removal of Hair without a Razor, from the Arms, Neck, or Face, as well as Sunburn or Tan. The activity of this depilatory is notable. It is easy and safe. It leaves a Whole Skin and a Clean Complexion.	**At 1s.** By Inland Post, 1s. 2d.
1892.	**SOLD BY THE PRINCIPAL** **DRUGGISTS.**	For Abroad at Foreign Postal Rates.

80,000. S.   91/1/92